GODS OF ASH AND AMBER

Seeds of Chaos
Book 5

AZALEA ELLIS

Join the Inner Circle**

Become part of the Inner Circle.

Instantly receive a free Seeds of Chaos novella, set between Book 2 and 3.

https://www.azaleaellis.com/newsletter

I will send you new release updates, exclusive content like pre-release or deleted scenes, as well as news about giveaways or contests I'm doing (signed paperbacks, posters, etc.) and other cool stuff I think you might enjoy. Sometimes I tell weird stories about my life.

Support me on Patreon

https://www.patreon.com/azaleaellis

Read along chapter by chapter as I write the next book in my current series, with early access chapters not available elsewhere, plus exclusive short stories/bonus chapters and other goodies.

To Jared. You are not alone.

Chapter 1

There are black zones of shadow close to our daily paths, and now and then some evil soul breaks a passage through.
— H.P. Lovecraft

I DREW a tremulous breath and held it for a moment, forcing my constricted chest to loosen. I had just finished explaining to my teammates that Pestilence wasn't the last of his kind, and the words hung like poison in the air.

After a horrible, silent pause, everyone began to speak at once, but I shook my head, unable to focus on their words. Exhaling, I scrubbed the tears from my cheeks. "I need a moment alone."

I spun, searching for an exit, somewhere to hide my face. With an idle thought, I dismissed the VR chip Windows notifying me that some of my Attributes had leveled up. I tasted iron and salt, probably from biting my tongue while seizing under the final puzzle band's influence. I spat the blood out of my mouth. My eyes caught on the bright crimson as it splattered onto the marble floor and I faltered, arrested by the memory of the vision I'd just endured.

Adam reached out to stop me from leaving, grabbing my elbow. "Eve, what do you—"

I yanked myself free of his grip easily. "Just a few minutes," I said, my voice almost pleading. "My mind's all—I can't think, I just need a moment. I'll be right back." Ignoring any other protestations, I hurried to a side door and opened it onto one of the balconies overlooking the gardens. The solar eclipse was still progressing, barely past the zenith of complete coverage, and the colors and shadows all looked wrong, like someone had superimposed different times of the day atop each other. I closed the door and leaned my back against it, my chest heaving with suppressed sobs.

I spat again to clear the remnants of blood from my mouth and looked over the Estreyan city. It was beautiful, all cut stone, metal, and crystal that only barely glittered. Only a few blocks away, signs of the street festival celebrating this "incredible" day were just beginning. People cavorted about, drinking, laughing, and wearing colorful outfits and costumes. The crowds pressed between the many street stalls grew thicker as my eye moved toward the grand square in the middle of the city. If I had been there, like Queen Mardinest wanted, Blue would not have been able to clue me in to the significance of this moment.

I ran my fingers across the sparkling, delicate crown that had woven itself through my hair and clamped down on my skull. Was the Abhorrent's new game piece already here, on Estreyer, or maybe Earth? If so, would I have felt it arrive, somehow? Felt the pure world smeared with a syrupy drop of taint? Or would I have been catering to the cheering crowds, oblivious? The dark blue sky, short shadows, and muted colors lent a dream-like quality to everything, and it seemed like I should be able to sense something different about the world, like something so monumental should have written itself across the sky in words of doom. But it was just an eclipse.

The vision had been figurative, like the two before, but the meaning was impossible to misunderstand and all the more terrifying for it.

Hanging suspended within darkness, lit as if by a spotlight, I had seen a checkered game board. White pieces were set up at one end. Nine of those pieces, the largest ones, bore the familiar symbols of the Seal of Nine. Arrayed around them were various smaller pieces. Their allies.

The darkness around the board, an abyss of black oil, rippled like someone had tossed a pebble into it. With dream-like intuition, I identified the ripple as one of the strange, warped distortions that had popped into existence over both worlds when Zed had torn Pestilence apart.

A new piece tumbled out of that darkness like a flipped coin, landing on the opposing side of the board. Contrary to my expectations, the enemy piece was not black.

Encased within amber, bright metallic shards formed a knotted mass of tentacles. The piece was small at first, but it grew, and continued to do so, until the shiny tentacles broke free from the amber, more a writhing alien creature than a game piece now.

One tentacle reached out into the darkness, then returned, dragging another small game piece onto the board. The second was different from the first, but I couldn't quite distinguish the symbol or form it carried within. This one began to grow, too. When it was large enough, both of them reached out and brought back more pieces. I only recognized one. Pestilence was already broken, his cicada husk washed-out and dead. But the other seven were whole, and beyond the edge of shadow that surrounded the board waited the ninth, the hand of darkness, the conductor.

The enemy pieces began to move across the board, and the white pieces moved to meet them. We fought and maneuvered, and one by one, each matched by a stabbing pang of loss and desperate denial within me, our white pieces were destroyed.

Finally, the Abhorrent's pieces stood atop the board alone, surrounded by the broken, ivory remains of their enemies.

Blood began to well up from between the checkered squares of the game board, spilling over the sides and down into the darkness. My vision followed one drop of crimson down and down, into lightless emptiness, until it swallowed me. I did not know how much time passed in the dark, with no eyes to see and no mouth to scream.

Finally, it ended, and I had seen again the faces of my teammates and the sparkle of their Seals, blood in my mouth and tears falling down my cheeks.

That was why I had needed a moment to myself.

With the previous two visions, there had been hints at a path to follow, clues for me to pick up on, mysteries to decode. They had been a guide. This one was not. It was a prophecy of *failure*, undeniable and complete.

What did that mean?

Had the Oracle given up? But even if so, why give me a vision like that? It accomplished nothing but spreading despair—and that seemed petty, even for her.

"Come down and talk to me face to face!" I screamed up at the sky, letting my Wraith Skill balloon out and take stock of everything within my sensory range.

She didn't, of course.

I slumped back down. I could hear the faint voices of my teammates in the throne room behind me, arguing about what little I had told them and whether to go after me.

"What if it's the opposite?" I murmured aloud, perking up. The Oracle was a manipulative bitch. When we fought the God of Knowledge, she had seemingly tried to force me to give up and let most of my teammates die so I could defeat the Abhorrent in the end. After I told her to shove it in no uncertain terms and ended up defeating Knowledge anyway, it seemed like maybe she'd actually been using reverse psychology or some other stupid thing, trying to get me to *refuse* to give up and escape. What if this was something similar, and the vision was supposed to catalyze me into acting as she wanted?

A horrible thought sprang up in my mind. What if the reason the Abhorrent's pieces were going to win now was because I hadn't listened to her then? She'd told me all my teammates would die eventually, even if I didn't abandon them. What if it *hadn't* been some weird psychological game and now I was seeing the results of my choices?

I shook my head forcefully, bending over the railing and closing my eyes. The sound of my own blood pulsing through me drowned out everything else.

I couldn't think like that. Dying earlier was in no way better than dying later. Plus, I couldn't imagine any way *I alone* would have been strong enough to defeat Pestilence, his analogues, or the Abhorrent darkness behind the curtain.

With a thought, I pulled up my Attribute Window, looking at

the numbers with a fear and greed that I hadn't felt since Pestilence. For a while, I had stopped caring about them beyond vague satisfaction when one of my Attributes increased, but now I bored into the data as if hoping some incredible power would mysteriously appear and save us all.

PLAYER NAME: EVE REDDING
TITLE: BEARER OF TESTIMONY
SKILLS: COMMAND, SPIRIT OF THE HUNTRESS,
TUMBLING FEATHER, WRAITH, CHAOS, VOICE

STRENGTH: 40
LIFE: 108
AGILITY: 50
GRACE: 42
INTELLIGENCE: 43
FOCUS: 39
BEAUTY: 23
CHARISMA: 53
MANUAL DEXTERITY: 11
MENTAL ACUITY: 45
RESILIENCE: 89
STAMINA: 45
PERCEPTION: 60

It seemed that, with the latest update, the Oracle had gotten rid of the now useless "Level" stat, since that only recorded the number of Seeds NIX had given me and was no longer a realistic measurement of my power or progress. She'd also combined Characteristic Skills with the main Skills. That was all irrelevant. Had I gained anything useful?

I suddenly had a few extra levels in Mental Acuity to go along with the vision, but the rest of my increases were natural, from practice or the simple propagation of the Seed organisms within my body over time. Compared to my levels when I had first become a Player, which were in the low teens at best, I was a powerhouse. Now, my Skills made me deadly to even the finest Estreyan warrior, and my Attributes were representative of my status as a godling.

But according to the Oracle, it would not be enough. I sighed and waved away the Window.

Of course, I knew I couldn't blindly trust the Oracle, but she had no reason to fabricate the warning itself. Whatever her purpose in revealing this bleak glimpse into the future, the fact remained that my teammates—and both worlds—were in danger.

But the vision was devastating. My fingers still trembled faintly. If I were to share it with the others, would it drive them to panic and despair? Perhaps a truncated version would be less damaging. I could warn them of the danger but leave out our destruction and the fatalism. They would help me fight, and maybe, somehow, we could subvert the future I had seen.

I shuddered at the thought of carrying the horrible weight of this knowledge alone. I had kept secrets and lied to them before—and then dealt with the backlash. Hadn't I learned by now? If the vision came true, and they died fighting because I had lied to them, it would kill me just as thoroughly as the Abhorrent's victory.

Without good information, how could my teammates make good decisions? What if they wanted to abandon the fight and run? I wouldn't stop them. They deserved better than my manipulation.

And maybe—maybe if I shared this burden with them, together we could find a way to overcome it.

I straightened, running my tongue across my too-sharp teeth. I gave the sky a small smile that bore no humor.

In a deep pit within me dwelt a rage that seemed to have no bottom and no end. Perhaps it had always been there, and I had been oblivious to its true nature. Or perhaps it had been created when Pestilence tried to consume me and I found I needed a godling's weapon and not just a human's mercurial willpower. When we'd defeated Pestilence, I'd thought it was over. I'd tried to tamp that rage down and forget about it, but it kept simmering just beneath my surface. It flared up now, sending ice and strength through my veins, and my claws gouged furrows into the stone of the balcony railing.

The cold rage was happy to do away with my fear; fear was useless to achieving my goals. I could run, or hide, or fight back like the knife edge of death, but whatever I chose, I would not do so as prey.

In the end, as I turned back and opened the doors to the throne room where my teammates waited, I did not know if my decision to tell them everything was born of honesty, cowardice, or plain recklessness, but I knew that if it were me in their position, I would choose to know the truth. Knowledge, no matter how terrible, was always better than ignorance.

<hr>

MY TEAMMATES' arguing, which had only grown louder in the few minutes I had been away, abruptly quieted as I reentered the imposing throne room.

"Adam, Torliam," I said. "We'll need shields against sight and sound."

They all shared worried looks as we silently gathered together within a spherical ink shield. Torliam's power gave us all a sickly pallor and left the air buzzing faintly as he canceled out any sound that reached the edge of the barrier.

"Talk," Adam ordered, his voice strained and his fingers flexing and twiddling as if wishing for something to fiddle with.

I left nothing out. I could feel hints of strong emotion through the weak blood bonds I shared with most of them, and more clearly through my mutual connection to Torliam. I struggled not to let it drag me down.

Zed bent forward, letting out a gasp of air as if someone had punched him in the gut. "The warps?" That was the term most of the Earth population had taken up for the mysterious phenomena. "They're a doorway to the Abhorrent? But those appeared when… when I tore Pestilence apart. *That's* why this is happening?"

Gregor's body blackened as he slipped into his Shadow form, his features losing distinction.

"This is a lie," Adam murmured numbly. "It has to be. A nightmare." He pinched himself, to no avail.

Torliam tucked the old book and scrolls he had been carrying under his arm. His shoulders straightened and his jaw tightened. I watched as he set aside the historian and scholar, embracing instead the warrior.

When Kris reached up and tugged at Torliam's pant leg, he

swallowed and forced some of the tension from his face. He used a wave of sky blue power to lift her up, allowing her to sit in the crook of his other arm as if it were a chair.

I placed a clawed hand on my brother's shoulder and cleared my throat, but my voice was still rough when I spoke. "This isn't because of you. If we hadn't killed Pestilence, things would be over already. We bought time, at least."

Sam's eyes were dark with the use of his Black Sun Skill, the shadowed orbs looking out from his face with the kind of nihilistic chill that I hadn't seen for a long time. "We bought time for seven more just like Pestilence to be born, all with their own little umbilical cords back to Daddy," he said dryly.

Zed flinched at the words, and Jacky glared at Sam.

Birch, whose head now came up to my elbow when he sat straight, laid his ears flat and let out a long, low whine. He moved one wing through the edge of Gregor's silhouette, but the boy ignored him.

The tailos turned to me, butting his nose up against the side of my arm. A feeling of concern bloomed in my mind, along with an image of me pulling the others close, tucking them under strong wings, and roaring out at the approaching danger fiercely. "*Protect*," Birch sent telepathically, mixing his instinctive impressionistic communication with the human language that he'd learned from growing up around us. "*Kits are scared.*"

I slipped a hand into his fur and squeezed. "I know," I murmured to him, taking comfort in his downy coat and the warmth of his body beside mine.

Kris's eyes had welled with tears and kept flicking from face to face as if the answer to some cryptic question was written in our expressions. "We're all going to die?" she whispered.

Jacky shook her head sharply and chopped a hand through the air to punctuate her words. "No! We're gonna do what we always do. We're gonna fight back, and we'll kick their asses. We already did it once, we know we can do it again." Counter to the confidence she expressed, her Struggle Skill activated involuntarily and her body grew slightly, reacting to the face of a threat she felt unable to handle.

The tears spilled from Kris's eyes.

Torliam tucked her closer to his chest and turned to me. "Was there no indication of how we might avert this future?"

"No." I shook my head. "But that *doesn't* mean there is no way. However the Oracle's power works exactly, I know she doesn't see a definite future. She sees possibilities and paths. So maybe the path we're on right now leads to that future. Or maybe she just plain made the vision up because she saw it would manipulate us into doing something she wants. We know she's lied before, and she's probably made mistakes, too—like when she didn't warn us about the monster attack at the Spire of Prophecy."

Zed had crossed his arms over his chest, his fingers pressing punishingly into his flesh as if he were afraid he might fall apart and was attempting to hold himself together. "It's just the one new…*thing* for now, though, right? What if we can close the warps before it gets big enough to pull its friends through?"

Jacky nodded furiously, popping her joints one after the other, seemingly oblivious to the way Adam's scowl grew more harsh with every fleshy *crack*. "That's a good idea. Maybe one of the gods could help us, too. Like the little guy did with Pestilence."

Adam snorted grudging agreement. "Seems like this whole thing should have been the gods' problem from the beginning, but they're just sitting around waiting for us to handle it."

I agreed, but kept my mouth shut as rage boiled up within me at the thought.

Gregor returned to normal, breathing a little too hard. "But what if we can't beat them? Could we run away? There are other worlds out there, right? Can't we just…evacuate to somewhere the Abhorrent can't reach?"

Torliam shook his head. "That is not how it works. The ways to those worlds are closed, for this very reason. If we were to somehow find a way to break through, we would only doom them as well as ourselves."

Gregor's voice cracked. "But…but, maybe they would have a way to deal with it. A way to fight back and win, or the means to block the Abhorrent and his game pieces off."

Torliam's expression grew melancholy.

Gregor saw and turned to me in desperation. "If not that, then what do we do? Do you have a plan, Eve?"

It was hard to force words up past the tight pain in my chest. "I don't have a plan yet, but I know we can come up with one. We just need more information to figure out what we're really up against and what our options are."

Gregor did not seem entirely persuaded, but he nodded, and some trembling tension left his body. "I can help, too."

"We need to catch the Oracle and force the truth out of her," Sam said, his voice the only one not filled with anxiety.

"Yes," I said. "And maybe we could find another manifestation of the God of Knowledge, or someone who could tell us what's going on here." All this time, we'd been working off vague information, but had been too ignorant to understand that fact and too busy attempting to survive one crisis after another to recognize our own ignorance. How many times throughout my life would I have to look back and realize how inadequate my efforts had been, how foolish and shortsighted my decisions? Had I improved at all, or would I continue to dig this hole of cascading consequences deeper?

"Where do we start?" Jacky asked, her intensity practically radiating outward from her enlarged form.

My scales rippled with a sudden thought. "I know who can tell us more," I said.

"Blue," Adam and I said simultaneously. I nodded at him, then added, "It knew the eclipse was significant, and that Pestilence and the Abhorrent were not the same. It offered its help." I turned to my brother. "Open the Veil."

Zed grimaced. "Should I…" He made a vague motion away from the rest of us, questioning if he should remove himself from the group.

I shook my head. "Blue will just have to get over its grudge. This is more important. Besides, it's not like you destroyed all the energy it'd been hoarding on purpose. If anyone, Blue should blame the Abhorrent for that setback."

With an unenthusiastic nod, Zed reached into the air and tore it apart. The cold grey light of the Other Place spilled through.

THE DUPLICATED ENVIRONMENT around the opening to the Other Place spread a few dozen meters in every direction, and one of Blue's gigantic eyes looked on from beyond the edge, the majority of the cosmic whale's body beyond clear perception. "I heard that, you cheeky morsel. Speak, and be grateful that I do not consume you and be rid of the trouble that trails you like a cloak," it said, its voice echoing like the cry of the whale I had named it for.

I raised my hand and set the air afire above it. Holding the flame aloft like a torch, I stepped through to Blue's domain.

The others followed me.

The fire struggled against the devouring cold, and tiny little ash-like flakes coalesced in the air around us, concentrated around my flame. Behind us, Zed closed the opening to the normal world. When we had first accessed the Other Place, before we understood Blue, we thought the copy of reality on the other side was just part of Zed's Skill. We had been wrong.

I hadn't yet pried much information out of Blue. After our fight with Pestilence did such damage to the creature's domain, it refused to speak to me beyond ordering more, hotter flame until I had repaid part of the debt of energy I had promised it. However, I had managed to gather that the Veil-Piercer Skill was very different from what we had first imagined. If not for Blue, those initial cracks Zed had seen in the world all around us would have led to a much deadlier something, or *lack* of something, beyond the Veil. We were very, very careful never to walk beyond the Other Place's edge, now that it was close enough to see.

This new understanding had led to some questions about how the portal to the God of Shaping and Molding's little realm had been in the Other Place, but then we speculated that there was *space* beyond the Veil whether or not Blue had filled it with anything we could interact with. The god must have hung his portal in that dimension with the expectation that any Skill based around piercing the Veil would be able to access it, knowing that one of the Seal of Nine would have such a Skill, by definition.

I let the flame flare brighter. Blue was fairly easy to appease, so long as you understood that at its core, it was a glutton. "Did you hear everything, then?" I asked. "I would prefer not to repeat myself."

"There was an echo in the air," Blue's voice resounded. Even without Zed opening the cracks, some tiny amount of energy, and along with it, information, could be sucked through, because the seal wasn't perfect. Over thousands of years, the energy bleeding through these cracks had been enough for Blue to build the Other Place up to the size it had been when we first visited, and as Blue consumed the energy, the information contained within that energy became a part of it, allowing Blue an unnerving insight into the places or people it concentrated its efforts on—like our team.

Blue's eye turned balefully toward Zed for a moment, but my brother only gave the creature a deep nod, and Blue said nothing.

Without further preamble, I spoke. "You knew the Abhorrent was not defeated. Did you know what the warps were? What would happen during the eclipse?"

Blue sounded impatient when it responded, its huge, amorphous form moving around our little copy of the throne room more quickly. "Of course he was not defeated. You destroyed *Pestilence*, as I said. Your inability to grasp basic concepts makes it clear to me how you failed to comprehend the situation in the first place."

Scowling, I let the flames die down a bit.

Blue swam closer. "Peace, peace, tiny one. What would you have of me? I am willing to aid you as I may…for a price."

"Before that, tell me about the Abhorrent." The edge of darkness surrounding us suddenly reminded me of the darkness surrounding the game board in my vision. They were not the same, I reassured myself silently. Here, light was able to penetrate beyond the edge, illuminating Blue for a short distance, as if the creature simply swam through deep waters.

"I do have some information, though my knowledge is limited. However…information has its price," Blue repeated.

My scales lifted and angled toward it, an involuntary sign of aggression. "If we die, Blue, there will be no one to open the Veil, no one left to repay our end of the bargain with fire. In fact, there may not even be anything left on this side of the Veil for you to eat. Because that's what's going to happen if the vision I saw comes true.

We all die, and the world goes with us. Do you think things will be better for you if the Abhorrent wins?"

The sucking cold drew at me more persistently for a moment, but I held my ground and kept that bottomless well of anger that spilled up into my stomach flaring bright.

Blue eased off, and after a few moments of silence, it spoke. "You must realize that the totality of existence is greater than you can imagine with your tiny mortal minds. You have seen enough evidence of this, I presume? While some places and beings are within your understanding, there are others that exist beyond your frame of reference, just as the stars are beyond the understanding of an ant. The Abhorrent is one of those."

Torliam hugged Kris tightly to his side. "What is it? Are there others like it? How do we kill it? Speak, creature!" he said.

I preemptively pushed energy into the flames until they flared high and bright, distracting Blue from the likely retaliation that would have otherwise dropped the Estreyan to his knees. "Please, Blue, excuse him. You must understand why this is so important to us."

"We've got more important things to deal with," Gregor snapped, stomping his foot somewhat dramatically. The way he shivered and wrapped his arms around himself undermined the impact.

The creature was silent for a while, but allowed us to remain in its domain while my flames assuaged its greed. Finally, it continued to speak. "I am a being similarly different from your species, though I do not know exactly what the Abhorrent is. It is the first of its kind that I have encountered, and before I could learn more, I was imprisoned *here*," it finished, its tone sharp with frustrated disgust.

I shot the others a warning look, urging them to remain silent and wait for Blue to speak on its own terms. We could not afford for it to refuse to help us out of vexation.

Though Torliam's expression was still mutinous, he remained silent, and Gregor only shivered and scowled.

"I do not remember my birth, or know of that concept in rela-tion to myself. I was not, and then I was. And after I *was*, I became curious, though at that point I did not yet know what curiosity was. I explored, and when I came upon interesting things, I ate them. After much of that, I came to understand that things could not be truly understood simply through consumption, and so I learned restraint.

"I came upon mortals, some like you, some different, and I learned. These flesh beings, the Estreyans, they passed me by while fleeing the Abhorrent. Of course, I did not know that at the time. I turned to travel with them, and, at first, they were curious as well, or at least not hostile. I restrained my hunger, so as not to destroy them before I could experience all they, their strange gods, and their world had to offer. However, when they realized that their flight from their old world had been futile, they grew fearful of all that was different, and especially that which was also powerful. And so I was imprisoned, and here I have existed, with only the tiniest morsels of life to keep the pernicious boredom at bay. Until the boy, of course, but see how that turned out." The huge eye glared down at Zed.

"Due to my imprisonment, my knowledge of the being they call the Abhorrent is limited. Similar to the gods of this world, or perhaps as a response to them, its power is vast, but faceted. Just as Chaos is an idea with many faces, the being they have named the Abhorrent has many limbs. I call them Avatars, as that is what they seem to be. I do not know what blocks it from fully entering the mortal realm, but its Avatars act in its stead. They do its bidding and spread its influence. When you used that reckless method to destroy Pestilence, the Abhorrent took advantage of the opportunity and created connections from the place *between*, where it exists, to the place here. Significant celestial events, such as this eclipse which happened simultaneously on both your worlds, allow for a weakening of the distinction between what *is*, and what *might be*. Now that the way is open again, it may do more than simply feed the single Avatar that had already gained a foothold."

It was too much for me. I had to speak, despite having warned the others against doing so. "So what do we *do*, Blue? Please, you must have some idea."

It hummed, the sound echoing like muted thunder under the water. "As you are, you cannot succeed. All of you—besides Eve, perhaps—are so very mortal. There is no escape, and there is no way to win."

Jacky shook her head frantically, stepping forward. "But we did kill Pestilence, right? We gotta be able to do the same to the rest of 'em. We just gotta figure out how to do it without making more warps or whatever."

"Must I remind you of the cost? Will you continue to rip this realm apart with each Avatar you destroy, reaping ruin even as society crumbles around you? In the end, you may fail even as you succeed."

I shuddered at the thought. Had the Abhorrent actually allowed, or even *wanted* us to destroy Pestilence the way we did, so that the other Avatars could gain access to our world? The timing, only a little more than a year before an aligned celestial event between two worlds whose time ran differently… That would not happen very often. What would the Abhorrent have done if things had gone differently? Would Pestilence have simply killed everyone directly, or perhaps he would have found a way to create a doorway for the Abhorrent without our interference? I could only wonder.

"I will remind you as well that you were only able to destroy Pestilence with my help to cut off his connection to the Abhorrent. I am disinclined to allow such damage to myself again, and with these warps, I would be at risk of notice if I were to attempt it. No," Blue reiterated. "With such mortal bodies, you have no chance."

I swallowed painfully. "You said I might be the exception to that, right? Because my body's been…rebuilt? Maybe I could do the same for the others, if we could find a way to make sure I didn't accidentally kill them while attempting it?"

Blue let out a snort. "Even you are not the rock of fortitude you believe yourself to be, Eve. You are a godling, not a god. However, I do remember something from before I was sent to this place which might help. I have not heard any whispers of it for a thousand cycles or so, but if it still existed, and you could avail yourself of it…" It paused and made a booming sound that might have been a cough.

I shared a look of frustration with Adam. "What?" I urged.

"Perhaps some of those Estreyan power crystals are in order?

After all, if I am to be your ally in this, I must regain some of my strength," Blue said.

I scoffed angrily, took a few deep breaths, and said, "A hundred pounds, small to moderately sized."

"A thousand," it rebutted. "As well as a doorway into the heart of a volcano. The boy can open one and leave it for me, perhaps with some minor maintenance."

"How am I supposed to get into the heart of a volcano?" Zed blurted out. "I'd die!"

I snapped my finger, pointing at Zed. "Exactly. Five hundred pounds of energized crystals, and if you can give us a way that Zed could survive being dropped into the heart of a volcano, we'll open a small doorway into one."

Blue sniffed. "Acceptable. This is in addition to the remaining Earth days of fire that you owe me."

"Of course." I nodded. "Now tell us."

"You will need to request the details from one of the mortals, but when this world was young, several times I heard mention of the 'fruit of life.' The mortals would quest for them just as they would quest for Bestowals from the gods. As I understand, these fruit grant long life and enough resilience to battle a wyrm. Will it allow you to defeat the Abhorrent? Likely not. But perhaps it will be sufficient to stand against its Avatars for some short period of time."

Some of the crushing weight lifted from my shoulders, and the tightness in my chest eased so that I could breathe deeply, despite the cold of the Other Place. My teammates shifted around me, letting out sighs and chuckles that were more about relief than humor. "Yes, *yes*." I turned a questioning look toward Torliam, but he shook his head.

"I have not heard of this," he said, giving a hint of an apologetic bow. "But I had not heard of Blue's origin or contact with the early inhabitants of Estreyer, either."

I waved a hand in the air as if shooing away a fly. "That's alright. We'll find out the details." I turned to Blue. "Is there anything else you can think of?"

"You must learn to use your own abilities, godling. Perhaps, if there is one force that could stand against the Abhorrent, it would be that Aspect of your own which matches it in terrible power. Chaos is change, both destruction and rebirth, and that primordial mud from which all of reality was molded. But there was another Aspect of it, which many have forgotten. Chaos is the formless void, the emptiness, the absence."

"The Void Aspect," I murmured.

"Just so," Blue said.

Jacky whooped and forced Zed to high five her. "Why didn't you say so in the first place? We got this!"

Gregor let out a sigh of relief.

Even Adam's face regained some color, though his scowl remained. "Find the fruit of life and teach Eve to wield the Void. Somehow I have a feeling it's not going to be that simple." Still, his tone of voice lacked the deep pessimism I had expected.

"I don't suppose you…" I said, raising my eyebrows hopefully toward the cosmic whale.

"Little crumb, I am not one of your gods. If you wish to learn how to use the tool in your hand, ask one of them," Blue said.

I grimaced. "Alright. What else? Do you know what power the one 'Avatar' that made it through has?"

"That is all. I do not have any knowledge of the Avatars that were previously confined beyond the *breaks*. You must not dawdle. With every moment, it will gain strength, exerting its will on the world."

I snorted. "Trust me, I have no plans to laze about." I turned and spun, motioning for Zed to open our way back to the normal world.

"Do not forget my power crystals!" Blue called out as we left.

Chapter 2

What looked like morning was the beginning of endless night.
— William Peter Blatty

ZED CLOSED the rip in reality behind us and we reset the privacy barriers.

"What's our next move?" I said, thinking aloud. "We need to get both worlds as prepared as possible, we've got to find the Avatar, and we need information about these life fruits and the Void Aspect of Chaos." I took a deep breath to settle my nerves and my racing thoughts, using Wraith to scan our surroundings and get a quick overview of the castle and any activity around it. I used the Skill so freely now, living without it would have been like being blinded.

The eclipse was only just ending. Had so little time passed? I felt like I had aged a month since I received the vision.

Torliam's eyes were closed, a deep frown of concentration on his face. When he opened them, he shook his head. "I cannot find this Avatar. I do not have enough familiarity for my Tracker Skill to know what to search for."

"I expected as much, but keep trying periodically as we gain more information." I cleared my throat and tried to make my tone calm and authoritative. "It would be stupid to run around trying to solve this all by ourselves. Our first priority should be to increase the magnitude of our resources and influence. We need Queen Mardinest, the delegates from Earth, and any Estreyan dignitaries who have access to surveillance or military resources. If there are any historians who are likely to know about this fruit, we need them, too. Someone should contact Ester from the Remnants, and we'll have to pull all the recorded data from the warps."

I took a deep breath and ran my claws through my hair, quickly tying it into a long braid that hung down almost to my hips. Both Earth and Estreyer had been studying the warps created by Pestilence's destruction, using multiple different forms of surveillance that recorded without pause, so if *anything* had come through, we should be able to find out. "Torliam, you have the authority to command the staff and guards, right?"

He nodded, already setting Kris down. "Yes. I will go to my mother's war room and begin relaying orders immediately. Many of the people we will need will be at the festival. For the rest, we can patch a secure comms link into the war room to allow them to participate remotely."

"Good. Message them all. We'll meet in the war room in, say, three hours. That should give enough time for some of the more distant people to get here, if they rush. I'll contact the queen and let her know what's going on ahead of time."

Adam pulled a folding datapad out of his pocket and inserted his fingers into the sides, which had been modified to allow him to control the device with his Skills rather than the touchpad surface. "I'm going to contact the warp site observation teams. I'll send you a Window with any discoveries."

"What should I do?" Gregor said.

"And me?" Kris piped up, pulling the tiny, old-timey aviator goggles she had taken to wearing down over her eyes. "My marionettes are on the way from my workshop. I'm ready for anything."

"You can help me," Adam said to Gregor. "We'll split the warp sites between us. It'll be faster that way."

"You're with Jacky and Birch," I told Kris. "Get our gear and the ship ready. Our first move will depend on the Avatar, but we need to be braced to respond immediately."

Birch nodded, fluffing up his fur and feathers to make himself look more threatening.

"On it," Jacky said with a nod, bouncing lightly on the pads of her feet as she visibly restrained herself from rushing off to start preparing that very second.

Gregor gasped, then groaned, leaning forward and holding his head in his hands. "Oh no!"

The rest of the team froze as we all turned toward the boy, but our alarm was quickly assuaged when he continued. "I only made full body armor for myself! I didn't even consider the fact that the rest of you might need any, and the stuff we have in the bounty vaults is good and all, but it's not even personalized, it won't work with your Skills..." He straightened, yet more horror settling into his expression as he touched the daggers at his sides and lamented, "I haven't even finished my Absurdly Sharp Blades!"

The boy was serious, but the way he verbally capitalized the names of his experimental weapon even at a moment like this caught me with a prick of unexpected amusement. "Besides the people who have to know, I don't want anyone else finding out about this," I warned. "Mass panic is the last thing we need right now."

"I can help with any panic," Sam said, the calm words sounding oddly threatening.

I coughed out a sharp laugh. "Hopefully we won't have to resort to that."

"Zed?" I asked.

He'd been staring into midair, but snapped to alertness at the sound of his name, speaking rapidly. "Is there any way to close the warps? The researchers requested my help at the beginning of their investigations to see if I could affect them, so we already know I'm useless there. But maybe one of the gods could do it, or we could invent some theoretical physics that would undo whatever...whatever I did?"

"You didn't do this," I snapped. "The Abhorrent did this. Sure, *maybe* he wouldn't have been able to if you hadn't killed Pestilence, but don't pretend your culpability is any larger than it is."

"Eve's right. You don't get to be a martyr, so don't be an idiot," Gregor said, shaking his head condescendingly. "Sometimes you can be a bit dramatic, you know." The hypocrisy of the statement seemed to be lost on the boy, and I shared a look of amusement with Adam over Gregor's head.

Gregor continued, "As for the warps, I doubt there's anything we can do…maybe if my uncle were still here, he could find a way." He swallowed, looking away. "But I'll look at the research. Maybe the Remnants can help, or…I don't know."

Zed forced out a smile. "Okay, okay, I hear you. I'll come with you to look at what we've got on the warps. Even if I didn't cause them directly, I'm still the one out of all of us who has the best chance of doing something about them now."

Gregor sniffed and nodded haughtily, appeased.

"I guess I'll go charge up my Harbinger Skill," Sam said. "Do you guys want your weapons coated in poison? I can do that while I'm at it, too."

Jacky shot him a thumbs-up.

After a quick check to make sure there was nothing else to discuss, Torliam and Adam dropped the little privacy bubble, and our group split apart, everyone moving with purposeful strides.

I made my way to a room in the hall that held Queen Mardinest's war room, climbed atop one of the tables, and sat down cross-legged. I struggled to calm both my body and mind for longer than I'd like to admit, but finally managed to focus my senses on my breath, then my heartbeat and the blood it sent pumping through my body, and then into my mind.

I found myself within the familiar mental construct, a mansion and grounds surrounded by a gigantic barrier wall. The final spark the God of Knowledge had Bestowed on me had tried to train me to defeat Pestilence within these rooms, full-nightmare-immersion style. The gigantic barrier wall and mansion were still there, but the eerie lighting and sinister, horror-film elements were gone. Memories of the things she'd put me through in my dreams still made me shudder, and I was pretty sure some of those phobias would remain for life.

Meditation had long been my response to being in over my head, and had become a habit I used both to center myself and to train my mind. Now, I used it to prepare for the upcoming meeting with the world's influential and powerful.

Adam, Gregor, and Zed found me a couple hours later, when I was well and truly settled, ready.

"What did you find?" I asked Adam.

His curly hair was fluffed up and fairly floating away from his head with static, his movements jerky with pent-up energy. "*Something* happened. There was a flair of exotic energy at the exact moment the eclipse reached full zenith on both worlds. It was across all the warps simultaneously, but nothing came through as far as we could see. I've got the teams analyzing the data more carefully, but for the moment, we've got *nothing*. It could be anywhere on either world. I mean, hypothetically, it could be swimming around in outer space somewhere next to a warp we haven't even discovered," he said bitterly.

Readings like that from the warps would have been strange and alarming, even without my vision, but pairing it all together with a complete lack of results left me reeling, as if I'd gone to take a step and found the ground fallen out from underneath me. I resisted the urge to ask Adam to repeat himself.

"Nothing came through?" Jacky said. "Does that mean the Oracle was wrong?"

"It's unlikely," I said. "I'm pretty sure I got the vision after the eclipse had already reached its zenith, so either the Oracle was lying, the Avatar is waiting for us to let down our guard to enter, or it's already here somewhere and hiding. There could be warps we don't know about, like Adam said, or maybe the Avatar's just invisible. It wouldn't be the strangest thing we've ever seen. Either way, we have to act as if it's already here, because it would be disastrous if we were wrong."

Gregor scowled down at the datapad in his hands. "They haven't discovered any way to affect the warps at all, let alone close them. I've had their data transferred to me, but I barely know what I'm looking at. I have to learn an entirely new field of science to have any hope of helping, and I'm a genius, but it's just not that *easy*!"

Zed was silent, simply shaking his head.

"Well." What else could I say?

Wraith could sense the crowd gathering in the war room down the hall. "I need to speak to the queen," I said.

As if summoned, the woman burst into the room like a warrior, the air practically shrinking back from the force of her presence. "Does anyone care to tell me what is going on? My son sent me an urgent message to leave the festivities as quickly as possible, and from the people spilling out the doors of *my war room*...I am not the only one."

QUEEN MARDINEST'S eyes flicked up to the glittering circlet wrapped around my head. I figured I could just come out and explain the situation, since she and a whole room of other people would have to learn what was going on in the next few minutes, since we needed their help, and Wraith could confirm no one was listening in.

"Bad news," I replied baldly. "Pestilence has siblings, and one just arrived."

She paled dramatically, and her hand fell instinctively to the dagger at her waist. I had to give the queen some credit; she was always ready to fight for her people—even when she shouldn't.

"This new Avatar of the Abhorrent is still small and weak, but without the Champion to repress its influence, we are all in danger. If it grows strong enough, it will summon more."

"And the quest?" she said. "What is this plan that you need our help with?"

"We can discuss more specific details later. For now, we need to *find* the new Avatar and start preparing and coordinating. We'll need every ounce of power we can gather."

Her eyes narrowed at my word choice and remained so as I explained the vision and our conversation with Blue. "That is not all. I can scent the secret on the air around all of you, and it smells of desperation," Queen Mardinest said.

"There is more, but it was not for any ears but our own," I said. Her Skill would let her know that we were keeping a secret even if I didn't tell her, but I had seen how she acted when she believed there to be no hope. That's what had led to her betrayal and the invasion of Earth. I would have hesitated to give her any ammunition at all to use against us...but despite how fickle, harsh, and disloyal she could be, she really did seem to have the best interests of her people at heart. As long as she believed me and the two of us were sincerely working together to save the world, I could trust her to do her side of the job.

Her expression had twisted with displeasure.

"Some secrets will damage you to learn them, Mother," Torliam said gently. "Eve acts wisely."

As far as the people I had assigned to covertly investigate her could tell, she really *hadn't* been involved in Blaine's murder. Everything she'd done to oppose us had been surprisingly bold and directly to our faces. Not that I either liked or trusted her. To the contrary, if Mardinest had not been in such a critical position as the queen of one of the most powerful countries on Estreyer, I would have gone out of my way to never meet her again after having her thrown in prison. But I could respect her strength, and once again, we needed her.

She glared at Torliam, her power flaring along with her nostrils, but she nodded. "The fruit of life? I have heard of this," she said.

Torliam looked to his mother in surprise.

She raised a haughty eyebrow. "Yes. Did you imagine that I was able to become queen with an empty brain?"

He cleared his throat and gave her a small bow.

"The fruit have not been accessible for over one thousand cycles," she said. "During my predecessors' reigns, there were a handful of attempts to obtain one, but all questers disappeared on the hostile level where the fruit grow and were not heard from again. That level is home to highly aggressive creatures. It is dangerous enough to be a restricted level, like that of the Spire, and I have not been so foolish as to send any there to die. I do not recall the details, but I will look up what records I can find for you. Now, what about this Void power? Is it the same as the Voids of Tartarus?"

I knew only that I'd once been threatened with teleportation into the heart of the Voids of Tartarus and began to ask for clarification, but Torliam spoke first.

"It seems likely, though we do not know for sure. It is supposedly one of the Aspects of Chaos, but I have not come across any records of any Khaos manifestation using a power that matches that description."

"I think we should contact Behelaino directly," I said. "She should know about her own power better than anyone else and should be able to teach me to harness it. She might even be willing to help us directly, fight with us. I do worry, though, that the Avatar could attack while we're off on some other level and can't return immediately."

"That may be a problem," the queen agreed, frowning thoughtfully. "Our communications systems do not reach to all levels, particularly those where it is not safe for the technicians to install the relay obelisks, or which cannot be accessed through any safe doorways. We do have some strong transmitters that can overcome poor conditions, but even with them you would need to be relatively close to the level's entrance to make contact."

Adam shook his head. "If we don't finish preparing to kill the Avatar, it doesn't matter if we return, because we won't be able to do anything."

"We don't know that for sure," Kris whispered. "We could at least hold it off, maybe, while people escape?"

Sam rolled his shoulders back. "I don't particularly *feel* it at the moment, but I'm sure without this Skill active I would be much more concerned about the populace. Have we considered that this Avatar is aware of us and the potential danger we represent? Perhaps it is only waiting for us to be absent and preoccupied to make its move."

My scales rustled and I had to consciously avoid clenching my fists so I didn't stab myself with my claws. The fact was, I hadn't considered Sam's suggestion, and it made the path forward even less clear in my mind.

Mardinest let her eyes trail over the group slowly, then nodded. "I have a suggestion that would allow you to, at the least, travel instantly to most major population centers on Estreyer as soon as you were notified of the need, and could be adapted to give you quick access to Earth as well." She paused, looking at me.

I raised an eyebrow, waving an impatient hand for her to continue.

"Ichi," she said simply.

"That bastard!?" Gregor burst out, catching us all off guard.

Jacky's head whipped toward the boy, her eyebrows raised as if she were scandalized…except I knew that *she* was probably the one who'd been cursing enough for it to rub off on the child. She turned to glare at Mardinest. "*Mierda*," she cursed, "you must be crazy. You didn't forget what he did to us, did you?"

My scales rippled with an involuntary shudder at the memory of that dark form appearing out of nowhere, followed by Blaine's blood splattering over my face. There were few other people, even on Estreyer, who would have been able to pull off the same feat. Considering Ichi's sudden disappearance and the way he continued to evade contact, the evidence was pretty damning.

At first, Queen Mardinest had suspected some of her political rivals, but if one of them had been the ultimate force behind Ichi's actions, there was no evidence of it, even to someone like her who could sniff out secrets. The reason for his attack on us was still a mystery.

"Explain," I ground out.

"I am very much aware of his betrayal," she said. "However, Ichi has a very useful Skill, and if he could be compelled in such a way that would allow you to trust him…"

"Do you have some sort of blackmail on him? After killing Blaine, I doubt simple words or even threats would be sufficient to ameliorate his antagonism toward us. Besides that, there's no way for us to keep him still long enough to talk to him," I said, a note of incredulity creeping into my tone despite my efforts to stay respectful.

Queen Mardinest had sent more than a few quick response teams after him, using Torliam to pinpoint his location, but as soon as anyone got close, Ichi used his Skill to disappear to some remote level halfway around the world, and they had to start from scratch.

"I agree, words cannot always be effective. But there is more than one type of force. For instance, if there were a way to *compel* loyalty, it would allow you to trust and work with him for the duration necessary, and afterward, to mete out the appropriate punishment," she said.

Torliam frowned. "*Compel* loyalty? If you mean what I think, that is illegal."

She sniffed. "Well, of course it is, but there are times when such a thing is necessary, for the sake of a greater good. As for illegality, who would prosecute this malfeasance? That is *my* job, is it not?" she said pointedly, one shoulder lifting in a nonchalant half-shrug. "All you would need is a portable, single-person Skill suppressor. Perhaps a talented runic technician could make one, or one of these Remnant Estreyans that have been secretly living on Earth. Alternatively, some sort of long-range sedative Skill that would force him into unconsciousness faster than he could react. From there, you can bring him back to the capital, and with a simple vow said from his lips, my contact will force him to fulfill said vow. The words need not be said willingly."

"Not willingly? Do you plan to torture him, then?" Torliam said.

She scoffed. "That is entirely unnecessary, when we have your brother. It will be painless. Reglium will compel his words, my contact will compel his loyalty, and when this is over, we can give Ichi a trial and mete out just punishment."

I shifted, frowning. Taking away someone's free will like that was even worse than what Reglium had done to us, and perhaps worse even than what NIX did to its Players. At least as a Player, I had been able to scheme against and betray my oppressors. If I had been compelled against my will to be truly loyal, I might have broken in the face of despair.

Seeing our discomfort, she waved a hand as if to brush it away. "This may not be pretty, but think of what is at stake. The greater good, the lives of so many, weighed against the life of a murderer and a betrayer. This arrangement would not be permanent, and you could even build that into the vow. Think of it like indentured servitude, a way for him to pay back some small part of the debt he owes you. In any case, please consider it."

QUEEN MARDINEST HAD EXPANDED her main war room to accommodate larger meetings since the city had become a political hub for both worlds in the aftermath of the war. The room was still packed, even with three out of four walls covered in screens showing the people who weren't physically present. There were a few humans, but it wasn't possible to communicate in real time between Estreyer and Earth due to the differences in the relative passage of time. We would need to speak to those on Earth separately. Many within the war room were questioning why they had been brought here so suddenly, and the tension was growing as politicians and soldiers clustered into groups like high school children in a cafeteria.

I was careful to keep my expression and body language free of any signs of agitation as I entered the room, attempting to seem sober and in control. I knew how critical these people and the response from this briefing would be in the coming days. Social graces were not my forte, and politics even less, but no one else was in a position to take charge of this in my stead.

I caught sight of Reglium in one corner and fought to keep a glare from my face. I had met a few more of Torliam's siblings, and there were none that I liked less than Reglium, despite his attempts to smooth things over with the members of the Seal of Nine after his mother's failure to get rid of us. That desire to burrow into our good graces reminded me of Bunny, and I thought it was likely motivated by the fact that Torliam was now by far the most popular member of the royal family, which could prove problematic for Reglium, who still wanted to inherit the crown.

Queen Mardinest entered behind me, followed by the rest of my team. Rumors of her attempts to keep us from defeating Pestilence had filtered out, so despite our continued alliance with her, she had struggled to maintain her status and political capital, and was under a lot of pressure from rival families. This new threat could either stabilize her position or see her ousted completely.

The whole room turned to me in a spreading ripple as people noticed others quieting and looking toward me and copied the behavior. With surprise, I saw that my mother was among the crowd, standing beside Eliahan and a group of the Remnants led by Ester.

Reglium bowed to me, and I gave him the shallowest of nods in return, barely a few degrees away from an obvious slight.

"We've called you all here today because I've received critical new information from the Oracle," I said loudly. The last sounds died, as if smothered by my words, but as I explained what we had learned—leaving out the dire omen of our failure and death—my audience grew agitated and the brief silence was broken by nervous rustling and frightened voices.

"This cannot be true," one man said.

"Perhaps it is not!" another agreed. "What evidence do we have of any threat, and yet they are asking us to promise *our* resources to an alliance based on this existential crisis? And of course, *they* would be the leaders of this alliance. It would be a shrewd political move to gain power over us." He nodded like a bobblehead, looking around for others who might support his words.

"But the crown," a woman said, motioning to the glittering bands across my forehead. "It is evidence that the Oracle gave her the final vision. There always was speculation about the godkiller's ability to complete the quest with only two out of the three gifts."

"How do we know that crown is actually one of the gifts?" the second man said. "It could be a replica meant to deceive us!"

"Oh, shut up, Dedric," someone else said. "The rest of us would like to get some actual facts from the people who know what is going on."

"How many did she say there were? *Seven* more? We don't stand a chance!" a human said.

"How is this even possible? I thought they killed the Abhorrent!" another said, her voice pitching toward a terrified moan.

"Are more going to just keep coming? Is there a whole race of these things out there?"

"A whole *race*? What even *are* they!?" someone else cried.

I raised my hands for silence, resisting the urge to demand it aloud and let Voice force the issue. I reached for that well of cold focus within, since the calm of meditation seemed to have slipped away. "This is real, and it is serious. We do not have time for panic. Fear does us no good, we must *act*." I scanned the faces in the crowd, meeting each gaze in turn. "Each of us has a part to play in the future of our worlds. Rise up, and take control of your own destiny, and the destiny of those you love. We are not beaten yet."

Chapter 3

We ask only to be reassured
    About the noises in the cellar
    And the windows that should not have been open.
    — T.S. Eliot

A HALF HOUR LATER, I'd answered the most critical questions and set the ball rolling to gather resources and information.

While the officials got to work, some leaving while others remained in the war room to use its equipment and take advantage of the security it offered, my teammates and I met with the Remnants and Queen Mardinest in a nearby secure room.

I'd been the last to slip away from the briefing, so they were all waiting for me when I arrived. As I closed the door behind me, Adam shot me a helpless look.

My mother was giving Zed a bear hug and babbling motherly things about how much she'd missed him and how tall he was since she'd last seen him a couple months ago.

Eliahan stood a few feet away from the two, ignoring my brother, who was looking at him over my mother's shoulder.

Queen Mardinest and her son Reglium were in some kind of glaring match with Ester, the leader of the Remnants. For the moment, it appeared to be a draw.

The Remnants' scryer, an ancient old woman, was jabbing her cane at Adam, scolding him for his rudeness in a constant stream of hoarse words.

Ester turned away from her staring contest as I stepped into the room, and even that innocuous movement seemed somehow a slight toward the queen.

Reglium's fists clenched, but he wasn't stupid enough to actually escalate. Ester was older, and probably stronger, than Reglium and Mardinest put together and had never sworn loyalty to the Aethezriels when they became the ruling family. Though many of the Remnants were eager to return to Estreyer, some of them wanted to stay on the island compound on Earth, which effectively made Ester, as their leader, the ruler of her own smallish —country.

Instead, Reglium turned to Torliam with an ugly sneer. "Brother. Never quite decisive enough to finish the matter the first time around, I see. Just like when we were children."

"And you never realize when the poison on your tongue will harm its wielder more than the target of your attack," Torliam replied.

Queen Mardinest reached out a hand to stop Reglium from retorting, and he flushed but complied.

Eliahan moved past my brother without a word to stand in front of me. He gave a small, smirking nod, the motion more for himself than for me, as if he somehow thought that he'd contributed something other than genes to my current state of power.

He bowed and greeted me, "Daughter."

My mother wasn't oblivious to the slight toward Zed, and shot Eliahan a glare past my brother's shoulder. Her eyes moved to me for a second, barely softening.

I gave Eliahan an informal nod, then walked past him to stand beside my brother. "Hello, Mother. How did you get here so quickly? Weren't you on Earth?"

"Mom came with the Remnants," Zed said.

My mother pressed her red lips together and frowned down her nose at me. It was actually impressive, considering how much taller I was than her. "It's no thanks to *you* that I'm here, that's true. If

Eliahan hadn't happened to be nearby and relayed the information, I wouldn't have heard anything at all before you dragged your brother off on another life-threatening mission."

Before either of us could say more, Ester stepped in front of me with a bow and a warm smile, seeming unaffected by the tension and worry most of the others carried visibly. With both women standing side by side, it was obvious that Ester was related to me, however distantly, since I looked more like her than my own mother. "Well met, Eve."

I crossed my arms, letting my scales flare up a little in warning. "Did you know about this? About what was going to happen?"

Ester frowned slightly. "I assure you, I did not."

"Your scryer didn't decide to keep this a secret because she thought telling us would lead to disaster, did she? *Again*, that is."

The ancient old woman coughed roughly, slamming the tip of her cane down on the ground. "Watch your tongue, youngster," she rasped, using a dialect of Estreyan that even I could tell came from a time before anyone else in the room was born. How much time had passed on Estreyer while she was trapped on Earth? Generations, at least. "We work for the good, and I am not so stupid as to keep silent about something which I do not understand. I have had premonitions of this day, of doom, but my sight has been clouded, and every attempt to scry an answer has ended in failure. I reported these results, but we, myself included, judged it most likely that I was simply foreseeing my own death. One cannot scry into a time where they will not exist, and I have always found the manner of my passing hidden behind a shroud. Yet I still live, and a dark day that I could not foresee has arrived. I fear what this means. Perhaps the enemy has learned a defense against the things that acted as its downfall previously."

"So it *is* the Abhorrent?" Eliahan said. His words sent a ripple of unease through the room.

"Yes," I said, gazing at him impassively. Had he hoped I'd been lying during the briefing, making it all up?

"Despair follows hope," one of the Estreyans murmured.

"The Spark will light the way, even in the deepest darkness," another said, laying her hand on his shoulder. She turned toward me with an expression of both fear and stubborn, willful belief.

I gave her a nod, suppressing an uncomfortable shudder.

"If you have information or resources which might help us, it is imperative that you join the efforts immediately," Queen Mardinest said imperiously, though I couldn't imagine any reason Ester or the Remnants would have refused.

Ester raised an eyebrow toward me but did not even deign to look at the queen.

"I won't let you involve Zed in this, too," my mother burst out.

We all turned to stare at her.

She raised her head almost as imperiously as the queen, the muscles in her jaw jumping but not an eyelash out of place.

"I'm not a kid anymore," Zed told her. "I make my own choices, and there's no way I'm just sitting back and watching. It's not like Eve's dragging me into—"

"You can't tell me all of this isn't because of her," she snapped. "I'm not saying everything is her *fault*, but I'm also not blind. She suddenly starts changing, losing all this weight and being so secretive, and before I know it you're both running away from home and relocating me to another city to try and keep me from sticking my nose into your business." Her tone had grown more angry as she spoke, and her last statement was a clear accusation.

My scales rippled. I resisted the urge to flinch away from my mother, even as she clamped her mouth shut as if to keep further bitter words from spilling out.

Ester reached out to grip my arm, heedless of the sharp, raised scales that sprouted from it, and turned slowly, staring down her own nose at my mother. "Your son is one of the Seal of Nine, and your daughter is the Spark, a godkiller, and defeater of the Sickness." Ester left her rebuke unsaid, but we all knew what she meant.

Zed rubbed the back of his head awkwardly. "I'm here because I want to be here. It's true, I might not have figured out what was going on if not for Eve, but all this stuff still would have happened, you know. At least now, I'm not helpless. It's not *Eve's* choice what I do, either."

My mother's eyes narrowed at the Estreyan woman, but she did not shrink back at all under the force of Ester's presence. "I would rather have a live child than a dead hero."

What did that mean? Did she think I had *chosen* any of this?

Torliam stepped forward then, so close he was almost pressing against the back of my shoulder. "Your tongue is venomous, woman, and you speak of what you do not understand. We are heroes, and champions, or we are *naught*. The enemy does not spare children. Heroes and innocents alike will fall before it."

My mother paled, though I did not know if it was from anger or fear.

Eliahan stepped up behind her in turn, scowling across our tense little group at Torliam. "You will not speak to the mother of my children so, Aethezriel. She has borne the line of Matrix—my line, and the line of queens. Know your place."

Queen Mardinest bristled, and the power of an overwhelming Charisma rang in her tone as she said, "It is the line of *Aethezriel* that rules now, Remnant."

"Peace. There are more important matters at hand," Reglium said, raising his arms and letting just enough of his power wash over the members of the room to interrupt any gathering Skills. "What aid can you lend?" he asked Ester.

"Our scryer," Ester said with a wave toward the crone. "Perhaps she will be able to aid your search for this 'Avatar.' Additionally, much of the knowledge we hold of runic technology seems to have been lost in our absence, so perhaps *we* can make some headway researching these warps. Even if we can be of use in no other way, be sure that we will lend our aid as warriors."

The ancient woman shook her head, gnarled hands squeezing and twisting around the wood of her cane. "It will not be enough. It was the Oracle who gave me my Bestowal. My power will not tip the scales if hers could not."

I swallowed, stealing a last glance at my mother before stepping away, suppressing my urge to pace. "That kind of thinking is useless." The words fell from my lips bold and clipped. I glared out at them all, and most looked away when I met their gaze.

"The Oracle is not infallible." When I spoke, Voice laced my words with power, not a blow of force but a steady wave. "She chose me because she knows this."

I let the silence stretch for a moment before continuing. "She chose me because I will continue on even if she fails, even if the gods crumble to dust before my eyes and the stars are swallowed up around me. And because I continue on, I will win." I half-believed the words coming out of my mouth, convincing myself even as I convinced them.

"The Oracle is not infallible," I repeated. "She did not give me a quest or hint at an answer, and that is because we must find the answer on our own."

"And how will we do that, child?" the old woman asked.

I hadn't had any real solution until I began to speak, only an intention to abort any defeatism before it started, but as I answered, a sense of relief and hope filled me, and I knew I might have found a clue, at least. "The Oracle once told me that she sees many paths and discerns which are most probable. She sees statistical likelihoods," I said. "So if we want to avoid her vision coming true, perhaps we simply need to act in a way that is statistically *unlikely*."

WE SPOKE FOR A WHILE LONGER, hashing out the details of personnel and resource allocation, and then sent a report to Earth explaining what we had discussed in the war room.

As we finally left, the others hurrying ahead, Torliam grabbed my elbow gently to hold me back. "It will be alright," he said, looking into my eyes. The two of us were almost the same height now. Someday, maybe I would look down on him.

"I know." I swallowed, turning my head away.

"Then perhaps you should allow yourself to believe it. I have some sense for your emotions, if you remember. Desperation is not the same as determination."

"You didn't experience it," I whispered. "The vision…it was a distillation of hopelessness."

He placed both hands on my shoulders as if to hold me steady. "This is not your first taste of such hopelessness. Yet, here you stand before me today. You have not lost until you have given up. Anything before that is merely a setback."

I let out a small snort of amusement, and some of the sick chill in my bones receded. "Alright. So we're going to win. We're all going to live, and when it's all over I'm going to kick the Oracle's ass for giving me that vision."

He squeezed my shoulders, a light, satisfied smile growing on his face. "Alright," he repeated with a nod, letting his hands fall away. He turned to leave, but this time I stopped him. "What about you? Are you okay?" I asked.

He rubbed a hand across his jaw. "It would be strange if I were truly 'okay,' but I have enough strength to continue fighting. I will be off," he said with a slight bow. "There is no time to waste." He strode away down the hall.

After a moment of aimlessness, I went to the castle library to research the Voids of Tartarus. I hoped we would find the Avatar quickly, but in the meantime I could prepare. No matter what, we would leave in the morning.

The Voids were apparently terrifying and mysterious, even to the Estreyans. I remembered the not-Eve, the little spark that Knowledge had left behind in my mind to teach me more about using Chaos, and the black oil-spill bubble she had started to create before I defeated her in that last dream session. Had she been about to use the Void Aspect of Chaos? Briefly, I regretted stopping her too soon, or not stopping Pestilence sooner. Perhaps that little spark would still be around to train me if the Sickness hadn't snuffed it out.

I thought of the methods she'd chosen to "motivate" me and changed my mind with a shudder. I'd literally rather walk through fire than be subjected to more of those horror-dreams.

I'd gone through almost everything relevant the library had about Void in connection to Chaos or Tartarus in only a few short, frustrating hours. There were Voids contained in Tartarus, which were deadly enough that a creature some sources said was a god and others called a monster—only ever vaguely referred to as the Warden—patrolled the level. Other than that, trying to find more, better information was an exercise in frustration. I sighed with relief when Queen Mardinest sent a data file to my link.

I unsnapped the clear surface from my arm and smoothed it out as I read everything she had pulled from the royal records about the "fruit of life." I took a moment to grumble to myself that I hadn't known about them when Chaos was eating me alive, before I'd learned to control it. I could only hope that obtaining them wouldn't be harder than destroying the corrupted manifestation of a god.

Most of the records were about the failed attempts to reach them and the questing parties that had disappeared in said attempts, with only a few delving into what exactly these fruit were. The descriptions were vague, saying only that they were irresistibly appetizing. After that, reports varied, some saying the fruit contained a source of endless healing and a piece of eternal youth, reminding me of the legendary ambrosia from my own world's myths. However, from what I could deduce from the more realistic descriptions of those who had eaten them historically, the fruit were more likely to have some sort of strong transformative power that constantly returned whoever ate one to their physical state at the time of consumption. This effect lasted for the equivalent of about three hundred earth years, weakening as time went on.

That was…much less impressive than I had been hoping for. Would taking the fruit mean that we couldn't get physically stronger or faster for the next three hundred years? What about the kids? Was it even *safe* for a child to take it?

When my temples began to ache with phantom pain and Chaos kept swirling up under my skin like a dog pulling against a leash, I stood up and strode off toward the gardens. I had to *do* something, or I'd go crazy.

Despite their name, the castle gardens were not just pretty plants, fountains, and hedge mazes, though there was plenty of that. Of course, on Estreyer the pretty plants were likely carnivorous or poisonous, the fountains held water sprites that would drown you and then eat the tongue out of your mouth, and the hedges moved around you in an attempt to keep you lost and trapped until you starved to death. The main attraction of the gardens, to me, were the training fields, sections of land with various terrain meant to aid in sparring practice and Skill control, and which no one cared if you happened to destroy.

I found Jacky already at our usual training field, which was mostly bare dirt and rocks, but had a medium-sized pond on the far edge that none of us had accidentally obliterated yet. She was meticulously outfitting herself with a set of body weights. Gregor had made them for her, cackling to himself about her not being so cocky about her strength after trying these out. She, too, would know the pain of muscle soreness, he'd promised me, then gone into some complicated explanation about charged magnetic fields not being the same as gravity. They covered her torso and limbs strategically and obstructed any major movement, in addition to being made of one of the heaviest substances Estreyer could provide. She tossed her head, flicking her short, layered hair away from her face. "You here to join me?" she asked, her Gravitational Autonomy Skill flaring as she rose up on to her toes.

I nodded.

She clenched and unclenched her fists, then snapped into a martial stance. "Then get started, already."

I complied, settling into a stance of my own. Her movements were short, quick, and powerful, using strength from her core to lend force to her strikes, while my own kata was more focused on graceful, fluid slices and stabs. "The others are handling the administrative tasks, and I just finished reading up on what little we know about these fruit and the Void Aspect. I hope Behelaino can help us, but I figure I'm going to need every ounce of control and expertise I can wring out," I said, adding a spike of Chaos to an elbow jab, while she stomped a small crater into the ground.

"That's kinda why I'm here too," she said, her voice lacking some of its standard verve. "The only thing I'm really good for is fighting, so I figure I better make sure I don't get rusty." She grew larger mid-strike, her fist ending up about an inch farther than it could have reached at her normal size. She followed this up with a backward leap that changed into a sideways roll halfway through as her Skill yanked her through the air with no leverage needed to change directions.

"You know that's not true, though, right? You're a fantastic fighter, but you're more than that, too. It's not all that you bring to the table." I spun out with a lashing kick. Cords of condensed Chaos followed in the wake of my strike, one wave, and then a second before my foot even returned to the ground, both fast enough to make the air whistle as they cut through it.

She snorted, but didn't reply. Her kata grew more powerful, and more unpredictable, changing course mid-movement in seemingly random directions that nevertheless always managed to end in a devastatingly powerful blow to an imaginary enemy.

"I'm serious, Jacky. I don't know why you tell yourself these stories about being inferior." I spun and jabbed my forearm out, and dark tendrils swirled forward, creating a shield as they went. I jumped away, following the shield with an explosion caused by a small area of super-heated air. I squinted as a few loose strands of hair whipped at my face in the small shock-wave, but I never stopped moving. I was carefully and deliberately practicing the movements Jacky had formulated to help me become a better fighter while forcing me to integrate both raw power and the fine manipulation of my Skills.

She blushed a little, moving faster and striking harder, till dust and pebbles sprayed up with every movement of her foot and the air snapped with the force of her blows.

"You're my friend, and you've saved my life more than a few times, but you also make me laugh, and you've spent a ton of time and effort training us. Seriously, you've gone above and beyond. You developed this martial kata *specifically for me*, Jacky!" I slammed a foot down, and the black flames of Chaos turned a small conic area in front of me into a spike field. The lake, which I'd been getting closer to as I went, rippled from the force of our combined movements and attacks, the water jumping about as if it were experiencing an earthquake. "Then you did the same for the whole team. I know how much time and research that took. I've heard the queen's guards talking about what a genius you are. I know that sword-Skill master from Aldavan tried to poach you. And…"

I stepped forward onto the lake, letting a burst of Chaos out from the pad of my foot as I brought it down. Chaos spread through a wide swath of water in an instant. Using a technique Jacky had thought up when researching my Skill to create my training plan, I delicately twisted the power spread throughout the water, forcing it to firm and still. When I placed my weight down, I sank only a little, never quite breaking through the surface tension of the liquid. It was like creating snow-shoes, or perhaps turning the area I controlled into a water balloon. By holding the molecules together unnaturally, I could disperse my weight throughout the water just enough that it could support me. It required the kind of fine control over Chaos that I had struggled to develop, and even with practice was very mentally taxing.

When I was certain I was not about to splash down into the water, as had happened more than a few times when I had started learning the technique, I grinned at Jacky. "I wouldn't have been able to do this, if not for you," I finished. "You're one of us, Jacky, and seriously, I'm going to have to kick your ass if you continue pretending we only keep you around to beat stuff up for us."

She ducked her head, covering her expression with a feathery section of her bangs for a moment, then looked up, grinning. "You, kick *my* ass? Don't get cocky just because you learned a few tricks." Still wearing her weights, she shrunk back down to her normal size, and, with a flare of power only obvious to Wraith's extra senses, stepped out on the water to join me. She, too, did not sink, though her feet got wet and seemed to stabilize a few inches beneath the surface.

She raised an eyebrow. "I've learned a few things, too, yeah?"

I let out a surprised laugh. "Are you serious, Jacky? I didn't even know you were practicing that! Awesome."

She crouched down, returning to her stance with a cocky grin. "Just imagine what I can do *without* the weights." She lifted her arm toward me and bent her her fingers in a "come-hither" motion like an action-move heroine.

I brought out Chaos, carefully ensuring that any hit from it would create bursts of colorful light with only a little heat rather than disintegrate her flesh, and sprang forward, a wide grin on my own face, our troubles temporarily forgotten.

ONCE JACKY and I had finished blowing off steam and were both covered in sweat and mud, we headed for Kris's workshop. The sun had set, and the stars were beginning to come out, twinkling brightly, each their own color to my enhanced eyes.

"How long till this Avatar gets big like you saw?" Jacky asked. She pushed her short, layered hair back like a film star, the crystalline symbol embedded in her hand glinting even in the darkness. It reminded me of a brand—a mark of ownership from the gods.

I was almost jealous of how consistently gorgeous she was, no matter how disheveled and filthy she might be. Even now that I'd met a few Estreyans with high Beauty and Charisma Attributes, she didn't lose in comparison. "I have no idea," I admitted, pushing open the door to Kris's workshop. "Hopefully a long time." I didn't say it aloud, but we both knew that without the God of Shaping and Molding to hold back the Avatar's influence, it might not take nearly as long as we hoped.

Within the workshop, which had once been a storage room, Kris stood atop scaffolding, her aviator goggles pulled down to protect her eyes. She was shaving away the edges of a gigantic marionette made of what might have been whale bone with what looked like a dagger-sized light saber, but was probably some kind of plasma cutter. The marionette was tall and slender, bipedal, with huge bone knives for fingers and forward-curving metal feet that would be good for speed and springy, explosive power.

Kris didn't turn when we entered, but she sent us a Window.

—GIVE ME A SECOND TO FINISH THIS UP. I'M AT A DELICATE POINT.—
-KRIS-

As she worked, I looked around the workshop at the marionettes. At least half of them housed a permanent spirit. They were doing chores and helping Kris with various stages of the production process. One waved to me, and I waved back, then did a double take when I saw a group in the corner that seemed to be playing with dominoes.

When Kris finished, she shut off her carving tool, carefully buffed the section of the marionette she had been working on, then turned to Jacky. "Eagle's nest?"

With a nod, Jacky moved beneath the girl and held her arms up.

With no hesitation, Kris jumped off the side of the scaffolding.

Jacky sprang up, caught her, and landed gently to set her on the ground.

A marionette Kris's size, less than a meter tall, jogged over and handed her a glass of water and a rag to wipe the sweat from her face, which she accepted with a nod.

Others gathered to show her little gadgets and the marionette parts they'd been working on, which she either approved or sent to the scrap pile. In the corner, these spare parts were being methodically broken down by a bovine-like marionette that chewed and separated the materials like a bored cow.

"Do we have an update?" she asked, turning to Jacky and me.

I shook my head. "No."

"We just wanted to check out your work, *chica*," Jacky said.

Kris nodded seriously, then went to the wall and pulled off a datapad that looked huge in her arms. "Okay. My inventory is still a little low. School gets in the way of workshop time, you know, and I can't just pass everything off to these guys." She looked up and added, "Even if they are learning," to reassure the marionettes, which seemed to be listening. "I have a lot of broad-utility and miniature forms, but not enough damage dealers or tanks. I had an idea for a kind of egg-with-legs form that would do search and rescue, and maybe I could even teach them to do basic first aid, but I've barely started designing the prototype. I think those might actually be the most useful, because no matter how much significance I put into my marionettes or what material I build them from, they will never stand up to something on the god-level. With search and rescue, me and the guys might really be able to make a difference."

I scanned the room again, my mouth slightly open. This was impressive, both more structured and more professional than I'd expected from a pre-teen girl. I used the Command Skill NIX had given me, which allowed certain privileges with the VR chips, to pull up her Attribute Window.

PLAYER NAME: KRIS MENDELL
TITLE: ONE OF NINE
SKILLS: SUMMON

STRENGTH: 2
LIFE: 13
AGILITY: 8

GRACE: 5
INTELLIGENCE: 12
FOCUS: 10
BEAUTY: 9
CHARISMA: 3
MANUAL DEXTERITY: 17
MENTAL ACUITY: 11
RESILIENCE: 12
STAMINA: 11
PERCEPTION: 8

Some of her physical Attributes, most noticeably her strength, had been lowered due to her diminutive body, but the rest, especially her Manual Dexterity, would be impressive even for an adult human. Still, with so little initial Seed material, her natural Attribute increases were stunted compare to those of us who'd glutted ourselves on NIX's—Torliam's—Seeds.

One of the marionettes, a small creature that looked a little like Pinocchio had, and who wore a handkerchief proudly around his neck, let out a series of rapid beeps from a small box attached to his chest. I thought it might have been super-quick Morse code, since Kris listened and then said, "Go ahead and get that started. No slacking off, guys. If I come in and find you playing games, some-one's getting moved to the no-limbs body."

I followed all of their gazes to the torso sitting sadly by itself in the corner.

The marionettes all shivered dramatically and burst into action, while the little guy with the handkerchief beeped angrily and waved his arms at them like a tiny tyrant.

I couldn't hold back a chuckle at the scene, and Kris shot me a wry smile. "They're cute, right? His name is Pino, and he's the foreman."

She was cute, too, but she was more than that and so were her creations. "Pino, short for Pinocchio?" I asked, thinking about the little puppet that had saved Kris's life when Pestilence destroyed her body.

She looked away, returning the datapad to the wall. "Well, kinda. Pinocchio's gone, and I'm living in what used to be his body, kinda, but I didn't want to just...forget him." Her head drooped and her shoulders hunched as she avoided my gaze.

I decided to change the subject and get her talking about something she enjoyed. There were no parents around to show interest and tell her how proud they were of her, after all. "So tell me about your latest design. Walk me through your process."

Her head lifted. She smiled up at me with surprise. "Oh! Um, sure!" Her shoulders drew back. "Well, I've always got a ton of ideas. I've been using the Seal of Nine fund to order rare and interesting materials from other levels, and you know I'm taking that runic engineering class on the weekends, which has been useful for adding significance and utility that would otherwise be difficult to integrate..."

She chattered on, showing off various projects and marionettes while Jacky and I listened. As she interacted with her creations, I saw how comfortable among them she was, and couldn't help but contrast that with the careful smile and straight back she wore around most others besides our team.

I resolved to redouble our efforts to find someone or a combination of someones who could return her to her full size. Every avenue thus far had led to disappointment, either failing outright or interacting dangerously with Kris's Seed core, which no longer circulated throughout her body like a human, instead coalescing in her chest. Still, maybe we had missed something. Truly impossible tasks did not exist, only those which had yet to be completed due to lack of cleverness or resources.

Chapter 4

The world outside had its own rules, and those rules were not human.

— Michel Houellebecq

EARLY THE NEXT DAY, with night mist still floating over the ground, we gathered on the airfield before Torliam's new ship. We would travel directly to the Shortcut anchor at Behelaino's Trial, and from there would fly the ship to the caldera atop her mountain. We hoped to obtain the Goddess of Chaos's aid before continuing straight on to the level where the fruits of life purportedly grew.

Torliam had hunted the creature that made up the body of the ship himself and used the most cutting-edge techniques to turn it into an air-fairing vessel. He had named her the *Swiftsure*. It was larger than *Lady Ladriel*, his old ship, by quite a bit. Enough for a main room attached to the open cockpit area, as well as a separate bathroom and small bedrooms barely larger than closets for each of us. Despite her size, she was also faster than *Lady Ladriel* and had an outfit of weaponry that would be effective against moderately dangerous threats.

I had taken every precaution I could think of. We were geared up with the best supplies money or influence could buy; what space in the ship's cargo hold was not filled with other necessities was stuffed with Kris's small army of marionettes; Blue had been paid his power crystals; and every competent, trustworthy person we could command or rope into helping was searching for the Avatar and preparing the worlds to fight.

We were ready to go.

With goodbyes that were more than a little awkward considering the things that had been said the day before, Zed and I had left our mother and Eliahan at the palace that morning.

I had asked Sam if he wanted to talk to his own parents, mindful that it might not be something to dread and avoid for him.

"I visited them a couple weeks ago, and I don't want them to see me like this, or worry endlessly. If I end up dying, fifteen more minutes of awkwardness between us won't change anything," he'd said with a wry smile.

Letting my head fall back, I looked up at the slowly brightening sky as I thought of Queen Mardinest's suggestion that we should force Ichi to help us.

From a pragmatic standpoint, the situation was too dire for a bit of squeamishness to keep us from doing the optimal thing. And it was true that Ichi's ability to instantaneously transport the entire team anywhere on Estreyer would be incredibly useful. Even just being able to get us to a Shortcut that would then take us to Earth would more than cut our response time in half, and would completely erase it if the emergency were on Estreyer. If his Skill would also work on Earth…

Still, the idea was distasteful.

From a utilitarian standpoint, hurting one for the sake of many was a good trade. But where did it end? I had no love for Ichi. I would beat him to a pulp, imprison him, and if he tried to fight back, I might even kill him. But this…it didn't feel the same. To be honest, it left my stomach feeling a little sick.

With a sigh, I shook my head and returned my attention to the present. I had told Queen Mardinest to go ahead with the production of a portable Skill suppressor. If we could find Ichi, something like a guided stealth rocket might be able to tag him with the suppressor before he realized the danger and teleported halfway around Estreyer to escape it. Whether I would use it to drag him

back to the capital and force him to obey us when the time came…
I didn't know.

Torliam, who I knew had spent all night receiving reports and
sending out orders through his datapad, checked over the *Swiftsure*
to make sure all the preparations had been completed correctly
while the rest of us waited.

Adam was creating a series of future Animus constructs on
small tablets made of various precious materials. He had created
each tablet by hand. Their value and subconscious significance to
him would boost the power of his Skill's creations.

Birch stood off to the side, practicing creating a little whirlwind
of Chaos around himself, which was slowly digging a circular crater
into the ground.

Jacky carried Kris, who had stayed up late in her workshop and
was now dozing off in the larger girl's arms.

Zed and Gregor were discussing ideas that would allow us to
subvert the Oracle's visions.

"That's a terrible idea," Gregor snapped at Zed. "Until we have
some good news to tell the citizen populations, or some actual way
that they can help, we should definitely *not* inform them of the
existential threat to all life. People are stupid and they act irra-
tionally, Zed. Have you even considered the consequences?"

"We'd never do it normally, that's what I'm saying," Zed replied,
ignoring the child's quarrelsome tone. "The Oracle wouldn't have
foreseen us announcing the truth to everyone. Maybe someone out
there has just the right combination of Skills or information that
we need."

Gregor snorted. "I'm not disputing that a handful of people out
there could be useful, but it's extremely unlikely that their useful-
ness outweighs the combined destructiveness of the *entire remainder*
of the population. What we should do is reach out discreetly to
those individuals with special Skills or education. Bad ideas don't
become good ideas just because we were unlikely to have chosen
them in the Oracle's vision. We need to come up with *good* ideas
that we simply would not have considered otherwise."

"And *how* do we do that?" Some frustration leaked into my
brother's voice.

Gregor's eyebrows scrunched together like two black caterpillars, but he didn't respond.

I stepped up beside them. "I think it might be as simple as continuing to search for solutions even after we think we've found an answer. So, say we try to come up with ten more ways to do something, even if we've already found a way that works. Maybe one of those other ways will be better in the long run. Or, if a couple different methods of accomplishing something seem equal, either we try both of them, or we randomize our choice by flipping a coin."

Gregor nodded with satisfaction. "Yeah, see, Zed?" he said, as if he'd given the answer himself.

I let out a small snort. "I refuse to believe that anything is impossible. Sometimes, though, you need to have made different choices in the past to change the present. Hopefully, we still have time to do that for the future. I'm trying to imagine if we could be doing something else, right *now*." We climbed onto the ship, then, and our conversation was interrupted by everyone settling in.

Going to see Behelaino seemed like the obvious choice, but did that mean it was the wrong one? Maybe I should have made up my mind about the forced loyalty contract and gone after Ichi right away? We might have been able to keep him sedated all the way back to the capital, even without a Skill suppressor. I just didn't know. It was like running blind, knowing there were knives in the dark, but unable to tell where they were before we cut ourselves on them.

The others gathered in the main room attached to the cockpit, and Torliam was of course at the controls, but I noticed Zed was missing. I found him fiddling with some equipment on the small cot in his room.

I knocked gently on the open doorframe.

He looked up briefly, then returned to his gadgets.

"What do you have there?" I asked, looking out the window as the Shortcut outside spun to life. It was more powerful than the one NIX had stolen, and large enough to transfer the entire *Swiftsure*, not just our bodies and whatever we could carry.

"Some sensory equipment," he muttered, not meeting my eyes.

I waited for more, and when it didn't come, said, "You've been quiet."

"I'm trying to figure out where we went wrong."

I stayed silent, waiting for him to continue on his own this time.

After a while, he did. "Like you were saying, sometimes to avert the current situation, you would have had to make different choices in the past. It wasn't impossible for this moment to be different, it's just impossible *now*. So what did we do wrong? Or if it wasn't us, when and where exactly *did* it go wrong?"

"I don't know. I think we've been running through all this blind, never really understanding what we were dealing with. We've been coping with immediate problems, and maybe by doing that we've been creating others. Or we've been cleaning just the surface rot and ignoring the deeper infection."

He let out a breathy half-laugh, tilting his head back. "When you say it like that, I guess this was bound to happen. I know, if I hadn't attacked Pestilence, you would be dead, or you'd be controlled and working for the Abhorrent. And that would be *worse*. But there had to have been a third option somewhere, right? I just don't know what it was, or where I would have had to make some previous decision differently, for a third option to open up."

"But you couldn't have done that," I said, struggling with the shape of the idea even as I expressed it. "We didn't understand. We had no reason to do things differently. We made decisions based on our personalities and the information we had at the time. Maybe it would have been different if we were more mature and experienced, if our information was more complete. But we didn't know any better. That's why we can see mistakes *after* the fact. The past... It's immutable." I paused, trying to make the words fit the concept. "I'm not saying there's no free will, but free will only exists in the future. Once a moment has passed, there's no way it could ever have been different, because it *wasn't* different. The people we were, with the information we had, they make the same decisions every time. But at least we can use those memories to make future decisions differently. This time around, we have to get all the answers. Once we truly understand what we're dealing with, then we'll be able to make decisions that don't lead to compounding problems."

He nodded slowly, looking back down at the equipment on his bed. "I think I get what you mean."

The Shortcut's eerie song built up, vibrating through everything, and then it snapped, and the view from the small window was different.

Zed stood and walked toward the common area, and I followed. "Don't worry, Eve. I'm not spiraling into depression or anything. I just want us to do better this time. I want *me* to do better this time," he said. "I'm *tired* of screwing up."

I gave his shoulder a brief squeeze, releasing it as we came within sight of the others.

I could see bright aquamarine water and white sands through the *Swiftsure's* wide cockpit window.

Adam waved me over to the corner where he was perched atop a two-seat couch that, like all the furniture, was melded to the floor so it would not fly around if Torliam needed to guide the ship into more extreme maneuvers.

I sat next to Adam, whose fingers were sunk into the sides of a datapad. Incomprehensible letters and numbers—data, or maybe an unfamiliar code language—scrolled past the display faster than any human eyes could take in.

"I'm looking at the data we've collected through satellites, terrestrial and marine seismic activity monitors, Estreyan communication beacons, instantly updating maps, predictions from both NIX's Thinkers and Estreyans with Skills that have access to heightened foresight abilities…and a lot of other stuff." He looked up at me briefly, his eyelids fluttering as most of his concentration remained on the data he was processing.

"We know the Abhorrent's Avatar, as Blue calls it, is somewhere on one of the two worlds. But there's seemingly no evidence of it. We are unable to locate it. There are a number of reasons why that might be, and I'm not sure which of them is worse. However, by the very act of existing, most things affect the world around them, and those effects create ripples. Data, if you have *enough* of it, can explain and model almost anything. So I'm trying to figure out a way to find the Avatar by the ripples it creates. I haven't done anything like this before, so it's a lot to get my head around."

"You're not trying to process all that data directly, are you?" I said.

"Of course not," he said, sounding insulted that I'd dare to even ask. "I'm creating a program that can flag suspicious activity on its own. I'm smart, Eve, but even with Seeds and Skills my brain is still limited. It would take me hundreds of years to go through all this, if not longer, and that's with my organic ability to recognize patterns and trends. This pad is connected remotely to a server room with a petra drive and eighty *yotta* of memory." The data scrolling past the screen slowed, and then he set the pad down.

It took him a few moments to continue speaking, and when he did, his voice was softer, almost quiet, as if he did not want the others to listen in, though none of them seemed to be paying attention to us.

"This whole thing… It was a surprise to all of us. This feeling of urgency, of the clock running out, it's familiar, but I'd almost forgotten it, after everything settled down, and with how busy we've all been. But I—"

He was interrupted as Gregor ran up. "Eve, I need you to give your clearance code. These idiots won't give me access to their Skill database, and I need it to compare known dimensional and quantum effects versus the warps."

I gave Gregor my code and was turning back to Adam to ask what he had been about to say when the ship stopped rising. The top of the waterfall-covered mountain came into view, a kilometer or so out from the wraparound cockpit window.

"We're here."

***

I STEPPED CLOSER to the front to get a better view. The white-sand beaches stretching out far below were different than I remembered, shot through with swirls of ochre and black sand. The plant life in the distance was also changed, now consisting mostly of blue trees which might actually have been giant mushrooms. However, the mountain itself was still the same. It was colossal, made of hundreds of flat-topped buttes and mesas gathered together and stacked into a tiered tower. Huge waterfalls spilled endlessly out from openings in the rock faces and crashed down the tiers, contributing to the thick veils of mist that rose around the sides and coalesced into dense clouds at the top.

Wraith could sense Behelaino's power at the center of the bowl-shaped caldera topping the mountain, though the clouds blocked my view. I thought I sensed her glow pulse in awareness of our arrival, many times brighter than I remembered. Then, she had been weakened from just causing a volcanic explosion of Chaos and using its black flames to cleanse the surrounding lands of Pestilence's influence. Looking back, it was still amazing that we had managed to steal the Seed core out of her chest, as weak as we had been.

I squinted down at the clear water below, searching for dark shapes cutting through the scattered lakes. It was almost nostalgic to remember the time a shark-like monster had nearly eaten me. "Approach slowly," I said to Torliam.

Birch stood beside me, his ears perked up and angled forward with interest. With a quick brush of his nose against my arm, he sent me what I thought must have been memories from when he was a hatchling. They were less visually and conceptually distinct than his normal communications, heavily focused on smell and touch. "*I hatched here?*" he asked.

"You did," I said.

His head swiveled, and after a moment his ears lost their perk. He sent me an even vaguer memory, and I heard the distorted sound of other tailos and the feeling of warmth and the occasional burst of mental connection that used no human words—a memory from when he was in the egg, with others of his kind surrounding him and attending to him lovingly. "*But there are no tailos here,*" he said.

"We didn't find you here. It was during a different Trial, before this one. It was in the middle of a huge desert, but your...*pack,* they lived in a copse of extremely tall, interwoven trees that soaked up liquid through their entire surface. When we arrived, monsters under the ground were attacking the roots of the trees to try and topple them, and these disgusting flying monsters called retchin had attacked the tailos. Our team—though there were less of us at the time—tried to help protect your pack, but there were too many enemies. The pack leader, who I think must have been your mother, gave your egg to me and tasked me to protect you, and we escaped with you."

"*Left pack behind? Pack all dead?*" He sent me the absence of Chanelle and Blaine to explain his concept of death.

I bit the inside of my lip, then winced as the pointed teeth at the sides of my mouth sank into the skin. My Seeds went to work repairing the damage right away. "It is likely they are all dead, but I don't know for sure."

He sent me a burning curiosity. "*Tell stories.*"

"I don't know a ton about the tailos," I admitted, feeling guilty that I had not researched his people enough to be able to answer his questions. *Of course* he would want to know these things. Any orphan would. "But how about this? When we're done with Behelaino, I'll tell you everything I can remember about that Trial, and we can look up more on the Net. And then, when all this is over, we'll make a visit to that desert."

He let out a small sound that was difficult to decipher, and then nodded.

Having arrived at the outer lip of the bowl-shaped caldera, Torliam let the ship hover above the stone ledge. "If you wish, we can disembark here, and I can have the *Swiftsure* circle continuously around the mountain till called."

I agreed, a burning excitement that held hints of anxiety filling my chest. The others began to descend, jumping from one stone ledge to another, but I simply jumped forward, off the side, and plummeted straight down.

I slammed into the stone below in the iconic three-point stance, hard enough to jar my joints and organs and bruise the parts of me that had made contact with the ground…but the ground *cracked.*

In the middle of the caldera, the column of steam surrounding Behelaino's semi-humanoid body exploded outward.

The force of the steam-filled wind sent my braid slapping backward and instantly drenched me in a layer of warm water.

When the wind died down and the steam cleared, I looked up, taking in Behelaino's impressive figure.

Her torso was rooted in the stone and boiling water before me, her body stretching upward a dozen meters at least. She looked slightly different than I remembered. Molded obsidian formed a spiked halo around her head, and the water that ran over her body in obvious defiance of physics, connecting her limbs and filling her torso, was now as black as the ocean on a moonless night.

The features of her face were still distinctly formed, and the stone near where her hips melded with the mountain still ran a bright liquid orange, occasionally sprouting different colored flames. I could sense her Seed core hidden within the water of her chest, as brilliant as a little sun, though still smaller than the one the God of Knowledge had held.

Before, there had been large flat-topped columns of stone that broke up the surface of the water and allowed us to approach and fight her, but now the space between us was only bright bubbling liquid with the glow of lava underneath.

Behelaino's voice boomed out with the slow, crashing impact of a rockslide. "Eve-Redding. You have grown, godling. It is good that you have come to pay homage to your ascendant."

I suppressed an awkward cough. Paying homage? Was that something I was supposed to have done? "Well met, Behelaino."

The others finally reached the base of the caldera, but on Adam's unspoken warning they stayed near the edge, as far away from Behelaino as possible. Disregarding Adam's order, Birch pranced up and let out a roar of greeting when he reached my side.

The water bubbled up and splashed him in the face, and he jerked back with a squawk of surprise, shaking his head. He laid his ears back and let out a small tendril of Chaos toward the water, seemingly just to show that he could, and then settled down beside me.

"You look slightly different." The goddess leaned down as if to get a better look, looming over me.

"I'll be as big as you when I grow up," I joked awkwardly, immediately cringing internally.

I hadn't been sure if she would get the joke, but she threw back her head and laughed. "You are bold as always. I did well, to allow your ascendance."

I paused as her stone eyes examined me, mulling over her choice of words. We had been quite naive the first time we climbed the mountain. I had more experience with gods and the power of

Chaos now. If I had a Seed core as big as hers, even if I were constrained to the form of a volcano and had just used the black flames to remake the land for kilometers in every direction, I would have had no trouble simply disintegrating a group of five early level Players. Our fight against her had been a test, not a real attempt to crush us.

"Thank you," I said, putting my gratitude into the word.

She dipped her head in acknowledgment, seeming to understand my meaning. "You destroyed the sickness that had plagued this land. This pleases me."

My scales shifted uncomfortably. "But we have not defeated the Abhorrent, and more of its servants come to enforce its will. That's why we're here, actually."

Her arms crossed over her chest, a human motion that I wouldn't have expected from her. "You came to me for strength before, willing to trade time for power. Is your conviction still as strong?" Her scrutiny gave pressure to the question, as if the air had grown heavier.

"It is," I said.

"I would test your will, godling. If it is lacking, naught may aid you, for any boons will be squandered and any weapons will slip from your grasp."

I flexed my fingers. "I've overcome more than a few trials to stand before you today. Anything you have for me will be no different. I'll prove whatever I need to."

"Send your subjects away so we do not harm them. You will fight me, and we will see the truth of your path to ascension."

Gregor let out a deep, aggravated sigh and turned to Torliam. "Just call the ship to come pick us up here. I don't want to have to climb all the way back up there."

Jacky gave me a thumbs up. "Be careful not to kill Behelaino, alright?"

Behelaino let out a scoffing rumble, and a shark burst out of the water, its mouth open to take a bite out of Jacky, but she jumped away and bounded up the side of the mountain, laughing with no real fear, and Behelaino did not attempt to catch her.

A relieved sigh rushed from my lips as I shared a smile with Adam, who rolled his eyes. Behelaino's mood could change with the swiftness of a lightning strike, but those of the team who had been with me while the goddess struggled to teach me to control Chaos seemed to have no true fear of her, or even, in Jacky's case, an appropriate amount of respect.

While my teammates vacated the mountain, I flexed and relaxed my muscles, preparing them for sudden action. The scales that covered my torso and extended halfway down my arms and legs shifted, and my clawed, animalistic feet scratched at the ground as I dug my toes in. I didn't need to activate Spirit of the Huntress, as it seemed the Skill never turned off, now, but I extended Wraith fully through and around the mountaintop.

I released Chaos, the thick black mist boiling eagerly up from my skin.

Chapter 5

We'd stared into the face of Death, and Death blinked first.
   — Rick Yancey

I WAITED for Behelaino to make the first move.

Wraith could sense the golems she had hidden, spots of energy that stood out against the overall glow of the mountain. Instead of attacking me directly, however, those points of power all swarmed toward Behelaino. Lava, water, and stone converged on her and leaped into place, fitting themselves to her body. They attached, twisting and turning and settling together with practiced coordination, building a massive, complex body. It looked like a scene from a film—some mecha transforming into its ultimate form.

I sprang forward with a leap that was as much physical as it was my Skill playing with the density of the air, accelerating so fast pebbles sprayed out behind my footsteps. You don't just politely allow your opponent to finish transforming into their super-self without interruption, not if you actually care about winning.

The water separating us had no platforms, but that didn't matter. Using the technique I'd been practicing, I let a broad net of Chaos spread from my feet as they slapped down onto the water and, with a delicate twist on the power, forced the water to firm and still for an instant, just enough for me to push off of it before sinking more than a couple inches in. Moving faster meant I could keep from sinking even with less of the liquid under my control, but it required much greater mental agility, since I had to keep reapplying the effect with each new step, maintaining perfect timing.

Chaos was change, but that didn't have to mean destruction. Under my will, it simply meant *control.*

The water was hot enough to be almost unbearable, even to my ultra-toughened foot pads. Molten heat glowed from underneath, and I wondered how the water managed to resist instant evaporation in an explosion of steam.

It took me less than a handful of seconds to reach Behelaino. I spun to evade even as I came within range, using the turn to lash out with a dark scythe of highly compressed Chaos contained within a slightly weaker coating.

It was good that I had been cautious, never intending to battle it out face to face, because a chunk of lava from Behelaino's side moved to defend without the goddess needing to move her limbs like a human with fully articulated joints would.

The scythe hit the lava, and, as I had created it to do, it exploded, the condensed Chaos within writhing out like an eldritch maw that gnawed away at anything it touched.

Much of the lava was destroyed or sent back onto Behelaino, but some of it splattered out toward me, and it forced me to create a shield of Chaos behind my swiftly retreating back.

A wall of water rose up in front of me to cut off my escape, so I thrust a wedge of Chaos forward to break through, sending it extra power as the water resisted being pushed aside or boiled off.

The resistance slowed me down, and I almost sank into the lake before I could regain speed and burst through the barrier. I slammed into the stone of the caldera wall at a full sprint, absorbing the impact with my legs and springing off again, sprinting toward the area behind Behelaino. I didn't expect this to throw her off, not with her newly revealed ability to control random sections of her body autonomously, but maybe it would slow her down and give me an opening.

This time, as I passed behind her, I condensed Chaos into solid, fibrous cords that formed a web, which fell in toward her like a pincer from either side. My Chaos was darker, without that almost shimmering quality that hers held.

Her own Chaos burst from her chest, dark and twinkling and unformed, but so abundant that it overwhelmed mine, eroding the condensed weave into mist, which quickly dispersed.

Before I made it past, the water rose up again, this time forming a column all around me. Simultaneously, the liquid underneath my feet rushed away so fast it created a whirlpool, like it was being flushed into a giant toilet, and took my footing with it. I quick-stepped, scrambling in a circle and lashing out with Chaos, but I was unable to build up any momentum to break through the barrier.

Below the water, Wraith sensed the orange burn of lava fountaining up toward me.

Gritting my teeth, I pushed off against the side of the whirlpool and leapt into the air. At the peak of my upward trajectory, I released a burst of Chaos, spreading the cloud of dark mist as far out as possible to grab as much of the low-density gas as I could. With a precisely timed application of power, I created a platform to push off of in mid-air, and then another, and another, and then I was out over the lip of the column of water she'd used to surround me.

I pushed off sideways, gasping from the effort of not only using so much power, but the mental speed and control it required to use my Skill in such a way. I sent a couple whipcords of Chaos lashing back toward Behelaino as I fell, hoping to distract her.

She blocked one, but the other left a deep gash in her back. The lava that had been rushing up beneath the whirlpool turned sideways to follow me, forming teeth and fins even as it leapt from the water. On my other side, one of Behelaino's gargantuan arms swung toward me, the forearm and hand unfolding as it whistled through the air like a much bulkier—and more solid—version of the net I had tried to use against her.

I was forced to keep climbing rather than let myself fall, her arm whistling past just under my feet, but while the lava shark reached the apex of its leap and dove back into the water, Behelaino herself had no such gravitational constraints.

The goddess had turned around to face me, or perhaps just

rebuilt her body facing my direction. I thrust off the air directly toward her, pushing a drill of Chaos in front of me.

It smashed into her head, but since her head was already unfolding to the sides, twisting into winged forms of lava, water, and obsidian, my attack did less damage than it otherwise would have. Still, it bought me the space to move forward, my foot touching down for an instant on the base of her neck. I used the opportunity to send a spike of Chaos right down through her body as I pushed off, and she jerked and lurched forward as if she'd lost her balance.

I touched down on the surface of the water on her far side and kept running as the winged creatures she'd created from her head flew after me, joined by darting orange forms following me beneath the water.

I reached the wall and made to jump off it again, but the plain stone flooded with Behelaino's power and my legs sunk into the wall like jelly, while the rock ledges above me began to fall down. Wraith took in the flying and swimming golems converging on me, the collapsing ledge above, and the stone that continued to tighten and harden around my legs, trapping me. My mind spun, trying to come up with a method to shield or free myself. I hesitated half a second too long.

The stone around my legs collapsed inward, and I screamed in pain as my bones creaked and my flesh bruised and squished like a soft berry under a foot. Chaos exploded out of me with no conscious control, devouring everything, but my lack of concentration meant one of the lava golems made it through, and though I destroyed it before it could do more than make the lightest burns on my skin, a huge rock golem following full speed in its wake slammed into me with the force of a train, crushing me against the outer wall.

It did not last long against the raging storm of Chaos around me, but it had already accomplished its goal, and I collapsed forward, coughing out blood and gasping breathlessly against the kind of pain that would only be made worse by screaming.

Across the water, Behelaino watched me, completely undamaged.

She sent a second wave of golems, some of them formed of

Chaos, and as I struggled to push myself to my feet, I sensed the remains of the wall behind me begin to break apart into even more enemy forms. I still had Adam's shields tattooed across my forearms, and a pair of wings inked into my shoulders, but the shields would not last long against Chaos, and the wings were not as maneuverable as the smaller flying golems. To use either would be a move of desperation, not a strategy that would allow me to win.

My legs were already healing, but it would take at least a half hour before I could walk normally, not to even consider *running*, and there had to be some internal bleeding beyond that. I wasn't down to the last dregs of my power yet, but I would need to use what remained strategically, not go around disintegrating everything she threw at me. She could keep that up. I couldn't.

Forcing my body to stand straight despite the pain, I used my only other option, hoping desperately that it would buy me the time I needed to come up with something better.

"Kneel," I ordered, the word resounding with a vibrating echo as Voice lent power to it.

The golems slowed, then stopped. The ones made of light-and-dark fire resisted, but I pushed more power into Voice, concentrating on the supremacy of my will. I had held off Pestilence. I could do the same to a few dozen golems. The golems made of Chaos dissolved in a shudder, and the others seemed to lose their animating force, dispersing into the water or returning to the base stone and lava from which they had been raised.

Trembling slightly and listing to one side, I stood surrounded by crude statues and puddles of slag.

I'd barely had time to breathe a sigh of relief when the ground beneath my feet trembled and the very walls began to shake.

The glow of Behelaino's power in my mind's eye thrummed and brightened like a fire that had been fanned and fed, and the delicately carved features of her face twisted into an angry glare. "I. Do. Not. Kneel," she said.

The world shook with her words.

"Oh, shit," I whispered.

THE CHAOS in Behelaino's core brightened even further as she prepared to attack, building up so quickly I knew there would be no chance to outrun it.

I unleashed my own power even as I dropped to one knee. I ignored the pain from my abused appendages and leaned a bracing shoulder forward. Rather than counterattacking, every drop of Chaos I could bring to bear went into creating a half-dome-shaped shield between me and Behelaino. I condensed it as tightly as possible and smoothed the surface till it reflected light like a molecularly perfect mirror, hoping that would let the shield deflect some of her attack rather than absorbing it head on.

The brightening of her power slowed as she reached the apex of her buildup, and I activated every single tattoo shield on my left arm at once, layering them underneath the shield of condensed Chaos.

Behelaino released her attack.

Chaos hit me like a geyser.

My shields scraped against the rock as I was pushed backward, and I dug them and my claws into the ground for purchase, squeezing my eyes shut and hunching my shoulders as the world tore apart around me.

The sound was so deafening it might as well have been silence, except for the pain in my ears and the blood that dripped from them. Through the layers of dark Chaos and ink shields and even my closed eyelids, my eyes still picked up colors I had never seen before, so bright and searing and sharp that I thought I might go blind. I could feel my shields wearing away, the first layer of Chaos being eroded like sandstone by a river, while Adam's shields popped, one by one, like soap bubbles. I had to withdraw Wraith closer to my body to avoid being completely overwhelmed.

I dredged up more power from within, feeling it sear through my bloodstream as I reinforced the Chaos shield, and then activated all the ink shields on my right arm as well.

Even so, by the time Behelaino's attack subsided, the only thing standing between me and her was a weakly shimmering barrier of my own Chaos, which dissolved as soon as I no longer desperately continued to fuel it from my rapidly emptying reserves.

The shaking and rumbling continued on for several long

seconds after her attack had ceased, and only after the mountain had settled did I unclasp my arms from around my head and rise from my kneeling position.

Half the mountain was gone. It looked as if some gigantic laser beam had cut away everything in its path, except for me and the small patch of ground underneath and directly behind me. The caldera now opened up onto clear air. Even the mist that had filled it was completely gone.

The super-heated water frothed and crashed between us as it rushed in to fill the space that had been emptied.

I remained alert but still, panting as I tried to regain some energy. A quick scan of the skyline found the faint outline of the *Swiftsure* on the far side of the mountain, safe.

Slowly, the rumbling died down.

I watched with Wraith for hints of an attack.

"You flicker like a used candle flame. Is this the extent of your will?" she said finally.

I straightened, despite the pain in my legs. "No." I was almost out of strength, but I had enough left to condense a few cords of Chaos, wrapping them around my torso like a harness and using their tips to lift me up from the ground, taking the pressure off my legs. Adam had done the same with his ink constructs when his spine had been damaged, so I knew it would work if I could simply keep Chaos under my control, and I had been practicing my control constantly.

Behelaino nodded, and the rumbling began anew. Except this time, it didn't stop at severe earthquake levels. The stone began to crumble and the water to jump. The mountain fell apart around me, and then its pieces floated up, as if Behelaino had decided that gravity did not apply here.

The ground under my feet rose and crumbled away, and as my mind stuttered in fear and awe, I was forced to use the cords of Chaos to grab onto nearby floating boulders to keep from falling through the three-dimensional minefield she was creating.

With a mental slap to myself, I stopped observing in awe and remembered that this wasn't merely a gratuitous display of power, but an attack that was likely meant to pulverize me. These floating pieces of the mountain were really just more extensions of her body.

The possible escape routes were constantly shifting and disappearing, and the power suffusing everything around me eclipsed my own by more than a dozen times over. I couldn't match it head-on, and if it continued much longer, I would run out of strength and might well end up dead. It didn't seem Behelaino was holding back this time.

Worse than that, though, if I lost here, I wouldn't be able to get her help against the Avatar and the Abhorrent. That was unacceptable, so I had to find a way to turn her wanton use of power to my advantage.

Her core shone bright to Wraith's senses despite everything, and I mentally mapped a path to it while I pushed more Chaos up through my burning veins, lengthening the cords wrapped around and extending out from me. I rolled my shoulders, cracking the joints, and with a whispered, "Animus," unfurled the wings Adam had settled under the skin there.

Rather than using them for flight, I used my harness of Chaos, yanking myself through the air in abrupt jerks, weaving through the minefield so quickly I felt like I would give myself whiplash. The gigantic wings wrapped around me, acting as a shield whenever I got too close to a floating chunk of stone, or blob of lava or water. When she attacked with Chaos, I countered directly, but my main defense was the speed and erratic nature of my movement.

In response, she spun the floating minefield around more quickly. Despite the agility the cords of Chaos afforded me, they were braced on the surrounding boulders, and any time something ran into their length, they either had to move or disintegrate it. It was the same for my body.

The space around me became a tornado of death with the eye closing in on me, but I continued to compress and guide my power with uncompromising focus. My wings disintegrated under the force of the attacks, and I was forced to use Chaos to shield myself. The Chaos harness had trouble keeping me afloat, let alone maneuvering me, as its anchors spun out of control. Still, I concentrated, my eyes closed against the whipping wind and debris, bruises beginning to sprout all over my body as I was struck and tumbled about.

A single tendril, so thin it was invisible to the naked eye, threaded up and out through the center of the maelstrom, where Behelaino's power was thinnest. From there it floated, almost weightless, through the air in a giant loop, curving around to finally approach Behelaino from behind.

Chaos, not my own, laced through the wind and tore at my skin and scales, scraping off flesh as if it were soft wood under sandpaper.

My eyes popped open. The invisible tendril snapped forward like a striking snake.

It took Behelaino less than a second to realize what I had done.

The tornado made of her mountain slowed, then stilled, a path from her to me opening up.

I wiped away the blood flowing from my nose, showing bloody, sharp teeth as I smiled at her.

That single, filament-fine tendril of Chaos that I had managed to get through without her noticing was sunk into the black water of her chest, encircling her Seed core in a clear threat. She looked down, her expression almost disbelieving, and then back up to me.

The debris scattered around me dropped, and I would have fallen with it, drained to the point I couldn't catch myself on the air alone, but Behelaino created a stone platform to let me ride down on.

Slowly, carefully, I withdrew the filament of Chaos, letting the remnants of unused power sink back beneath my skin. It was hard, really, but as I collapsed across from her once more, the space between us divided by a field of steaming boulders and pools of lava, I heroically resisted the urge to say, "I won."

If she got angry and decided to swat me, I was too exhausted to defend myself, after all.

YOUR AGILITY HAS INCREASED!
YOUR FOCUS HAS INCREASED!
YOUR RESILIENCE HAS INCREASED!

I IGNORED THE WINDOWS, dispersing them with an absent thought.

The towering goddess tapped irritated fingers against her sides as she stared down at me. "I concede your will is acceptable," she finally said. "But you used your little subject's skin-painting ability to shield yourself instead of relying only on the strength which you could rightfully call upon."

"I look at it differently," I said with a shrug. "Anything I can manage to use is power I rightfully call upon. I will use everything I have access to. It's about *winning*, not following some set of arbitrary rules or looking good."

She nodded slowly, her body casually shedding the modular additions as the golems sank back into the water and concealed themselves against the stone, leaving her again slightly different than she had been before. As Khaos, she likely had no set form. "Your path resists constraint, as does mine, but though you grow closer to ascension, godling, it seems you will not follow the mold of your ascendant. You are not simply of Khaos," she declared, enunciating the "K" and "H" separately. "Perhaps your path was threaded with the greater power of another, or perhaps your mortal will simply diverges from the concept. In either case, you shall not be called Khaos, should you ascend fully." She let out a huff, almost knocking me off my shaky footing with the force of the breeze. "It is no surprise. New godlings often diverge. Darkness and the night were both born from me, after all."

I bit my lip gently, remembering a few of the things Torliam had told me. I was descended from the line of Matrix, who were said to have some distant relation to the God of Shaping and Molding. After the little god had seemingly fallen to Pestilence, Torliam's Tracker Skill had pointed to me when he tried to find him. But...I was pretty sure I didn't have any Seeds except those from Torliam and the Bestowals from the gods.

"Call your subjects back, if you wish," Behelaino said. "They will be safe, now, and we may speak of your troubles."

I did so, and as my teammates returned, she used a few broad strokes of Chaos to fix some of the destruction our fight had caused the mountain.

"Did you win?" Jacky asked as she jumped down from the *Swiftsure*.

"Enough to convince Behelaino to help," I said. I knew the goddess could have killed me if she really wanted. I still wasn't strong enough to win a one-on-one with an immortal being. If my teammates had been allowed to fight with me, though, the odds might have shifted.

This time, the others didn't stay as far back, gathering on either side of me.

Gregor scowled as he looked me up and down critically, then turned to Sam. "Fix her," he ordered.

With a huff of exasperation, Sam laid a hand on my arm and took the worst of the damage from my legs, then sat down to allow his body to heal the wounds he'd assimilated.

"Thanks," I murmured.

"Don't you think that test was a little overboard?" Adam asked, clearly unable to decide if he was more worried or angry. "I legitimately thought you were going to die when she unleashed that beam attack." His eyes flicked toward Behelaino before continuing. "Seeing that the goddess doesn't seem to know the difference between a real fight and a sparring match, we were just about to come down and join you."

"Goddess or not, you would have not survived if you truly maimed or killed Eve," Torliam said, addressing Behelaino directly.

Jacky nodded, too, opening her mouth to add to their comments.

Before she could do so, I cut her off. "Are you guys seriously trying to re-start the fight I just finished? Behelaino's agreed to talk to us, so just cool it."

They shared looks with each other, seemingly unapologetic, but at least they didn't continue antagonizing the goddess standing in front of us.

Behelaino shook her head disapprovingly. "You must learn better control of your subjects, godling. Perhaps removing their mouths would teach them the appropriate lesson."

Gregor lifted his hands to his mouth in horror, staring up at the goddess, wide-eyed. "Remove my mouth?" he whispered.

"That will not be necessary, I think," I said. "Let's just return to the matter at hand. Each moment is precious." At Behelaino's nod, I explained, once again, the vision and our talk with Blue, though this time I told the whole of it. "Blue said the Void Aspect of Chaos might be able to stand against the Avatars."

"It is possible," she agreed with a rumble.

I swallowed hard. "Will you fight with us, then? I haven't learned to use that Aspect of Chaos yet. Perhaps with your help, we can avert the end of the world."

An aftershock caused me to flinch with alarm, but Behelaino seemed calm. After a moment of consideration, she said, "Khaos is one of the few truly greater powers. From me, many other gods were born, and each of my Aspects is both great and terrible. Of those Aspects contained within me, the Void is both the greatest and the most terrible, for it cannot exist unbound without swallowing all that is not itself. It was the first. No mortal language has the words to explain it, for it is the antithesis of mortality as it is the antithesis of existence. We may only speak around it by explaining what it is not." Even talking about it, Behelaino seemed to grow stronger and stranger, her presence causing my hair and scales to prickle upright and a cold sweat to sprout from my palms as something in my hindbrain urged me to run away.

My teammates seemed to feel it too, some of them having shrunk back or hunched down, and even Jacky, with all of her disregard for the threat Behelaino manifested, was white-faced, her fists trembling at her sides.

I forced my breath to remain steady and my scales to flatten, though I could not stop the cold sweat or the pounding of my heart. "But you can control it. Estreyer hasn't been swallowed by the Void, which I'm pretty sure exists in Tartarus right now."

The black water flowing along and connecting her body pulsed, drawing my gaze as if I could sense something else staring out of it. Her head tilted to the side, but her movements had lost the faint hint of humanity I had noticed earlier. "I am Khaos. Though you see me in this form before you, I may *be* constrained. I do not *constrain.* Even if I were capable of changing my own nature so, the Void is barred from me."

In the silence that followed this statement, Torliam spoke, saying, "What do you mean?"

"I am the Goddess. The one that came before, and was formed. I am change. I am destruction and birth. I am Khaos constrained by order, the formlessness shaped, and only thus does all you see before you exist. The Void is part of me as well, but since the greatest of the gods first came together to create, to meld our power, it has been shunted aside and confined, and my oath given that it will never be birthed from me again. Even we cannot remove its existence completely, and this is the only reason that some remnant of it is imprisoned within Tartarus."

As fast as the disappointment hit me, desperation rose up in its wake. I clenched my fists hard enough that my claws sank past the toughened skin of my palms, shaking my head in denial. I paced back and forth for a few seconds, avoiding the stunned and dismayed faces of my teammates, then spun back to her. "What about me? I'm not the goddess of Khaos, and I never made any promises, but I can use your power. You could just teach me."

She shook her head, and I continued on desperately before she could deny me aloud. "This is important, Behelaino. No matter how dangerous Void is, it can't be worse than what the Abhorrent is going to do. If the world will be destroyed either way, we should at least choose the option that *attempts* to save it. It's not just the mortals that are in danger, you understand? The Abhorrent goes after the gods, too, and maybe Pestilence couldn't infect you, but he got the God of Knowledge and dispersed the God of Shaping and Molding, and this new Avatar might not be something you're so easily immune to—" I cut off as she raised her hand, palm facing toward me.

"With only mortal perception and memory, you cannot access the Void. Even now, you use Chaos in singular, distinct expressions, not truly. If I were to eschew this form and attack you with my essence unconstrained, you would have no defense. You do not understand your power. The idea of Chaos as infinite is one you do not, and, I think, *cannot* understand."

I returned to my pacing. "Maybe the God of Knowledge could teach me? He gave me a Bestowal that was teaching me how to use Chaos better, and I think she was about to show me the Void, but Pestilence destroyed the Bestowal before we could kill him."

She leaned forward, a frown on her face, to peer more closely at me. "Tell me of this Bestowal and its use of my power."

When I had explained, she drew back and made an angry sound that was more like the lightning-strike of cracking rock than a human vocalization. "This teaching-dream did not use my power, nor could it teach you to use the Void. It merely gave you a hint to the existence of this Aspect based on Knowledge's understanding of its effects. Even that fool has not touched the Void, and he was not yet born in the beginning." She paused, the anger slipping from her face. "Perhaps, if there *was* a way to let you touch the Void, to submerge yourself in it and experience it without dying or losing your sanity... Once you had been forced to comprehend the immortal infinite, your understanding stretched and expanded, you might be able to call upon a piece of it."

Perhaps sensing the immediate shift in my mood, she crossed her arms and admonished, "This is no way to *win*, godling. If you attempt this, you will surely die. If you do not die, you will lose yourself. If you do not lose yourself, you will lose control of the Void as it eats away at your mortality, and then it will swallow the world. It is only another way to fail. Find a different path."

Her admonishment subdued my exuberance but did not crush it completely. Chaos should have killed me, eventually, and yet here I was.

Pestilence was supposed to have been impossible to defeat, and yet everyone who had been under his influence was cured.

Why couldn't this be the same?

"What about the fruit of life?" I blurted. "If I took one before attempting to experience the Void, could it keep me alive?"

Her scowl grew deeper. "It may," she conceded. After a heavy pause, where she glowered with a surge of frustration and distress that was expressed almost physically by the aura of power lashing around us, she continued, "But if I am to let you attempt such a thing, I will have a vow from you and yours. If you wish to access the Voids, you will go to Tartarus. If, somehow, you manage to live, you must vow that you will not return if your will cannot contain the Void. If it overcomes you, eats away your mortality and your sanity, you must preserve the world and all within it. I would have your vow that you will not become the end you attempt to avert."

WE ALL AGREED to give the vow readily, but Behelaino's apprehension only grew as she carefully formulated the binding words we were to speak.

"The mortals may lie and betray," she said, "but they are your responsibility. Your word must be your bond, godling. I care not for the stakes, for the circumstances, for any excuse you may think of. You will keep both the word and the spirit of this vow."

"I will," I said.

Water lashed around as if being blown by a strong wind, and the mountain trembled. "Speak, then," she said.

"Neither by action nor inaction shall I allow the Void to exit Tartarus without being covered with the aegis of my will, sound of mind, and conviction. Neither by action nor inaction shall I allow the Void to consume the realms of the gods that have come before me, and my will shall stand always as a shield against this power's spread. I will uphold both the word and the spirit of this vow. So mote it be."

I didn't feel particularly different after saying the words, except for the conviction that settled in my chest. This was a promise I would not break, by choice if not by compulsion.

I opened my mouth to ask her if she had any other ideas of how we might defeat the Avatars, but the rumbling of the mountain around us had not stopped, and Behelaino's limbs were flexing restlessly. I was only halfway through my question when her core began to glow brighter in my mind's eye with gathering power.

"The risk is great," she said, her voice strained, slightly absent. "My own vow constricts, my bindings wake from slumber. Can you be trusted, godling? Your will may be great, but your recklessness is just as much so."

Torliam stepped forward, blue mist wafting subtly off him and spreading out as a shield around us. "I am calling the ship," he murmured to me.

"Perhaps I should kill you here," Behelaino said, her tone what someone might sound like if they were contemplating whether to have Chinese or pizza for dinner.

"You can trust me," I called to her, while mentally I ran

through a slew of curses and readied my own power to respond as best it could. I sent a message to the others via Window.

—When the ship arrives, no dawdling.—
-Eve-

—No shit.—
-Adam-

"I WILL BE responsible with Chaos, all forms of it," I promised Behelaino, not even quite sure what I was saying except that I was stalling for time. "I have been before, and I'll continue to be. I may have endangered myself a few times, but I don't just recklessly use my Skills in ways that could hurt others. People I don't *mean* to hurt, that is."

The *Swiftsure* arrived with a speed that did credit to its name, stopping nimbly and allowing us to scramble into the open door.

Torliam lunged for the cockpit even as the *Swiftsure* began to rise on its own.

"Strap in!" I yelled.

We each threw ourselves into a seat, slamming our heads into the braces meant to keep us from getting whiplash and throwing the safety harnesses around our bodies. Birch leapt into the seat next to me and I did my best to secure him within a harness, and though it didn't fit his feline shape well, I hoped it would keep him from tumbling about the ship's interior.

A spherical shield, visible only as a faint shimmer in the air, flickered to life around the *Swiftsure*, and then Torliam cranked one of the cockpit handles all the way back.

We shot upward so fast my back cracked as it compressed against my seat, slamming through a barrier of water and lava, then pulverizing a couple boulders. A wave of Chaos swept after us like a tsunami, and though it brushed the edges of the shield, causing it to glow under the strain, Torliam avoided the worst of it with a flesh-rippling jerk to the side.

Once we were away from the immediate threat, maybe a kilometer out from the mountain—though that wasn't nearly far enough to save us if Behelaino was determined—Torliam adjusted a couple more controls, then pressed a button and shoved the throttle all the way forward.

Breaking the speed of sound is actually quite unpleasant. Especially when it takes you less than three seconds to accelerate to that point.

"Brace!" Torliam ground out, changed the shape of the shield to a conical point instead of a sphere, and then increased the speed even more.

My guts lurched backward as we sprang forward, outstripping the volcanic explosion of Chaos that spewed out of Behelaino with the literal wrath of a god.

The shield glowed visibly from the pressure it was under as it forced the air out of our way.

Gregor whimpered and turned to Shadow to relieve himself of the sensation.

Once our speed stabilized, the pressure receded, and we all breathed a sigh of relief.

Torliam looked at the screen that displayed the rear view and frowned. "That eruption was more like the shock-wave you'd expect to see from one of your Earth's atomic bombs than any volcano. Her power broke the sound barrier, too. If we were a little slower, things might have gone poorly." He patted the *Swiftsure's* control console fondly, as if praising a favorite animal.

The terrain underneath sped past almost faster than I could take it in.

"Why did she suddenly attack us?" Sam asked. "She was the one who suggested a way for you to use Void."

"I don't know," I admitted, "but maybe it had something to do with the vow she took? About not birthing the Void again, or something like that? I'm not sure she was entirely in her right mind."

Jacky shrugged, flicking her bangs back. "Well, she's *Chaos*, no? You can't expect her to be the *same* all the time. She changed her mind."

When we had gone far enough that not even the most pessimistic person would believe we were still in danger, Torliam allowed the ship to slow, which was perhaps more disconcerting due to the feeling of being thrown against our harness straps for so long it felt like the ship might malfunction and fall out of the sky. It used too much energy to keep up those speeds long term.

Torliam contacted the capital for any updates, but they had none. They, in turn, were eager to hear about our mission, so Torliam let them know that, while we hadn't managed to receive direct help from Behelaino, we had learned the means to accomplish what was necessary, and were now heading for the fruit of life.

The rest of us removed our harnesses and Birch mewed weakly as I extricated him from the straps, which had become entangled in his wings. Around me, the team did their best to relax, all clearly trying to calm their frazzled nerves.

Zed pulled out his datapad, and Gregor, who was peeking at the screen, said, "That's a paper on post-human genetics."

"I know," Zed replied, raising his eyebrows as if to say, "What's your point?"

"You're doing homework?" Jacky asked incredulously. "Now?"

"Post-human genetics is an easier problem to solve than the end of the world, and if we do somehow defeat the Abhorrent and the world still exists when this is all over, I don't think being part of the Seal of Nine is going to excuse me from school. Not if I ever want to be a real medic. It just…it gives me something to focus on, you know?"

Gregor gave him a skeptical look. "Let me know if you need help understanding anything."

With a playful snarl, Zed hooked his elbow around the boy's neck and started grinding his knuckles across Gregor's scalp till he pleaded for mercy and escaped to my side, where Kris was already crouched at my feet, scratching Birch between his wings.

Watching Zed on the pad, a thought came to mind. "Was everything okay with the schools when we pulled you out for this mission?"

Gregor snorted. "Did anyone even bother to let them know?"

I blinked. *I* hadn't, but I assumed *someone* had.

"I handled it," Jacky said from across the room.

I gave her a grateful nod. It was hard to focus on little things like school when there were apocalyptic forces bent on wiping out the universe to deal with.

"It's not like it matters," Gregor said smugly. "I hacked Miss Jenkins' lesson plan the first week of school, did all the assignments early, and now I just turn them in one by one. I had to jailbreak my school link so I can spend the class time researching something actually useful rather than following along with whatever mundane thing she's teaching."

—DID YOU KNOW ABOUT THIS?—
-EVE-

Jacky shook her head after reading my message, though she didn't seem particularly surprised or upset at the revelation.

I couldn't blame her. I myself wasn't sure how to react. Gregor was in an advanced class containing some of the smartest children on Earth, so I would have thought they would be prepared for precocious children. Was the teacher oblivious, or was she purposely allowing it to give him a chance to learn things at his own level? If she paid any attention to him, she must have understood that her class wasn't meeting his needs. But if she did know, why hadn't she contacted us to discuss it? We were Gregor's legal guardians, now, after all.

Then, of course, there was the part of me that wanted to shrug it off like Jacky and focus on our mission. Zed had a good point too, though; if there was still a world when this was all over, Gregor and Kris would need to be a part of that world, not just a part of our team.

I turned to Kris, keeping my tone conversational. "Do you do that, too?"

Kris looked up to search my expression, but I kept any consternation from it, and she returned to her fiddling. "Gregor hacked my lesson plans, too, but I haven't finished working through all of them yet. I've been too busy with the workshop. Mostly I do pay attention during the lessons, because they won't even let me bring any of my tools or supplies with me, and they said none of my marionettes could attend, even though the spirits do understand some things. Of course, I bring small marionettes anyway, hidden in my pockets and stuff. It would just be stupid not to. What if something happened?"

75

Gregor nodded and gave a slightly vindictive smirk. "Right? Everyone else would be completely useless, flailing around like little kids. None of them even have any survival or self-defense training. I don't know how their parents stop worrying about how oblivious and weak they are long enough to let them out of their sight."

"Does your teacher realize you're bored?" I asked.

"I'm not sure if she knows or not," he said, sounding extremely uninterested. "She keeps cooing over me and saying how brave I was and how I'm a hero and all that inane stuff. Some of the other kids realized I wasn't following the lesson, and one of them threatened to get me in trouble, but like I said they have no training *at all*. I phased a Shadow pencil through his hand and told him I could do that to his brain, and he went off *crying*. They stopped threatening to get me in trouble after that, but they're still so *juvenile*," he sneered.

I blinked twice. Phasing a pencil through a fellow student's hand and threatening to kill them? What was the appropriate response to something like that?

Before I could think of a reply, Kris began speaking again. "Gregor thinks it might help, but I don't really want to threaten my classmates. But I am considering it, if only to get them to stop *touching* me without my permission." She pulled her hand away from Birch as if suddenly questioning her right to pet him, but he pushed his forehead into her open palm and she resumed her scratching. "It's like they don't realize I'm human, too, and not an animal, just because I'm small."

"I actually had an idea about that," Gregor said to Kris. "Just use your Skill on them. Once they feel their soul tugging them away the next time they touch you, they won't dare to do it again."

"Yeah, that'd probably do the trick," Jacky agreed, apparently oblivious to the questionable morality of Gregor's suggestion.

"Is there no one at school you get along with?" I asked tentatively.

Both of them thought for a moment, then shook their heads. "Not really," Kris muttered. "We don't fit in, you know? They're not *like* us."

I had known they didn't have any close friends their age, but I hadn't considered what that really meant. I wasn't sure what could fix something like that, either. Gregor, we might be able to move up a few grades so he'd be challenged, but what about Kris? We'd chosen to put them in classes with human students because Estreyan children were likely to treat them like the biggest celebrities since Elvis, while on Earth at least they might have some hope of a more normal school life. Perhaps that was a mistake. After all, they weren't normal kids, and they'd likely never live a normal life.

When Torliam slowed the ship again, I looked out the cockpit window onto the opening to another level, and thoughts of school and a life outside of the Seal of Nine were pushed out of my head. It was the most obvious connection between two levels that I'd seen so far. Two carved stone arches met in the middle, creating a round, weathered portal that stood impassively in a rocky field, as if the Estreyans of aeons past had created a frame for the door to this level. Faint hints of chiseled symbols still lay on the stone's surface, too worn to make out the words. The archway's opening buzzed with little bright yellow motes that looked like static, but I could faintly make out a clearing and then trees on the other side.

Dead bugs and animal carcasses were scattered around and piled up on the ground in front of the archway connecting our level to the other, an obvious clue that the static was dangerous, but the real problem was the portal's size. It was much too small for the *Swiftsure* to fly through, even with the smoothest of maneuvers.

Interlude 1

Reed glanced at the clock before turning back to the link sitting on his bedroom desk. He was supposed to be doing homework before his friends came over, but he was procrastinating with the much more interesting Net. When the aliens had attacked and the truth about everything came out, Reed had watched the news with a mixture of fear and horror like everyone else, but, though he would never admit it aloud, he'd been more than a little excited, too.

Finding out that the world—if not the planet *Earth*, exactly—wasn't so small, with the fairy tales and the mystery explored right out of it…it was like his childhood had come roaring back to life. The world was still full of stories to be told.

Welcome to the Earth Defense Force message boards.

You are currently logged in, ReedItAndWeep.

You are viewing thread: "Sightings of the Empowered—West Coast Players"

ORIGINAL POSTER "FIGARO" SAYS:

So there have been a lot of posts and threads lately about the people who got alien superpowers through those secret genetic engineering experiments. I thought it'd be a good idea to have one place where we could talk about it. This thread is for the West Coast. Now to be clear, there's been a lot of different names being bandied about for these superpowers and the people who hold them, but from what I can tell, most of them prefer to call themselves Players, and their powers Skills. The capitalization is important, apparently?

If you've been keeping up with the scene, you know about the lawsuits and the way the government's been scrambling to get the Players under official military contract. Some of them agreed, but a lot of them want nothing to do with that (And I mean, can you blame them? I definitely wouldn't.) Some are going "independent," if you know what I mean.

Sightings should be accompanied by films or pics (or it didn't happen.)

I'll move the best of your links <u>to the repository</u> for visibility.

It already has the best video I could find on the bank incident with those ghost things, as well as the waterpark uprising, the Eighth Reaper, the mysterious red flicker people think might be a woman, and, of course, the Seal of Nine group.

Discussion is welcome, but please try to keep it civil, guys. We don't want the mods cracking down and locking the thread.

POSTER "OUTERLAND" SAYS:

I hear the Red Mist (Because, seriously, the "red flicker?" She deserves a cooler name than that.) is actually using a Skill to speed up her relative time versus the rest of the world. If you check the individual film frames on that street scene you can see her clearly. I don't think there's any way a simple speed Skill would allow her to *walk* so fast she causes that wind in her wake. Check it out, the stance difference between a walk and a run is very clear. She's strolling.

POSTER "BREAKFAST SOUP" SAYS:

Who cares about the Red Mist or Red Flicker or whatever you want to call her? Most boring Skill ever, she can't even *do* anything when she's moving that fast. I'm more interested in the Seal of Nine. Does anyone have complete dossiers on them? I want details about their Skills. And please tell me you guys aren't overlooking the fact that apparently there are real-life, walking and breathing *gods* on Estreyer! Apparently, if you can impress one, you can get a Skill of your own. If only the cost to use one of the Shortcuts wasn't so high, not to even mention the waiting list…

POSTER "NECKTIE" SAYS:

Saw one of the Empowered at the grocery store the other day. Weird looking fella, for sure. Not sure if it was because of his power or if he wasn't totally human, or what?

POSTER "BETZOMBIE" SAYS:

Breakfast Soup, I am looking for more comprehensive information on the Seal of Nine, too. The official stuff is totally vague and sterilized, as you probably know, but I've spent some time compiling reliable information from quite a few different sources. I've done some speculation, but that's clearly noted and separate from the provable stuff. It's got pics and film, too, mostly candid.

Here's the <u>link</u>.

Also, you are quite right that many people don't seem to be focusing on the most important things. I'm searching for anyone who has some Seed material. I'd settle for the stuff that does basic physical empowerment, but ideally I'm interested in a Skill. I'm willing to pay. Contact me by PM, no spammers please.

Reed downloaded the compiled dossiers to his link for later perusal. Out of all the Players out there, the Seal of Nine were still his favorite. Their abilities were on another level, and when they stood together in their battle costumes, they looked like they should be on the poster for an action film, but it was also because they actually *did* something useful with all that power.

Plus, it was fun to listen to them give interviews, especially the leader, Eve Redding, who was even cooler than his best friend Demi. The gorgeous Jacqueline was probably using some sort of secret Skill to make herself that beautiful, but he was still hoping they'd put out a poster series so he could hang her face on his wall.

And, of course, they had an actual Estreyan on the team, who was apparently a *prince*.

They reminded him of characters from one of the stories he and his grandfather used to make up when Reed was little. Those stories had featured fey warrior princes—who were, perhaps, a little too bloodthirsty for a child that young—double-edged sentient swords, and starborn peasant girls who rose up and took over the country. It was too bad that his grandfather died before getting to see all this. He would have loved it, too.

Of course, Reed wasn't the only one interested in them. Puzzle band jewelry was everywhere, and the week before, he'd seen an advertisement for crystalline dermal implants that would look like the symbols the Seal of Nine team had embedded into their skin.

He shuddered. He wasn't *that* much of a fan.

POSTER "STARVASCULAR" SAYS:

Can anyone explain to me why Kris Mendell (I think they call her the Summoner) is so freaking small? It doesn't look like a birth defect, but they're so vague about it whenever someone asks.

POSTER "LOVERJOY" SAYS:

Summoner is crazy cute. I just want to dress her up in doll clothes and take pictures of her.

POSTER "OUTERLAND" SAYS:

@ LOVERJOY
Creep.

POSTER "YESTERYEAR" SAYS:

Betzombie, you do realize the Seed material will basically rewrite your DNA and that it kills anyone who doesn't have enough alien ancestry, right?

POSTER "HOLYSTONE" SAYS:

Interspecies breeding is disgusting, and an abomination. Those who are part alien should just go back to Estreyer. Earth is for humans.

POSTER "55FINGERS" SAYS:

LOL wut?

POSTER "OUTERLAND" SAYS:

HolyStone, you realize *you* could have Estreyan ancestry, right? They are reproductively compatible with humans, just a little bit bigger than us. In fact, if you got rid of the Seeds they pass down to their offspring and kept those offspring from coming into contact with any Seeds, they'd be mostly indistinguishable from humans except for the size and the extra fingers. Apparently they first visited a few thousand years ago, so I'd be truly surprised if the majority of Earth's population didn't have *some* Estreyan blood by now, whether or not it's expressed.

Reed sighed and skimmed over the next couple pages as the thread temporarily descended into arguments, insults, and rants until the moderators wrangled it back on course. Mention of his city,

Leighton, drew his eyes to one of the next posts, and he slowed to read in detail.

POSTER "SNOWBELLS & WHISTLES" SAYS:

Has anyone considered that there might be other ways to gain powers or Skills or whatever you want to call them? There's that one guy who says he can talk to bacteria after touching one of the warps, and isn't it strange that the government is so interested in them? They've got them contained and they don't let the public in, maybe because they're afraid we'd all get powers if they did. The warp in Vancouver would be most accessible for most of this country, I think.

POSTER "GENETICS-PHRENETICS" SAYS:

Snowbells & Whistles, I gather you think it's unreasonable to keep civilians away from the unexplained phenomena that have killed several people that came into contact with them, and which could just as easily give you cancer as any special Skill? That guy who can supposedly talk to bacteria is either lying, got driven insane by the warp, or got the shittiest power *ever* at the risk of his life.

More to the point of this thread, did you guys hear about the Scorpion? He's been wreaking havoc down south, and I'm pretty sure <u>that's</u> some kind of sand-control Skill.

POSTER "BETZOMBIE" SAYS:

Genetics-Phrenetics, pretty much *any* Skill you get will risk your life, according to what all the Estreyans and Players have to say. If there's a way to do that by touching a warp rather than risking my life petitioning a god in one of their Trials, it seems like less hassle overall.

Reed was skeptical that the warps could actually grant people Skills just from touching them. There was one on the outskirts of

Leighton, and one of the local nonprofit channels streamed a live feed of the strange distortion just hanging there in the air twenty-four hours a day. When the warps had first appeared, he'd spent more than a few hours just staring at the film stream, hoping to see *something*. He hadn't, and as far as he knew the scientists who were occasionally caught on camera visiting the warp in their protective suits hadn't, either.

If you really could get Skills just from touching one, the military, at the very least, would have had a whole line of volunteers queued up to stick their hand in. And everyone knew about the people who had died messing with them, not to mention the handful of people who'd just disappeared. Personally, he thought they might be a portal to elsewhere somewhere very, very, dangerous and not conducive to human life.

He shook his head and returned to reading.

POSTER "MAXXX" SAYS:

I got approved to visit Estreyer!!! I've hired a guide, who doesn't have a Skill because he's not a warrior. Of course, he's still nine feet tall and able to bend a steel bar with his bare hands. (He sent me a film as part of the job interview.) I just wish customs weren't so strict, because I'd seriously love to bring back a pet. Have you guys heard that they have dragons there? I heard they're called wyrms, but I'm pretty sure it's the same thing. It would be so cool to raise one of my own.

POSTER "BETZOMBIE" SAYS:

Maxxx I'll buy that travel ticket from you. I can make it worth your while. PM me.

POSTER "CHINCHILLI" SAYS:

1. New film of some contract Players doing a drill, <u>here</u>.

2. Strange phenomena caught by drone. It's not West Coast, but you guys will still find it fascinating, <u>here</u>. Pretty

sure it's a Skill effect, some sort of illusion. At the right angle, the city is mirrored in the clouds, upside down. Alternate dimension, another Earth?

POSTER "DEVON MILLER" SAYS:

Chinchilli, that's not a Skill. It's a natural phenomenon called a fata morgana. Basically a rare and complicated mirage. You know when you see a reflection of the sky on a hot road, that shimmering that kind of looks like water? This is the opposite of that. There's a long history of folklore based on them. Get schooled, kid.

POSTER "ZODIAC DRAGON" SAYS:

I just saw Doctor Deer on the news. Is there firm confirmation that it's a Player? Because really, he just looks like a deer wearing clothes and glasses. Here's the <u>link</u>.

Reed was just leaning forward to follow the link to the film clip of Doctor Deer, who had been appearing randomly and escaping the enforcers with dependable hilarity, when the door to his bedroom burst open.

The door slammed against the wall and sent a rattle through the entire room.

Reed jumped and let out a little scream.

His best friend stood boldly in the doorway, a hand on her hip and a provocative grin on her face. Her wine-red lips only stretched into a bigger grin at his reaction. "Catch you looking at something you aren't supposed to?" she said, walking in and leaning over his shoulder to look at the screen.

He leaned away from the boob pressing against his shoulder, his wince turning into a scowl when her grin only brightened. "Demi, would it kill you to knock? Or, you know, at least not slam my door open so hard my house is in danger of crumbling from the impact?"

She frowned in disappointment at the innocuous Net page

displayed and thankfully gave him some space. "Your house isn't *that* old."

"It *is* that old," Reed muttered, but he didn't keep the argument going, as his other best friend followed Demi's path of destruction up the stairs and into the room.

Lucas gave a much more normal greeting in the form of a nod and a "Hey, Reed. Whatcha up to?"

"Just on the EDF forums," Reed replied. "I was reading about Players. Looks like there's a group of independents forming up a bit south of here, and Doctor Deer was sighted again."

Lucas shook his braided head, dropping his backpack and sitting in one of Reed's chairs. "I don't get why you're so interested in that stuff, man. It's never gonna be *us* waving our hands and shooting lightning bolts, you know."

Demi stuck her tongue out at Lucas. "Blasphemer." She flopped back on Reed's bed and spread her arms and legs like she was trying to make a snow angel from the covers. The old wooden frame creaked in protest. "Did Doctor Deer escape?"

Reed shrugged. "He always does, but I haven't watched the film clip yet."

"So do you think he's an actual deer, or a Player disguised as one?"

"I've been thinking, what if he's not a Player at all, but also only kind of an actual deer? What if he's part of the Skill of a Player who is using him as a decoy? He could be a projection. It would explain how someone managed to get him dressed like that, if the clothes are part of it."

"A decoy for what? Like, robbing banks? And if he was already wearing the clothes when he transformed, that explains it just as easily."

With a sigh, Lucas interrupted before either of them could sink further into discussion. "It looks like rain outside. Clouds have been getting more ominous. Are you sure we should go to the market today?"

"This is the only day all three of us can make it this week, remember? Besides, I'm pretty sure my dad said it wasn't supposed to rain," Reed said, getting up and pulling aside the curtain at his window to peer up at the sky. Despite that, it was true that clouds were hanging low and grey over the city like a depressing shroud. Along with the way all the plants on the street seemed to be wilting, even the grass in his neighbor's beloved postage-stamp yard, it produced an almost eerie atmosphere. He caught Demi and Lucas sharing a look behind his back. "What was that look for?"

Demi pursed her lips and hopped off his bed to stand in front of the small silver mirror attached to the wall. "It's just...I know your dad is a weatherman, but you *do* realize he's wrong like half the time?"

Reed crossed his arms over his chest. "That's not his fault, you guys! You know that. Predicting the weather isn't an exact science, it's about probabilities, not absolutes." Lucas and Demi each gave him an identical pointed look, like they'd practiced for just this occasion. "He's not any worse than any of the other weathermen, at least," he grumbled.

Demi fluffed up her short hair and blew a wink and kiss at the polished-silver mirror, then took out her makeup kit and began to refresh the redness of her lips and the dark stuff around her eyes that made the blue in them stand out even more.

From his chair, Lucas watched her surreptitiously.

Reed mentally shook his head at the other boy. Demi was gorgeous and playful and liked to flirt, but she would never be interested in either of them. They were *friends*. He'd gone through his own phase of having a crush on her, but thankfully he'd gotten over it. Demi might not be interested in them, but she was a great wing-woman, or at least she would have been if Reed could be as bold as her and just talk to a girl he didn't know without tripping over his tongue out of nervousness.

She frowned at the mirror, then tried unsuccessfully to pry it off the wall. "It's stuck," she complained.

"It's been that way since we moved in. Mom joked that it must be a load-bearing mirror."

"It's also tiny."

"It's an antique, from before glass existed or something. You do realize it's literally polished silver? Of course it's tiny. I don't know why you're even using that thing. Go to the bathroom instead if you want to actually be able to see yourself," Reed said.

She frowned, then opened her mouth wide and breathed out

on the surface before polishing it with her sleeve. She turned around, looking behind herself, then back to the mirror, still frowning.

"What?" Lucas asked her.

She shook her head. "I think I will go to the bathroom," she said. "I've got to piss, anyway."

Lucas winced at even the hint of vulgarity, but Reed just grinned.

When she returned, they all ran down the narrow stairwell into the kitchen, which was the only room in the ancient house that had been fully upgraded. His dad had wanted to maintain the history, but his mom was an amateur chef. "I refuse to cook on a wood-burning stove that would be more fit for a *museum* than a modern kitchen, Herman!" she'd said, and that was that.

His mom was using big mitts to pull some fancy pastries sprinkled with cheese and herbs from the state-of-the-art oven. "Is anyone hungry?" she asked, smiling brightly.

Lucas immediately sat down at the kitchen bar. "Always, Mrs. Phillips."

She took out three plates and began to pile them with food, even though she'd already given Reed a snack when he got home from school. "These are gougères which I've put my own little twist on. As you can see, I've brushed a garlic oregano butter sauce over the top, along with a sprig of cilantro, and the cheese filling is a mix of smoked havarti and goat cheddar with just a touch of minced shallot."

Reed tuned out most of the explanation.

His friends gave outrageous moans and declarations of the cheese puff's deliciousness and his mom's status as the best cook in the world, which only caused her to smile wider and continue to pile food onto their plates.

"It's good," he agreed when she turned to look expectantly at him.

Lucas smacked the back of his head lightly. "Don't listen to him, Mrs. Phillips. It's more than good."

Demi nodded emphatically. "If I were ten years older, Mr. Phillips would have some competition for his wife," she said with a wink that made Reed's mom cover her mouth as she let out an embarrassed laugh. "You know half the reason we come over here so often is for your cooking. Reed's just ancillary to that."

"Hey!" he said. He turned to Lucas for support, but his second best friend's mouth was too full to talk, so he only gave Reed a pitying shake of his head.

"Go call your father down from his office," Reed's mom told him.

The narrow stairs creaked as Reed ran up them. He found his dad at the desk in his office. "Mom wants you. She made fancy cheese puffs."

As his dad turned off his link and got up from his desk, Reed said, "Are you sure it's not going to rain today? The clouds…"

His dad sighed deeply, looking at the window, which was letting through the gloomy grey light from outside. "Yes. Well. That was somewhat unexpected. Perhaps…take an umbrella with you," he finished with a grimace, muttering something that sounded like, "the station will be getting more angry letters about this, I'm sure."

Reed turned back to his room to grab the family-sized umbrella he kept in his closet. It would be big enough for the three of them, if they needed it.

When he entered his room, the little mirror attached to the wall caught his eye. He frowned, looked around the room, and then stepped closer to it. He'd thought for a moment that he saw something move in the polished silver.

The reflection looked a little off, dirty and grungy, like someone had added an age filter to the image. He breathed on the silver and polished it with his sleeve, and when he looked again, it was clear and normal. He would have to get out the silver polish to keep the tarnish away. He looked around the room again to reassure himself that really, nothing had moved. He'd always had a bit of an overactive imagination.

Chapter 6

All the world will be your enemy, Prince with a Thousand Enemies, and whenever they catch you, they will kill you. But first they must catch you, digger, listener, runner, prince with the swift warning. Be cunning and full of tricks and your people shall never be destroyed.

— Richard Adams

TORLIAM LANDED the ship a couple hundred meters away from the archway leading to the other world-level of Estreyer, and we got out.

"How could no one have thought to mention this?" I said.

"I can only imagine they did not know," Torliam said. "There have been no recent expeditions to this level, and the records were clearly not detailed enough."

I recalled what I'd read, and realized that the mentions of brave quester's various mounts and steeds might not have been just extraneous information, but a useful hint about what size of ride could get through the archway. "Well, I guess we'll be on foot, if we can figure out how to get past that static. Maybe the marionettes can help carry some of our supplies?" I asked, turning to Kris.

She nodded, frowning. "Static?"

Using Wraith, it was easy to find the cause of the yellow fluff.

"Yeah. Looks like runes are carved into the archway on the other side," I said, using a claw to scratch a copy of them into the ground for Torliam's perusal. "They're charged, so I'm assuming they're the source."

Kris stood beside Torliam to peer over the diagram I'd copied.

"You say you see a barrier? This is designed to kill anything it touches, I believe, and would explain all the dead creatures lying here, but to my own eyes there is nothing but the level entrance," Torliam said.

"Really? I—" Turning to look at the archway again, I realized that he was right. My eyes saw nothing but empty air. It was Wraith that noticed the static; the use of the Skill was so familiar to me that I hadn't even thought to distinguish it from my physical senses. "Oh. It's some sort of Seed glow. I've never seen it like this, though. There aren't any Seed organisms, and"—I took a moment to search the limits of my reach—"there's no one around using a Skill."

Torliam's frown grew deeper, and he rubbed a hand against his neatly trimmed beard. "Are you sure it is Seed glow you see, and not some other energy? That is…impressive."

Adam and Gregor were interested, but Jacky bounced impatiently on the balls of her feet. "So, how do we get through?" she asked.

"What about shielding as we go through?" Adam asked. "We've got a few different Skills that could handle that, in addition to the ship's force field."

Torliam's frown remained. "Perhaps."

"Let's just test it," Gregor said.

Everyone agreed that was a good idea, but we didn't want to put ourselves at risk to do so. We ended up capturing a nearby rodent-like animal and rolling it through inside a shield ball made up of Torliam's, Adam's, and my own powers.

The ball went through just fine, but when the shields dispersed on the other side, the creature within sprawled on the ground, quite dead.

"Surprising," Torliam muttered.

Adam, Gregor, and Kris nodded almost simultaneously.

"What type of energy is that?" Gregor asked. "I don't understand how it penetrated everything. Are you sure it's not some kind of Skill?"

"Maybe if I understood what I was shielding us from, I could create something specifically meant to protect against it," Adam said, taking out his modified link and inserting his fingers in the side.

Torliam gave him a dubious look. "It may be more efficient simply to disable the runic device. One of your ink constructs or Eve's power would be able to get through the barrier and perhaps destroy some of the runes."

Kris frowned and pointed at one of the runes. "Isn't that a pressurizer? I heard those are used in bombs. Without the repeating circuit, will it blow up?"

"Wow, good eye," Gregor said, giving his sister a surprised look. "Even I didn't notice that."

"You're not in my runic engineering class," she said, not appearing pleased with the compliment.

"An explosion won't actually destroy the connection between the two levels, right?" Adam asked Torliam.

"That should not be an issue, but we do not know what the released energy might do. Even if we retreat far enough that it does not reach us, though I do not know how far that would be, what if it is the type of energy that will linger in the surroundings, like your world's nuclear radiation?"

"We're going to have to disable it without triggering an explosion," Gregor said, his face so serious as he scanned the symbols that, for a moment, I was reminded of Blaine.

"Why don't we just use the Other Place?" I said.

Their heads all turned to me simultaneously.

"Even if the barrier still exists in the Other Place, Blue might be able to drain whatever's powering it, right? I can't sense it drawing any power from elsewhere, it all seems to be self-contained, so I imagine eventually it should just run dry, right?"

"It cannot hurt to try," Torliam agreed.

Zed poked a finger into nothing and wriggled it around. "Hear that, Blue?" He peeled back reality with ease, opening up a jagged hole in the air.

Nothing happened immediately, but Blue's voice filtered through faintly from the other side. "I can taste the heat. There is an end to all heat, if you eat long enough." Wraith could feel the replica of the archway in the Other Place. It ended abruptly at the level opening, as if the other side didn't exist all, and I speculated this was because the two levels weren't actually adjacent to each other, simply connected by the opening. It made sense, of course, because if I walked around to the other side of the archway, I'd still be on this level. It was simply a window, a doorway.

The aura of cold around the opening increased, and I could sense the static barrier's power flutter in response. The lack of true adjacency wouldn't stop Blue from draining the barrier, it seemed. "Let's give it some time," I suggested.

While we waited, Jacky plopped down beside me, laying her head on my crossed legs without asking.

I had been meditating on the Chaos within my body, but was thoroughly distracted by her sudden intrusion, and opened one eye to look down at her.

She grinned up at me, willfully oblivious.

With a sigh, I opened both eyes and ran a hand through her hair in a light scratching motion, as if she were a dog. She was tough enough that my claws wouldn't simply slice her up.

"Tell me about the fruit," she said, like a little child asking for a bedtime story.

It only took me a few minutes to go through everything I'd learned, because frankly, there wasn't much information on them. When I finished, I could sense that the tension in her neck hadn't subsided, though her expression was still lighthearted.

"More questions?" I asked, keeping my tone light but giving her a knowing look.

Her eyes flicked around to the children, neither of whom seemed to be paying attention to us. "We really need them to work," she said. "For the kiddos, I mean, yeah?"

Moving my hand from her head, I tapped my clawed fingers rhythmically against my scales, taking a moment to gather my thoughts before answering. "Yes, though I am a little worried about the part where the fruit might not allow either of them to grow into adults for the next three hundred years. We'll need to bring this fruit back and get it tested before we give it to them."

Jacky ran a hand through her hair in a stressed motion that reminded me starkly of Adam. "Right, but without them, the kiddos are *squishy*. With what you saw…I mean, we just…we gotta make sure we're careful with them."

I squeezed her shoulder. "I know. We'll keep them safe. If not the fruit, then we'll look for something else. I won't be reckless with any of our lives."

It took hours for Blue to drop the barrier, much longer than I'd expected, and Blue's domain grew a couple inches in every direction from turning the absorbed energy into a replica of matter. Whatever was powering the Seed-glow static began to replenish itself almost immediately, though I didn't see how that was possible.

Kris's marionettes piled out of the *Swiftsure's* cargo hold through the side hatch, securely loaded up with all of our supplies. "I was prepared for this," she said with no little amount of pride, straightening up atop Birch like some kind of warrior princess riding her steed into battle.

We were still wary of the archway, so we put up a series of shields as we walked through. Only after reaching the other side did Zed allow the rip in reality to close. We left a communicator beacon on the other side, near the camouflaged *Swiftsure,* to bounce signals through the portal and allow us to keep in contact with Earth and the capital as long as we didn't get too far away from it.

I turned to the new landscape, Wraith moving instinctively even as my eyes tracked over our surroundings. We were in the middle of a clearing filled with deep green moss fed by a bubbling spring. A few hundred meters to the west, a forest sprang up abruptly. The lack of smaller trees at the edge indicated the border was at least partially unnatural. The forest was dark and foreboding, the trees reaching up till their tops disappeared into thick clouds that seemed to be centered above the forest and thinning out to the east. I caught signs of monsters flying among the obscuring clouds above, both numerous and powerful. My scales rose at the threat, but either none of them noticed us, or they simply weren't interested, because they made no move to approach or attack.

To the east, the moss gave way to grass, which continued for a few kilometers at least, till Wraith couldn't reach and I couldn't see over the horizon.

Torliam pointed to the forest. "The fruit are that way, I believe."

"*Of course*," I muttered sourly. "We'll have to go through the forest. It's too dangerous to fly through those clouds." I explained what I'd sensed above. There was no way ink construct wings would be enough.

Gregor squinted into the darkness between the towering trees. "Is *that* any safer?"

"Surprisingly, yes. It might look scary, but there don't seem to be many dangerous monsters, at least on the edge here. I'm sure it's not going to be *safe*, but at least nothing in there can send us plummeting to our deaths."

Once the decision was made, we set off into the dark, looming forest, leaving the relative safety of Estreyer's main level behind.

THE TREES and the darkness their canopy created felt unnaturally thick at first, oppressively so. There was little undergrowth, just some moss and fungus, and the small creatures that populated this part of the forest either ate that or each other. There were a few larger, more dangerous monsters, but none that were a match for us, and most of them seemed to realize that, running away as we approached.

A snake of questionable intelligence, bigger around than any of us, spat a jet of acid at Jacky, but she avoided it with an acrobatic flip that ended with her boot stomping down on—and entirely *through*—the snake's skull. The accompanying spray of blood turned out to be acidic, too. Torliam was able to get it off her, but his Skill scoured her skin like extreme exfoliation, and she complained of dryness and itching till Adam threatened to bathe her in mud if she didn't shut up.

After only a few kilometers of walking, when we reached approximately the edge of the area I'd originally been able to scan with Wraith, the trees thinned and the canopy far above let through dappled light that fed the suddenly rampant undergrowth. I frowned, squinting up at the sky. Had the cloud cover disappeared?

I still sensed obscuring condensation high above, so where was this bright sunlight coming from?

Overall, the forest had metamorphosed into something out of a fairy tale, almost as if we'd crossed a barrier into a completely different place.

Mushrooms in bright neon colors and psychedelic patterns grew on tree trunks and among beds of decaying plant matter. Chameleon tree frogs let out chirps that sounded like chimes or beautiful songbirds, while the actual songbirds sounded like babbling brooks and pseudo-harps. Fractal vines swirled their way up and across the tree trunks.

One plant changed color to match the vibrations caused by touching it but was severely poisonous. A vine tried to sneak up behind us and steal Birch. One silver plant seemed to be made of pure metal, with leaves sharp enough to slice right through flesh if you brushed up against it carelessly.

Even the tree bark looked subtly fanciful—designed rather than natural. The decaying plant matter gave off a pleasant earthy smell that mixed with the peaches-and-cut-grass air of Estreyer in a way that seemed to forcefully siphon away stress. I was suspicious that some kind of sedative or hallucinogen was floating around in the air, but even Sam didn't seem to be immune, playing with pretty much everything we passed in the guise of testing it for poison.

All of that might have passed without too much suspicion, but what we stumbled upon next was bizarre to the point of surrealism, enough to make me suspect I'd been drugged and was hallucinating.

I wasn't the only one who stopped in my tracks and stared in disbelief at the creature prancing through the beams of light between the trees ahead of us.

It was a moose. A pale green, glowing moose, wearing armor. It was also singing, but my ears refused to make sense of the words because I was too gobsmacked by the—also pale green and glowing—music notes that floated out of its mouth with every word and hung about its head for a few seconds before fading away.

"Mama's little calves were lyin' in bed
One was sick and the other half dead.

Mama called the doctor, an' the doctor said
Feed them calves some grass, you silly butthead."

The moose seemed to notice our presence at that point, dipped its antlers to us in an acknowledging bow, then bounded off, trailing musical notes as it went.

"Oh my god," Kris said. "That was—was that—?" She turned to Gregor, wide-eyed.

He met her gaze, equally astounded. "Moose? Your moose, the stuffed animal?"

I let Wraith flare out to search for the source of what had just happened while swirling the Chaos in my bloodstream a little faster in the hopes it might help fight off hallucinogens or mind-controlling Skills. "You recognized it? Explain."

Kris's mouth opened, but for a second she just shook her head mutely. Finally, she spoke. "Um, it's the moose from one of the children's books my mom used to read us. It goes around singing like that while searching for its lost babies. Except, well, those aren't the original lyrics. Those are the ones Gregor and I made up instead, 'cause we thought it was funny. I was just thinking about how I missed Moose, and then he appeared! But not the stuffed version, the real thing. How is that possible?"

I could find no source of danger around us, and, unless it was incredibly subtle, no poison or Skill was affecting my mind. "We all saw that, right?" I asked. "The same thing? A big, green, singing moose with music notes coming out?"

My teammates all agreed.

So it had been real, at least, or at least as close enough in definition as I wanted to get. I sincerely doubted that was something Estreyer had created all on its own, which just coincidentally matched a very specific, silly variation of one of Earth's children's books. "Whatever created that is reading our minds," I said aloud. I sent Wraith on another search of our surroundings, this time more meticulous, searching for some detail I'd missed.

With a spark of realization, I looked up again. Sunlight, where there should be none. The trees had dispersed and the forest had become more friendly. "Was anyone thinking about how they wished the forest wasn't so dark and ominous when we walked in?" I asked.

Gregor tentatively raised his hand, as did Sam, and Birch raised a wing.

We had probably all been wishing that. "Whoever or whatever is doing this might not be able to respond to our thoughts instantly. I'd suspect they were just trying to subtly phase in the responses without us realizing, but after the moose, that's absurd," I said. "So the delay between our thought and the response could be a clue." The third option, which I kept unspoken, was that their mind reading range was simply longer than Wraith's reach.

"So what do we do?" Jacky asked.

"We keep going," I said. Wraith had found nothing with the more detailed scan. "Guards up, be ready for an attack. We don't know what we're dealing with, here."

A few kilometers later, further than the gap between the edge of the forest and its sudden metamorphosis into a fairy tale woodland, we came upon a hotdog tree. Hotdogs, cooked to slight crispiness and still sizzling, hung from the branches like fruit.

Birch's ears perked up. He sniffed exaggeratedly while licking his chops.

It smelled amazing, even more so than it should have, and I had to grab the tailos by the sleek fur at his neck to stop him from wandering closer. "Did you wish for this?"

He whined and ducked his head with embarrassment, but was still drooling and had to lick his chops again.

I sighed. "No one go near it. We're circling around. Try wishing for these fruit of life, or to meet whatever's behind all this. If you see something that's abnormally appealing or that might be a response to something you were thinking about, avoid it and let me know. Definitely *do not eat it.*"

We didn't come upon anything that Torliam identified to be the fruit of life, though there were various delicious-looking fruit another few kilometers on. I was beginning to see a pattern in the distance between these strange phenomenon, which lead me to suspect my initial conjecture about whatever was causing them had been missing some crucial element essential to understanding this forest.

I pulled Wraith in closer to my body, searching only for danger in the immediate kilometer or so rather than stretching it to its limits through the woodland. I let us walk for a while, and then I noted what was at the edge of my sensory range at that moment. I asked everyone to focus on their strong desire for a chocolate guitar.

Low and behold, slightly more than one kilometer on, we discovered a chocolate stage with an entire range of elaborate chocolate string instruments, some of which were actually playing themselves. Eight chocolate chairs and one giant dog bed lay invitingly beside the guitars, and my mind struggled with a clamor of different desires. I wanted to play music, relax in the chair that was meant for me, and eat delicious, creamy, decadent chocolate. I wanted to gorge myself on it till it was seeping out of my pores.

My mouth began to water nearly as bad as Birch's had, and I had to swallow before speaking. "Look away. Cover your ears. We're going around." When we'd gotten far enough away that the allure had cleared from our brains, I explained the results of my experiment. "Unless whatever's behind this is just screwing with me, I think it might not be able to change things we are actively observing. Wraith has a pretty big range. If I wanted to risk pulling it in entirely, we might find a gingerbread house or something equally absurd just beyond the next group of trees."

"It's observing us while making sure we can't observe it," Adam said, his tone half-question, half-statement.

I tugged irritably on my braid. "Also, it's likely this is some sort of attack, trying to make us let down our guard by giving us exactly what we want. It's all way too appealing, when it should be alarming. It's not just reading our thoughts, it's tugging at our minds."

DESPITE EVERYTHING, we still made better time than even elite human forces could have hoped to before stopping to make camp during the darkest part of the night. Along with whichever team member was on guard, Kris's marionettes spread out around the edges of the camp to keep us safe. The marionettes didn't need to sleep at all, after all, and we were all growing increasingly on edge at the consistently more brazen attempts to divert us from our quest.

In addition to the fantastical, illogical, wish-fulfilling things we kept stumbling upon, we also had to fend off more normal attacks from the forest's flora and fauna. Most were easily dealt with and equally uninteresting, but there were a few surprises.

A swarm of bat-squirrels tried to ambush us as we walked beneath their community, but a flat wave of Chaos cut through tree and squirrel alike, so thoroughly there wasn't even any wood dust or bits of dead, carnivorous rodent left to rain down on us.

Later, a group of semi-transparent flying fish seemed a little too interested in us, until Sam started using Black Sun on any looking our way and Birch conjured a gust of Chaos-laced wind to scare them off.

Despite the incessant attempts to kill or entice us, Jacky found a way to make even this journey an opportunity for training, insisting that we all used our Skills constantly, even frivolously, because the difference between life and death could be one degree of mastery. When use of our power was so easy it was instinctual, we'd be able to think about something else in the middle of a fight, and that might keep us alive.

A few days into our journey, Adam woke me in the middle of the night.

I was awake immediately, my claws flexing even as I gathered Chaos to lash out at whatever danger was encroaching, but he pressed a hand to my mouth and shook his head. "Shh."

Wraith sensed nothing amiss among the camp. Frowning with confusion, I relaxed.

He took his hand away. "Nothing's wrong. I found something I want to show you. Come on."

As I rolled out of my tearaway sleeping bag and got quietly to my feet, I shared a silent nod with Zed, who gave me a thumbs-up and returned to staring out into the night, on watch against danger or ambush while the others slept.

Adam led me to a small pond a few hundred yards away from the camp. Blue and green glowing flowers with petals shaped like four-leafed clover surrounded the banks. It was like a scene from a fairy tale, with the glow glinting off the occasional ripple on the water, the petals swaying gently in an almost unnoticeable breeze.

He sat down on a fallen log at the edge of the little clearing and looked at me with an expectant smile. The crystalline puzzle band across my forehead reflected faintly in his eyes.

Slowly, I lowered myself down beside him. We were both silent for a while. "It's beautiful," I said.

He nodded, shifting a little with nervous energy, but didn't speak.

I watched the glowing flowers, letting my thoughts turn over slowly in the silence of the dark. We were reaching the edge of the range from which our overpowered communications device could still receive the signal bounced off the relay beacon beyond the archway, but Torliam's Skill told him that the fruit were still further on. I worried that if we kept going beyond the range of easy contact, we would return to find the world in ruins.

There had been no progress in finding the Avatar, which meant we had no idea of its abilities or power, either. It could be guiding a meteorite toward Earth at that very moment, or preparing to evaporate the oceans, or be traveling through time to assassinate me and my teammates when we were still babies...or *anything*.

More than anything, I wanted to talk to the Oracle. She had to know more about the Avatars and the Abhorrent, and I needed every ounce of information I could get about them. Plus, I really wanted to curse her out.

"So." Adam cleared his throat. "I've been thinking."

He paused, and while I was waiting for him to continue, I noticed faint shadows moving in the dark undergrowth, which Wraith immediately identified as ant-like bugs with big mandibles and slits in the carapace on their back.

My blood ran cold, and I held back a shudder, pulling my feet away from the ground just in case.

The bugs went straight for the flowers, crawling up the slender stems to reach the petals. They put their mandibles to quick use, cutting off the petals at the base. Then the tiny little monsters shoved the severed petals around to their backs, clamping down on them with the slits in their carapace to create little glowing wings.

In less than a minute, the ants had beheaded all the flowers and used their makeshift petal wings to fly, rising up with lazy flaps like Franken-butterflies.

I stood abruptly and let out a broad scythe of Chaos without even fully considering it. It engulfed the pond, what remained of the flowers, and even the nearest of the surrounding trees, scouring everything with little particles of destruction. When it dispersed, the pond was half-gone, the surrounding earth bare, and the trees were missing their bark, leaves, and smaller branches…but the bugs were gone, too.

Adam's mouth hung open, his words stillborn on his lips. He turned to look at me, surprise and dismay painted clear upon his face.

"I hate bugs," I said with simple vehemence. I doubted I would ever get over that, after the nightmares and Pestilence. I realized I was panting and took a few deep breaths to calm my body's reaction, glaring out at the little clearing as Wraith searched for any ants that had escaped. Of course the forest was filled with insects, but whatever these had been, I didn't sense any more of them in our immediate surroundings. Belatedly, I turned back to Adam. "Right, you were saying?"

His mouth closed and he shook his head. "Nothing. I was just going to let you know that the search program I've been creating hasn't found anything yet. We'll be going out of range soon, so it won't have any updated data to work through until we finish here. We should hurry."

I tilted my head to the side and waited in case there was more, but he let out a huff and turned back to the camp. "Let's go back," he said.

I grimaced. He was probably perturbed with my wanton destruction of the little secret place of beauty he'd found. I could imagine, if you weren't traumatized by memories of bugs eating into your flesh and burrowing beneath your skin, or suffocating you to death, or crawling into a humanoid pile and taking the shape of your friend who Pestilence had just murdered… Well, if you didn't find them viscerally horrifying, the sight of little flower-butterflies swarming up in the darkness might have been beautiful. Or something.

I shook my head at Adam's foolishness and followed him back to camp in silence, but a suspicion crept into my mind. "Wait. Adam, did you *wish* for that place?" I asked, irritation lacing my tone.

Adam scoffed and rolled his eyes, stomping off without replying.

My brother, still posted up at the edge of camp, had opened a small rift to the Other Place, which was emitting grey light and freezing the humidity into ice crystals in the air beside him. It looked like he was feeding bits of something into the opening. "Peace offerings," he mouthed silently. "I think it's working."

Birch lifted his head, opening one lazy eye as Adam plopped down beside him. He snorted scornfully.

"Oh, shut up!" Adam snapped, wrapping himself in his sleeping bag without another word to me.

I moved to sit beside Zed.

Zed popped one of whatever was in his hand into his mouth. My eyes couldn't make it out, but Wraith could. It was berry from one of the silver bushes scattered throughout the forest. A frown grew on my face as I sank down beside him. "Did Sam test and approve those?" I asked.

Zed popped another metal berry into his mouth and then put one into the Other Place, as if he were giving a treat to an animal. "I programmed some of my nanites into the surface of my tongue to catalogue everything I eat. It's safe, and some of the components can be used by the nanites. They'll handle disposing the rest, too. I don't want to be reliant on that nutrient paste forever, you know."

"Ah." I hadn't considered that, but it wasn't a bad idea. Now that Zed had access to the nanites and could more or less program them himself via his VR chip, creating what equated to minor Skills—like his preternatural ability to aim projectiles and learn languages—would be easier. We were silent for a few more minutes, and then I said, "I think it might be the forest itself that's reading our minds. Or at least I have found no clues that point to anything else. I think it's trying to stop us from reaching the fruit."

He nodded thoughtfully. "So it's all one big sentient organism?"

"Well, the woodland is not part of a god's domain, and unless there's something close to us that even Wraith can't sense, or something that manages to consistently stay farther away than I can reach, I don't see how else this could be happening. It's not that crazy of an idea, actually. Remember when we first escaped NIX, and our ship was downed by that sentient storm? Estreyer is wild in more ways than one."

"If that's true, I bet things are gonna get a lot worse when the forest starts getting desperate."

He was right.

Chapter 7

No live organism can continue for long to exist sanely under conditions of absolute reality.
— Shirley Jackson

WE'D BEEN TRAVELING for less than an hour the next morning when the woodland dropped any pretense of playing nice with us.

Kris and Gregor were trying to drag Sam into developing an injectable oxygenating compound that could be inserted directly into the skull cavity.

"Think of all the lives you could help to save," Gregor cajoled, gesticulating to emphasize and punctuate his words. "We only need to keep the brain alive until it can reach someone with a healing Skill. The compound will be perfect for Kris's rescue-pod marionettes, but not *just* them! Hospitals can use it, and emergency response teams. If the compound is stable, people could even have it as part of their first-aid kits at home and in their vehicles! Horrible, debilitating accidents no longer need to be deadly!"

Inwardly, I thought there probably weren't enough Skill-based healers to keep up with demand if the world ended up with what amounted to brains in jars, their entire bodies needing to be regrown around them, but it wasn't a bad idea.

Maybe a problem like that would even spur the people in

charge of NIX, or any similar organization with the ability to get humans into a Trial, to screen for people likely to gain more useful Skills out of their Characteristic Trial, rather than just warriors. Really, there should have been some push for that from the beginning. I didn't understand the decisions of the Thinkers who had condoned such senseless waste of life in the Trials. Then again, they'd given *me* a healer.

I looked to Sam, who was still unconvinced by the kiddos' argument and was shaking his head at them, and felt a hint of unease that slipped away before I could grasp the reason for it.

Gregor was undeterred by his lack of success. "So, what's your actual problem with helping us out?" he asked, frowning severely up at Sam. We edged around a patch of thick bushes with thorns as long as fingers.

Sam's head rolled lazily to the side. "I have a few. One, my Harbinger of Death Skill doesn't create positive effects. I can't just pop out some serum that simulates a working circulatory system without needing to be re-oxygenated or circulated. It's meant to torture, maim, and kill. Two, you realize suffocation isn't just a function of a lack of oxygen? Have you heard of carbon dioxide poisoning?"

Gregor waved these arguments away as if they were little more than flies. "That's all workable. I've already taken into account that anything you create with a positive effect is going to have side effects. Pain, at the least. It'll still be a good jumping-off point for further development, and in the very worst-case scenario, as long as the side-effects don't cause long-term damage, it would definitely still be a better alternative than *death*."

"And how would you even get my Skill to respond with something like that? That seems like a very…esoteric form of damage. I'd be more likely to create something that suffocates or kills brain cells." The faint rustling of the surrounding leaves mixed with animal noises and what I thought was a distant burbling brook, creating a calming background susurration that almost felt like music.

Gregor and Kris shared a look. She shook her head minutely, but the boy turned back to Sam and started talking without any hesitation. "Well, maybe first we try suffocating you and see what happens. Zed brought that scanning equipment so we'll be able to monitor your Skill's response really closely. If simulating the problem doesn't work, we see if we can get you to pick up a version of the solution as damage. We have an oxygen tank. Some tinkering, and I can have you breathing straight oxygen. Or we could literally just insert the gas into your bloodstream. The medical kits have blood transfusion equipment, just in case. If none of that works, I guess we'll just be a bit slower with development. I'm sure I can figure it out, and you'll still be useful as a guinea pig to ensure the final product is safe for mass consumption."

Sam's expression had twisted into a look of stunned horror at the boy's explanation. "You want to…*torture* me?" I caught the hint of amusement in his tone, though it seemed neither of the kids did.

The group turned toward a path worn through the underbrush by animals. The leaves swayed around us as if in a subtle breeze, seeming to point the way.

Gregor raised his eyebrows, ignoring Kris's frantic motions for him to be quiet from Sam's other side. "You do realize how your Skill works, right? Maybe if you had more control—"

One of Kris's marionettes ran up and kicked Gregor in the ankle, and as soon as the boy shut up, she reached up and grabbed Sam's hand. "We don't want to torture you," she said sweetly—a little too sweetly, to be honest. "Don't think of it like that. That'll just make you feel bad. This is to help people. It's really important. Plus, you get hurt a little to help heal the rest of us all the time. At least with this, you don't have to keep doing it over and over. Once we figure out the compound, we'll handle the rest and you'll have helped every single person who gets saved with it, with barely any actual healing done on your part."

I couldn't help it. I burst into a fit of giggles.

My eyes widened. I clamped a hand over my mouth to stifle the sound, straightening as everyone turned to me in surprise. I was Eve Redding. I didn't *giggle*. What was going on?

The others grinned at me, and Birch let out a little chortle.

I looked around, frowning. Were we still going the right direction? I hadn't been paying attention. I realized suddenly that Wraith hadn't been stretched to its limits, actively searching ahead, but just hanging about the group lazily. I had grown used to the soothing smell of the air, so I couldn't tell if it had grown stronger, but I felt relaxed to the point of silliness, on the edge of falling into another giggling fit.

I tried to feel alarmed but couldn't quite manage it. I reached for my anger instead. That could not be suppressed, flushing through me with a cold-burning strength that sent blood to my cheeks, set my heart to pounding, and left my fingertips tingling. The allure of the enchanted woodland fell into the background. "Group shields!" I called.

Despite not sharing any of my alarm, my teammates were well-trained. All of us, including the marionettes, gathered together near Torliam and Adam, who created a double layer of protection around us, blocking out the forest almost completely. "Clear the air, Torliam," I commanded, already turning to the marionettes to search through the supplies they carried.

"What's going on?" Sam asked, an anxious frown growing on his face as he caught the gas masks I tossed to him.

"The forest is trying to lure us somewhere, subtly. I'm not sure exactly how it's doing it, maybe a combination of airborne sedatives and hypnotic suggestions. I'm not even sure how long it's been since it started, and I have no idea where we are or what direction we're going." I turned to the Estreyan, who had finished clearing the air within our sphere of protection. "Torliam?"

He closed his eyes briefly. "You are right. We have turned away from the fruit."

The marionettes around me shifted uneasily and started gesturing to each other, but little Pino let out a few commanding beeps and they settled.

"What's the plan?" Jacky asked, crouching down onto her heels. "I can tear up a few trees till it gets the message to leave us alone?"

I found a package of noise-cancelling earplugs and tossed them to Adam to hand out. "That's the last resort. We don't know how strong it is, or how it will react to that. I'm thinking it upped the ante because we were getting a little too close to the fruit for comfort. Let's see if we can push through. We'll go on the offensive once we have to, no sooner. We have to get all the way *out* of here, too, remember."

We used a rope to tether everyone except the marionettes

together, so none of us could accidentally wander off, and then set off again, partially shielded from the allure of the woodland. I kept my eyes closed, and would have had the others do so as well if I thought I could get away with it. When we came to barriers or obstacles, we bulldozed right through them with our Skills. Torliam checked periodically to make sure we were still going the right direction.

Whatever mind was controlling the forest seemed to grow more desperate, eschewing subtlety for blatant attempts to stall or kill us, and despite our determination, progress slowed.

After one of the trees literally tried to topple over onto us and I'd been forced to disintegrate it with Chaos, Adam pointed into the gloom above us and said, "Are you sure it would be more dangerous above the tree line? It might be a little difficult to climb all the way up there, especially if this place tries to stop us, but it would be a lot faster afterward. I could create a few constructs ahead of time, built for speed and maneuverability. We could probably get the fruit and be back to the level opening in less than a day."

I frowned, considering his argument as we kept moving slowly through the increasingly hostile forest. Not long after, we came to a semi-clearing, where the trees grew less closely together. Just as I was looking upward to gauge the feasibility of climbing up above the canopy, a gargantuan shadow blocked out the light. It was too big to see the edges with my eyes, what with the trees blocking visibility, but Wraith could make out its shape. I ducked instinctively, though I realized immediately afterward it was very unlikely the monster could see or sense us all the way down here.

The others ducked as well, looking up for the source of my alarm.

I cleared my throat. "Pretty sure that was a wyrm," I said. No one needed to be reminded of the creature that had almost killed us at the Spire of Prophecy. Wyrms were almost unkillable, constantly adapting to resist any damage you managed to cause them, and relentless in pursuit of their prey.

"So I vote we *don't* go up there," Gregor said.

IT MIGHT NOT HAVE BEEN an actual wyrm," I offered. "Wraith can't quite reach all the way into the clouds. I can sense *signs* of monsters, but I haven't actually *felt* a wyrm. What if it's just the forest messing with us, trying to make sure we don't leave?"

Adam tugged at his hair in frustration. "Or what if the clouds are just another part of whatever this is, and when we go up there we get swarmed and eaten? Nothing I create can outrun a wyrm."

"A wyrm infestation would explain why this level is so deadly," Torliam conceded. "However, it seems strange that we would see signs of one *just* as we were considering leaving this forest. Perhaps it is only a ruse meant to keep us from escaping."

I sighed, rubbing the back of my neck. "How much farther to the fruit, Torliam? Can you tell?"

"We draw closer, but I cannot be specific. Another day of travel, at most."

"We keep walking, then," I said. I didn't know that the forest had thrown all it could at us, but I doubted anything on the ground could be worse than a wyrm. I considered climbing a tree to see if I could scout out the area above, but the risk of being caught by a wyrm, and then relentlessly pursued until one of us was dead, was at this point greater than the threat of the forest.

The enchanted woodland grew meaner and darker, losing all pretense of fairy-tale allure. At points I had to drill through trees growing too closely together to walk around or completely wipe out swaths of mushrooms spitting deadly spores. Branches fell from above and fallen leaves concealed holes and thorny spikes. The animals attacked and distracted us with increasing regularity. The bugs swarmed about constantly and probably would have stung or bit at us, if I'd let any of them live.

But in truth, none of that surprised me as much as the little platform of sticks Wraith sensed, lashed together between two tree branches, far enough above that I wouldn't have been able to see it with my eyes. Everything the forest had created until that point was either boldly fantastical or arguably natural. The platform looked both out of place and entirely mundane.

A couple of Kris's marionettes succumbed to a giant carnivorous plant's crushing grip, but their bodies could be held together with extra effort from her Summon Skill, so losing a few limbs and getting snapped in half didn't actually kill them, allowing her to do makeshift repairs.

The next clue to the truth of this place was some pebbles, hidden beneath fallen leaves, laid out in a decorative array that seemed unlikely to be natural. Yet another, the remains of a small fire, which seemed like it probably would have spread beyond the few inches of ash that remained, if it were natural.

"I think people live here," I said, rubbing a pinch of ash between my fingers. "We're getting closer to them, and since we're tracking the fruit, I don't think that's a coincidence. Maybe they're the ones controlling the forest. They could have been feeding stories to the outside world about the dangers of this level, while in fact they themselves are the danger."

The group speculated about this for a few minutes, until Kris, who'd been quiet until then, said, "We should try talking to them."

I turned to look at her, as did the rest of the team.

She ducked her head a little under the scrutiny at first, then fiddled with her aviator goggles and forced herself to straighten. "If they're people, we don't *have* to fight. Sure, maybe they've been attacking us and trying to stop us from getting in, but if they're people, that means they're *sentient*. We don't have to fight," she repeated. "So why don't we try and talk to them? This could be the other way, the thing the Oracle didn't see! We don't fight, we talk, because normally we wouldn't care. So we try something different, right? That's what you were talking about, a way to change the future. What if we could pay for the fruit? Or do a favor for them to get it?"

"Seriously? After all this shit we've been going through? They started it," Jacky grumbled, crossing her arms over her chest. "They should be apologizing for trying to kill us and give us the fruit so when we save the rest of the world, we save them, too. No?" she asked, looking around for support.

Birch let out a cough of agreement.

Gregor sighed and shook his head. "Do you really want to fight against those death particles? Let's resort to threats as a final option only."

"It's not a threat," she said. "It's just the truth. Besides, threats aren't the final option. Beating them to a pulp and just taking the fruit is the final option."

Kris glared at her. "Typical. Don't you realize that's probably what the Oracle expected us to do? Right?" she added, turning to Sam for help.

Without Black Sun active, his empathy was at full strength. "Well, that hasn't been the case for all the obstacles we've ever faced, but I will agree that when you have a hammer, every obstacle seems to be a nail. Trying something different is a good idea. If we can keep these people alive by doing so, that's even better. It says something about your character when you get used to collateral damage."

Kris crossed her arms and nodded. "In the films, the person who talks about needing to break a few eggs to make an omelet is always the bad guy."

"Are you trying to live your life like you're in a film?" Adam muttered, but he didn't object further.

I considered Kris's argument. The idea of *paying* for the fruit, whether in gold or favors, had a bit of an absurd ring to it. I had simply never considered that it was something we might do. But she had a good point. If it was possible to negotiate rather than fight, we should try that first, because it was the least likely choice, and there was always the other option if things didn't work out.

"Alright," I said. "We'll try talking."

Kris looked almost surprised, but grinned brightly and straightened even further from her seat atop Birch's shoulders, where she had strapped a makeshift saddle for herself.

After a few more hours of struggle, literally cutting our way through the forest, the behemoth trees gave way to smaller ones, and then to green fields and rolling hills broken up by burbling springs. The water bubbled up cold and clear from the ground and cut through the land like silver veins. It made me apprehensive.

The rolling hills grew larger, and at the top of one I could see the beginning of a new forest, the space between us covered with smooth boulders half-submerged in short, mossy grass. I raised a hand to stop my teammates, opening my mouth to warn them of the danger ahead.

Sam had been periodically activating Black Sun as we traveled, using it in conjunction with Harbinger to accrue a healing charge by harming the flora and fauna we passed. He was trying to get used to the effects it had on his mood and personality.

One of the lumpy stones under the turf raised its head and turned toward us, staring directly into Sam's black eyes.

Chapter 8

This inhuman place makes human monsters.
  — Stephen King

THE GIANT TURTLE-LIKE CREATURE, which was nearly as large as an elephant, stretched out its neck and let out a bugling roar in response to Sam's inadvertent attack.

Every grass-and-dirt-covered lump hibernating in the field in front of us stirred and began to rise. They weren't turtles disguising themselves as boulders. Rather, they were rock and earth and moss formed in the shape of turtles. They lacked the resistance to Wraith that flesh and blood beings had. I could feel the earthworms and other burrowing bugs still crawling around inside them, agitated by the sudden movement. They reminded me of the rock giants that had protected us from the sentient storm when we'd first escaped NIX, dormant and formless until given blood in exchange for their protection.

Estreyer, in its way, was alive. Some places more so—more wildly—than others.

"Oops?" Sam said, the flushed, slightly sweaty skin of his cheeks seeming out of place in contrast to the blackness that had overcome his eyes, sclera to pupil. He shrugged. "I guess we have to kill them all, now?"

The first turtle shook off the clumps of dirt and grass that had grown over its body like camouflage and turned toward us, its bump-covered face twisted into a scowl. It sucked in a sudden breath—with more force than should have been possible—and Sam reeled backward to avoid both the sudden pull of wind and the shocking cold that froze the liquid in a conical area in front of it solid. That area included the damp grass and ground, the previously invisible humidity in the air, and a chunk of Sam's side.

Sam screamed, but the noise cut out an instant later when he fully released Black Sun. It seemed to numb the pain, or at least make it so that he didn't *care* about the frozen patch of skin on his side. Sam's face relaxed. He turned that cold, black-eyed gaze on the turtle, his side healing even as the creature, still staring as if in challenge, slumped to the ground.

The deep breath of air the turtle had taken in seeped out, setting the surrounding terrain on fire and pushing the smell of baking clay out toward us. It had lost control of whatever breath attack it had used, I assumed. All that heat it had taken from the air could cook even a two-ton turtle if applied directly to its internal organs. Its eyes grew glassy, and it did not move again.

I carefully turned away from Sam, keeping tabs on him only through Wraith. Accidentally meeting his eyes wouldn't kill me, but when he was like this, he might not hold back his attack quickly enough to avoid hurting me. "It might be a trap," I said. I strained Wraith, reaching out beyond the comfortable edge of my range, gaining a bit more distance in exchange for losing most of my overall area and detail.

I found them, camouflaged and hiding beyond the rocks in the far trees, almost as if they knew exactly what my Skill was capable of. "They're here, watching," I said, pointing them out to my teammates on a mini-map Window.

The rest of the previously hibernating creatures were undeterred by their nestmate's death.

It didn't matter. Once, this might have been a difficult fight, but we were stronger now, and they were nothing compared to Pestilence. I was more concerned with the people waiting for us on the other side.

"We don't want to fight!" I yelled, projecting my voice as loudly as I could. "Let us talk!"

I didn't know if they just couldn't hear me or weren't interested in talking, but they didn't respond.

I stayed on the defensive as the turtles attacked, writhing tentacles of Chaos lashing out at every creature that neared, sending them crumbling to the ground in flaming or frozen pieces.

The turtles retaliated with their breath attacks, sucking in all the warmth in an area and then releasing it again as beams of heat so powerful they set even the air afire. They were quick, for turtles, and their energy-manipulation attacks almost instant, with no dramatic windup required.

Kris's marionettes had been trailing through the forest behind us, but now they rushed up to the edge of the treeline and waited, ready to spring into attack or defense against any unexpected dangers. The kids were forced to retreat back toward the marionettes at Jacky's insistence, despite their pouting. The rest of us could handle this without putting them at any unnecessary risk—even if neither Gregor nor Kris appreciated being sidelined and would probably whine about it later.

Adam tossed me a cone of ink, and I held it to my mouth before yelling again for a ceasefire, still to no response. Perhaps they would be more willing to talk to us once their last defense had been destroyed and they had little other option.

Torliam's sky blue power lashed around him, shielding himself and Zed.

My brother stayed behind the shield and sniped the creatures with almost perfect accuracy, sending any exposed turtle heads splattering into oblivion at a distance none of the rest of us could reach.

Torliam, like Jacky, jumped straight into the fray, killing with direct blows. He remained clean due to his power, but Jacky quickly found herself covered in dirt. She didn't seem to mind, grinning brightly even as mud formed in the cracks between her teeth. Both of them still had a level of martial prowess that I couldn't hope to match, flitting around with whistling speed and hitting with enough force to shake the ground just as strongly as the stomping movements of the mammoth-sized monsters.

Sam strolled around with a bored gait, and whenever he made eye contact with one of the turtles it would slump to the ground. He didn't waste any of the destructive energy he'd saved. Not being made of flesh, many of his Harbinger Skill's destructive effects were ineffective on the giant turtles anyway.

One creature stomped atop the dead body of a former companion and leaped off like a professional wrestler jumping from the top turnbuckle, shooting a heat beam at me as it fell. I killed it, but that didn't stop the fall of its crushing boulder-body, which was likely what it had been aiming for.

I projected Chaos from my feet at an angle, creating a platform of hardened dirt and air, and sprang out of the way. When I landed again, my clawed feet sent dirt and grass spraying up from the turf.

Behind me, the rock turtle's corpse crashed into the ground with such force that I was nearly thrown from my feet, and probably would have been if not for the structural adaptations my feet had gone through.

I could still sense our audience on the very edge of my range, watching the fight.

—Kris, send your marionettes to circle around. Keep them far, keep them hidden. I don't want our real targets to escape.—
-Eve-

The girl nodded, not even looking in my direction, and her minions moved.

That was when the ground started to shake in truth, the type of rumbling, bucking quake that gave me flashbacks to Behelaino's anger and made me feel as if the earth were literally going to rise up and walk away.

Which is exactly what it proceeded to do.

At first, even I, with my multi-kilometer sensory range, couldn't understand what was happening.

The ground in the distance, where the rolling hills once again gave way to trees, *broke*. It shattered along what seemed to be fault lines, echoing with cracks of wood and stone that sounded like the breaking bones of giants. Throughout the forest, as far as the eye could see, flying creatures burst from the trees in panic, filling the skies with their raucous cawing.

The land continued to rise, and I thought for a moment that an island that stretched as far as the eye could see might be trying to rise up and float away, thrust into the air by a giant column of earth. Then my perspective realigned, and I realized I was looking at a leg. At that point, I could see the overall shape, and with a stunned blink and an absent scythe of uncondensed Chaos toward an enemy, I realized the island was actually just the back of another turtle.

The creature had been resting under the ground long enough for trees to grow and die and grow again, rivers to run through the land, and any hint of what lay beneath to be concealed. An entire forest grew from its back, the trees swaying and trembling as it moved. Dislodged rocks and dirt spilled from its sides, joined in a couple spots by waterfalls that had once been rivers.

"Fall back!" I cried, using both words and a VR Window to make sure all of my teammates were able to receive my message over the deafening sound of the titanic turtle's movements.

As quickly as possible, we retreated through the field of fallen opponents, the two-ton, elephantine rock turtles now seeming tiny compared to the behemoth monster behind us.

"Should we run?" Gregor said, his knuckles squeezed white around the handles of his daggers.

The behemoth moved slowly, almost as if in slow motion, but I doubted we'd be able to outrun it, even so.

The smaller turtles continued to attack, but Zed shot them down before they could get close enough to use their freezing, scorching breath, and I turned my attention from them to focus on the more pressing danger.

I shook my head. "Maybe we can pierce the brain. If we can get through the skull and drop me inside, I should be able to just start scrambling everything around me like an egg. Adam, I don't want anyone on the ground. Start on backup flying constructs. This could take a while, and we might run out. Everyone, keep in mind this thing could have those energy-transferring breath attacks, too. Don't stick around if it turns its head toward you, and I want you shielding at the slightest sign of danger. Torliam and Birch, we'll be the strike team…" I trailed off as, contrary to my expectations, the behemoth did not pursue us. In fact, each stomping, earth-shaking footstep had turned it in the opposite direction, and now it seemed to be moving away.

"Oh," I breathed. "They're retreating."

"They're running with the fruit," Sam said.

"We're gonna chase them, right?" Jacky said.

My eyes narrowed. "They wouldn't just run. Not when they've seen that these things can't hold us off. They can't be confident enough to think the sight of their giant turtle scared us away. So there will be a rearguard."

I turned my attention away from the behemoth as Wraith sensed several more rock turtles rising up and heading our way. The turtles were surprisingly quick once they had time to get up to speed, and their charge could be heard even through the earth-quake-tremors of the titan's slow steps. On their backs rode the camouflaged rear-guard I had sensed watching us before.

"They're coming, guys!" I called.

We grouped up defensively and waited for them to arrive. I considered going on the offensive and taking them out, but hesitated as Kris's argument replayed in my mind. What if this small choice could change the future? I would at least *try* until there was no other option but to kill them all in self-defense.

Kris's marionettes came out from the cover of the trees, their hands raised in the air in the human gesture of non-threat.

Our opponents were not nearly so hesitant. They had closed much of the distance between us, enough that I could make out a bit more detail. What I had thought was camouflage—rocks and wood and feathers—turned out to be their actual bodies. Each of the riders was different from the others, and they looked more like the bodies Kris might create than any organically grown being. They carried large bamboo-like tubes on their shoulders, carved with runes. The tubes were comically large against their small frames, like oversized rocket-launchers. One of the creatures stood atop their turtle's back, lifted their tube, and aimed at us.

It shot a ball of yellow static that quickly opened into a spinning fractal shape that expanded as it flew toward us.

I immediately recognized it as the same invisible-to-the-naked-eye static that had covered the archway and killed anything it touched. The order to scatter was on the tip of my tongue when the fractal net seemed to reach the edge of its limits, and, unable to stretch apart any further, it broke into pieces and dispersed. We scattered anyway, just in case, but by the time it should have reached us, the static was no longer killing every bug, blade of grass, or patch of moss that it touched, reassuring me that there was a range limit to it, at least.

Still, if they'd been just a bit closer, and us too slow to move, it could have killed us. Anger surged in the pit of my belly and rose up through my mouth in a vibrating roar as Voice gave weight to my words. "Stop! I wish to speak peacefully, but if you wish to fight, I will join you. When we are done, you will be dust, and I will walk over your remains."

My teammates stumbled away from me, pressing their hands to their ears, and the echo of my words was almost a visible ripple in the air, shivering through our opponents' bodies and onward till it dispersed into the distance.

The rock turtles stumbled and fell to their knees, and their riders were not much better off. They took some time to regroup and seemed to argue with each other. Though I could hear what they were saying from this distance, and it had the same lilt I associated with Estreyan, I couldn't understand them. I belatedly realized that maybe they hadn't been able to understand me, either, and had no idea I was trying to negotiate from the beginning.

At my side, Torliam cleared his throat, muttered a few variations of a word I couldn't understand, and then yelled it out to them. As a group, they turned to us, their body language showing obvious surprise.

In the Estreyan I could understand, Torliam said, "It seems my guess was correct. It looks like they speak a language that split off from a very old dialect of Estreyan. We should be able to communicate, with some difficulty. I have called for peace."

"What's the Old Estreyan word for parlay?" I asked.

WE FELL into an awkward standoff with the enemy group. Neither of us attacked, but we also did nothing but stare warily at each other.

"Someone has to make the first move," I muttered. "Open negotiations, or whatever." More than a little reluctantly, I withdrew Chaos, letting it roil beneath my skin, ready but outwardly unthreatening.

Torliam moved up beside me, a stubborn look on his face that told me I wouldn't be able to get him to stay behind without physically incapacitating him.

We'd only closed about half the distance to the other group, walking slowly, when the one who seemed to be in charge raised a hand to us and yelled something.

Torliam frowned and mouthed the word the creature had yelled. "Stop," Torliam said.

I obeyed, raising a questioning eyebrow.

A little slowly and awkwardly, he called out something in return. I understood a few of the root words, but I couldn't understand the entire sentence or grasp its meaning. The non-flesh creatures didn't seem to understand, either, and Torliam was forced to add some pantomime to the words to clarify his meaning, blushing a little under his tan and avoiding my gaze as he did so.

Eventually, he got the point across, and, after a short discussion, the leader urged his rock turtle mount closer to us. We met between two mounds of rubble, one frozen and the other still smoldering.

As far as I could tell with either my eyes or Wraith's sensory abilities, the leader was made of hundreds of smooth river rocks fitted together into a humanoid shape, using no mortar or adhesive to affix the stones to each other. Microscopic filaments of light flowed over and through his body in waves, as if invisible fiber optics had been woven within him like veins. In fact, I only labeled him a male at all because he didn't have any bumps on his chest, while some of the others did. He was short and stocky, coming up to about mid-thigh on me. None of the creatures were big, but each was different from the others in their own way, except for the flow of tiny lights pulsing over and through them. One seemed to be made of hand-pulled copper wire, one of butterfly wings preserved in tree resin, and another from what looked like sun-bleached bird skulls. Most, though, were not quite so exotic, and were made of some variant on carved wood or stone.

I wondered how the creatures could speak, or for that matter *move* at all. They had no lungs, no muscles or flesh, and did not glow with any Seed power that I could sense. I assumed it must have something to do with the tons and tons of tiny runes carved into them, on the insides where you wouldn't normally be able to see.

I bowed to them, adding slightly more respect to the motion than was necessary. They probably didn't know who I was, after all, and we had basically invaded and attacked them without provocation. I didn't bow *too* low, though. That would be a sign of subservience or insecurity.

The river-stone creature returned my bow, just a little too shallowly to be truly respectful. He introduced himself, quite aptly I thought, as River Pebble of the woodland guardians.

He pointed to Kris's marionettes. With Torliam's help translating, and a lot more pantomime, we were able to communicate. "The not-flesh creatures. Are they your companions?" River Pebble asked.

"They are one of my teammates creations," I said.

River Pebble requested to speak to Kris, and she joined us, still riding Birch, with Jacky following behind her like a bodyguard.

In stark contrast to how they'd greeted me, River Pebble and his entire group of warriors bowed to her, bending all the way to a ninety-degree angle. When he looked at her, the miniature light-streaks made his eyes sparkle. "We did not know that a creator was among the group. The traps, they are to keep out the other flesh-eaters and those who would bring ruin to the homeland. Are you truly the creator of all these children?" He waved to the few dozen marionettes arrayed behind our group on either side.

She grinned and nodded, crossing her arms and puffing out her chest proudly. "Yep! I have a Skill for giving them spirits, but the design and creation are all me, all from scratch."

"I can see that you are both wise and skilled," River Pebble said, bowing again to her. His little rock eyes seemed to examine me closely. "Are you also a creation of Creator Kris?"

My eyebrows raised. I shook my head. "No."

The little row of pebbles over his eyes rose, too. "Truly? You look…different from the other flesh-eaters."

"I've gone through a few changes from what I first looked like. I have a portion of the Seed of Khaos, and after almost dying a couple times, this is my new, stronger body. I'm a godling."

His expression soured, and he paused for a few seconds before turning back to Kris. "Creator, you are the most honorable of your companions, though oppressed and kept from leading. Please, with honesty tell me, can this one," he pointed to me, "be trusted with negotiation?"

Kris's eyes widened as Torliam gave the translation, and Jacky scowled at the creature. "We don't mistreat Kris, you stupid rock pile," Jacky growled under her breath.

Kris looked to me, then back to River Pebble, adjusting the aviator goggles on her head. "We're the good guys. We weren't trying to attack you just now, we'd already agreed ahead of time that when we found you we wanted to talk instead of fight."

River Pebble's companions shifted, looking at each other and murmuring, till a sharp gesture from him quieted them.

"We're here because we need help. We're fighting against the Abhorrent, and we heard there was something on this level that would help us."

"This is trouble beyond my strength, Creator Kris. If I may have your word that there will be no further harm attempted, I will call our most honorable leader out to meet you. You are sure that the others will not try to…*eat us* or anything, truly?"

She frowned. "Umm, I think there's some sort of cultural misunderstanding. We don't eat people, really. Go ahead and call your leader, you're safe as long as you don't try and sneak-attack us or something."

None of them seemed interested in getting the rest of us to confirm her words. One of the woodland guardians spoke into a runic device strapped around their wrist, but even Torliam didn't seem able to keep up with what was said. Shortly afterward, the behemoth, which had already lumbered several kilometers away, leaving a cratered depression in its wake that stretched out like a dried seabed, stopped fleeing and began to eat the trees like they were broccoli.

While we waited, the woodland guardians talked with Kris. When they went up to interact with the marionettes, she had to explain that most of them couldn't speak aloud and used gestures to communicate, except for Pino, who had his little beeping box which only she could understand.

The woodland guardians seemed to find this sad, but consoled her that it was still amazing to be able to create so many of them, and talking wasn't the most important thing anyway, and that they were sure the marionettes were still happy.

I had a sneaking suspicion everything we said was being relayed back to their leader.

It took almost an hour, during which time I called the rest of the team forward to join us. I was beginning to worry the creatures were gathering a follow-up attack force, but their leader finally appeared, swooping out of the sky on the back of a small winged lizard. He was made of molded vines, most of them old and brown, but a few green and sprouting the occasional leaf. He looked over our group, and without hesitation, moved to stand in front of me.

He introduced himself as Weaver.

"We do not wish you here. Can I persuade you to leave peacefully?" he asked.

"Yes. We came here for the fruit of life—one for each of us, nine total. Give us those, and we'll leave right now," I said.

He considered me for a moment, then said, "No."

I doubted Torliam had translated such a simple sentiment incorrectly, but I still asked, "No?"

"No. We guard the fruit, and it is precious to us. We will safeguard it from flesh-eaters and foreigners to the last, though you were to kill us all."

Jacky cracked her knuckles, her eyes flicking about as she took note of the number and location of the guardian creatures.

—ARE WE GONNA GO WITH MY IDEA NOW? THE BEST DEFENSE IS AN OVERWHELMINGLY POWERFUL OFFENSE, YOU KNOW. —
-JACKY-

Zed moved his hands toward the guns at his sides, ready to draw them on a moment's notice, and Gregor did the same with his daggers.

Birch bristled, feathers and fur rising to make himself look more threatening. Unlike when he'd been a small cub, it was effective. He added a low growl, and the woodland guardians closest to him stepped away, resting their hands on the large tubes that shot that killer yellow static.

"Be calm," I said aloud, adding onto the words with a Window for those of the team who had a VR chip.

—Just wait and watch, gather information.—
-Eve-

We were not in an advantageous position, so close to their weapons. We could probably slaughter the whole group of them before they could retaliate, but only if we truly caught them by surprise. And even if we succeeded in that, we did not know if there were more traps waiting to kill us, or some other way they would keep us from accessing the fruit, which we still hadn't *seen*. If we really couldn't win with negotiations, we needed to keep smiling, withdraw, and attack after thorough reconnaissance.

I locked my eyes on Weaver's. "That may be so, but perhaps you should reconsider what is at stake here," I said. We both knew it was a threat, I could tell from the way his light streaks sped up, like a quickening heartbeat, but I continued with a slightly more innocuous explanation of my words. "The Abhorrent does not care for the distinction between my people and yours. We have destroyed the first of its Avatars, Pestilence. Another arrived on the day of the eclipse, and with time, it will grow strong enough to bring through its brethren. This is a catastrophe that will spare none, and it is the *responsibility* of all who have the power to stop it."

He paused before asking what seemed to be a non sequitur. "Who are your progenitors, godling?"

"Khaos," I said, then paused. "And maybe the God of Shaping and Molding, too, though much more distantly. We're not totally sure about that, and he's not around to ask anymore."

"You are not becoming Khaos, nor Shaping and Molding, and not even a simple mix of the two, I think. I cannot give you the fruit, but you can *earn* it."

I raised an eyebrow, waiting for him to explain.

"You lead this group, despite not being a creator, and if I am correct, also being a flesh-eater," he said to me. "However, you listen to the wisdom of your creator, and your creator trusts in you. You have done much harm here, but you stayed your hand before the final attack. Because of this, if you are able to prove your worth before us all, to show that you understand the way of our people and the worth of a different path, we may gift the precious fruit to one who does not spoil all that they touch."

A lot of fancy words, but it all came down to just another quest, in the end. I gave him a deep nod. "I'm willing to try, at least. Tell me more."

DESPITE THE WAY Weaver had phrased it, for some reason I was still expecting him to want money or favors of some sort, perhaps for me to kill some powerful monster that was threatening their town or agree to some treaty that would keep other Estreyans from entering the level once we left. But it turned out that was just my own bias talking.

"Our people greet the beginning of each new lunar cycle with an exhibition as the sun sets. One prepares a demonstration, and the rest gather to watch and receive enrichment. If you are able to understand us, your demonstration will enrich our spirits and enliven our minds, and will confirm that you are worthy to receive the fruit of life."

"A demonstration?" I echoed. "What exactly does that mean?"

Torliam and Weaver went back and forth for a bit in Old Estreyan, before Torliam explained, "The contents of the demonstration are up to you. It seems to be something like your Earth's concept of a 'talent show.'" He'd grown interested in my planet's films and television, and made the connection with a proud grin.

"Things like dancing or singing?"

"Only sometimes, but yes. The point seems to be to move the

hearts of the audience, to cause them to feel emotion or think deeply, to broaden their horizons."

I tried to keep my dismay from showing openly. "And how am I supposed to do that?"

Torliam's mouth quirked up, entirely unsympathetic. "I am sure you will figure it out."

"The next demonstration will be held in thirteen days. You may reside among us until then," Weaver said.

"*Thirteen* days?" I shook my head firmly. We'd already spent a few days traveling, and that would make it almost three weeks since the eclipse, in Estreyan time. "We don't have that long to wait. The Avatar is growing stronger with every moment—"

Weaver stopped, his small, lightweight body giving off the aura of a deeply rooted boulder. "Thirteen days. If you can come to understand us, you will know that there is a goodness to experiencing all things in their rightful time."

He hadn't said so, but I could sense the hint of threat underlying his words. If we couldn't wait, I would fail their test before I even began, and they wouldn't give us the fruit. In fact, they would probably attack in an attempt to eliminate the threat we posed. "I'll do it," I said.

Weaver welcomed us to their land under the stipulation that we do no harm and bring no others here without permission. He required agreement from all of us, not just Kris.

"That means no eye curses, got it?" Jacky said to Sam, elbowing him in the side. "Think you can manage to do that?"

Sam grunted in pain and glared at her. "I definitely can."

She gave him a half-skeptical, half-threatening look, but moved ahead and ignored him as he sputtered defenses.

The behemoth turtle, which had been still, turned around. It let out a deep sigh of apparent irritation, which flattened a broad swath of giant trees and blew away a small mountain, despite not using a breath attack like its smaller counterparts had. It turned around and very, very slowly, walked back and settled down in the same place it had arisen. With a final rumble, the land returned to rest, the only evidence of the behemoth's existence the broken fault-lines around the edge of its shell.

The woodland guardians escorted us through the remains of the battlefield and onto the land atop the giant turtle. As we followed them into the woods, Kris was the only one who didn't seem tense and distrustful. "Why?" she asked Weaver. "I mean, why won't you share with foreigners?"

Light motes sprinkled through his body, and he paused before answering. "We shared, when the flesh-eaters first arrived. We were well-intentioned and naive, and when they ate of the fruit, gluttony grew within them. They wanted more, with no care for the tree or the needs of our people. We did not know warfare, and so the best and brightest of us, created so carefully and loved so deeply, were killed."

Weaver turned to look at me again, something hard in his voice. "We learned to kill in turn, learned the perfidy of the flesh-eaters. They grew wary, and yet their greed did not dissipate. We were taught the same lesson many times, each betrayal slightly different than the last, until we understood that we must safeguard our land and the precious fruit from all outsiders." He looked to Kris. "We have allowed these others onto our land only because of you, Creator. We did not know there were any like us on the outside."

Kris frowned, seemingly thinking deeply. "Are there only a few of the fruit, then? Not enough for you and us both?"

Weaver nodded, walking into an area where leafy vines hung down so thickly from the branches above that it felt almost like swimming to move them aside as we passed through. "The fruit are the spark of life given to each new child. They grow slowly, and if the creation is unworthy, they are wasted without bringing life to it. Without them, our people would fade until the light went out of the last of us, with no children. I am curious to learn how you have given life to your own creations, without them."

Kris blinked a few times, then looked around at her marionettes with wide eyes. "Wait, so you guys are all…" She cleared her throat. "I mean, does the fruit have a spirit in it? It's a way for you to summon spirits into bodies?"

The old, dry vines above Weaver's eyes drew down in a frown. "Some say this is the case, but I do not believe the spirits of the dead are held and reborn from within the fruit. The fruit simply spark life, and the spirit is formed in the living. But who can know, truly?" He paused for a moment, letting the question linger. "Perhaps, Creator, you pull the spirits of the dead into your children?"

Kris shrugged her tiny shoulders. She didn't look so out of place next to these diminutive creatures, I realized. "Kind of, but it's hard to explain. The spirits aren't souls or anything like that. They're imprints, energy left behind by things that happened or trees that lived a really long time or a lot of people feeling something strong in the same place. There's an echo of people when they die, but mostly it fades away and mixes together with everything else pretty quickly."

The guardians escorting us started chattering, too quickly for Torliam to translate.

"We would be most pleased if you would spend some time with our elders and sages, Creator. I am sure they would be very interested to learn more of your children, and of these spirits."

"Well…" Kris bit her lip. "I don't mind, but we really need those fruit. We don't want to hurt you or keep you from creating… children, but, um, you realize everyone everywhere is going to die if we fail?" Her eyes flicked to me almost unnoticeably before she clenched her fists and hardened her tone. "The Abhorrent wants to kill you just as much as it wants to kill us, and we're going to *lose* if something doesn't change."

"That is up to Eve Redding. We would also be interested in learning how you bypassed our protections," he said, stopping as the curtains of vines opened onto a village.

The rest of us also stopped as we exited the barrier of vines, looking out onto the guardians' village, which was as storybook-like as the rest of the woodland. Houses had been built into and out of the surrounding greenery, with little cobblestone paths on the ground and stick and vine bridges weaving through the air above. Runes were everywhere, carved into walls, painted on doorjambs, and chiseled into the cobblestones of the paths that wound throughout the village. It was obvious that runic technology was part of every villager's way of life, not something any specific engineer did, but something that all of them tinkered with in their spare time. It made sense, considering they themselves seemed to be built around incredibly complex runic designs, and creating more "children" would require mastery of the practice.

The citizens of the village, most of them small, and each different and fantastical in their own way, gathered among the trees and burrows and woven huts to watch us.

There were many signs of the major earthquake that had essentially just hit the village, though less damage than would have been caused to a place that used more urban construction methods. The woodland creatures watched us with as much suspicion, fear, and anger as curiosity.

Weaver lifted his arms and called out loudly, "The outsiders meant no harm, only wishing to visit us and ask our aid against a great danger. Despite the outsiders destructive powers, none of those who stayed behind to guard our escape were harmed, and among them walks a creator. Please, welcome them. They will stay with us until the exhibition, during which their leader will share her thoughts with us."

This did not seem to mollify the villagers, but they didn't do anything but watch us with fascinated distrust, like you might watch a boil being lanced and drained. Had they never seen a human? They seemed, more or less, to be modeled upon the same outline. Bipedal, two legs, two arms, though there were some exceptions.

The only ones who received anything like a positive response were Kris, Birch, and the marionettes. The marionettes waved and nodded to the villagers, who greeted them tentatively in return.

Pino seemed particularly pleased by the attention, strutting around beeping and bowing like some sort of celebrity.

Weaver brought us to the base of a truly gargantuan tree, its trunk as wide around as any skyscraper and reaching just as high. "We have no living quarters that will accommodate your entire group. Perhaps, Creator Kris, you would allow your children to dwell among the village with the other guardians? They would be well-received, and it might help your cause for the others to associate them with your flesh-eaters."

Kris was surprised, but agreed readily enough. "They've got all our supplies, though, so we'll need them to drop that stuff off first."

I was in favor of the idea, both to build goodwill, and because, if we had a marionette in half the houses, we were effectively holding all the citizens hostage in the event that things went…poorly.

Weaver pushed aside a door of living vines to reveal a cramped staircase that wound up and around the inside of the tree's bark. Bowls filled with glowing water lilies were set into little alcoves and provided enough light to see the steps in front of us. We passed a few floors without pausing, and I used Wraith to scout the rooms that seemed to fill at least half of the tree's interior, mostly workshops and living quarters with balconies looking out over the village.

Weaver led us to a large room half a dozen stories off the ground. Sleeping mats sat along the beautifully carved walls, and a wide balcony looked out onto the village below.

Torliam and I stretched upright with relief, having had to hunch almost completely over to get through the staircase and hallway.

"The rest of you may stay here," Weaver said. "You may look out upon our people and visit among them as you please. Some might be distrustful, so I ask that you remember your vows of peace." He turned to me. "If you would like support in the demonstration, please reach out to us. Perhaps you will find that learning our ways can help you to choose your path. Remember, without the agreement of the people, there will be no fruit given."

I pushed back the tangled, flyaway hairs that had escaped my braid and let out a sigh, the soothing green smell in the air not enough to assuage my tension. "Is there a record of previous demonstrations that have been well-received? Do you have anything like a library?"

Weaver clasped both hands over his little cane and shook his weathered face. "Our library holds different information, and though you would surely gain much wisdom from reading the thoughts of our most learned, it does not have specific records of the monthly exhibitions. These memories are held in the minds of my people. We pass our learning on to our children as we raise them. If you wish knowledge, speak to the elders and the masters, learn from the children and the creators. Their minds hold all that you could need, if only you are able to listen."

I only managed to partially suppress my scowl. It was obvious from all the not-so-subtle hints that he thought me foolish at best, malicious at worst, and very likely to fail this little test.

Birch looked to me, then to Weaver, and after a moment of hesitation crept forward and touched his nose to the woodland creature's hand.

Weaver's expression fell as he looked up at the tailos in surprise and dismay. "Has the outside world fallen so far? The last of your kind…" He shook his head. "We were not allies of the tailos, flesh-eating creature, but we do have memories of them. Come with me, that you might learn of your history."

Adam, who had slouched against one of the beds, immediately straightened. "I'll go with you," he said, not even bothering to hide his distrust.

Weaver seemed amused by this. "Very well, human. Perhaps your head could use some filling, too. I will go dig around and see if there are any translation devices left in working order. It has been long since we needed one."

Weaver took a couple more minutes to explain our quarters and the village amenities. He seemed to find the fact that flesh-beings sloughed off dead flesh and gathered bacteria in places like our armpits embarrassing and distasteful. He gave us all a strong sugges-tion to clean ourselves of the accrued travel-dirt in a nearby stream.

I didn't think a bit of sweat and dead skin cells was enough to warrant such a response, but we all went to do as he suggested. When we finished, Birch tugged impatiently at Adam to get him to return to Weaver and the promised information about his heritage.

Weaver had dug up enough translation devices for all of us. We affixed them to our shoulders and prepared for the coming battle. "Let's go make friends, guys," I said.

Chapter 9

Hope not ever to see Heaven. I have come to lead you to the other shore; into eternal darkness; into fire and into ice.
— Dante Alighieri

TO MY RELIEF, I found that not *all* the woodland creatures were reluctant to talk to me. Just most of them. I walked around the village, waving and smiling and introducing myself, and though a good number only stared or closed their doors, others examined Torliam and I with curiosity, shook my offered hand, and asked a few questions.

Torliam stayed a few steps behind me despite the translating tokens on our shoulders, his body language as unthreatening as a giant warrior's could be.

It didn't take me long to start distinguishing the children from the adult guardians, although the younger ones didn't seem to be any smaller than the others. The adults were obviously doting toward the young, who had a childish exuberance and curiosity that reminded me of Birch as a cub. There weren't many children, and a quick mental calculation told me it was unlikely their population was growing quickly, and might even be declining, depending on their life spans.

Weaver's initial response kept me from being open about our

need for the fruit of life, but I explained to everyone who would talk to me that I would be participating in the exhibition in thirteen days and that I was hoping to learn about their favorite demonstration from the past.

This was a topic that the villagers were happy to discuss. Aside from a few games, the exhibitions were the only form of mass entertainment they had. The exhibitions were a Big Deal. What stood out to me was how, beyond the skill and expertise of the performer, the creatures always mentioned how they *felt* while watching, or the musings it stirred in them afterward.

I supposed, living such an insular life, they would cherish anything that could introduce new ideas or feelings.

While I mingled, I kept Wraith active and searching. I noted the layout of the village and any defenses they had. I searched for the fruit, but didn't find a hint of them.

A couple of the guardians kept their hands near weapons when I approached, and others held one hand up, palm facing out to me, in some sort of warding gesture. Those I left alone, unsure of the sign's exact meaning, but confident that they didn't want to speak. Some were bold enough to ask questions about the world beyond, and I drew a small group of listeners as I described some of my less death-defying experiences with Estreyer's wonders, and showed off the ring, armband, and crown that were the Oracle's gifts.

When the sun began to set, I made my way back toward the huge tree in the middle of the village, where it seemed pretty much every other creature in the village was also gathering. At the base of the tree, in front of the stage settled in between two of its roots, I found a group of woodland guardians surrounding Adam, patting whatever part of him they could reach and making soothing sounds.

"I'm *fine!*" Adam insisted to the group, clearly frustrated. "That's just the way my Skill works, it's not even a big deal!"

They shook their heads sadly at each other, obviously not believing a word Adam said. One of the guardians was crouched down, covering his face and shaking in grief.

Adam jostled his way out of the group and stalked over to me. Sparks jumped from his hand as he ran it roughly through his hair. "I keep trying to tell them my ink constructs aren't actually alive, I just imbue them with traits when I create them to make them *seem* that way."

I smirked at him. "Let me guess. They think you're a 'creator,' too, and that your little ink children keep dying after enjoying only a few minutes of life."

He groaned in answer. "I'm not sure if this translator device is broken, calibrated improperly, or if they just refuse to accept my words as the truth."

A stocky, stone creature passed by, then, patting Adam on the back of the knee almost hard enough to buckle his leg. "You need not try to hide your sorrow with bluster," he said, then moved on to join the gathering.

I let out a snort of amusement, and then quickly straightened my expression into solemnity when a couple of the nearby creatures shot glares toward me. I patted Adam sympathetically on the shoulder. "Poor guy." Before he could respond, I walked off. Despite my teasing, I was pleasantly surprised by his progress integrating with the villagers. No doubt his Animus Skill had been the catalyst there, but he'd made more progress by accident than I had with hours of effort.

Gregor had his own group of gathered villagers. The boy was standing at the edge of the stage, using the screen of his datapad to show pictures. "This is called a skyscraper," he said. "The base structure is made of steel and cement."

The villagers *oohed* and *ahhed* with interest, and I watched with amusement as Gregor ran through a few presentations that seemed like they'd been prepared for school.

Kris and her marionettes were as popular as I would have expected, and Birch made friends showing off Chaos, his Gale Skill, and giving some of the youngest villagers rides atop his back.

The woodland guardians liked to gather for socialization every evening at the base of the central tree, but had no need to eat. I figured that was fine, since we'd brought more than enough rations for our group, but they had some knowledge of Estreyans, even if most of them weren't old enough to have met one, and they understood that we did eat.

A group of them enthusiastically brought out a platter of nuts, berries, and bare roots, then stared at me and my teammates expectantly.

Jacky pouted about the lack of meat, but the rest of us ate the offered food readily enough.

After dinner, I took out the long-range communication device we'd brought with us and attempted to get a signal from the relay beacon we'd left at the entrance to this level. I got only static.

I wasn't sure if the math said it would help, but just in case I took the device with me as I climbed up the central tree. I hadn't made it halfway up, but was already higher than most of the forest canopy, and the signal hadn't grown stronger. I decided not to try to reach the top.

When I returned to the ground, one of the woodland guardians who I'd met earlier asked me what I'd been doing. Pondslider was taller than many of the other guardians, and made of little magnetic shards of iron which she could mold to some degree to change her form.

When I explained, she grabbed the comms device out of my hand, poking and prodding at it unabashedly. "You come with me," she said, motioning to Torliam and me with two fingers. "I will help you fix this," she added.

Torliam and I followed her into a little house, both crouching to avoid banging our heads on the ceiling. He looked around at the half-finished projects scattered haphazardly about with shrewd eyes. "She seems to be a runic technician or engineer. This is quite surprising, fascinating, even… It is proof, at least, that they had extensive contact with my people some time in the past, to have picked this up. I am not familiar with any of the formations she is using, but they seem quite elegant. Perhaps these guardians have preserved some of the lost knowledge of our ancestors."

"We do not preserve, we develop *better* technologies," Pondslider snapped, obviously offended. "Stupid flesh-eater," she muttered to herself. She spent the next few minutes shooing us around as it seemed we were always in the way of the tool or reference she needed. It took her less than an hour to take the comms device apart, polish out and re-carve some runes, and add a separate power crystal. The extra innards meant she had to pound the outer covering into a more lumpy shape to make it fit back on, but she handed the smashed-up device back to me proudly. "Now you can talk to the outside."

I checked for a signal, and sure enough, it came through clearly. I was quite impressed.

When I said so, Pondslider waved my words away and leaned in to look at the device's screen. "Have you heard of the thing called… 'sky sharks' before? I heard the outside has them. Ask them," she said, gesturing to the device expectantly.

I looked to Torliam in confusion, but he was smiling at Pondslider with the kind of ease I hadn't seen from him since we'd arrived here. "Sky shark is an old term for the *kulia*. I have hunted and sent the aether through their bones myself, you know. We arrived in the *Swiftsure,* as sleek and deadly as she is beautiful."

Ah. They were talking about the Estreyan air ships.

"*Swiftsure*? Where is it?"

"Unfortunately, we were forced to leave her behind at the entrance to this level, for fear that she would be damaged flying through your deadly traps."

Pondslider was undeterred. As the two of them jabbered with shared excitement, I turned back to the comms device.

There were a couple messages waiting for me from Queen Mardinest and Earth, basically just saying that they were still mobilizing, but that there had been no updates.

I sent out a video call request, and after only a couple minutes of waiting, Mardinest connected from her end. The quality of the connection was grainy, but I was ecstatic just to be able to get updates at all.

"Is everything okay?" she asked without preamble. "Do you have the fruit?"

"We're alright," I responded with similar speed. "No fruit, yet, but I'm working on it. I met another race of creatures here. Did you know about that?"

Either she was a very good actor, or she truly hadn't, because she paused to process my words. "Are they dangerous?"

"As dangerous as any other sentient race with access to runic technology of the kind I've never seen before."

A muscle in her jaw tightened as she gritted her teeth. "I see. Is this the obstacle keeping you from the fruit?"

I shot a quick glance to Torliam and Pondslider, but neither seemed to be paying attention. "In part. They're willing to listen, but changing their minds involves proving that I understand their culture and getting a vote in a couple weeks."

Her brows drew down. "Reinforcements are ready to go at any point, at your request. Stealth or overwhelming force, whatever you think best."

"No need for that," I said, keeping the "yet" unspoken. "Any news on the Avatar?"

"None. We are searching ceaselessly. To be truthful, this ability to remain hidden so completely is worrisome. I have been placing my hopes in the possibility that we have not found it yet simply because it is so weak, whatever damage it might be doing is still unnoticeable."

That was a nice thought, but I knew this new Avatar wasn't like Pestilence, whose connection to the Abhorrent had been stifled and his power suppressed by the God of Shaping and Molding. The new one would grow violently. We'd considered focusing all our search efforts on the warps nearest the places that a full, rather than partial, eclipse had been visible, but that could just as easily be irrelevant, and by now the Avatar could be anywhere.

"We haven't revealed the reason for our movements, but it has been impossible to keep them completely unnoticed," she continued. "The people are beginning to wonder, and there has been speculation, some of it…unfortunately accurate, if not in the details. There are only so many conclusions one can come to, if they know enough of our undertakings. I do not know how long we will be able to keep the truth hidden. Do you think…perhaps we should be forthright, rather than allowing the danger to be revealed some other way? It could mitigate panic if we were seen to be proactive."

My scales shifted as my muscles tightened with stress. "Not yet. Let us at least get the fruit, first. We need some positive progress to show."

"Two weeks?" she said, the skepticism obvious in her voice. "That is a long time to keep a secret of this magnitude."

"That's your job. I'm doing mine. Find a way," I said.

She let out an irritated huff. "Very well. Is there anything else, Godkiller?"

I knew I was being somewhat unreasonable. It was impossible to keep a secret when so many people had a piece of it. Two weeks was likely going to be too late to stop the truth getting out ahead of us, if rumors were already spreading. On Earth, at least, there had been an increased focused on investigative journalism and uncovering high-level secrets and corruption after everything that had happened with NIX. People would be digging. "Nothing else," I said. "Contact me immediately with any news."

She signed off, and I stared down at the blank screen for a moment before tucking the comms device back in my pack. "I'm going out," I said. "Thank you, Pondslider."

I sent Adam a Window to let him know I'd found a solution that would let him continue to access information for his search algorithm, and marked Pondslider's house on a mini-map.

Instead of returning to the giant tree, I moved toward the edge of the village, walking along the thick vine curtain that enclosed it. I let my awareness stretch out, Wraith leisurely curling around both above and beneath the ground like some huge invisible creature, taking note of every inch within my range.

It took me almost an hour of walking to reach the other side of the village. I was becoming concerned at my lack of success when I discovered a cobblestone path leading out of the village on the far side, opposite where we'd been let in. A couple stout woodland guardians loitered beside it, their ruse of lazing about ruined by my ability to sense the yellow-static cannons half-buried and camouflaged beside them. They were guards.

A more thorough examination of the path showed the runic traps laid around it and throughout the forest on either side. Someone was serious about protecting whatever was at the end of that path to put such serious traps so close to the village.

It was growing dark, and the village was emptying as people returned to their dwellings for the night. No doubt someone would check in to make sure we were comfortable in our room and that none of us were wandering where we shouldn't be.

I turned back to the gargantuan tree, already planning an excursion for later that evening.

I WOKE WITH THE MOONRISE, in the stillest hour of the night. Taking a deep breath of the cool, humid air, I listened, but heard only the slow breathing of my teammates, the faint sounds of the forest, and the tiniest crackle of electricity.

"Adam?" I whispered. It was his turn to keep the night watch. It wasn't that we thought the woodland creatures meant us any harm, but letting our guard down would just be an invitation for things to go wrong.

He turned toward me, his face lit from below by the light of his datapad. "Are you ready?" he whispered back.

At my nod, he reached over and touched Kris, waking her easily.

Torliam and Kris had both agreed that the traps on the path itself were meant to capture nearest the village, but grew increasingly lethal farther along. We'd considered trying to avoid the path entirely, walking through the forest alongside it, or even using ink wings to fly over it, but judging by the suspicious lack of non-plant life around the path. They'd tried to figure out how the runic arrays woven through the surrounding forest were accomplishing that, and failed utterly. "It is not safe to attempt," Torliam said. "At least the traps on the path can be deciphered."

The cobblestones themselves were the key, and they needed to be traversed correctly, as if each were a note of music on a huge instrument. However, the traps also triggered at the presence of any living being.

"Not any living being," Zed had said from the corner, carefully massaging his muscles with pain-relieving cream. "I bet it just catches beings with a heartbeat or something, right? 'Cause *they* don't have one."

Torliam confirmed this theory.

Gregor patted Zed's shoulder. "Good job, that was pretty clever."

Zed squinted at Gregor suspiciously. "Was that…a genuine compliment? Not backhanded, about how even simpletons manage to think out of the box every now and again. Or maybe how you noticed that three minutes ago and you're glad I'm able to see the obvious?"

Gregor scowled at him. "What are you talking about? I give genuine compliments all the time!"

When Zed raised his eyebrows skeptically, Gregor's mouth fell open in outrage. He looked around to all of us. "Tell him, guys!"

Most of the others awkwardly avoided his gaze, and Jacky let out an unladylike snort of laughter. "I'm not gonna lie for you, kid."

When he looked to me for help, I asked. "How often is 'all the time'? I mean…it does happen, sometimes."

Unsatisfied, Gregor *humphed* inarticulately and crossed his arms over his chest. "I see." He turned his head away for a moment before snapping, "Well get on with it, then. If you two die from lack of preparation tonight, you'll do so still under the impression that I'm some sort of…*curmudgeonly cretin*!"

Sam had to clamp a hand over Jacky's mouth and half-suffocate her to keep her howls of laughter from waking up the entire village.

Zed grinned at the younger boy. "I wouldn't say it's that bad. I mean, you're virulently villainous. Odiously obnoxious. Repugnantly rotten. Peevishly—" Zed cut off abruptly as Sam used his free hand to muffle my brother. Zed's grin only grew bigger as Sam took his hand away. "Whew, that was close. I have no idea what goes with 'peevishly.'"

Gregor was still scowling, but the edges of his lips twitched with ill-repressed amusement. "Peevishly penurious," he said smugly, letting his arms fall to his sides and the smile reveal itself.

Jacky's laughter resumed, and Sam pinched her nose while keeping her mouth covered. "If you don't get ahold of yourself, I'll tickle you till you can't breathe," he warned her.

She swallowed down her amusement with fearful haste. "Anything but that," she whispered once he'd released her.

Birch let out a sleepy grumble and climbed into my lap, which he'd grown much too big to properly fit on, then covered his head with his paws and proceeded to go to sleep.

Adam let out a deep, put-upon sigh. "Can we get back to business here?"

"If you would stop distracting the group, I'm sure we could," Torliam had said.

Adam's jaw dropped and his eyes widened at the accusation, and he was about to retort when Torliam revealed a teasing grin.

"So funny," Adam said, deadpan.

"Thank you," Torliam replied smugly. When I'd first revealed my suspicions about the location of the fruit, Adam had wanted to come with me, and grown irritated and snappish when I denied him. Instead, once we had deciphered the nature of the traps along the path, Kris had insisted that *she* would come with me.

"Torliam might be better at runes, but he doesn't have a VR chip so Eve can show him the hidden runes easily, plus he's big and conspicuous. Also, I'm the one with the marionettes, and they don't have any flesh or blood to set off the alarms, so the path won't recognize that one happens to be carrying us. I'm the best choice to go with Eve. Plus, if we do get caught, I'm also the one the guardians are least likely to try and kill on the spot," she'd argued, pulling her aviator goggles down over her eyes and crossing her arms stubbornly.

Her point was well made, and I agreed to bring her along. We'd planned for a while longer, then gone to sleep to make sure we were fresh later that night.

Once Kris was awake, she called one of the few marionettes housed with us instead of among the villagers.

The short, crablike minion obediently skittered over from the edge of the room, dipping down in front of us as if giving a little bow.

Kris motioned to his back. "We can ride him."

I stared dubiously at the creature's many legs, the scales on my back rippling with a shudder of unease.

It looked like a bug.

I looked around at the other marionettes bunking with us, hoping to find an alternative, but most of them were small, definitely too small to support my own over two-meter-tall frame.

I searched to see if anyone or anything was monitoring our room. I found a guard in the hallway outside, so we left via the balcony.

The flat-backed spider marionette crawled down the outside of the tree on its own, and when we'd made our way stealthily through the village and out to the hanging curtains of vines on the far side, I finally settled atop it, hiding the way my innards lurched with revulsion.

Our mount skittered into the thickly hanging vines, which we used as cover as we carefully circumvented the guards. The marionette crept out a few dozen meters behind the guards, where the cobblestones began to vary in color. It moved with careful steps, strictly avoiding the stones that would bring traps snapping shut on us here, and deadly static rays shooting toward us later on.

We'd only deciphered the sequence as far out as Wraith had been able to catalogue during my earlier excursion, and after a few kilometers came to the point where Kris and I needed to solve the cobblestone puzzle on our own.

Well, mostly Kris. I was starting to understand some of the runic patterns we'd seen most often, but I was far from competent.

Our speed slowed further as I sent Kris the runes Wraith sensed under the ground via a constantly updating Window, and she worked to decipher them as quickly as possible.

Her face showed signs of strain after a while. "It's getting harder," she admitted. "I'm not sure what to do, here. Are we supposed to make a little jump and avoid this row altogether? Or should we be using only the far left stones for the next few meters?"

I looked over the hidden runes again, but the only thing I could be sure of was that *something* would trigger a response—which wasn't very useful.

Instead, I turned my attention to the surface of the path. Visually, except for the rainbow-like colors of the stones, there was little difference. However, to Wraith, concentrating closely rather than stretching wide, even the tiny molecules that made up the surface were visible. Places where little remnants of bone had been left behind, scrapes and scuffs, and even dirt that was slightly more compacted beneath certain stones. "The left side," I said. "That seems to be where everyone else has been walking."

Kris stared at the path, then slowly swiveled her head toward me. "If you could just do that, why have I been straining myself to figure this out!?"

I rubbed the back of my neck. "Well, I didn't consider it, at first. Besides, I could be wrong, or it could be a trap, so you'd better keep confirming the answer, anyway."

Despite that, simply following the steps of the creatures who had walked that path before us sped our progress up significantly. Soon, the path led through the woods and into a rockier, hilly area. I was careful to ensure none of these rocks were secretly living creatures hibernating halfway beneath the ground.

When we reached the end of the trapped area, we diverged from the path, climbing up the side of a large hill and then following along beside the path as it climbed and wove through the terrain.

I could sense us getting closer.

There was no oppressive weight of power, no rising glow that had been absorbed by the very earth and air like I noticed when we approached a god.

I couldn't quite grasp what I was feeling, other than perhaps a heightened awareness of the world around me, and a magnetic pull that came from somewhere beyond the next rocky peak. The air had an unnatural quality, and I didn't know if I was imagining that it was thicker, but I was conscious of the feeling as I breathed it in, as well as the smell of lightning.

When we arrived, Kris and I crawled off her marionette, keeping low. "Stay down, and keep your eyes closed until I tell you it's safe," I said. This situation felt a little too similar to our excursion to spy on the God of Knowledge, and I didn't want to take any risks.

Kris did as I said, though the expression on her face told me she didn't like it.

Looking over the edge of the hill in front of me made my heart clench almost as hard as seeing the God of Knowledge for the first time had, though for completely different reasons.

I was crouched above a small valley with a clear stream running through the middle, lush moss covering the rocks, and a little tree growing beside the water.

When I'd heard of the fruit of life, I'd expected a tree like the one in the center of the village behind us, something towering and mighty, and maybe the fruit would be made of gold or pure Seed material.

Instead, it looked like a bonsai tree. It was a little bigger than the type some fancy businessman might keep trapped in a pot on his desk, but still shorter than Kris. A few tiny little fruit glowed among the branches like stardust, and I could have sworn that the tree had rustled as if turning to face me just as my head first poked over the barrier between us.

I took a slow, deep breath of awe. The world felt dense with the weight of anticipation. I could simply go forward and pluck those fruit. It was impossible to imagine they would taste like anything other than the ambrosia of the gods, an elixir of wellbeing and electricity.

A sharp pain in my leg drew my attention away from the little tree. I turned to see that Kris was literally stabbing me in the leg, a knife sized to fit her hand pried between my protective scales. I realized only then that I'd stood and already begun to climb down the other side of the hill into the valley.

My claws flexed, and I snarled at her, instantly enraged by her assault. How dare she turn on me when our goal was in my sight? The fruit—

Kris had her head turned resolutely away from the tree, the eye closest to it closed so that she didn't accidentally catch a glimpse. "Eve? Eve! Can you hear me? Stop looking at it," she begged, digging the knife deeper.

The anger left me as swiftly as it had come on, like fading thunder after a lightning strike. I scooped her up in my arms, keeping her turned away from the tree, and lunged back up and over the mountain. I kept going until we reached the path again, only stopping when we'd made it back to the nonlethal area of traps.

<hr>

Chapter 10

<hr>

Stare at the dark too long and you will eventually see what isn't there.

— Ilium Troia

"THANK YOU," I said to Kris. "I'm lucky you were there."

She nodded, her scowl not leaving her face. "You could have gotten hurt, Eve! What if I hadn't been able to get your attention?"

I considered her words for a moment. "I don't know what would have happened," I admitted. Maybe it would have been fine, as long as the villagers didn't find out, but anything that could influence my thoughts had to be at least a little dangerous. With the way I'd been thinking, would I have left any fruit for the rest of my teammates? Devouring them all myself while in a fugue would have invalidated the entire reason for our visit.

When we got back to the others and told them what had happened, they all forbid me from going back by myself.

"I wasn't going to do that, anyway," I said with exasperation. "If we're going after the fruit, we should probably all go together, so no one's left behind in danger. Maybe Kris's marionettes or one of Adam's constructs could do the actual gathering, so no one gets mesmerized. Then, if the guardians have a problem with it, we can be gone before they have a chance to respond."

"I still think we should gather more information before we do anything rash," Adam said. "I don't like all these surprises. What if the fruit are different from what we were told, too? What if these creatures have some way to keep us from escaping this level? A lot of things we're not even thinking about could go wrong."

I turned away, facing out over the balcony. I tugged on my braid with my claws as I thought things through. After a few moments, I turned back to the others. "You're right," I said, nodding to Adam. "Let's give it at least a couple more days. Worst-case scenario, I end up doing this exhibition. We should have a plan in place in case that doesn't go well and we need to resort to force, though. If one of you could make it a priority to figure out their yellow death static and how to keep it from killing us, that would be great."

We set out to prepare and gather information as soon as the sun rose. The plan was to be subtle about our intent, couching questions in harmless curiosity about the woodland guardians and their culture. I wished China were still with us. She was great at this kind of thing.

We gathered information on the strength of their warriors, their weapons, and their defenses. We asked about the enchanted forest. We watched for watchers of their own, blatant or subtle. In between that we told stories of Estreyer and Earth, and received stories from them in return. It would be going too far to say that they accepted us, but the majority of them seemed less wary of us, almost all of them were deeply curious about the outside, and a few individuals like Pondslider even seemed friendly. It would take time for anything more.

Within a couple days, I felt like we'd learned enough to be reasonably certain that we could steal the fruit and get away with it. As long as we didn't trigger any alarms or get trapped in a static field, the main trouble would be escaping back through the archway quickly enough afterward.

I was sitting on a branch of the enormous tree, looking out over the village below and contemplating our next move, when a guardian made mostly of waxy feathers poked its head out of a nearby window cut into the trunk and waved at me. "Weaver wishes to speak with you, human. Come, I will lead you to his sanctum."

I rose and walked nimbly back along the branch, leaping toward the window and swinging my body inside by the upper edge. I would have asked what Weaver had called me for, but the feather creature that had come to fetch me was one of those less friendly toward us. I didn't want to deal with half-answers and sneers, so I followed silently.

The guardian led me to a large room, one of the few with a ceiling high enough for me to feel comfortable. Shelves filled with bark-and-paper books lined the walls, and in a small adjoining room, Weaver sat at a desk fiddling with some silver thread.

My attention, however, was drawn to my brother, who I was surprised to find in the library, sitting hunched over a child-sized book. "What are you doing here?" I asked Zed.

He looked up from the delicate paper pages in front of him distractedly. "Researching. Did you know Weaver has created more children than anyone else here? I've been picking his brain about the process, and he said I could look through these books to learn more." He looked back down to the page in front of him, taking notes on his datapad. "It's obvious these people are made of nonliving, organic material, but did you just think that was odd and move on, or did you stop to wonder *how* that actually works? They have no organs or muscles. They have no brain. And yet, they're alive."

I moved to look over his shoulder. "So what does it mean?"

"Well, two things. First, they're manipulating the properties of matter and energy somehow to move their bodies. Basically, molding physics like play-doh. I don't understand how they do it at all. But secondly, they use light rather than electrical impulses to transfer thoughts. They don't have neurons receiving and acting on those impulses. They don't get nerve damage, and as far as I can tell, there's almost no delay whatsoever. Have you considered exactly what it is the Seeds do to our brains to increase our Intelligence or Mental Acuity? How are you able to process all the information that Wraith gives you without having a seizure?"

"You think the two are connected?"

He nodded, flipping through the pages rapidly to point out

different sections of ancient Estreyan that I couldn't read fast enough to follow along. "When you first start to gain levels, the things you can do are theoretically possible with genetic modification or enhancement, and then later with new organ and bone structures—or basically cybernetics. But after a certain point, or when you consider Skills like Chaos, that doesn't really make sense anymore. Now, I admit, I really have no idea what I'm talking about, but these people *do*, and if I understand what I'm reading…" He took a deep breath, and looked up at me. "Eve, where does the power come from? These people don't have a single Seed in their body. What's running their thoughts?"

I could see the reason for his interest. "Do they know?"

One side of his mouth twitched up in a smile, and he leaned back, letting a little of the excited tension drop from his shoulders. "Well, I'm not sure we have a word for it. Somewhere else. I'm not sure if it counts as an alternate dimension? Those little light motes you see are weaving in and out of somewhere else, moving information and energy. I'm trying to figure out exactly how they've managed to offload their brains like that. They do it for their children, and maybe the Seeds are doing something like that for you, but if we could understand what's happening, maybe…" He closed his mouth, shaking his head. "Well, maybe we could improve."

"We'll have to ask Torliam about it," I said. "Some of the Estreyan scientists must have studied this before."

Zed snorted. "Eve, the Estreyan books I've read about how Seeds work all talk about aether, the primordial nature of the gods as an existence from before time, and the higher and lower powers. It's like…they're not doing systematic experiments. There aren't any widespread tests or theories that are able to predict the Seed-created phenomena ahead of time. They *pretend* to understand, just like Hippocrates pretended to understand when he came up with the four humors as a medical theory."

"I didn't know you were so interested in all this."

He let out a slightly bitter huff. "The only reason you're not interested in this is that you *have* Seeds, and they just work for you without any need to think about them or examine *why*. You can just pull up a virtual status screen and get your abilities quantified. If you had programmable nanites instead…"

"The boy is right," Weaver said, standing in the doorway to his little office. "But this is a failing of most foreigners. Come, human. Let us speak in my sanctum."

Zed waved an irritated hand at the two of us and returned to his note-taking.

Weaver closed the door behind me when I'd entered his office, then walked over to the open-air balcony looking out over the village. He stood there for a few increasingly awkward moments, facing away from me.

I wanted to break the silence, but that would be admitting discomfort, giving him some small advantage.

Finally, he spoke. "I know you plan to take by force what is not given freely," he said.

I felt my pulse quicken as nervous energy suffused my muscles and my instincts prepared my body to defend itself if necessary. How did he find out? Were we being monitored more closely than I had realized? Perhaps they had some sort of listening device that Wraith couldn't pick up, or maybe one of my teammates had given something away accidentally. By the time I realized it would be smartest to feign ignorance, too much time had passed in silence for it to seem believable.

Weaver turned and waved me forward. "Come, stand beside me. I wish for you to see what I see."

I did as he bid. The village was beautiful, admittedly, light dappling down through the canopy above like speckles of gold, houses woven into the trees and mounded from the ground, and each of the creatures different, yet working seamlessly together.

I barely noticed it over the itching in my claws and the adrenaline in my blood. As far as I could sense, there were no warriors waiting outside Weaver's office, no snipers hiding in the trees, nothing out of the ordinary.

"You should not be so surprised," he said. "I needed no tricks to deduce this. It was obvious to me, from the first moment we heard of your intrusion into our land. It was only made clearer when we met. Your eyes track us and your muscles bunch like a predator ready to spring. You are a flesh-eater, perhaps even more so than the rest of those you bring with you. If not for the respect young

Creator Kris has for you, I would have never opened our home to you."

I thought that reasoning was a bit naive. There were tons of different Skills out there, many of which would probably meet these creatures' definitions of "creation." Plenty of those people would also be morally bankrupt and ready to slaughter every one of the woodland guardians for a single precious fruit.

Something of my thoughts must have shown in my expression, because one of Weaver's gnarled eyebrows rose. "You think me naive?" He chuckled. "Perhaps that is so. Only time will judge. But I am not ignorant of the ways of you flesh-eaters. I am old. I have seen much, and remember more. I know what misguided desires drive you, and I also know that there is the ability for growth and change within you, just as your bodies grow and change throughout your lives. It is my wish that you learn to act based on respect, not simply desperation, and *earn* rather than steal. This Avatar has not shown its face yet. There is time." Each of his words were slow and deliberate. "Perhaps, as you stay among us and study our values to gain our approval, you will learn the worth of our ways and begin to walk in our footsteps." He sighed. "And perhaps not. However, whichever outcome is destined, I cannot allow you to harm my people or my home."

My scales rose like the hackles on a dog at the implied threat, and I forced them to settle down.

"So, I will bribe you," Weaver concluded, turning his back on the village below.

That was not what I expected. I did my best to hide my surprise, this time. "With what?" I said. If we could get the fruit early in exchange for not causing trouble, that would be best, but it seemed unlikely, with how adamantly he'd refused us earlier.

"With knowledge," he replied simply. "Did you think us dimwitted, because we do not live as your people? Your brother has the right of it, though he has not grasped the full worth of the books I have allowed him to access. We are rich in ways that the flesh-eaters have failed to appreciate simply because we do not conquer and demand, but are content to live and understand."

"Knowledge about how Seeds work? Can you teach me how to use the Void Aspect of Chaos?" I almost salivated at the thought.

"More than that, but yes. Our people were here long before the first immigrant arrived, with their gods and their powers. They chose this world, which was only a single planet then, for its synergy with their own abilities. I can teach you to use the Void, but most importantly, I can teach you how to become a goddess."

I sucked in a sharp breath.

He nodded. "Just so. And I can tell from your reaction that the outsiders have not grown any wiser in the time that has passed. The first—and *best*—step in any war is to gain knowledge of yourself."

I resisted the urge to fidget or pace as electrical excitement surged through my body. "I agree. If you can truly provide such information, my companions and I will remain until the day of the full moon at least, and we'll leave the fruit to your judgment."

He let out a dry snort. "I will believe none of your lies, human. This is the same assurance you already gave me. If you were able to keep your word even when it did not benefit you, I would not be hearing this promise again now." He shook his head ruefully. "No, you will stay as long as it benefits you, and *if* we grant you the fruit, you will leave peacefully. If not, you will take it by force, having also gained what knowledge we have to offer."

He wasn't wrong. The stakes were too high for me to leave empty-handed, though the kind of information he was offering might be even *more* valuable. "So what would you have of me?" I said.

"Believe your promise," he said. "Tell me that if you are not deemed worthy, you and your people will leave without harm, without the fruit, and you will not return. I understand, a little, what those you call the gods are. Believe so strongly that when you tell me, I am forced to believe as well, because I know your words have imprinted their truth on the world."

I blinked down at him as I realized what he was really saying. He wanted me to promise with the weight of a godling behind my words. He wanted me to promise with the same strength that had burnt Pestilence out of my body.

To do so, I would need to believe those words so strongly that there was no room for a divergent thought in my mind, no allowance for any other possibility. It would bind me to my promise just as surely as a bomb implanted in my brainstem.

"That depends on the worth of your knowledge," I said. "And I won't promise to leave right away, or to never come back. At the most, I'd promise to do no harm, and not allow others to accompany us if we returned."

He stared at me silently for a few moments, little sparks of light surging through his body as he thought. "Alright. Come, then, and judge the value of our knowledge." He turned and opened his office door, waving me into the little library. "You will vow once you understand what we offer."

———

WEAVER WAS RIGHT. When I'd grasped the broad overview of what the woodland guardians could teach us, I knew it was more valuable than a fruit that would make us more durable. The fruit would allow us to fight an Avatar outside of Blue's domain without dying.

The knowledge…maybe—*maybe*, it would allow us to *win*, to defeat the Abhorrent.

So I made the promise, on the condition that I could keep trying to earn the fruit if I failed the first time.

Adam had muttered something about my promise not binding *him*, which earned him a glare from me, and a warning that I would stop him if he tried.

"But what if this is the reason we lose to the Avatar? Don't you think Weaver was playing you? How likely, really, is it that all these things are going to vote that you're one of them and deserve nine of their precious fruit?" he snapped back.

"Acting with honor is never the wrong choice," Torliam said.

Normally, I would disagree with that, or at least with the standard definition of "honor," but in this particular instance I was happy for the support.

Gregor couldn't seem to decide whether or not my decision had been uncharacteristically smart or unusually stupid, and so kept switching back and forth. "Is this the most *likely* of good choices?" he wondered, staring at me skeptically.

"I'm not really sure," I admitted. "But if we'd wanted to kill all the people here, we probably could have taken both the fruit and the contents of the library, and had Torliam and Zed decipher them over time."

"We could still do that," Adam muttered, ignoring my sharp look.

"However," I continued a little more loudly, "the guardians may have *insights* that aren't written down. Or, maybe the time saved not having to translate every single book will be critical. Because that would take a lot longer than guided study until the exhibition. I've thought this through, and it seems really unlikely I would have taken this path if I hadn't had that vision. We wouldn't have negotiated with them in the first place, and maybe we'd have the fruit already, but we probably wouldn't have gone through the library or realized that the people here could have anything important to offer besides the fruit. We could have flipped a coin to randomize the choice, but I figured this was the best way to take *both* good options."

"I don't know the answer, and I don't care if we leave now or later," Jacky said. "But if we're stuck here, we're gonna be training to fight, too, not just reading books."

"I don't mind staying," Kris agreed with a happy grin.

"I agree," Sam said. "And I'm glad you're calling them *people*, now."

I bit my lip. "Yeah," I said. It was an admission, and we both knew it. It was easier to plan to hurt someone when you focused on the differences between them and yourself, rather than the similarities.

Our first lesson with Weaver was a revelation.

He had asked for all the details we could provide about our quest to defeat the Abhorrent, and then sat us down in the small library outside his office, accompanied by a few of the most knowledgeable villagers.

"The so-called gods of Estreyer are little more than their titles," the old creature said. "I mean that literally. A teeming mess of self-replicating viruses with the ability to siphon power from elsewhere and convert it into an effect. What that effect is, is based entirely on what you might call the gods' *core directive*."

I remembered the marble-like spheres of Seed material that NIX used to give out. They had required us to make a wish before injection. The Seeds had recognized our desire, and followed it.

Weaver continued, "Another way to put it would be that gods have control over their specific domain, the concept behind their creation, the spark of their sentience. All lesser abilities are a dilution of this, a jumbled mess of priorities with enough dissonance that sentience beyond the brain of the mortal host organism will not form."

He paused to let his words sink in, and I swallowed with a suddenly dry mouth. "Are you saying that to become a god, or a goddess in my case, the Seed of Chaos within me needs to gain sentience of its own?" The thought disturbed me, and then I realized why. "What happens to my own mind?"

"You are partially correct. It is not unheard of for a mortal godlike to grow into yet another iteration of their progenitor, but that will not be you, I think. Why would the others have gone to such trouble to create you, if not to reach for something *new*? What title, what *concept*, have they been lacking?"

The tension in the air grew palpable as we waited for him to answer his own question.

He shrugged. "I do not know." He interrupted our disappointed sighs and groans with a raised finger. "But I do not need to know. That is something that must come naturally to you, Eve Redding, if you are to keep your own mind. You must be in harmony with your power, and your will strong enough to match it, if you wish to retain consciousness beyond the will of your Seeds. We can help you to prepare for contacting the Void and train you to strengthen and stretch your power, to bend it to your will rather than its own."

Once we had a basic grasp on the more theoretical portion of their instruction, Weaver and the other elders took us down the tree and into the tunnels and rooms woven between its root system. The room we entered was covered in runes, literally. It reminded me of an old typewriter, or maybe a printing press, with blocks of runes on tracks that allowed them to be rearranged in nearly infinite configurations. I doubted any Estreyan engineer on the planet had this kind of grasp on the technology.

Weaver caught my expression of awe. "We were born to this. As

I said, they chose our world for its affinity with their nature, the ease with which their virus was able to access energy. Our people are the same, only we came to be naturally, efficiently, without the waste and the binding restrictions. Truthfully, when they first arrived, we felt sorry for them, such unnatural, hackneyed things, crippled by their own nature."

I kept the expression from my face, wondering how much of what he said about the gods was true. Hackneyed and crippled was not exactly how I would have described them, but then again, they weren't exactly *normal*, were they? Not by human standards. Did I want to be defined, controlled, by a single concept? I was more than Chaos, more than Shaping and Molding, more than Knowledge. Were the gods more, too? I pressed a hand to my abdomen, feeling that bottomless well of cold rage within me. Was that my Seeds, taking on a purpose of their own?

I let my hand drop, pushing the apprehension away. "You say you run on the same energy, but I have a Skill that lets me distinguish Seeds and the power they wield. It's like a glow. I haven't seen anything like that on you. It's part of why I didn't notice you earlier, actually."

"Waste," Weaver spat. "That is what you see, I would guess. They are inefficient. As I said, *unnatural.*"

The guardians guided me through a series of tests, exercising my Skills not so unlike what NIX had done, but without the cruelty.

I wondered about the first of the guardians. It seemed unlikely that something like them would just evolve from nature, runes and all. Yet they insisted they had been here before this world was multiple levels, before the Estreyans and their gods arrived. And all evidence pointed to them telling the truth about pulling the energy that powered their thoughts and movements from somewhere *else.* They didn't eat, or photosynthesize, or even, as far as I could tell, do something more exotic, like consume and rip apart atoms for the power of their bonds. Maybe they really were a natural occurrence, and it only surprised me because I didn't fully comprehend how unlikely and amazing it was that sentient *humans* had evolved from single-celled organisms.

"These levels, the Attributes you see in your mind," Weaver said. "They do not exist. A true representation of your strength would be complex, a fractal of ever-changing, interconnected data. It is a construct of your worldview that only serves to hold you back. It is the same self-imposed limitation that makes it more difficult for you to use Chaos for certain things. We will try to break you of these limitations."

I suppressed a grimace. I recognized the tone of those words. Weaver was going to enjoy this, the sadist.

Interlude 2

Welcome to the Earth Defense Force message boards.

You are currently logged in, ReedItAndWeep.

You are viewing thread: "Serious Discussions—The Science of Alien Magic."

ORIGINAL POSTER "GENETICS-PHRENETICS" SAYS:

When I first saw evidence of Skills in action against the alien invaders, my first thought was, "Oh, shit, the world has turned into an action movie, and I'm one of the faceless background characters that gets killed without any lines." My second thought was, "How?"

I've gathered a lot of examples and tried to piece together the puzzle of what exactly Skills are, what these alien Seeds are, and how they work. I consider myself a pretty smart person, and this is tangentially related to the field I work in. However, at the end of over a hundred hours of research, I've come to the conclusion that physics does not work how I thought it did. I don't understand, and maybe that's because, without the ability to speak Estreyan, I don't have access to the information I need. Or maybe that information is being restricted by our government as a military secret. Or maybe, this is one of those instances of sufficiently advanced science seeming indistinguishable from magic, and us humans are missing three or four intermediary revelations about the nature of the universe that are necessary to understand these fantastical, spectacular powers.

I'd like to open up discussion with those of a similar mindset in the hopes that gathering those with different backgrounds and expertise might provide what we're missing. Are there any Estreyan linguists on the board? Any mathematicians or advanced physicists? Any Players with Skills that seem impossible, or some mental ability that allows you to bridge this gap in understanding?

POSTER "POP-TARTS LOVER" SAYS:

Genetics-Phrenetics, I don't have the kind of expertise you're looking for, but can this also be a place for speculation about individual Skills? I saw Glaze in real life yesterday. He looks normal, seems normal, and I watched him shake someone's hand, but as you know, he leaves icy footprints behind after every step, a couple of which ended up shattering the concrete from the sudden change in temperature. I took a film messing around with one of the footprints, check it out here. I was wondering how this possibly works? Where does the heat go?

POSTER "ZODIAC DRAGON" SAYS:

I'm basically a layman, too, but I can contribute to speculation about the mechanics of individual Skills, if not the higher-level discussion about how Skills themselves are possible.

A couple possibilities came to mind, Pop-Tarts Lover. One, Glaze might not be producing heat naturally any more. What if he's cold-blooded, like a lizard, and the heat he's sucking up from the pads of his feet keeps him warm and active? Or, what if he's secreting some sort of substance from his skin that causes that reaction? Like, something similar to saltpeter and water, but more violent/potent.

POSTER "GENETICS-PHRENETICS" SAYS:

I don't mind speculation about how individual Skills would work, but the problem is that much of this speculation leads right back around to the greater question of how *any* of it works.

Zodiac Dragon, other than Eve Redding herself, I haven't seen evidence of other Players experiencing *permanent* physiological changes. It's not impossible, but it seems unlikely that Glaze has become cold-blooded in response to his Skill. Even cold-blooded animals generate heat as a by-product of metabolism and movement, it's just that they don't produce *enough*, so they use external sources of heat as a supplement.

As for the second idea, that's already been disproven. Some college students who live in his city did a report on it. No abnormal substances have been reported in his wake.

On another note, I just learned about something pretty cool. Some of the information NIX gathered while doing their dirty deeds has been unredacted and released to the TXGen institute for study. I'm really interested to see what they're able to glean from the Players' genomes, specifically when contrasted against normal humans, and those who have the gene but were never given a Seed.

POSTER "NINJA PIRATE WARRIOR" SAYS:

I've heard some interviews where Players say that they eat a lot, like four to ten thousand calories a day. Perhaps their bodies are using that energy to power their Skills?

POSTER "DEVON MILLER" SAYS:

Ninja Pirate Warrior, unless Players are doing fission reactions or some other more efficient method of extracting energy from food, I don't think even one hundred thousand calories a day could explain some of the things that have been caught on camera. It's not a bad theory, though. Maybe the Seeds really do deconstruct food more efficiently than the human digestive system.

POSTER "HAIRY-POPPINS" SAYS:

What if they're absorbing some sort of exotic energy that we just can't detect, like gamma rays?

POSTER "NINJA PIRATE WARRIOR" SAYS:

Really??? *Gamma rays?* What century do you think this is, Hairy-Poppins?

POSTER "HAIRY-POPPINS" SAYS:

I said *like* gamma rays. I'm not a scientist, okay?

POSTER "SERIAL-PESSIMIST" SAYS:

My city is doing a volunteer DNA test drive for the public, and there's been all that controversy about whether they're allowed to do that without permission. Because of recruitment laws or something? But I noticed they say if you're over the age of 25, even if you have the Estreyan gene, there's no point getting tested, unless you're interested in donating sperm or eggs. You guys probably also heard about that family that's trying to raise support to get their ten-year-old son a Seed, since he has the gene, and you're more likely to survive the younger you are.

The whole eugenics debate is for somewhere else, but I'm interested in the age limit. I'd wondered previously why NIX didn't just *recruit*, you know? How does age matter? Is it just because you're more resilient while younger? I wouldn't think it would make *that* much of a difference, as long as the adult was healthy.

POSTER "JANET MASON" SAYS:

Serial-Pessimist, those parents are heinous. A ten-year-old is too young to make that sort of decision on their own, even if the risk of death is low at that age. Even *NIX* didn't go that young. That poor child's parents would probably sell him outright if they thought it could get them more money and fame.

POSTER "HOLYSTONE" SAYS:

I agree, Janet. It's blasphemy. It's bad enough they had the gall to pass down their corrupt genes to the child, but now they want to give him completely over to evil by sowing the Seeds of the devil in him.

POSTER "ALIEN77" SAYS:

Wake up, sheeple! The supposed "aliens" are really just brainwashed citizens from the slums. The government experimented on them in Base37, which is located in the Mariana Trench. This whole big reveal and the supposed Estreyan planet is just a hoax! It was the government that attacked us! It was just an excuse to wipe out some of the population and get us more firmly under their thumb! Mark my words, the next time they want to take away more of our freedoms, they'll just start another "war" with the Estreyans, and all the sheeple will be so scared they won't have any trouble passing their new indentured-servitude laws!

POSTER "BETZOMBIE" SAYS:

Alien77, seriously, we've heard your rants more than enough. Please. Stop. Isn't the fact that people are actually *traveling* to Estreyer enough proof for you that it exists? I bet you'd deny Skills were a real thing if you could manage to twist the facts enough, too.

And Holystone, I just… I can't even. It would serve you right to find out that you're also a carrier of the gene.

POSTER "GENETICS-PHRENETICS" SAYS:

Guys, could we please get the thread back on track? We just got a warning from a moderator…

POSTER "POOP HAPPENS" SAYS:

Betzombie, stop trying to shovel your shit over everyone's eyes. I may not agree with Alien77, but it's obvious to me that you're—

Reed sighed and exited the thread. A frustrating number of these discussions digressed into arguments and personal attacks, and eventually the moderators always suspended the ability to post. His grandfather would have said something about stupid people ruining everything for the rest of them. The man had often advocated for taking the warning labels off everything and just letting natural selection do the rest.

Reed had been hoping to get a little more insight into Skills and what they could realistically do, after an idle comment from Demi had sparked his imagination.

Their trip to the local market a few days before hadn't been interrupted by rain, and despite the gloomy, ominous clouds that continued to hang low over the city, the last few days hadn't rained, either. "A new Player must have moved to Leighton," she'd joked. "He's stopping it from raining."

He hadn't thought much of it at the time, but while Reed was brushing his teeth that morning, his dad had stepped into the bathroom to straighten his tie before heading down to the broadcast station. His dad had sighed deeply, the practiced smile he shot the mirror more than a little strained.

Reed spat the foam out of his mouth. "More complaints?"

His dad sighed and gave Reed a wry smile. "The forecast for today is cloudy with a chance of Cthulhu attacks, because apparently my meteorology degree was worthless." He flicked the curtain away from the bathroom's little window and pointed out at the dark clouds. "Four days of that, and not a single drop."

Reed had frowned and gotten lost in thought as he stared out at the clouds, wondering if Demi's offhand comment had held some truth. He turned to ask his dad about it, but the man had already left while Reed spaced out.

Reed had gone to his room and turned on his link to search the Net. His results had been…unimpressive at best. Most people were just spouting their own ideas as if they were fact, and the reliable information was sparse. Still, the idea had him intrigued.

Could it be possible that a Player was somehow behind the clouds? They could simply be stopping it from raining, as Demi had said, or even creating the clouds themselves. But why? And what else might they be able to do? Floods? Lightning strikes?

If Reed was truthful with himself, he knew the giddy feeling in his chest had more to do with his imagination than any actual proof, but he'd always wanted to meet a Player.

His eyes skimmed across the thread titles until he found another that interested him.

You are viewing thread: "Seal of Nine Movements & Government Mobilization"

ORIGINAL POSTER "ANTIGONE" SAYS:

I'm worried the site may be pressured to take this post down, if it is as relevant as I *hope* that it's not. In case I'm right, *here's* a link to a place where we can discuss current events privately.

I used to consider myself a bit of a conspiracy theorist, all in good humor. Then I experienced the past couple years and all those things the "crazy," "paranoid" people were talking about suddenly got blown wide open with black and white proof. Now I'm constantly afraid I'll find out that's not the end of it. I've realized that I didn't actually *believe* the conspiracy theories before, because I wasn't properly afraid. Now, I know that being watchful against corruption and secrets from the elite could be a matter of life and death for the rest of us.

I realize this may be controversial, but this could be very important information, so please refrain from arguments and personal attacks that could get the thread closed, and remember to save the private link.

Four days ago, a large percentage of Earth's high-level military and governmental leaders were simultaneously called into top-secret meetings. Sources say these meetings were mirrored on Estreyer. Since then, they've been quietly scrambling like drones from a kicked anthill. It's still early days here, but as you know, time moves faster on Estreyer than it does on Earth, so we can get an idea where this is heading. They've had a couple weeks to work over there, and—

Reed heard footsteps coming up the stairs at the end of the hallway and turned away from his link's screen, rubbing at his temples to relieve the headache that he hadn't noticed building.

His mom carried a little tray with some artfully arranged fruit slices into the room and laid it on the desk beside him. She frowned down at him. "What are you doing? That doesn't look like homework."

Reed knew the answer was obvious, but she waited for him to admit it aloud, anyway.

"If I catch you slacking off again, you're grounded, mister," she warned. "It'll be no Net access for you for the next week. That should help you focus." With her hands on her hips, she looked around the room and gave a displeased huff. "How are you supposed to get anything done in this gloom?" She strode over to the window and yanked open the curtains, pursing her lips at the weak grey light that filtered into the room, leaving it not much brighter than before.

Catching sight of his mom in the silver mirror, Reed simultaneously gasped in horror and attempted to stifle the gasp, causing him to choke on his own spit. He tried not to cough. He felt instinctively that he shouldn't draw attention to himself, that he should play dead and pretend he hadn't seen anything, but his lungs refused to comply.

As he coughed violently, his mom turned away from the window. "Are you alright?"

He nodded, waving her away when she moved closer to pound on his back. "I'm fine," he gasped out as soon as he could. "I just forgot not to breathe and swallow at the same time." He tried a grin, hoping it looked normal.

She smiled widely. "Silly boy. I'm going back down to the kitchen. I've got a whole party to finish making appetizers for. Don't make me come back up here and punish you, okay?"

He nodded rapidly, giving her a thumbs-up.

As she walked away, he stood carefully from his chair, his knees slightly bent in case he needed to dodge or something. He sidled away from his desk, his eyes flicking between his mom's back and the silver mirror attached to his wall.

With his eyes, he could see his mom, barefoot with her hair in a bun, her slender shoulders covered by the sweater his dad had bought her for her birthday.

In the mirror, she was different. Her head was larger, her skin paler and smoother, like grimy porcelain. Her ears were simple lumps on the sides of her head, and her hands and feet were stubby, missing the fingers and toes, like some sort of simplified puppet.

But that was nothing compared to her face, which he'd seen when she walked past the mirror to open the curtains. Large black buttons had replaced her eyes, and a wide, childish smile exposed teeth that were large and tombstone-like, and cheeks that were too plump and peachy to be real. Her skin was smudged with the rust and grey colors of old blood and soot.

As his mom stepped down the stairs, Reed pressed a hand up against the wall to keep himself from falling as his heart pounded like a fleeing jackrabbit. Once the dizziness had passed, he moved forward, just enough that his own profile was displayed in the mirror.

Chapter 11

Despite my ghoulish reputation, I really have the heart of a small boy. I keep it in a jar on my desk.
— Robert Bloch

"AFTER WE ESCAPED BEHELAINO, we flew to this level's doorway, and for a moment we were truly stumped by the deadly barrier you had set up," I said, looking out over the gathered villagers from where I sat cross-legged at the edge of the stage. I had found them to be ravenous for exciting stories, and after a few days explaining the basic situation of the outside world to them, one villager had asked me about the wyrm we'd encountered, having heard Jacky brag about it. That's when I got the idea to start story night, where I told them, in installments, everything that had happened to me since NIX first captured me in the alley.

I continued my story, moving on to the enchanted woodland. "If we had less experience, or our quest was any less important, maybe we would have been enticed by the forest's allure and lost our way. But we knew that if we failed, it would mean not only our own destruction, but that of everyone we had ever met. Parents full of joy at the first breath of their child, lovers who have only just found each other, friends who have walked hand-in-hand for a life-time, men and women who wake up to the sunrise and let it fill them with energy as they embark on their daily quests to make the worlds better." I was laying it on a bit thick, but I'd found the villagers only loved it more when I added some melodrama. "And then, finally, we found you, and you took us into your home with courage, kindness, and compassion. But we have to leave, soon. The Avatar is still out there, and the Abhorrent behind it. We must fight it, for if not us, who?" I bowed my head and covered my face as if in distress, inwardly hoping that my story had swayed a few more of them to our cause.

After all, for us to get the fruit meant that nine of them would not, and I needed them to *want* that.

I stood and returned to our room in the tree, leaving them to quietly discuss our quest, some of them moved to emotion, and some of them still stubbornly convinced that the Abhorrent was not their problem.

Two weeks had passed faster than I would have thought possible, and though each day left me more worried about the Avatar, all updates from both worlds were the same: There was no sign of the enemy, and the citizens were growing suspicious and antsy.

When not preparing for the exhibition, I spent much of my free time under the elders' tutelage, meditating and stretching my abilities to their limits. They, to my disappointment, agreed with Behelaino that I didn't seem to be able to comprehend the Void, and without that could not wield it. But they had ideas about limbering my mind so that when I did encounter the Void, it would be less likely to rip through my consciousness. I spent a lot of time trying to wrap my head around theoretical ideas they postulated, meditating on abstracts or impossibilities, and exercising Chaos in ways that were distinctly not destructive in order to deepen my control over it.

The hardest exercise they gave me was something I hadn't expected at all.

"Define Eve Redding," Weaver had said. "Who are you? What are you? Catalogue yourself so completely that if I could shape you from mud and breathe life into you, no one, not even yourself, could tell the original."

I found this to be much more difficult than expected. With Wraith I could see myself and describe my physical characteristics in a way most people could not, making that a simple task. But how do you define a personality? A lifetime of memories? I tried to ask Weaver for help, but he only gave me a look of vague satisfaction at my struggles and told me to keep trying.

The rest of my teammates got a little bit of advice on Skill use from the guardians, but mostly they were restricted to the informative lessons. I was aware of the possibility of the woodland guardians using the knowledge of our Skills against us, but the potential benefits seemed to outweigh that danger. Zed loved the theory and knowledge, and made his own deal with the guardians for extra lessons on his own power in exchange for letting them research Veil-Piercer and the creature Blue, who had managed to bring down their death-static barrier.

As the full moon grew nearer, I spent more time preparing for the show and less time on the theoretical lessons. My absence there mattered less than I would have wished. No matter how much effort I put into it, my mind could never work like Gregor's, Zed had nanite chips that could handle the translation and any necessary mathematical calculations for him, and Adam simply thought faster than I could, which made a big difference over time.

Jacky had long since grown frustrated and antsy with our lessons. She had no interest in the theoretical and there was little the elders could teach her about fighting, so she decided to pass the time by teaching the guardians some martial kata. She seemed surprised to find they were more interested in the meditative aspect of the martial arts than the ability to destroy another living being with their bare hands.

Kris and Gregor drew Pondslider into the development of their oxygenation compound, and Pondslider jumped into the project with enthusiasm, dragging Sam along. She took the three of them on expeditions into the enchanted forest to gather research materials, and I even found her helping Kris with the creation of some of the girl's rescue-pod marionettes.

Birch was more interested in any records of the tailos the guardians could dig up, and I often found him curled up in a comfortable chair with a paper and bark book, turning the pages with small, directed bursts of wind. Of course, I also saw him running down the village's main pathway, towing a sled full of village children who were laughing so hard they struggled to hang on, or play-acting as the evil dragon in mock fights against them.

The day of the exhibition, Gregor woke early and shuffled over to me, shifting awkwardly and letting out little hesitant sounds.

Such reticence wasn't like him. "What is it?" I asked.

"It's been kind of nice, staying here," he said, scuffing his foot against the ground. "None of the people here think I'm stupid just because I'm young, and there's so much to learn, and I get to decide what I want to research, and—I just—"

I frowned. "You want to stay here?"

He shook his head swiftly. "No, that's not what I mean. Only, when this is all over, when we go back, do I have to go back to school?" Before I could respond, he continued. "Listen! I'm not just saying that because I don't like it. Well, it's true, I don't like it, but I also have good reasons! There's nothing there for me to learn. The whole standardized schooling system in inefficient. Our curriculum is juvenile and full of busy work. The children are stupid and I can't respect them enough to make friends with them, if you were hoping I'd learn how to socialize or something. I'm mature enough to go to war for the fate of the world, apparently, so shouldn't I also be mature enough to choose my own learning system? I'd do much better in a self-directed study course that's more hands-on, maybe with a tutor or two that have done actual work in the fields I'm interested in. My teacher hates me anyway after I used a static field to stick her dress to her chair so she couldn't get up. A diploma is useless for me, it's not like I'm ever going to get a normal job where they care about that stuff, and..." His rapid-fire barrage trailed off and he panted for air. "And I'm asking seriously. Can I not go back to school after this is over?"

"That was...quite the list of reasons. You've certainly thought this through."

Gregor nodded silently. His fidgeting had stopped but his fists were now clenched.

"Well"—I gave him a single nod in return—"that's that, then. I'm not sure what we'll end up doing, and it's likely you'll need to meet certain requirements for both schooling and socialization, but I'll bet we can find something that suits you better, as long as you're okay with those stipulations."

He let out a shuddering breath, and I only then realized that he'd been holding it.

"Were you that nervous? You could have come to me about this sooner, you know," I said with a frown.

Instead of replying, he reached forward and grabbed me around the legs, burying his head in my stomach. He'd grown since the first time he did that, but then again, so had I.

I reached down and ran my clawed fingers through his hair, combing it gently. "I'm sorry I didn't notice you hated it so much," I said softly. "I'm stupid like that sometimes. So when I am, you just need to point it out, okay?"

He nodded into the scales of my stomach, which I kept flat to avoid cutting him. After a few seconds, he withdrew. His eyes were dry, and he wore a wry little smile. "Yeah. I'll definitely tell you when you're being stupid. Like…right now, don't you think you should be practicing for the show? If you don't manage to impress everyone in the audience, or at least a majority, we're not getting those fruit. It's kind of a big deal."

I blinked down at him.

His smile widened, and he winked at me.

"You cheeky brat!"

With a gleeful laugh that made him sound like a little boy again, he ran away, avoiding my grasping hands as I lunged toward him. Gregor's head was turned over his shoulder toward me so that when the door opened and Jacky stepped through, he collided with her.

I expected him to bounce off and maybe get hurt, since Jacky combined aspects of both the proverbial immovable object and unstoppable force, but instead, at the first hint of unexpected contact, Gregor flickered into his Shadow state.

He ended up on Jacky's other side, having passed directly through her body.

She let out a gasp and shuddered, whirling on him. "Don't *do* that!"

He returned to corporeality and shrugged innocently. "It was an accident. Besides, if this was an ambush, you would have been caught unprepared."

When Jacky's glower deepened, he seemed to realize the error of adding on that second sentence. "Err, I mean, I'm sorry," he amended.

"It's time for training," she said. Her windblown hair, the streaks of dirt and sweat-turned-mud on her face, and a couple rips in her baggy clothing told me she'd already been training for a couple hours. "We'll see if you can manage that a second time."

His shoulders sagged. "Do we have to?" Before she could respond, he glanced to me and straightened into a stance that might have been imposing if he'd been about four feet taller. "I want to go to the library instead. It's the last day here, and we can do training any time. I won't get to take any of those books with me, and if Eve's performance goes well, I probably won't get to come back. This is more important."

The wooden floor creaked as Jacky's weight increased, though her size stayed the same. "Training is always a priority," she said. "Without my training, half a year ago you woulda flattened yourself running into me, no? Three hours of work today might be the difference between this Avatar slicing you in half and you having to watch your severed legs twitch two meters away as your upper half bleeds out…and going Shadow fast enough to escape, or maybe even get a counterattack in."

I grimaced. While Jacky wasn't wrong, it seemed a little excessive to spell it out so gruesomely for the boy.

Gregor seemed completely unfazed by the imagined scene. "We've been training till we drop every single day we've been here!" he complained, pulling up his sleeve to reveal the green and purple splotches on his skin, then lifting his foot awkwardly for her to examine. "I'm still totally covered in bruises, and my toes still hurt this morning. I think maybe you injured them when you stomped on my foot. I need time to rest and recuperate, too. Training all the time isn't good for your body."

She nodded, her eyes trailing over his limbs. "Well, your point about over-training might be right…if you were a normal human. But we have Seeds. We'll take you to see Sam, if you're really feeling it, and he'll get you fixed up before all this procrastination makes you miss any more time with the books." Changing tack, she added, "I'm even helping to subvert the 'bad ending!' I created a whole list of possible things to train, even if some of them seem like they're less likely to be useful, and I'm using some dice to pick which one we're gonna work on," she said proudly.

Gregor was only stymied momentarily. "But what about mental fatigue? Sam can't do anything about that. Plus, I'll be distracted thinking about what I'd rather be doing, and so I won't get the optimal improvement from training right now, anyway."

She cracked her knuckles. "Distracted? You'd better not be distracted, cause that leads to making mistakes, and making mistakes leads to getting *dead*."

"How about this?" he said quickly. "We do one hour of training, and I do my best and focus completely, no distractions, and then I go to the library."

"One hour? I was planning on four."

"*Four?*" His jaw dropped, and he shook his head in childish denial. "No, no, that's way too much." I could tell he was casting about for another argument. I opened my mouth to interject when he burst out, "Even Kris is tired, you know? I saw her falling asleep while she was trying to design a new marionette last night. How about an hour and a half of training, and then when I go to the library I stay in my Shadow state the whole time and only let my fingers solidify long enough to turn the pages? It'll be endurance training."

"Hmm..." Jacky crossed her arms over her chest, seeming unconvinced.

Gregor tugged at her elbow, leading her through the door. "Okay, then, it's settled. Let's hurry up and get started. I bet Kris is playing with Pino and the others down at Pondslider's workshop. We can pick her up on the way."

Jacky allowed herself to be pulled along, but when she turned to tell me, "Good luck, Eve," the smile I'd been expecting was absent from her face, and her eyes and voice held a hint of poorly disguised tension.

Birch rolled his eyes at Jacky and Gregor's backs, then hopped over to my side and mewled like the cub he no longer was, fluffing out his wings and begging to be scratched.

Torliam looked up from his bed at the other end of the room where he'd been sitting and tapping notes into his datapad. When their footsteps and Gregor's running chatter had faded away down the hall, Torliam said, "The boy loves you, you know."

I looked away, rubbing the back of my neck awkwardly. "Well, the feeling's mutual." Of course I loved Gregor, just like I did the rest of my teammates, but it was embarrassing to say the words aloud.

Torliam smiled, setting aside his datapad and moving to stand beside me at the balcony. "You thought the boy would wish to stay."

I nodded, raising a questioning eyebrow and crouching down to scratch Birch's belly as he rolled onto his back.

"I would not mind staying here longer. Perhaps, some day we could return. For me, this village offers an escape from palace life and politics, as well as the kind of opportunity for research and insight that any historian or archivist would give a limb for. It is a rare opportunity, indeed. For you…this would be a good place to raise the children, do you not agree? With comms access to the outside world, they could easily finish their schooling remotely, and both of them feel at peace here. There are no reporters or paparazzi, and my mother could not be constantly volunteering you for polit-ical events. You could pursue…whatever you want." His tone was careful, almost cautious. He met my gaze searchingly.

"Well, I suppose," I agreed. "Jacky doesn't seem to like it very much, though. Maybe if she could set up a training dojo and take on students, she'd feel less restless here. And Sam probably wouldn't want to stay, either, since there's no one here to heal."

"Once this is over, our lives will all be our own, to make our own choices with. Even if they did not wish to stay, your agreement with the guardians ensures they could at least visit."

"Hmm. I'll think about it. We should ask the kids."

He turned to face the balcony, hiding the slightly too-big smile on his face from my sight—but not from Wraith—as if he'd just won some sort of victory but didn't want to gloat about it.

I reached out to nudge him. "What are you grinning abou—" I was distracted as shouts from below filtered up to our balcony. I moved forward to look down over the railing.

A human—Adam, judging by the ink constructs appearing and immediately disintegrating all around him as he waved his arms wildly, stood in the middle of a crowd of screaming villagers, contributing with his own unintelligible shouts.

"I'd better go see what this is about," I said, vaulting over the edge of the balcony railing.

———

I SLOWED my fall on tree knots, balcony railings, and branches on the way down, but I still hit the ground hard enough to jar everything from my toes to the tips of my hair. I rose, groaning, and only then remembered the last time I had done something similar, and the regret that had followed.

I stood at the edge of the rabble, my arrival having gone largely unnoticed. I cleared my throat loudly, and when that did nothing to calm the ruckus, sent a burst of Chaos into the air above and exploded it.

The *boom* rolled out through the air, leaving sweet silence in its wake.

The crowd looked around until they caught sight of me, and then slowly parted and turned to face me, leaving Adam in a little circle of clear space within.

"What's going on here?" I said.

Belatedly, a few more of the ink constructs dispersed, drawing shudders and a few muffled whimpers from the nearby villagers.

Adam's expression wavered between belligerence and shame. "I had to show them that my ink constructs aren't actually alive, and even if they *seem* to have personalities or thoughts, that's only because I *made* them seem that way!" His voice rose as he spoke, until his yell at the end made some of the villagers flinch back. This only seemed to make him more angry. "They treat me like some sort of disabled invalid who's been in a tragic accident that everyone except me can remember!"

"Ahh…" I said, looking around at the crowd. It was true. I'd noticed the consoling looks, the whispers, and the way they acted as if he would snap and fall into a sobbing mess at the slightest trigger.

Still, couldn't he have just dealt with it? The guardians' refusal to accept his statements to the contrary was plain willful ignorance…but they obviously thought he was just putting on a brave face, which only made them pity him more.

There were few *worse* times he could have chosen to lose control of his frustration. We had only half a day remaining before the exhibition and the vote the villagers would hold to decide our fates.

I sent Adam a Window message saying just that.

As his eyes flicked across the empty air in front of him, reading my words, some of the belligerence slipped away.

I turned to the diverse group surrounding us. "Adam overreacted," I said. "He can be a bit grumpy, and as you know we're here on a desperate quest to save our world, the stress of which would be enough to make anyone snappish. However, you all have been behaving badly as well." I raised my hand to forestall any objections, but to my surprise, none of them tried to pipe up in denial. I continued. "You're right, Adam is a creator." I ignored his expression of outraged betrayal. "But he is not a creator of living beings. Do you consider the plants to be people, simply because they turn toward the sun? Is a stone alive just because the flowing water rolls it along the river bed? Do you mourn it when it ceases to move? They do not have feelings of love or compassion, and do not ponder the meaning of their own existence. Adam's creations are the same. They have the instincts that he places in them as he creates them, but no more than that. They have no fear of their own deaths. They are not like us. The way you've acted toward Adam has hurt his feelings."

"Hurt my feelings?" he muttered, still incredulous.

I shot him a sharp look. "Yes, hurt his feelings. He feels both ostracized, because of the way you've been treating him differently, and demeaned, because you won't accept his words about the nature of his own creations as the truth." I was laying it on a little thick, but I could see the looks of dismay and shame that took over the villagers' expressive faces, their awkward shuffles and muttering, and I knew it was working.

—It's damage control. I wouldn't have to do this if you'd just held your tongue for one more day. Think of this as you doing your part to make sure we all get one of the fruit. Take one for the team.—

-Eve-

Aloud, I said, "Adam, I understand why you were upset, but I still think you should apologize for the way you acted."

I could hear him grinding his teeth, and he stared at me a little too long to seem completely willing, but eventually he turned to the crowd and said, "I'm sorry."

Grudging and perfunctory though it was, it set off a round of reciprocal apologies. The villagers crowded in to give Adam handshakes and friendly pats, and I escaped the scene as silently as I could, ignoring Adam's gaze burning into my back. The fallout from the altercation seemed minimal, and it occurred to me that the chance for these villagers to come to terms with Adam's abilities might even bond them to him—to us—and make them more likely to vote in our favor.

My scales rose with nervous apprehension, and I forced them to smooth back down, going over the show I'd planned in my head again. I thought longingly of the fruit, then trudged back up to our room. I had to practice, and I didn't want anyone outside my team catching a glimpse and ruining the surprise.

Torliam was still there when I returned, and set aside his work to watch the one-woman show I put on, giving me last-minute critiques and reassurance.

I was interrupted when the communicator device began to call for my attention, and a chill crawled up my back, tightening my muscles all the way up to my neck. I had spoken to Queen Mardinest only that morning. Why would she be contacting me again so soon? It took me less than a second to accept the call.

She wasted no time on pleasantries. "The Remnants' *scryer* has died."

It wasn't what I had been expecting, and I felt momentarily off-balance.

"The woman was attempting to scry the location of the Avatar at the time," she continued.

Ah. There was the sinking feeling I'd been bracing for. "Did she succeed?" I asked.

"No. Or if she did, she had no way to let anyone know before it killed her. It is only evidence of what we already thought. The

Avatar is somewhere in the mortal world, and growing stronger. I do not think I can hold off the press conference any longer. It must be today."

"The exhibition is today. I won't have the fruit until this evening at the earliest. If things don't go well…" I trailed off.

"Perhaps it is best if you simply do not attend the press conference, then. We can say that we do not wish to tip the Avatar off to our grand plan, which is why we waited to tell the public, and also why you are not present. It even has the benefit of being partially true."

I took a moment to consider. My presence would serve as a good stabilizer to Queen Mardinest, who was still working to regain the trust of the people, but better to not appear at all than to have no results, or to pretend at results only to unwittingly give the Avatar information it could use against us. "Alright. You handle it."

"Perfect. I'll be sure to impress on everyone how seriously we are taking this, and that you've been working ceaselessly. Perhaps I'll make up a misleading anecdote about our conversation when I attempted and failed to patch you into the press conference remotely. Something heroic." She smirked.

I let out a small huff of amusement and nodded. "That other thing we talked about, is it ready?"

"Ready and waiting."

"Good. I'm signing off. The next time we talk, I'll have the fruit."

AS THE SUN approached the horizon, yellow beams of light slanting sideways through the canopy above, I descended to the gathering spot at the base of the tree and took my place on the stage set within the hollow between two hill-sized roots.

Every creature in the village, even the ones I'd not seen out and about previously, gathered around, all the little tree stumps and moss-covered rocks used for seats. There was chatting at first, but it died down quickly. Every face, each different in its own way, turned toward me expectantly.

My heart fluttered within my chest. I'd given speeches before, but nothing like this. This was a performance meant to be judged not on the persuasiveness and charisma of my words, but on the artistic and emotional merit of something I'd created. I looked toward my teammates, standing at the edge of the communal area, and with a slowly controlled exhale, let Chaos billow out through my skin like thick rain clouds.

The clouds of destructive power rolled over the stage dramatically, harming nothing. They spilled over onto the ground, some spreading along the edges of the crowd and some rising up to act as a veil against the light of the sunset.

There were exclamations of surprise and murmurs of excitement, but none of the villagers shied away from Chaos as it partially enclosed them. Pondslider even stuck a hand in and wriggled it around, forcing me to put a little extra concentration toward keeping her undamaged. It crossed my mind that if I really had wanted to betray and harm the guardians, if my promise to Weaver had held less power, this would be the perfect opportunity to do so.

On the simple stage before me, I gathered Chaos into four different animal shapes…and set them alight. They were more light than heat, and stood out vibrantly against the backdrop of darkness. I'd wanted to do nine animals, to match my group, but I didn't have the control to handle that many. The main character was a tiny fox with comically large ears, accompanied by a bickering raccoon, a skittish deer, and a puffy little owl.

With every ounce of my concentration bent to the task, I created a small patch of black scenery and set everything in motion.

I'd decided to tell a classic story, one so ingrained in the human psyche that we'd told variations on it billions of times. The people here may not have been made of flesh and blood, but they felt, they cared, they had their struggles and triumphs just the same. The same stories that spoke to us would speak to them.

They also had no television, so they wouldn't be inured to the awe of special effects.

My fire animals moved happily, going about their normal lives, playing and squabbling amongst themselves. I hadn't been able to figure out how to mold vibrations into recognizable sound, so they used body language and pantomime to communicate, like a silent play.

The group of friends left their village, going out into the dark forest, where they found an ominous cave. Within, a small round egg glowed on the ground. The group gathered around it with excitement.

Out of the vague background, a hunched, scraggly, black figure crept out, wearing a tattered cloak of darkness with a hood that disguised its head.

The animals examined the egg, unawares.

The cloaked figure, obviously an evil enemy, had the villagers making small sounds of distress as it crept toward the bright animals. One of the audience members even tried to warn the creatures, calling out to them as if they could hear him.

With sudden inspiration, I had the cloaked figure freeze in alarm and the animals look around with their ears perked up, the little owl lifting a wing to the side of its head as if to help it hear better. The large-eared fox turned toward the audience, ears swiveling slowly as if trying to pinpoint the location of the sound.

The villager called out his warning again.

The cloaked figure's head snapped around, facing right toward the audience member. I brightened a single curved arc under the hood, revealing a smile as distinct and wide as the cheshire cat's.

The villager fell backward off his tree stump with alarm.

Seeming to hear nothing, the animals shrugged and returned to their examination of the glowing pebble.

A couple more villagers piped up, but by then it was too late.

The enemy sprang on the animals, spreading out spindly arms, its tattered cloak flaring like ominous bat's wings.

My main characters jumped, tripped, and let out silent shrieks of horror as the dark figure reached for them.

Stumbling and shaking, the owl managed to keep the deer from being caught, and they all ran.

Once they'd made it back to their village, the fox revealed the egg, which it had sneakily scooped up as they were escaping.

All was well again, for a while. The other villagers in my silent play, vaguely shaped like the rest of the background scenery, were very impressed with the egg, but dismissed the tale of the dark, cloaked figure, some even mocking the main characters when they tried to talk about it.

"It's true!" one of the young audience members called. "I saw it!"

But the background characters of my play couldn't hear them.

When the cloaked, gnarled figure crept unnoticed into the village, there were more warnings from the audience. It reached out and grabbed one of the background characters, surrounding them in a dark embrace. It grew larger, and when it released its victim, only ashy dust fell to the ground.

The audience grew increasingly involved as the enemy continued to victimize the little village, calling out to the four animals as they tried to figure out what was happening to the disappeared people. A few close misses between the main characters and the enemy, which grew with each secretive murder, had the audience gasping and screaming. Finally, a group organized to scream their warning simultaneously.

The large-eared fox made an expression of understanding and turned to explain what it had heard to its companions, but the enemy, now towering and dripping blackness, had heard the audience, too.

It left no time for my main characters to escape, pouncing onto the fox, tearing at its ears. The deer rammed the black figure with its stubby antlers and the owl raked at the darkness under its hood with sharp claws while the raccoon pulled the fox free.

The animals escaped again, but this time there was no safe village to run to. They took the egg with them into the forest, only stopping once they could run no longer.

The fox's head looked even tinier, with its ears ripped half to shreds, and it collapsed.

I let the flame creatures fade away on that desperate note, giving myself a bit of relief from the concentration as I moved the scene back to the village, where the enemy was continuing to attack the fleeing villagers.

Some audience members were crying, and my mouth twitched into a small smile of satisfaction.

I cut back to the scene of the four friends in the forest, letting my fox stir and wake. Its companions were as morose and defeated as I could make the molded fire forms look, their bodies of light drooping and dimming, but the fox was uncowed. It helped the others to stand, then placed the glowing egg on the ground between them.

After a short, silent pep-talk, they formed a circle around the egg. One by one, they each stepped forward and touched it, causing its glow to brighten until it was almost painful to look at. When the light died down again, instead of an egg, a small creature rose up. It had large, owl-like eyes, big fox ears, a fluffy deer's tail, and raccoon hands, a fusion of all of them. Its ears swiveled toward the sounds of the audience, and I carefully aligned the gaze from its big eyes to meet the unblinking stares of a few of the audience members.

Together with their new companion, the characters marched back to the village, where the black enemy had set up a throne in the middle of the main street and had the remaining background characters kneeling before him, their stooped forms twisting and growing dark.

When the animals arrived, they paused for a dramatic standoff, and then charged valiantly. They were tossed aside like rag dolls. The fusion creature's attacks were the most effective, the only one able to withstand a blow and deal damage in return. But alone, it wasn't enough.

The fox took a kick to the ribs that sent it flying off the stage where it landed among the audience.

The nearby audience members moved to check on it, tentatively touching the warm flames, which I was careful to ensure couldn't burn them.

The fox lifted its head feebly and struggled, but couldn't manage to stand.

The black enemy sent the raccoon flying, too, one of its little forearms bent at a wrong, broken angle. Then, the enemy moved to the edge of the wooden stage, looking out at the audience, and began to descend.

The other flame animals rallied and attacked its back desperately, but to little effect.

The audience members closest to it scrambled off their seats hurriedly, as if afraid it would reach out and give them the embrace of death, too. Even as they backed away, their eyes never left the scene.

The enemy approached the fox, who still couldn't stand.

The fusion creature sprinted forward to block the enemy off before it could reach the fox, and was joined by the others, even the little raccoon with the broken arm. Their expressions were determined, their glaring faces unwavering.

The dark creature's bright smile only stretched wider from within the shadows under its hood, and it reached out and snatched the deer, enfolding it in an embrace.

The deer struggled, and the others leapt to its aid, trying desperately to free it. They had no success, and the deer's kicks weakened, its flame dimming.

The fusion creature looked around desperately for help, and then its owl eyes locked on one of the nearby audience members, a female made of brightly colored feathers.

I let that moment draw on until everyone had a chance to realize what was happening, and then the creature reached out one of its raccoon paws and grasped the woodland villager's hand.

The villager gasped in delight-tinged awe. It took her only a second to gather her wits before turning a threatening scowl onto the much larger enemy. She threw an awkward punch, but despite the feeble nature of the attack, its black form dispersed into wispy smoke where her feathers had touched. The enemy dropped the fading deer in shock, reeling back from the attack.

After that, the outcome was inevitable. A second guardian ran to the first, then two more, and within moments the entire audience was roused. They mobbed the villain, which flailed uselessly against them, until they had dispersed it completely into smoke.

The main characters gathered their wounded and limped back to the stage, and, once the audience had given up on stomping angrily at the trampled ground where the villain had dispersed, and seemed able to focus, the play continued.

The main characters recovered. The background characters went back to their homes. The fusion creature joined their group as a new friend. They kept watch for the black villain, but it did not reappear. The play ended on a bittersweet note. The animals visited the makeshift graves of those who had been consumed, mourning the fallen. Still, they stood tall and bright, and they looked into the darkness without fear. I let the Chaos spread over the stage and around the audience disperse.

The woodland guardians were entirely silent, staring at me, standing alone on the stage where the story they'd become so engrossed in had just faded away.

As the last of my power faded away with the story, I realized that my breaths were ragged, my fingers trembling, and sweat was dripping into my eyes. The pool of energy within my belly was much diminished, maybe even more so than when I'd fought Behelaino, and I felt faintly dizzy from the strain of superhuman concentration. The lack of response worried me. If that wasn't enough to get us the fruit, I really had no idea what I could do better.

From the back of the crowd, Jacky let out a loud whoop and began applauding wildly. The rest of my audience followed suit.

$$\underline{\hspace{10em}}$$

Chapter 12

$$\underline{\hspace{10em}}$$

Spring, if it lingers more than a week beyond its span, starts to hunger for summer to end the days of perpetual promise.
— Clive Barker

WEAVER CAME up on stage to hold the vote, and I had to remain standing beside him, hoping the trembling in my knees wasn't visible.

By this point, the entire village was aware of what we wanted and why we were here. Some of them weren't happy about it, and I knew at least a few of those individuals were waiting for fruit themselves. They had been waiting to try to create a life, a child, for a long time, and if we got what we wanted, they'd be waiting even longer. Others wanted to help. Some were simply afraid of what might happen if they refused, conscious of the threat we posed despite our attempt at seeming friendly. Whatever their reasons, I was happy for every vote in our favor.

Weaver asked for a show of hands.

The crowd shuffled a bit, and a few hands rose into the air. Not nearly enough. The woodland guardians looked around at each other, and a few more hands rose.

My heart fluttered, a sick, dizzy feeling spreading through me.

Pondslider huffed angrily, her own hand raised high and proud.

"You would let the darkness win?" she demanded loudly, her bold glare meeting the eyes of those around her.

There was more shuffling, and though a few more hands rose, so did a discontented muttering. "To give the fruit of life to an outsider is blasphemy," one of the villagers said, arms crossed stubbornly across their chest. "No matter how pretty their illusions."

At least one villager lowered their arm.

The sick feeling settled in my stomach.

"*Outsiders* to not participate in the exhibitions." To my surprise, the one that had spoken was Weaver's assistant, a feathered villager who had previously seemed to dislike me. "Outsiders do not walk in the company of a creator. Outsiders do not treat us and our ways with respect and acceptance, and they do not *ask* for the fruit when they can *take*."

More hands rose, at that, but I couldn't tell if it was a majority.

Beside me, Weaver lifted his own hand. "I have seen something new, this day, and I felt it in my heart," he said simply.

More hands rose, and more after that, and a bubbling, heady relief washed away the fear in me. My legs wobbled, and I had to draw upon the pool of cold inside me, just a little, to keep from collapsing.

The majority of the audience's hands rose in approval. It was far from all of them, which put a silly pang of disappointment into my stomach, but it was enough.

I stepped shakily down from the stage, accepting congratulations and enthusiastic comments about the play from the villagers until my teammates joined me. As the sky fully darkened and the moon rose, the villagers lit a bonfire and began their celebration. I saw more than a few of them pantomiming the play they'd just seen, retelling the story to each other, already eager to experience it again.

We stayed outside with them until the fire burned out, though Gregor and Kris were both struggling to stay awake. A faint pang of paranoia made me contact Queen Mardinest for an update, but the only thing to worry about on that end was still the lack of news itself.

As the embers dimmed, Weaver made his way over to us. "The fruit will be ready for you in the morning, if you can wait."

For a moment, I considered denying him. We'd earned the fruit, and according to my promise I could go pick nine of them myself if I wanted, but I remembered the strange allure of the little tree with stardust hanging from its branches. It might be best to avoid putting myself in that situation again, and besides, we all needed to sleep. A few hours wouldn't make a difference.

So we went back to our room and faded into a peaceful night's rest, and as the morning turned from black to grey with the approach of sunrise, Weaver appeared, handing each of us a little rune-carved box. Within each, on a soft bed of velvet, sat a shiny fruit. I picked mine up. In my hand, it was harder and heavier than I'd expected, and resembled a miniature, metallic apple more than the stardust I'd likened it to before. It smelled like ozone, but the urge to immediately shove it into my mouth wasn't there.

"The fruit work best when they have been freshly eaten," Weaver said. "If your enemy is as powerful as you say, perhaps it would be best to wait until the time is at hand."

"How do they work?" I asked.

"It is named the fruit of life for a reason. In flesh-beings such as yourself, it will automatically heal wounds and imbalances in the physical body, until it loses the ability to pull further energy from the planes beyond. Unlike the *Seeds*"—he sneered the word—"the fruit allows a natural lifespan of a few hundred seasonal cycles, as there are no little viruses within replicating themselves constantly to replace those who have lost the ability to gather energy. It is safe for young and old alike to consume. It can heal even the most heinous of wounds, but cannot undo true death."

"What about Kris? Will it stop her from being able to return to her natural size, if we find some way that would otherwise work?"

"I do not know. We have no record of the fruit being used on one such as her."

I nodded, tucking the fruit away carefully in a little box stored securely within my pack. "Don't lose them," I warned the others as they each stashed their own fruit away.

Adam rolled his eyes.

As we gathered at the outskirts of the village, our group seeming much larger with all of Kris's various marionettes standing with us once again, a large portion of the woodland guardians came to see us off. They were still most friendly to Kris, treating her marionettes like people, too, but I got my share of well-wishes and plenty of comments about the play. Even Adam exchanged his goodbyes peacefully, despite some awkwardness between him and the villagers who'd witnessed his ink-construct-killing spree the day before.

Kris cried a little, hugging those she'd become closest to, and her marionettes dragged their feet as we finally left, their shoulders sagging.

"Come back with your sky shark next time!" Pondslider called out, waving her spiky iron arm wildly. "And do not forget to message me!"

We moved much more quickly on the way out than we had the way in. Gone were the traps and the animal attacks, the moving trees, and even most of the bugs. The enchanted forest seemed to have lost any desire to forestall our journey. Despite the seemingly friendly nature of the gesture, I was suspicious, and examined our surroundings even more carefully for better hidden traps. We were leaving with the guardians' precious fruit, after all, and at this distance they'd be safe from any immediate retaliation against an attempt to kill us. A wily enemy might have decided it was safer to simply retrieve the fruit off our dead bodies. However, when I didn't find anything, we sped up again, and reached the opening to the other level in less than a quarter of the time it had taken us to reach the village in the first place.

They had even turned off the static barrier, which I now knew I had only been able to see because of the inefficiencies in energy transfer. We still went into the Other Place before walking through, though.

The camouflaged *Swiftsure* was waiting for us. There was a clear sense of shared relief as we each stepped inside the familiar craft.

We had decided to leave the communicator relay beacon set up outside the archway. The small obelisk would let us communicate with the guardians without the ordeal of traveling to their village again. Pondslider, in particular, had been insistent that the children and Torliam remain in contact with her.

As we flew away from the small stone archway, Gregor asked, "What now?"

I looked at the rearview screen on the control panel, watching as the yellow static barrier reappeared across the entrance behind us. It was a good question. "We make a pit stop," I said. I gave Torliam the coordinates to a spot only a few kilometers away.

When we arrived, I hopped out of the *Swiftsure's* side door, carefully maneuvered to a patch of dirt that looked no different from the rest, and picked up an invisible box. Some fiddling turned off the camouflage effect. I carefully entered in the long password Queen Mardinest had given me, and when the box hissed and revealed a seam, I opened it.

Within rested a bulky harness made out of over a dozen different metals. When I focused harder, Wraith could sense the thousands of runes carved on the inside of each strap.

Sam hopped out of the ship and moved to my side. "Is that it?"

"Yes." I'd had Queen Mardinest commission this device to stop Ichi from using his Skill. It had taken a while, but when it was ready, a trusted courier had dropped it off at this location, ready for me to pick up as soon as possible. She had also included what looked like leg shackles and a cylindrical device that confused me at first, until a closer inspection with Wraith showed that it was meant for Ichi's hands. With both hands held inside and bound in front of him, it would keep him from using even his fingers. She'd thought of everything, it seemed.

"Are we going to do…what she suggested, then?" Sam's voice was filled with distaste.

"I don't know," I admitted. "Maybe. If we have to. First, though, we have to find Ichi. Otherwise the point is moot."

He didn't look happy, but he followed me back to the ship without saying anything.

I settled back into my seat against the wall and strapped in.

"Find Ichi," I told Torliam.

Jacky let out a whoop of excitement, and Adam groaned in relief. "Thank god."

Torliam flew the ship at the highest possible speed that wouldn't leave its power drained in case of an emergency. Ichi moved frequently, with no constraints on distance, so we had no time to waste.

We passed swiftly over a series of beautiful and strange landscapes that I had no time to ogle at. As visually arresting as the scenery on Estreyer could be, the danger was always equal to the beauty, but neither aspect of the alien environments appealed to me at that moment. After a while, Torliam turned to look at me, giving me a significant nod and beginning to slow the ship.

I gripped my harness and braced my feet against the floor to fight the sudden dragging force of our deceleration. "He's here?" I asked.

Birch, who had been playing a game on his datapad using condensed, carefully non-damaging Chaos tendrils on the touch-screen surface to make up for his lack of humanoid digits, looked up immediately and chortled an excited, questioning sound.

Torliam's fists were clenched tight around the steering controls. "Yes. I did not want him to hear the ship parting the sound barrier, so I made sure not to get too close. He has not reacted, at least not with any significant move to flee."

I flexed my fingers and let out a slow breath. "Alright. Close in slowly. Stealth mode. Point me in the right direction and I'll see if I can't reach him with Wraith."

Torliam did so, and everyone in the ship fell still and silent as we crept closer, as if a too-loud voice might alert Ichi, despite the fact that we were still many kilometers away.

It took another hour for us to get close enough for me to find our target with Wraith, though we were still too far to make out details. When I did, Torliam landed the *Swiftsure,* and we all exited. Outside the barrier of the ship's hull, my Skill was less impeded, and I could make out the fugitive Estreyan's prone form within a makeshift campsite. "He's sleeping," I whispered, also succumbing to the air of sneakiness the others had taken on.

We had spent several hours over the last couple weeks developing a series of plans for different possible situations we might encounter when we tried to capture Ichi. Finding him sleeping and unaware was one of the best possible scenarios.

Gregor quickly checked his armor and settled his hands around the handles of the blades sheathed at his hips, though according to the plan, he wouldn't be interacting directly with Ichi until the man was secured.

Sam spit into a small cup, and Adam Animated a small

cluster of mite-like bugs that he'd tattooed onto the back of his hand for this moment. They rushed into the cup, coating themselves in and gulping down the paralytic, soporific saliva, then sprang onto the back of a small ink bird, nestling into its feathers.

Adam lifted the bird into his hands and launched it in the air. It fluttered frantically for a fraction of a second, then took off like an arrow. "White-throated needle tail," he said. "Fastest bird in the world over short distances, and mine will keep that speed till it dissipates. It should be able to get them there in time."

I watched with Wraith as the ink construct sped across the barren land. The bird reached Ichi's camp with a couple minutes to spare on Adam's time limit, and slowed enough to let the mites jump off as it circled around.

Ichi stirred, and my heart clenched in my chest, but he didn't seem to wake.

Less than a minute later, the mites were on him, dragging their disgusting little bodies across his skin and depositing the dried residue of Sam's saliva on it. They waited, just in case, because I'd been worried that if they woke him up, it wouldn't take effect quickly enough to stop him from completing at least one teleport. He'd pass out whenever he got where he was going, sure, but then we'd have to find him all over again, hoping that we made it in time, that he was still unconscious, and that nothing else had killed him while he was helpless.

If we didn't manage *that*, then he'd know we were after him, and would undoubtedly become even more paranoid, increasing the frequency of his random teleportations and improving his other security measures.

But he didn't wake, and when the minuscule constructs bit down, releasing their payload into his skin, he jerked a little, but didn't even get his eyes open before slumping back down bonelessly.

ONCE I CONFIRMED that Ichi was down, we jumped back in the ship and hurried to reach him. I was grateful that he didn't have some powerful sensory Skill in addition to his teleportation Skill. It would have been impossible to catch him.

We searched the campsite for traps, then put the Skill-suppressing harness and the other restraints Queen Mardinest had sent us onto his limp body. With our target secured, we waited.

The team spread out around the little camp, but our eyes never left Ichi for long. The dark mood suffusing all of us was not lightened any by the small campfire.

My scales fluffed out a bit to ward off the cold.

I couldn't help but wonder how the Skill-suppressor actually worked. Did the Estreyans even know, or were they just copying runic patterns they'd long since ceased to understand? It seemed like negating Skill use would probably require some understanding of how Skills worked beyond the level of the "four humors." Would it work against me, and Chaos? Would it work against a god? Somehow, I doubted at least the latter.

It was too bad there wasn't anything similar we could use against the new Avatar.

"He's the one who killed my uncle?" Gregor asked, staring at Ichi's face.

"Why else would he run?" Adam said, his eyes dark and his fingers crackling with thin filaments of electricity.

Sam frowned. "Correlation doesn't always equal causation. He might have run for another reason. It's possible he didn't do it, but he knows who did and he's afraid of being silenced."

Adam snorted. "Occam's Razor. The simplest explanation is usually correct. We could have protected him, if he really was innocent. He could have come to us for help."

"Things are not always as simple as they seem," Torliam said, his arms crossed. "That said, I believe he is guilty. Now I want to find out *why*, and get the details. Are there accomplices? Was he commissioned to do this by someone?"

Kris, for once, wasn't spending her free time working. Her marionettes were spread out all around us, scattered beyond the edge of the fire's light. "If he tries to escape, I'll make him *hurt* for it," she said to Gregor.

The boy nodded to her. "Good."

Jacky bounced nervously on her feet. "But we're gonna have to keep him around for now, right? So he can *poof* us around in case the Avatar shows up? It doesn't feel right. What if he tries to kill us, too?"

"Well, if we take him back to the capital and force him to make a binding promise, we won't have to worry about that," I said.

Sam gave me a searching look, and I turned my head away. I didn't like it, either, but how else was I supposed to trust a murderer among us, even if he was restrained? And we needed Ichi's Skill. The time it could save, the freedom of mobility it gave us… It could make a critical difference for hundreds of thousands of innocent lives. Maybe more.

While I was still mentally gnawing on my conflicting aversion and desperation and trying to settle my own mind, Ichi woke.

He tried to keep us from noticing, his breathing still slow and shallow, and his eyes closed. His muscles tensed a little, not enough to move anything, just a test to check the remaining strength of the paralytic in his blood.

"He's awake," I announced, foiling whatever plan he was concocting.

He opened his eyes, looking around as much as he could without being able to raise his head from the ground.

I had expected him to leap into immediate rage, to struggle or spew angry words at us, but he didn't.

He took in his situation—bound, Skill-less, and surrounded by powerful enemies—with a small sigh and a tiny, wry quirk of his mouth. His words started off a little clumsy, as his tongue was still numb, but grew nimbler as he spoke. "So you have captured me. I knew a day like this would come eventually, but I admit it still caught me by surprise. I suppose you will execute me? Or, perhaps, torture and then execute me?"

Ichi didn't know about the Avatar. He probably had no way to keep up with the news while on the run. Otherwise, he might have realized that our team coming after him directly at such a critical time was about more than revenge.

Torliam's voice was heavy with condemnation and anger, enough to put pressure on even those of us who it was not directed at. "You admit you murdered Blaine Mendell, then?"

Ichi let out a scoffing laugh. "Yes! I murdered Blaine Mendell, just as you murdered my wife!"

I frowned, sharing a look with Torliam, but he only shook his head.

"What are you talking about?" Adam snapped.

Ichi's eyes widened, and he struggled to sit upright as he looked around at all of our faces with astonishment. "Do you murder so many that you can no longer remember them all? My wife's name was Ni. She was assigned with me, by the queen, to guard you." Another bitter laugh rose up from his throat, though his expression bore only pain. "She was on your side! She believed in you and your goodness, your destiny," he said, looking at me. "She had pleaded and cajoled and even managed to convince *me*. I should have known better. The only reason we had not yet acted to help you escape was my own wariness that the queen would discover our betrayal if we moved too soon. And then, before even a single day had passed, without one word of warning, or even a *threat*, you killed her."

As he spoke, I remembered. Ni had been the one with the Skill that would have allowed her to track us. I'd killed her to keep her from doing so, never considering that it might not be necessary.

Ichi had popped out of the darkness and shot Blaine without warning. Blaine's head had burst like a watermelon. Quick, violent, and at least relatively painless.

It must have been similar for her—my hand seemingly appearing out of nowhere as I reached out from an opening to the Other Place. I had sunk my claws into the back of her neck, released Chaos into it, and ripped back a handful of bloody mush. Now, I looked down at my hand, remembering the feel of dried blood in the creases of my skin and under my nails.

She wouldn't have suffered very much, with part of her spine and most of her neck missing, but there must have been at least a few seconds of confusion and fear as she bled out and her brain shut down.

That was why Blaine had died? As a punishment for my thoughtless brutality?

Interlude 3

Reed didn't look at the silver mirror directly, keeping its reflection in his peripheral vision as he leaned forward to see his profile. He'd braced himself ahead of time, so he didn't jump at what he saw.

He couldn't help the quickening of his breath, though, and his heart continued to pound. An off-white mask was molded over his face, made of paper mache or plaster. The eyes were just dark holes. Long fingers protruded around the mask's edges, wrapping around his head and holding it tightly to his face.

When the reflection didn't react to his scrutiny, Reed turned his gaze fully toward the mirror. While looking in the tarnished silver reflection, he realized he could *feel* the mask, too, its spider-like fingers tightening around his skull ever-so-slowly. Without warning, he reached up and tore at it, prying back its grasping fingers with all his might, clawing at its plaster surface.

It struggled against him, and it almost felt like he was tearing off his own face as he pried it off, but finally, with a few suction-like *popping* sounds, he dashed it against the ground.

He looked down to find it, but there was nothing there, no horrible mask lying on the floor at his feet. With that realization, he moved more quickly than he'd imagined he could, snatching his desk chair and placing it beside the wall. As he scrambled up onto it, the higher angle allowed him to see the reflection of the floor in the mirror.

The plaster mask had risen up on its finger-like legs and was skittering around confusedly. It didn't seem to know where Reed had gone. He watched it in horrified silence for almost a minute, wondering if he should try to stomp on and kill it. But if he got down from the chair, he wouldn't be able to see it any longer, and maybe it would attack him and reattach itself to his face.

Before he could figure out the best course of action, it skittered out the door, turning toward the bathroom next to his room and disappearing around the corner.

He listened carefully, but heard nothing except the sounds of the city outside.

Reed continued to stare into the mirror, his eyes flicking around the room reflected in it as he searched for more danger. The mirror version of his bedroom was even gloomier than the real thing and looked like it had been abandoned for a couple years, allowing grime and spiderwebs to accrue. Rust-colored water marks stained his walls, as if the roof had been leaking for a long time, and the plaster was cracking.

He realized he'd seen those rust stains before, in the mirror. Thinking back on it, this wasn't the first time he'd been alarmed by something it had reflected. Over the last few days, he'd thought he'd seen shadows moving at the corners of the room, and he'd even caught a glimpse of the finger-legged mask scuttling in the darkness under his bed.

Each time, after some time had passed, he'd simply *forgotten*.

Reed shuddered, goose bumps rising up all over his back and arms. There were scratches on his face, as if he'd clawed himself, or perhaps, as if teeth on the inside of the mask had abraded his skin. The adrenaline was starting to fade, and he felt strangely exhausted and weak, more than the aftermath of his panic seemed responsible for.

Had the mask been *feeding* on him?

Reed forced himself to take long, slow breaths. He hadn't had a panic attack since he was a young child, but he still remembered the feeling. When the buzzing in his brain quieted and he no longer felt like he might fall off the chair, he forced himself to acknowledge the obvious thought. There was a possibility that he was hallucinating—having a breakdown—going insane. Was this what paranoid schizophrenia was like? He looked at the scratch marks on his face again, which were slowly fading from prominence. That was good, because he was instinctually worried what might happen if that thing wearing his mom's body found out he'd discovered and removed the mask.

Reed checked the floor again, then carefully stepped off the chair, walking backward until he found his link sitting on the desk behind him. He hesitated before going to the call screen. The consequences of acting as if what he'd seen was real and being wrong were embarrassment, maybe some therapy, and having to deal with awkwardness and worry from his family and friends. But the consequences of ignoring it as if it were fake, and being *wrong*... That could be way, way worse. He thought of the pale, lumpy ears attached to the side of his mom's reflected head, the black buttons in place of her eyes. He had to press a hand to his mouth to keep himself from whimpering. Was his mom *awake* inside there?

He wasn't sure he could even imagine the worst-case scenario, but it probably was something like his family dying, or the mind-controlling creatures in the mirror taking over their bodies and minds for good. What was a little embarrassment compared to that? He couldn't deal with this on his own. He needed help.

Hesitation gone, he called Demi and Lucas, shakily telling them to come over to his house as soon as possible.

Demi agreed immediately, noticing the urgency in his tone and asking if everything was alright, but Reed only told her they'd talk about it when she arrived.

Lucas was a little more resistant, saying he still needed to go to his weekend orchestra practice.

"This is more important," Reed insisted. "Skip it. Trust me, please. I'm—I need your help. Get here as fast as you can."

While he was waiting for his friends to arrive, he kept his eyes on the mirror. It was obviously old, and the decorative pattern around the edge was black and tarnished. No glass lay between him and the polished silver back, which wasn't as smooth or clear as the mirror in his bathroom.

He considered the possibility that the mirror itself could be making him crazy, showing him illusions. But if that were true, would that mean his *memories of forgetting* the other strange things he'd seen in it had been planted just now? The mirror had been there for years, since long before they'd moved in, and he'd never had anything like this happen before. Something had changed in the last week or so, and that meant it probably wasn't the mirror.

Demi arrived first, greeting his mom like normal as she passed the kitchen, then running up the stairs.

Reed watched her approach in the mirror, giving her a relieved smile that she didn't return.

She stopped in the doorway to his room, looking around. Her eyes passed right over him. "Reed?"

Cold fingers of fear ran down his back. "I'm here," he croaked.

Only then did she seem to be able to see him, though she squinted as if it was difficult. She smiled, dropping her purse on the floor. "Oh, there you are." She didn't seem to find anything strange about the situation, which Reed found even *more* creepy.

"Come stand over here, I want you to see this," he said. When she got close, he stepped back, moving her between him and the mirror so that both of them could look at it at the same time.

Demi didn't seem to recognize what she was seeing at first. She had a pixie cut, but in the mirror her hair was dark, stringy, and hung all the way to her hips. It was dripping wet and fell forward to cover so much of her face that Reed could barely make out her eyes through it. A sack-like dress, also dripping wet, covered her stylish outfit, flapping a little as if she stood in a strong breeze. She smelled of brine and old seaweed.

After a couple seconds of shock, she tore at her hair and the sack-like dress, much like he'd done when he discovered the mask.

Reed helped her, ripping the fabric apart while she pulled at the hair. "Keep looking in the mirror," he warned her.

Once the ghastly parasite was detached from Demi, Reed had to catch her to keep her from collapsing to the ground. He wrapped one hand around her shoulders, letting her slump against his chest, and used the other to force one eyelid open. "Keep looking in the mirror."

He could barely make out the parasite crawling across the floor as it moved farther from them. At the doorway, instead of following the other one into the bathroom, it crawled into Demi's purse and disappeared. The bag didn't bulge any more despite the size of Demi's parasite, as if nothing extra was hiding inside.

It took Demi a few minutes to recover her strength. "What was that?" she asked, her voice low and strained with suppressed emotion.

"I don't know," Reed admitted. "But…do you remember when you were over at my house a few days ago? You were doing something with your makeup, and you—you saw something in this mirror, right?"

Her eyes widened, and she nodded slowly. "The hair. It was…growing."

"I've seen things that shouldn't be there, too, but I think something has been making us forget. The mirror helps us see the truth and remember. It's okay to look away for a little bit, but I don't know exactly how it works, so for now it's safer to keep your eyes on it. Plus, if one of those things comes after us, we'll have no way to know if we don't see its reflection."

"What are they?" Demi wrapped her arms around herself, shuffling back and forth to check the far sides of the room in the small silver mirror.

"It's got to be something to do with a Skill. I did consider that maybe the mirror was making it all up, but that doesn't explain the memory loss, right? It makes more sense that it's showing us the truth, and those things are feeding on us, or something."

"We need a bigger mirror," Demi said.

Reed shook his head. "I think this one is special. I haven't noticed anything in the others. Also, heads up, my own—well, I'm going to call it a parasite, for now—my own parasite went into the bathroom, so you might want to avoid going in there." He had a suspicion about what it had gone in there to do, but he didn't want to take the risk to verify it.

"Who would be sick enough to do something like this? What would have happened if we hadn't gotten those *things* off in time?" she asked.

"I don't know," he said. Her parasite had been much bigger than his, almost covering her whole body, and her reaction after getting rid of it had been similarly worse. He remembered his mom, who, except for her hair, seemed to have been completely subsumed, and a new worry bubbled in his stomach. Had someone targeted his family and friends? Or maybe it was some sort of infestation from Estreyer that had slipped through customs. Being invisible and intangible except when revealed by a silver mirror and forcing people to forget your existence, even if they did see you, would be very useful for creatures like that.

"One of them has my mom," he said, relief at the admission mixing with dread. "A big one."

"We'll save her." Demi gripped his hand.

He explained his speculation about the parasites' origin to Demi. She thought it was more likely to be a Skill, because they were a long way away from the nearest Shortcut, and customs was so strict they required people to go through a decontamination shower and subsequent quarantine before being released. The two were discussing the possible size of the affected area when Lucas arrived.

He didn't have as hard a time noticing them as Demi had.

Reed waved him over to stand in front of the mirror, but Demi said, "Wait. Close the door behind you, Lucas."

Once the other boy had complied, she crossed her arms over her chest. "Let's try to get him to answer some test questions, first."

Lucas rolled his eyes. "Guys, I'm tired and I'm not in the mood for any games. I had a perfect attendance record before today, so if this is some sort of prank, I'm going to be pissed."

"This isn't a prank," Reed assured him, still looking at him through the reflection.

"Are you having trouble seeing us?" Demi asked.

Lucas frowned like it was hard to understand the question, but after a few moments of consideration, he nodded.

"Reach up and touch your shoulders. Do you feel anything there?"

Lucas's frown grew heavier. "Why are you guys looking away from me?" he said. His arms rose halfway, but then dropped again.

"Touch your shoulders," Demi repeated.

Lucas's movements were slow, and when he finally complied, his hands clearly touched the two small heads growing out of his flesh on either shoulder.

Reed looked away from the mirror for a quick glance at the

"real" world, and only saw Lucas's hands resting flat on his own shoulders, directly *through* the base of where the two heads were in the mirror. The sight made his brain itch, and he quickly turned his eyes back to the silver reflection. "Do you feel that?" he asked.

Lucas winced and moved his hands up to rub his temples. "Something…" He trailed off, and when he took his hands away, they fell back to his sides. "You guys are irritating me. *Normal* friends don't treat each other like this. Something seems wrong about you…" His tone was a little too flat, lacking real emotion, and the faint frown that had been on his face since he arrived was gone. He hadn't once looked in the mirror himself, despite how they'd been talking to him while facing it the whole time.

Reed tried to hide his shudder, sharing a quick glance with Demi in the mirror.

"Sorry, Lucas. Come stand beside me," she said, holding an arm out towards him.

Lucas hesitated, and Reed said, "We didn't mean anything by it. Don't be upset." His heart was beating so loudly that he was afraid Lucas might hear it from across the room, and he tried not to tense his muscles noticeably as his friend approached.

When Lucas got close enough, Reed and Demi both grabbed one of his arms and pushed him closer to the mirror. It only took a few seconds for the other boy to snap out of whatever mind-control he'd been under.

He screamed, and Demi clamped a hand over his mouth to muffle the sound, but Reed was sure his mom would have heard the noise even down in the kitchen.

The miniature heads growing out of his shoulders had thin skin and undeveloped eyes, like a fetus in the womb, but their mouths were fully developed and were whispering an unintelligible string of words into Lucas's ears.

Reed and Demi wasted no time ripping them off and tossing them to the floor, then waited, their own ears strained to make sure the sound hadn't alarmed Reed's mom. When they heard no calls from the kitchen or footsteps heading toward the room, they relaxed, and Demi took her hand away from Lucas's mouth.

"What the hell is going on!?" Lucas whispered.

They took a couple minutes to fill him in, all three standing in front of the mirror now.

"I haven't been sleeping well lately. Nightmares," Lucas said. "I bet it was because of those things…whispering constantly…and I had no idea what was happening. Even when you were asking me questions and making me touch them directly, it was kind of like a dream. You know, where strange things happen but either you don't even notice, or you somehow come up with explanations as to how it all makes perfect sense."

"Should we call my mom up now?" Reed asked.

"I think we should do a couple more tests first. I just feel like we're missing something," Demi said, one arm squeezing her opposite forearm reflexively. With a deep breath, she turned away from the mirror. "If something goes wrong, or I start acting strange, you guys can help me. We need to know if we can stay lucid if we look away from the mirror for longer stretches of time. Do the parasites just come back? Is the person behind this aware that we got free?"

Reed hesitated, but nodded. This had started days ago, at least. A few more minutes to make sure they could save his mom properly would not change anything. "Alright," Reed said, inwardly a little ashamed that Demi would be the one taking such a risk rather than him. "Don't worry, we'll save you right away if something happens."

They waited, but she was fine even after a few minutes away from the mirror. She eyed her purse, which was lying on the ground by the door. Lucas's parasite had crawled inside it and disappeared, just like her own. Demi turned to Reed. "You said yours went into the bathroom?"

He nodded, then said hesitantly, "Is there a mirror inside your purse?"

She caught his meaning immediately. "There is. Do you think…?"

"It seems likely. If they just wanted somewhere dark and hidden, they could have crawled under my bed."

She took a deep breath and squared her shoulders. "We need to check." Despite her attempt at a brave facade, her voice quavered.

"I'll do it," Reed said quickly.

She shook her head. "No. Lucas started getting hostile at the end there. What if you decide to attack us? I'm not as strong or big as either of you. You'll have an easier time restraining me and forcing me back to the silver mirror. Maybe…maybe you'll be able to ask me some questions." Without waiting for either of them to respond, she walked forward and kicked gingerly at her purse.

It didn't react.

Reaching out with two fingers, she grabbed it by the bottom and lifted, spilling its contents over the floor.

The compact mirror within clattered against the old wooden floorboards, appearing all the more sinister for its apparent innocence.

Demi picked it up with trembling fingers, moving back to stand beside the two boys.

Reed grabbed her free arm, just in case.

"Don't look at it," she warned, then began to narrate. "I'm opening it. The mirror itself looks normal. Now I'm holding it out and turning it so I can see myself. There's nothing on me, I look nor—no, there's something crawling up my back, it's—" her voice choked off like something was strangling her. She spoke again after only a short pause, but now all the alarm was gone from her tone. "My lipstick needs a touchup."

In the silver mirror, Reed and Lucas could see the dripping hair and formless dress draping over Demi and settling down, like a bird going to roost in its nest.

Reed resisted the urge to rip it back off her; she'd wanted them to ask her questions. Despite it being her idea, his insides still wriggled with guilt at the thought of leaving her under its influence for even a second.

Lucas's darker skin turned almost green as he paled. "Do you remember what we were talking about earlier?"

"Sorry, I wasn't paying attention," she said.

Reed's throat and mouth were dry, and he swallowed painfully. "Is there anything you want, Demi? What's your goal?"

She giggled. "My goal? Well, I just want to do normal things together."

There it was again, Reed thought. Slightly too much emphasis on "normal." Were the victims being mind-controlled to avoid standing out? "What's normal, Demi?"

"We could do our makeup together?" she asked, her voice sweet.

Normally, he would have thought she was joking if she said such a thing, but now it made him tense. Was she trying to get him to look in a mirror? A non-silver mirror, that is? "Hypothetically, Demi, if I told you there was a parasite latched on to you controlling your mind, what would you do?"

She tensed, then turned slowly toward him, glaring at the side of his face while he continued to look at her reflection. "That's a very abnormal thing to say, Reed."

That was enough. He nodded to Lucas. Reed turned to Demi and tried to force her to look at the mirror, while Lucas struggled with the parasite.

She fought against them with all her might, scratching at Lucas's eyes with one hand while she tried to shield her own from the sight of the mirror with the other. She kicked Reed in the leg and ripped herself free from their grasp, lunging toward the door.

Reed didn't waste any time being shocked at the amount of strength Demi suddenly possessed. He lunged after her, slamming into her back just as she turned the handle of his bedroom door. The door shuddered in its frame, but he'd caught her, and with Lucas's help, they kept her from screaming as they dragged her back to the silver mirror, where they ripped off the soaking hair and sack-dress controlling her.

Reed tossed it away, and it crawled into the compact mirror, which Demi had dropped sometime during their struggle.

She once again seemed weakened, even worse than the first time. Her entire body shivered uncontrollably, and she couldn't support herself.

They moved her over to lie on Reed's bed, and when Lucas saw she was bleeding from the nose, he grabbed a tissue and awkwardly wiped her face.

His mom yelled up at them not to roughhouse in his room, and he called back down a quick "Sorry!" to her. "This is bad," Reed said, his eyes drawn to the bright red blood against the white tissue, standing out even more against the gloomy backdrop of his room.

Lucas snorted. "No shit."

Demi recovered after a few minutes, turning away from them and scrubbing what might have been tears from her face.

"Are you okay?" Lucas asked.

She gave him a derisive look and ignored the question.

Standing with some difficulty, Demi crossed the room and gingerly picked up the compact mirror, which she carefully closed without looking at. She walked over to the window, opened it up, and hurled the small mirror as far away as she could. She panted for a few seconds, then said, "Well, at least we've confirmed how it works."

"My mom will have to come up here on her own," Reed said. "The mirror is attached to the wall somehow, and there's no way we'll be able to drag her up the stairs if she's fighting against us."

He poked his head out and called down, asking her to come to his room, hoping his tone was normal enough not to make her parasite suspicious.

"I've got my hands full down here, honey!" she said. "Wait till this is finished."

"It's important," he tried. "Can't you just step away for two minutes? I need your help."

"These appetizers aren't going to make themselves, and the courier is coming to pick them up in an hour! If you're not bleeding to death on the floor right now, you'll have to wait," she called back, obviously distracted.

Reed knew from experience he couldn't change her mind. He moved to the mirror, trying to dig his fingers between it and the wall. It wouldn't budge. Should he start screaming like he really was bleeding out on the floor at that very moment? She'd have to come running for that, right? Once she understood his motives, she wouldn't be upset at the deception.

"We need to call the enforcers," Lucas said, derailing Reed's speculation.

Demi snorted. "You think they'll do anything? They're all corrupt. And even if they haven't been bribed to look the other way, how are *they* supposed to deal with this?"

Lucas threw his hands up in the air. "Well, we have to do something! We're not equipped to deal with this. People are in *danger*, Demi! This isn't the time to fantasize about playing hero. This is a job for professionals. They're paid to deal with stuff like this."

Demi glared at Lucas, and Reed stepped into the familiar role of mediator, making a calming motion to the both of them. "Guys, we're on the same side here. It's just the tension making us snappy."

Lucas looked away first, mumbling, "Yeah, sorry," and Demi responded with a small "hmph," and a nod.

"Lucas might be right," Reed said. "I know we always hear stories about how corrupt they are, but that's mostly in the slums, right? We're in a pretty good area and my dad has some influence, so they won't think they can push us around. I think the likelihood of them being so corrupt that they won't even do their jobs is pretty low. The risk is worth it, in any case, because it's not like we have any better options."

"I'm calling, then," Lucas said, already tapping on the link wrapped around his forearm.

The local enforcers station answered quickly, the standard "What's your emergency?" opener spilling out rapid-fire in a woman's voice.

Lucas carefully explained that they were under the influence of what they believed to be a Skill from a nearby malicious Player.

"Please be advised, false reports of harmful Empowered activity is punishable by a fine and up to five years in prison," the operator replied in a somewhat bored tone.

Lucas stared at the screen in astonishment. "I'm not making a false report. We're not absolutely sure it's a Player, but other than an infestation of some Estreyan monsters, we can't think of anything else it could be."

"Are you in immediate danger?" The woman's voice still sounded bored.

"Well, not *immediate*," Lucas said.

Demi frowned and shook her head at him, then started talking instead. "We *are* in immediate danger. Weird things that look like they came out of a horror movie are latching onto people, erasing our memories, and controlling our minds. They're mostly invisible, and once you look in the mirror you forget all about them. We know for sure at least four people have been affected, and we suspect more. Three of us have been able to escape the effects, but they seem to have been siphoning our energy or something, and it's likely that people are going to start dying."

Reed shuddered to hear it said aloud, though he'd known it was true. He tried not to think about that happening to his mom, downstairs with no idea about the thing violating her body and mind. He determined that he really was going to start screaming frantically for her help, as soon as they finished with this call. He could lie on the ground in front of the mirror, with Demi and Lucas waiting on either side of the door to grab her when she entered the room.

This time, the operator seemed a little more alert. "You say you've been able to escape these effects? How did you do so? And please give me the information on other individuals you suspect have been compromised."

Demi explained about the mirror and Reed's mom.

"I thought you said looking in a mirror caused this Empowered to regain control over you?" the woman said skeptically.

"No! Haven't you been listening? Looking in a normal mirror does that. We have a pure, polished-silver surface that seems to repel them. Don't you have a protocol for something like this? Our entire town could be being brainwashed and siphoned dry right now. We need manpower! Get a specialized team, or a squad of contracted Players here to deal with this! If you send some low-level bicycle enforcer, you're just going to be spreading the infection. Quarantine us all if you have to, I don't care!"

"Please remain calm, Miss. Getting agitated won't help me do my job." There was the sound of tapping, and then the woman confirmed the address they were calling from. "I can't authorize a specialized response of Empowered for something of the size you're suggesting until I have an official request from one of our own people. We do have a task force assigned to investigate extraordinary incidents, though, and they should have both the equipment and training to avoid... I mean, they've got glasses..." Her fast-paced, clipped tone slowed like cooling molasses.

Reed, Demi, and Lucas shared a look of dread.

"Close your eyes!" Reed called into the link.

There was a long moment of silence.

The call cut off.

"Oh my god, whoever is behind this already got to the enforcers," Demi said.

Lucas shook his head. "We don't know that."

"So you think she just hung up on us?" Demi rolled her eyes.

While disheartening, that was actually the preferable of the two possibilities. "Call back," Reed said. "Maybe you'll get somebody different. Tell them to listen to the recording of this call first, and maybe that will make them a little more wary."

Demi crouched down and held her hands in her head. "But did you hear her? All they're going to do is send a group of normal enforcers. Even if they are trained to handle Skill incidents, all it takes is one of them to flash around a mirror to the others, and it's over. Actually, if I were the one behind this, I would have taken out the government and law enforcement *first*."

"We have to try, at least," Lucas said, already calling again.

The distant sound of the front door opening and closing made its way up to them, signifying the return of Reed's dad from shooting the first weekend weather report. His mom would be calling them down for dinner soon, and he really didn't know how they were going to deal with that, sitting right next to her and knowing that something else was controlling her body. Was his dad affected, too? He really, really hoped not. His dad would be able to help them if he could think normally. He would know what to do.

He discarded his plan to start screaming hysterically. Both his parents would rush to his room if he did that, and if both were infected, they would be too much for him and his friends to handle. Instead, he opened the door and called down, "Dad? Could you come here? I need your help with something."

"I'll be up in a few minutes!" the man called back.

Reed was as relieved as he was anxious. He scanned the room in the silver reflection quickly, just to make sure nothing was sneaking up on them, then moved the chair back to his desk and sat in front of his own link. "I'm going to search for other avenues we might use to ask for help," he said. "Keep an eye on me, in case it's not just mirrors that are dangerous." The screen had an anti-glare coating, so there wouldn't be any reflections, at least.

He quickly exited the EDF board thread he'd been viewing and submitted a search query for "mind-control Skill emergency hotline."

He found a page with a list of emergency numbers and quickly saved them all to his link. He would go through every single one until he found someone who was both willing and able to help, if he had to.

An infographic took him to an article giving basic procedure on how to recognize and handle Skills that fell into the very broad category of "mind control."

> Skills that deal with the cognition of others are frightening even to think about. The idea that someone might be able to erase your memories and replace them with false ones, brainwash you into becoming their patsy, or take over your body is the stuff of horror films.

Reed skipped past the rest of the introduction, looking for information relevant to his own situation.

Lucas and Demi were arguing with the emergency operator, who was insisting on returning their call to the original woman they'd spoken to. Demi had gotten frustrated enough to demand to speak to their manager by the time Reed found something that seemed relevant.

> While some Skills are very difficult to counteract, none are completely without foils or ways in which the user can be defeated. Even the Estreyan gods are not omnipotent, though a human civilian has little chance against an aggressor of such strength.
>
> If you find yourself against an opponent with Skills, the first thing to do is run and request help from those better equipped to deal with the situation, such as your local enforcers. If that's not possible, best practices can help keep you alive, with your sanity intact.
>
> Act to neutralize, not capture. An Empowered, even seemingly incapacitated, is dangerous.
>
> Pain can help to forcefully reset your senses. If you

suspect you are affected, creating a small, painful injury on yourself may be able to "snap you out of it," so to speak.

If possible, move in a group with allies. Use an "eyes on" policy, with all companions maintaining constant visual contact with each other, and, if possible, the enemy as well. Each ally should be in sight of another at all times. No one should be allowed to move off on their own, even to turn a corner or enter a nearby room.

Against Skills that use illusions, invisibility, or sensory confusion, place a hand on the shoulder of the ally closest to you. This touch anchor can help to ground you in reality.

Use passwords to identify allies. Ideally, these passwords should be single-use, and each person should have their own. Consider using a set of rules that allow you to create call-and-response passwords on the fly, rather than needing to memorize one that can be overheard and stolen. Any time the eyes-on protocols are broken (you lose sight of an ally, or separate and meet again) passwords should be in use, even if your ally's subversion or replacement seems impossible. The impossible is possible.

Allies may narrate their actions to each other, in whispers if security is suspect. This may also take the form of a running call-and-response, based on rules such as the passwords above. If, at any point, an ally goes silent or breaks correct response procedure, assume they are compromised.

Allies who act against the predetermined plan or are not able to provide the *correct* password should be incapacitated at the first sign of deviance, regardless of how sure you are that they have not been compromised. When dealing with a Skill that affects your cognition, even *you* cannot be trusted.

Attack from a distance. Many Skills that affect cognition have a limited range.

If your enemy is a group containing multiple Empowered with seemingly similar power levels, the one able to disrupt your cognition takes priority.

Some Skills of this nature will have very specific rules, such as only being useable in the dark, requiring the Empowered to have a belonging of the victim's or some of their hair, or losing control if their victim suddenly encounters something that "triggers" them, that is, reminds them of the truth or jars them into confusion such that they start questioning their current circumstances.

"No, don't put me on hold—" Lucas pleaded, throwing up his hands in frustration when the operator did just that.

"What did I tell you?" Demi said gloomily. "Even if they're not corrupt, they've been compromised."

At this point, Reed had to agree with her.

Lucas was stubbornly unconvinced, though. "They could be mobilizing right now and too busy to talk. I'll wait until he picks up again."

Heavy footsteps drummed on the creaking stairs, and after a couple firm knocks that had Reed closing down the Net page and Demi and Lucas asking the emergency operator to wait a moment, Reed's dad opened the bedroom door.

The three of them stood, facing the man with apprehension.

His eyes swept over the room and its occupants with a hardness that bordered on suspicion.

Reed turned enough to see his dad in the wall mirror. His heart sank a little. He'd hoped, for some reason, that the man would be free and able to help them figure out what to do. He'd hoped his dad would be able to protect him.

Instead, the silver reflection showed flesh that seemed to be melting. Big, milky, blind eyes popped up from under his dad's skin like pustules, some bare and some still covered by a thin layer of skin. They varied in size, but none of them had eyelids, so they all stared constantly. Two larger, bulging eyes had emerged from the drooping skin of his face, one near his jaw, and the other high on the opposite cheekbone, close to crowding out his real eye.

Demi greeted the man with a too-cheerful wave. "Hi, Mr. Phillips! Umm, come on in. We have something to show you."

His dad, or the thing controlling him, didn't hesitate to deny her. "No. I think it's time for you two to go home. Your parents must be worried." It wasn't even dinnertime yet, and both Lucas and Demi's parents probably expected the two to eat at Reed's house, but none of them pointed out this obviously fictitious excuse.

Demi shared a look with Reed, and he hurried to say, "Okay, that's fine, but actually all three of us need your help, so maybe we could do that first? It won't take very long." He glanced toward the silver mirror, wondering if they should try to overpower his dad.

"I don't think so. Reed, it'll be time for dinner soon. Your friends need to go home." His eyes skimmed the room again, and Reed almost thought they caught for a second on the mirror.

Lucas, in a surprising show of bravery, said, "Now!" and leapt at his dad, grabbing for an arm and trying to yank him fully into the room.

Reed and Demi followed his lead, Reed grabbing his dad's other arm, while Demi grabbed his head, trying to force him to look toward the mirror.

The man head-butted Demi, his eyeball-infested face smashing right into her forehead, sending her reeling back.

The arm Reed was holding lifted him effortlessly, twisting around to grip his shoulder and toss him to the ground.

His dad gripped Lucas by the throat, his expression only mildly irritated as he choked the boy, ignoring his quickly-purpling face and the frantic clawing at his hand as Lucas tried to pry back the fingers digging into his flesh.

"Dad, stop!" Reed yelled, scrambling back to his feet.

As if only then realizing quite what he'd done, the man's eyes widened, and he released Lucas's throat. But he grabbed Lucas's arm instead, then reached forward and did the same to Demi. "Your friends are leaving now, Reed. Say goodbye," he said, dragging them from the room roughly enough they barely kept their feet.

Reed followed behind, horrified and at a loss for what to do, pleading with his dad without really listening to the words spilling out of his mouth.

The man ignored him. His dad was big, and he worked out frequently to be able to maintain his television figure while still indulging in his mom's cooking. He had no trouble manhandling a couple teenagers.

Reed berated himself despairingly. They should have freed his mom first. Maybe with her help, too, they could have overpowered the man.

His mom turned to watch as his dad dragged his two best friends down the stairs and over to the front door. "What's going on, Herman?"

What could Reed *do*?

To his surprise, his dad stopped at the doorway and released both of them, gesturing kindly for them to put on their shoes and jackets. He loomed over them still, though, leaving no room for escape. "Just some roughhousing, dear."

"In the *house*?" She wagged a pair of stainless steel tongs at him reproachfully.

Reed's eyes caught on the utensil's reflective surface. He looked away quickly, just in case it counted as a mirror and he ended up catching a glimpse of himself in it. That would turn a bad situation into a hopeless one. But it gave him an idea. While his friends slowly put on their outside clothes, he hurried for the old cabinet in the corner of the dining room, where his dad kept the antique silverware. The larger pieces were on display, but hadn't been polished recently, so he had a hard time judging what type of reflection they showed. He grabbed blindly from the drawer within, stuffing a handful of spoons into his pocket.

"Let me help you with your jacket," he said to Demi.

She rolled with his improvisation easily, and Reed managed to slip the spoons into her pocket.

His dad's eyes lingered on the pocket, and then flicked to Reed, and for a second his heart sank. But he only called back to his mom, "Boys will be boys. You know how it is, dear." He thrust Reed's friends out the door hard enough to make them stumble.

His mom sighed at that and returned to her cooking, and that was as much a sign that something was wrong as anything else.

His dad hated that platitude and said it was only a way to eschew responsibility for bad behavior based on gender stereotypes. Plus, Demi wasn't a boy. It was like a cry for help, disguised in his words. But neither Reed nor his mom were in a position to change anything.

He grabbed Reed's arm, and for a moment, Reed thought he would be evicted from the house as well, but his dad jerked a bit, his hand twitching, and instead, he pulled Reed back from the doorway and slammed the door closed. They stood there in silence for a bit, and then, slowly, as if he had to pry each finger up with sheer force of will, his dad let him go.

Reed stepped away immediately.

His dad turned and went back up the stairs without another word, retreating down the hallway into his office.

Reed turned to his mom, thinking maybe he could try with the silverware on her, but she was chopping up vegetables with a big knife. He swallowed, and instead ran back up to his room. He called Demi, since Lucas's link might still be occupied with the call to the enforcers.

She answered immediately. "The spoons work," she said. "But your parents… I'm worried about how strong your dad's parasite was. How much has it drained them? Even I—I'm not feeling so good, still."

Lucas's voice, sounding a little farther away, said, "Why didn't you say so? What's wrong?"

She ignored his question. "They might end up needing medical help. Also, I'm kind of worried about my own family. I want to check on them, and if they're not too bad, maybe I can save them. My parents would be able to help with your dad."

"Maybe the enforcers would actually listen to an adult," Lucas muttered bitterly.

Reed felt sick, but he nodded, then realized they couldn't see him and said, "Alright. Don't split up. Maybe you can sleep over at Demi's house, Lucas. Keep your heads down and travel quickly." As the Net page had recommended, he told Lucas and Demi to both keep up a running commentary about being lucid or speculate about the Player behind this, because as soon as they lost lucidity, they would forget pretty much everything to do with the truth the silver mirror had revealed, and the sudden change in topic would be an immediate indicator of danger.

Reed pulled the silver butter knife he'd filched from his pocket as he listened to his friends ramble. The reflection off the blade wasn't nearly as clear as the mirror in his room, but with it he could make out the phantom cracks and invisible bloody handprints on the walls, so it at least did something.

Maybe, if someone killed the Player behind this, it would release the victims without hurting them? He doubted he'd be able to do it, even if he knew who they were, but he'd at least be able to tell the enforcers.

It only took a few minutes for Lucas to stop professing his own lucidity.

"Lucas just froze," Demi said. "We're at the corner of the central square, and he's looking up at one of the screens on the side of the building behind me."

"Don't look, Demi," Reed said.

"He's not doing anything. Just staring. There's a crowd, they're all watching it. This is bigger than we…thought. It's…" Her voice took on that familiar molasses quality as she trailed off.

"Close your eyes! Close your eyes and take out the silver from your pocket!"

There was no response. He could hear the sounds of traffic and the advertisements coming from the large billboard screens that girded the buildings around his friends. He called their names over and over, pleaded with them to look into the reflections from the silverware they'd taken, to close their eyes, to run, anything.

After a few minutes, by which time Reed was planning to throw caution to the wind and go after them himself, the call disconnected.

He called again, but there was no answer.

Chapter 13

I am like a small creature swallowed whole by a monster, she thought, and the monster feels my tiny little movements inside.

— Shirley Jackson

I TRIED to push the sudden dizzy feeling of guilt away, but it crawled back up into my stomach and clawed at me even more viciously. Ichi's label for it—"murder"—wasn't wrong. I'd accepted a lot of negative things about myself, even embraced them, but I'd always considered my actions reasonable, even justifiable.

But this time was different. I hadn't known Ni was an ally, but did that mean she had deserved to die?

Obviously, I had decided at some point that she did, because I'd killed her—no, *murdered* her.

Combined with my roiling thoughts, Ichi's condemning gaze was too much to bear. I stepped back and turned away, my sharp scales raising their edges to ward off further intrusions. "I—I'm recusing myself for the moment. Stay here to question him," I told the others.

Adam reached out as if to grab my arm, but Chaos was there, a harness of condensed darkness wrapping around my body while prehensile tendrils yanked me away faster than my legs would have been able to carry me.

I caught Kris's expression of shock and dismay and Gregor's quickly crumpling glare as I passed.

I traveled in a wide arc, only stopping once the light of the fire was a distant orange spark against the midnight blue horizon. I stood with my back to it, looking out into the cold night.

I didn't cry, or scream, or collapse.

I let black flames roil out of me, spilling down like heavy fog on a cold morning and spreading out across the ground. I turned my mind to creation, and when I finished, the ground as far as the human eye could see was filled with stars, and my emotions had settled. I hadn't really put stars into the ground, just turned it into an opaline mineral that reflected flame-like sparkles from the light of the rising moons.

"I can't keep reeling from this kind of thing," I whispered to myself. No general in the army could start crying and apologizing every time they got one of their soldiers killed, and what my team was doing was more important than any war in history. Then again, they weren't soldiers, and I wasn't a general.

I'd done my best to rationalize ruthlessness, because it was the only way I saw to survive. I prioritized myself and those I cared about above strangers. Everyone did the same, I was just upfront about it. It's not that I didn't understand that strangers were people, too, that their lives held meaning, and that their actions had consequences, but I'd purposefully kept myself from dwelling on those types of thoughts, afraid they would make me weak.

I'd been forced to see and comprehend the consequences of my actions before. Each time, I felt ashamed, maybe even devastated, and then I picked myself up and tried to fix things. But had I *learned* anything? I'd promised myself, back when a little boy had died in my arms as a newbie Player, that I wouldn't act so as to be left with regrets, but I kept breaking that promise to myself.

Everyone was the hero of their own story. To someone else, I was the villain, that horrible monster that rips from them what they most cherish.

I gritted my teeth, taking a few quick breaths as my thoughts tried to shy away from the truth. I needed to be honest with myself, at least. If I was in the same situation again, without knowing my captors were secretly on my side, would I act the same?

Footsteps, surprisingly silent for the weight they carried, came up behind me. Torliam stopped by my side, looking down at the sparkling field I'd created. He didn't speak.

I supposed it wasn't too surprising that he'd found me so easily, with the blood-covenant bond between us.

"Are you here to console me?" I asked.

"Do you need to be consoled?"

I looked up at the stars above my head, imagining the expanse between me and the most distant twinkles. Some of them were dead already, and yet their light was still reaching me now. "I don't recognize myself in the mirror, sometimes," I said instead of answering. "I'll flinch before realizing this strange, alien creature is me. When this is all over, I don't think I'll ever be able to go back to a normal life. I wonder, has my mind changed as much as my body? Would the human Eve even recognize me?" I swallowed. "And…the thing is…I'm not sure I actually care, or if I'm just pretending to myself that I do, because it's frightening to admit what I've become."

Torliam sighed and moved a little closer, so that I could feel the heat radiating off his arm. "You have changed. The human Eve might not recognize you. But you are more beautiful now, for all your strangeness."

I turned my head toward him, raising an eyebrow.

"Nuance, contradiction, and suffocating depths of darkness. That is what you are. There is as much warmth as cold in you, and that is why you draw us to you."

"And if I were to destroy that which was most precious to you? If I turned your world to madness and fear? Would you still think that I'm beautiful?"

He gave me an inscrutable smile. "A bad action does not negate a good one."

"The opposite is also true."

"Yes. And so, perhaps you are a villain. Yet, you may still be the villain who saves the world, and a hero to those who have gained more than they have lost. And to some, those who know you best, you will be neither a hero nor a villain."

What would I be, then? I considered asking, but in the end kept silent.

Mercy and compassion were a weakness, but they could also be a strength. I knew that. I also knew that they were a risk, only suitable for those strong enough to afford them. There were two types of strength that allowed you that sort of freedom: You could be so powerful that the risk of compassion backfiring was only a negligible threat. Or, you could have enough mental fortitude, enough bravery and commitment to your ideals, that you could accept the risk, even knowing that it could destroy you and those you cared for.

Something inside me had settled. I turned back toward the distant campfire and began to walk, my footsteps even more silent than Torliam's.

AS WE APPROACHED THE CAMP, I sensed through Wraith that Jacky, Kris, Gregor, and Birch were still gathered around Ichi. "Where did Adam go?" I asked, frowning and already starting to compose a VR Window to him.

Torliam tried and failed to suppress a sheepish grin. "When you left, he wished to go after you, but did not want to alert you that he was doing so. I may have pointed him in the wrong direction."

"So childish," I muttered.

Torliam's lopsided grin only widened.

Through the empty darkness, we heard the sounds of someone in the camp screaming with hysterical laughter that bordered on sobs.

Without even pausing to share a glance, Torliam and I both sprang forward. I used tentacle-like cords of Chaos to pull myself faster, leaving Torliam well behind.

Some of my teammates stared blankly out at nothing, others had collapsed into tears. Even the marionettes were affected, creating a pile of incapacitated forms all around Ichi.

Sam was crouched down in the middle of this living shield wall, holding Ichi on the ground while staring into his eyes. Sam's eyes were black, from sclera to iris, all the way across.

In the time it took me to arrive, Ichi went from hysterical laughter to sobbing despair, then to shuddering, gasping fear. No sane mind could switch between emotions so completely and with such speed; I knew it must be Sam's doing, but if he'd just wanted to incapacitate Ichi, he could have made him depressed to the point of complete apathy, like he'd done to the others. This was torture.

Zed was circling around at a distance, his gun raised but not yet able to get a clear shot at Sam past the barrier of our other teammates and the marionettes.

Gregor's black silhouette was standing over Kris's collapsed form at the edge of the camp, protecting her. "He's killing him!" the boy yelled to me.

Zed and Gregor—and Adam, who wasn't there—were the only remaining members unaffected by Sam's Skill.

—I DON'T HAVE ANY NONLETHAL AMMUNITION. DO YOU STILL
WANT ME TO TAKE HIM DOWN?—
-ZED-

I shook my head, and my brother pointed his gun away, still ready to respond if something went wrong.

I didn't bother sending Adam a Window calling him back to the camp. He would have heard the commotion and was no doubt already on his way.

Torliam would be there soon, too, but I didn't want to wait to stop whatever Sam was doing even a second longer than necessary.

I reached out with a wave of Chaos, surrounding Sam in a quickly condensing bubble of darkness.

Sam tried to grab at Ichi to bring our captive into the bubble with him, but I had enough fine control over Chaos to forcibly rip his hands away. If I happened to grate some of Sam's skin off in the process, well, that was an accident.

I shrank the barrier of condensed Chaos around Sam till it was vaguely human-shaped, keeping him trapped, then moved forward to carry everyone else away from him.

Zed and Torliam helped, and when Adam arrived, he joined in after a moment of dismay.

Adam sent a drilling glare toward Torliam for his deception, but didn't say anything to either of us.

Ichi was huddled in a shaking ball within his restraints. He'd never had a chance against Sam.

"What happened?" I asked Zed.

"I'm not totally sure," he answered, a hint of mania in his tone. "Ichi was saying how we all deserved it, or something, and Sam's eyes went full-black. He started torturing Ichi, and Jacky tried to stop him first, but he dropped her before she could even lay a hand on him—eye contact—then the rest of us…well, you saw. It all happened really quickly."

I nodded. It was difficult to defend against an attack that affected you as soon as you saw it. Even if you could keep your eyes closed, you'd still be incapacitated as soon as you touched him. Gregor's Shadow state apparently protected him from even psychological damage, but I was surprised my brother was still alright when even the marionettes weren't.

I let Sam sit inside the bubble of corrosive darkness while I waited for everyone else to recuperate. I was fairly sure my teammates would be okay.

Ichi, on the other hand, fell into an uneasy, twitching sleep, and I could only hope that whatever Sam had done to him wouldn't be permanent.

Gregor tended carefully to Kris, stroking her hair and feeding her a sip of water from his canteen. Neither of them seemed to be paying much attention to either me or Ichi. I would have liked the chance to discuss Ichi's revelation with them, but unfortunately Sam's attack had made the delicate situation even more messy.

Jacky glared toward the bubble of Chaos, sitting there silent and ominous in the middle of the camp. "Kick his ass and get his head back on straight," she told me, clenching her fists and blinking away angry tears.

I prepared my mindset, letting some of that implacable rage from the pit inside me rise up to make me unbreakable. I nudged at it mentally, like I'd nudged the empty spot in my gums where I'd lost a tooth as a child—curiously. Did it feel like godhood? I couldn't tell. When I was ready, I expanded the size of the confining barrier and strode right through it like it was a soap bubble.

I warmed the inner layer and converted motes of the Chaos to light, which floated like glowing pollen against the ink-black bubble around us. Only then did I meet Sam's empty eyes. I felt a bit of apathy and fatigue, but he didn't attack me actively, and his Skill did nothing to the steel core of anger. "You've done something very stupid," I said.

He remained seated on the ground, crossing his legs. "I was *helping*. I didn't hurt the rest of the team, just kept them from interrupting my work. Every minute counts, you know, Eve. I can break Ichi, snap his will and make him listen. We don't need to go back to the capital and deal with Queen Mardinest or her vow-binder, we can just head straight to Tartarus. I can keep an eye on him, and I'll keep him under control for as long as we need. He deserves it." Sam's tone was cool, almost amused, except for the hints of anger that slipped through when he spoke of Ichi.

I stared down at my teammate for a moment, then joined him on the ground, crossing my scaled legs to mirror him. "What made you push Black Sun so hard? What were you feeling, right before?"

Sam blinked, shifting a little. "I was angry."

I had thought so. "You're still angry," I said aloud.

He gave me a small frown. "No. Black Sun suppresses emotions. I am logical."

"If you were making decisions solely based on logic, you wouldn't have attacked Ichi. You were angry, and you used Black Sun to try to deal with that anger. But I've been watching you, Sam. Black Sun doesn't get rid of everything you are normally, or negate all the goals you held before you activated it. There's a sort of momentum. I'd bet your restraint was the weaker of the two urges. So what you really did was get rid of the inhibitions keeping you from *acting* on that anger."

He shook his head, his frown deepening. "No, that's not how it works. Black Sun clarifies my mind. I stripped Ichi of his mental defenses because it was the most logical action, and without the bindings of morals and feelings, I realized I could act on it."

"Oh, really? Because if that were true, you must have realized there was no way you could actually keep Ichi under control constantly. One, Black Sun isn't a total mind-control Skill, so you'd be relying on the *hope* that you can torture him so thoroughly that he gave up any inkling of fighting back against us or sabotaging us, along with plain old *luck*. Two, you can't keep Black Sun active indefinitely, so what happens if Ichi decides to rebel while you're taking a break? Three, without this Skill active, you're going to be horrified by what you've done and refuse to continue. So once you'd finished torturing him and turning him into a gibbering mess…*if* you didn't make him lose his mind entirely, we'd *still* have to go back to the capital to make sure he didn't betray us."

Sam opened his mouth as if to respond, but closed it again without speaking.

"So, Sam, I understand why you did it. Anger, the desire for revenge, that's a perfectly legitimate emotion. Still, you screwed up."

After a pause, he gave me a small nod. "I'll turn it off." He tensed, as if bracing himself for the volatile flood of returning emotions, but I raised a hand to forestall him.

"Not yet." I stared at him for a long moment. "I'm worried that things like this are going to keep happening if something doesn't change. I can't tell you to stop using your Skill, but I also can't allow you to continue to be a liability."

He didn't relax, though his wariness had turned toward me instead of himself. "And so?"

"I have an idea. This is about as deep as I've ever seen you under the influence of Black Sun. While you're still here and you understand what it feels like, I want you to relate to your normal self. Not everything he does is out of naivety or stupidity. There are good reasons for him to believe and act the way he does. There are consequences to actions. Think about them." The words felt like they were for me as much as him. I paused, letting them hang in the air and sink in. "Then I want you to come up with a series of rules. Promises that you make to yourself, which you will keep *whether or not* you feel like it. You agree to them now, and then you will turn off Black Sun, examine them again, and see if you can agree to them then, too."

The blackness of his eyes seemed to ripple, as if something were swimming in their depths. "What's the point of this? I'm not a godling, Eve, I won't be bound to my promises like you."

"You will if you *decide* to be. If you had your emotions, honor would probably be a good enough reason. Without them… Consider the benefits of consistent action. It will help you avoid the consequences of rashness, because that's a weakness of this Skill, one that it disguises by its very nature. When you least feel like following the rules is when it will be most important for you to do so. And right now, while you're not bound by emotion, that's when you'll be creating them."

I stood. "Take some time to think. I'm going to keep the barrier up, just signal me when you're ready to come out. Try to look contrite when you do. The others are pretty upset with you." I turned and walked back through the Chaos barrier.

Muddy thoughts about promises and the power they could hold swirled through my mind. What was it that Weaver had said? "Believe so strongly that when you tell me, I am forced to believe as well, because I know your words have imprinted their truth on the world." What, then, if I made a promise to myself? A binding oath to follow through with something. Sam may not be a godling, but I was. If, as Weaver suggested, such a promise could imprint itself on reality, could a wayward thought be manifest into a certainty through force of will alone? Was this, perhaps, the true power of the gods?

The idea was too big, and I found immediately that I was having difficulty in wrapping my mind around it. Besides, I already knew that making a promise wouldn't guarantee the result if it was something outside of my control.

Starting over, I considered the thought from a different angle. If, somehow, I had access to a Skill that would allow me to send even the most basic information back in time to my past self, I could create causal time loops which would allow me to, in a way, game reality.

Needing an example for myself, I made up a game in which there were a thousand numbered boxes, and within one sat a hunk of gold, but I was only allowed to open a single box, and I didn't know which box held the gold. I could decide—could promise myself—to send the number of each box I checked, along with whether or not it contained the hunk of gold, back in time to myself. If I checked the wrong box, I'd get that information *before* I started checking, and so could skip that box and check the next one, then send the new result back to my past self.

Before I even started checking the boxes, as soon as I promised to do so, I would receive information from a future version of myself telling me exactly which box to check. Then all I'd need to do was check that box, verify the presence of the gold, and then send the same answer back in time. The alternate versions of myself that had checked all the wrong boxes would exist as their message, the pure data they had revealed about the world, but the timelines they existed within would never happen.

The important idea was that it became possible to actually force-compute the best of all possible choices, based on pre-determined criteria… Except, of course, that such a Skill didn't, to my knowledge, exist.

I stopped mid-step. I blinked. Someone said something to me, but they weren't bleeding or on fire, so I ignored them.

My hand smacked loudly against my forehead. I'd almost skipped over the *actually* important idea. I *did* know someone with a Skill that was basically time travel. What was predicting the future if not another way to say you were sending information into the past?

The Oracle could see all those threads of probability.

With a strong enough determination to find and send her a message, no matter what happened, I could control every possible future where I managed to stay alive long enough to do so. She would see all the different possible futures converging onto that eventual conversation, as long as I kept my promise to myself. By doing that, I could send the current version of her a message. Theoretically.

I took a couple deep breaths, closed my eyes, and said, "I'm going to find the Oracle, even if I have to keep searching for her until I die, and when I see her, I'm going to tell her that I wanted to talk to her at this moment, which at that point will be the past. Right here, right now. If possible, I'll use Ichi's Skill to find her more quickly. I'll ask her to please meet me here, even if it no longer makes sense within that timeline." If this worked, it was just further proof that the future wasn't immutable. Whatever may have been predicted could be changed.

I opened my eyes to find Zed staring at me with consternation. "What?" he said.

I looked around, but found no signs of the Oracle. I sighed.

"Well, I have to search for the Oracle and give her a message," I said. I was feeling disappointed, but the whole point of making the determination was that I would do it even if I'd already learned that it wouldn't work, because otherwise it wouldn't work. Still, now that I'd calmed down a bit, it felt more like I was playing a prank on myself than coming up with some clever idea. I turned around, planning to check on Ichi, when the ground began to shake.

I felt the undulations through the pads of my feet and flexed my clawed toes to improve my traction. A few hundred feet out from the little campsite, a white ripple spread outward through the dead ground, followed by a surge of thousands of slender white threads that shot up and fell together, creating an egg-like cocoon.

A section of the cocoon fell away, and the Oracle stepped out.

Chapter 14

The Devil pulls the strings which make us dance.
 — Charles Baudelaire

EVERY MOVEMENT the Oracle made as she approached the edge of our small camp released music into the air.

My teammates stood back warily, preparing their Skills, hands inching toward weapons. Ichi, still incapacitated, was ignored in favor of the greater threat.

I released Sam from the shield bubble of Chaos so he could help us if necessary.

I cleared my throat awkwardly as the Oracle arrived in front of me. "Umm… Could you meet me at these coordinates, about ten seconds ago?" I said.

Her stone eyes seemed to always look sad somehow, though the tear grooves worn into her cheeks were dry. "You are clever, godling, to request my presence this way. If you ever do it again, I will kill you."

At one point, that threat might have made my knees buckle. Now, I smiled. "Well, maybe you could give me some other way to contact you? I promise I won't do it this way again…unless the fate of the world is at stake."

Grudging amusement mixed with the anger on her face, but she simply nodded. "You have questions, Eve-Redding. Ask them quickly, for there is not enough time."

"Was this always going to happen, or did we—did *I*—screw up somehow?"

"Defeating Pestilence would never have been the end, though there are other paths you could have taken which would have given you more time to prepare."

I sighed and bowed my head, feeling my shoulders droop as some of the weight of doubt fell away. "So the last time we met— you telling me to abandon the others to the God of Knowledge so I could live and grow to defeat the Abhorrent—that was just reverse-psychology?" It still made me a little angry to think of, but this wasn't the time to get in a fight. I needed information from her. "But *why*?" I couldn't help adding.

"Because you were telling the wrong story to yourself. I saw your path straying from the one we needed, as you began to believe that you were selfish and self-serving, and changed to match that internal narrative. You would have abandoned the world. You should have realized by now, godling, that words have power. This is true even for mortals, but especially so for us. I had to give you a shock so you would change your inner story."

It took me a few moments to fully process what she was saying as I tried to reconcile the idea. Was she telling the truth?

While I was thinking, Adam spoke. "So have you been manipulating us this whole time, then? Have any of our choices actually been our own?"

She tossed him a dismissive glance, the slight movement giving off the sound of wind through reed flutes. "I do not steer your every movement as if playing with dolls, mortal. It would be coun-terproductive, and a waste of my resources. I may be a goddess, but there is much to do, and we are not all-powerful. At most, I simply provide choices. Sometimes, those choices are misleading, but I never force action. If Eve had chosen to let you all die and escape the fight with my father, I would have kept my word and started searching for another candidate to be the Spark."

She'd told me the last time I saw her that I was not the only option for deliverance among the mortals, but she simply saw me succeeding more often than the others. It was...*relieving* to be reminded of that. But I also remembered the visions I'd seen in the Spire of Prophecy, of the failed versions of the Seal of Nine before me. "We're not special. *I'm* not special," I said. "But how many times have you tried and failed before?"

She stared at me for a moment before answering. "We have been trying since only slightly after our creation. In human years, it has been millennia upon millennia. A longer time than a short-lived mortal can truly understand."

I nodded, letting some of the cold anger seep out to buoy me up. "It's quite too late to try again now, don't you think?"

Once again, there was a pause before she answered. Wraith could sense the cold sweat beading up on my teammates' skin from the combined pressures of our power in the air. "Success with another is...unlikely." There was a weight of grief in the last word that told me what she really meant was "impossible." "But as long as I exist, *we* exist, we cannot stop trying. It is our primary purpose."

Torliam raised his head from its slightly bowed position as if the movement were an effort. "Why do you not fight the Abhorrent directly? Surely, if all the gods would join forces, it would stand no chance against you."

"If only that were so." Water welled up from her stone eyes and slid down the lines in her cheeks.

A cold foreboding spread through me, partially my own, and partially traces of my teammates' emotions coming through the drop of my blood that lived within them. I realized we'd been wasting time on useless questions. "What is the Abhorrent?" I asked with numb lips.

"There are no words to describe it properly in the languages of mortals, for it is *other*. The question you have asked is the reason behind my own birth, the reason that Knowledge and Time joined to create me. I see the web of existence, and through it, myriad paths of the future. However, I was created to look *back*, beyond my own creation, beyond the birth of the first god, to the time before. Reconstructing a single past, discarding all untrue possibilities while so far separated by both time and space, it is like trying to read at night by the light of a single star."

I thought about what the woodland guardians had taught us of the Seeds, and I speculated, but I waited silently for her to continue.

"There is no end to the cleverness of mortals, nor to their curiosity," she said. "Beyond the *breaks*, there are eldritch creatures. They team like tadpoles in a drying pond, ever-hungry, ever-searching, and *alien*. Unlike your myths would suggest, mortals existed long before we gods. Their cleverness grew almost fast enough to keep up with their curiosity, but your wisdom has always been weaker than your greed. The mortals opened a doorway to the *breaks*, and as they looked through, a small creature on the other side looked back. It was hungry, and so it entered the mortal world, and the mortals were afraid.

"It had not known thought before, nor emotion, or any of the concepts mortals believe to be so universal. At that point, from them, it *learned*. Even now, I cannot tell what might have happened, if by chance, it had learned differently. For it learned fear, and fear's companions, and as it learned, it became."

Her words seemed to penetrate deep into my bones, making them shudder and grate against themselves like nails on a chalkboard, and I knew she could not be lying.

"The mortals were not all foolish, and they realized the danger of their actions quickly. They did not know it was too late already, but even so they did not try to undo their mistake, only to create a counter to it. They studied the Abhorrent, small and only beginning to grow, and they marveled at it. They knew better than to bring through another of its kind, but they craved its power. They imagined godly servants and all-powerful weapons. They imagined these in the hands of their enemies. They imagined the Abhorrent of the future.

"And so, with cleverness now lost to time, they created the first god, meant to be a counter to the Abhorrent. It was only a single Seed, a combination of alien material and mortal virus, and bound to a concept just as the Abhorrent was, extending invisible, hungry mouths not to the place beyond the *breaks*, but to other universes deemed disposable. Yet that Seed multiplied, and also learned, and together the many parts of a whole took form and gave voice to thought. The mortals experimented, creating brothers and sisters for the first god. While they worked, the Abhorrent grew. Then the mortals became desperate to undo what they had wrought, to send the creature that had *learned* and *become* back where they had found it and to close the doorway. Even as they sealed it away, it destroyed them, and their world, acting only as its nature demanded. And so the gods walked a dead world alone."

The Oracle paused, looking around warily, and the rest of us shuffled and took the opportunity to gather our composure.

I motioned for the others to draw closer to the little fire and added some more fuel onto it to ward off the chill shivering its way through their cores.

Turning back to us, the Oracle continued. "Due to the nature of the concepts embodied by the first gods, they felt the urge to create. And so the first of those you know as Estreyans came to be, flesh formed in the image of our own creators, but also bearing a piece of ourselves. We cleansed the world and breathed life into it again as we were able, and as we continued to learn, our mortal children multiplied, lived, and died. It was a time of hope."

I wondered how humans could look the same as Estreyans. We were not even so different from the woodland guardians and the gods themselves. The same features and basic body structure seemed to indicate some connection to these ancestor beings that had created the gods. I wanted to ask, but, remembering her warning, decided that it wasn't the most relevant question under a time limit.

"The time of hope did not last long. Though exiled, the Abhorrent could not forget, could not go back to the unwritten half-consciousness of the time before it learned of fear and mortality. It knew the door existed. And as you know, Eve-Redding, a door has two sides."

I suppressed a shudder.

"We saw hints of its presence, and so we gathered the mortals, and we ran. We built this new world, giving it wonder and struggle and all the things a mortal needs to grow. But we could not escape the Abhorrent, for darkness lives in the hearts of all mortals, and we had brought it with us. I was created then, to search for an answer. I saw what the gods who came before had already known, that none of us had the ability to undo the Abhorrent. We could only hope to create a new god, one with just the right synthesis of mortal concepts to allow it to do so in our place."

"And that's me?" I whispered.

"No. But it could be."

"I need to become a god before being able to defeat it?"

"Yes. The *right* god."

"How am I supposed to destroy the Abhorrent? I mean…what do I—*How?*"

"You have already discovered the way. You know how."

"What?"

"Ask another question. Time runs short."

I opened my mouth to ask where we could find the Abhorrent's current Avatar, but she raised her hand to forestall me.

"You must not ask this question now. Think of another, and quickly." Once again, she looked around as if searching for danger.

I couldn't help but look around, too, but I saw nothing. Still, something in the back of my mind told me I was being watched, and I remembered the sudden monster infestation at the Spire of Prophecy, and the Remnant *scryer's* sudden death. Could the Avatar somehow sense our focus on it?

"How do I survive the Void? How do I control it?"

"Millennia ago, before they were stranded, I gave those that now call themselves the Remnants a quest. They have been diligent. They will fulfill it, and you will fulfill this one."

She waved her hand, and an ephemeral quest Window popped up in front of my face.

THE TOIL OF GENERATIONS
RECEIVE A GIFT FROM THE REMNANTS ON EARTH. IN TURN, GIFT IT TO ANOTHER.
COMPLETION REWARD: INCREASED CHANCE OF SURVIVAL
NON-COMPLETION PENALTY: ENTER THE VOID ALONE

"Can you be less cryptic?"

"*Foolish mortal,*" she hissed vehemently. "I thread the needle-head of success while buffeted by a sea of possible destruction. My words are chosen with the utmost care." Without waiting for my response, she strode right past me and through the camp.

My teammates made way for her, and though she stepped directly into the campfire on her way through, she didn't even seem to notice. She grabbed Ichi, ignoring his wide, panicked eyes and Adam's call of, "What are you doing?"

She carried Ichi back to the gigantic spiderweb egg-sac and took him inside.

"What is she doing?" Adam asked me.

I sent Wraith tentatively squeezing in through the walls, but couldn't make out much detail within because of the blinding strength of the Oracle's Seed glow. Both the goddess and the man were silent, standing in front of what looked like a birdbath. "She's showing him something, I think. Everyone, let's get ready to go. I don't want to be waiting around once she leaves."

Only a few minutes later, the side of the egg-sac opened up again, but Ichi came out alone, unattended by the goddess. He wasn't wearing any of his bindings or the Skill suppressor. He was trying to hide it, but I could see the signs of tears in his eyes and pale sweat on his forehead. As he walked toward the camp, the egg-sac of giant spiderwebs splashed back into the ground like water and disappeared as if it had never been there, and the Oracle with it.

Ichi patted his chest and ignored the tension among the rest of us, strolling toward the *Swiftsure*. "Well, let us go. I could take us to the nearest Shortcut directly, but I doubt you want to leave your ship behind." He paused, his bloodshot eyes sweeping over us. "I still despise you all, to be clear. But she said we did not have the leisure of being enemies if we wanted to make it to Tartarus on time."

"WHAT DID SHE SAY TO HIM?" Torliam murmured to me as we followed the man who'd been our captive only minutes before into the *Swiftsure*.

"She said nothing, only showed me what could have been, and what might be," Ichi said over his shoulder in a tone than failed to be truly nonchalant. "It was convincing. But then, I suppose she already knew it would be."

"So you're on our side, now?" I asked.

Kris turned away, hiding her face, and Gregor scowled at Ichi as if he could impale the man with his gaze alone. The boy's fingers played at the blades sheathed at his waist, obviously wishing he could.

I sat down and strapped in beside Ichi. If he tried anything, I would be ready to stop him.

He gave me a look of contempt. "No. We merely have the same goal for the foreseeable future. When this is over, I plan to decry you as a murderer and have you stand trial."

Jacky glared at him. "Then you're gonna join her up on the stand, no? At least Eve had a reason. You just murdered Blaine for revenge."

To my surprise, after a moment of hesitation, he nodded. "Yes. I chose my revenge knowing the consequences."

Gregor scoffed, stopped in front of the Estreyan, and spat in his face. His fingers hovered over the long daggers at his side as he waited for Ichi to retaliate.

Ichi wiped away the spittle from his cheek, giving it a look of distaste. "Postpone your hatred, child."

Gregor turned his gaze on me, faintly accusing. "We're just going to trust him all of a sudden?"

Ichi spoke before I could. "Of course not. Do not be foolish. But the Oracle has vouched for me, and as you can see, I am free and have not taken the chance to flee or to harm you, despite plenty of provocation." He shot a dark look toward Sam, who, still under the effects of Black Sun, gazed back unflinchingly. "Feel free to hate me. I will do the same toward you. But we must not sabotage each other. And besides…you all were never going to go along with the mind-control, anyway. This is just saving some time in between."

Under Torliam's command, the *Swiftsure* lifted off and flew away, on course toward the nearest Shortcut to Earth.

"I'm not sure that's true," I admitted to Ichi. "I still hadn't made up my mind, and the Oracle can be wrong. I don't know what she showed you, but I'm willing to accept your help only because the stakes are so incredibly high that I would do almost *anything* to give us a better chance." Pausing, I met the Estreyan's eyes and let Voice fill my next words. "But let me be clear. You don't need your legs and arms to use your Skill, and if you put any of my teammates in danger, I will make sure it doesn't happen a second time."

Closing his eyes, Ichi settled himself in his seat and pretended to be at ease.

I glared at him, along with most of our teammates, but the conversation fell away, replaced by the discomforting roil of too much emotion confined in too small a space.

I considered what I had learned from the Oracle. Specifically, the idea that I already knew how to kill the Abhorrent. Another one of its kind, from beyond the breaks, could probably do it, or at least lock it in a stalemate, but it would have to start out much stronger than the initial Abhorrent was, because there wouldn't be time for the new one to grow before the Abhorrent realized the threat. It was a dangerous idea, and besides, I knew somehow it wasn't really the answer.

I did have an idea about how you might kill such a creature, but I was conscious that we still knew nothing of the Avatar. It could be anywhere and do anything, and even Pestilence had been able to gather information on us without our knowledge. It was dangerous to put thoughts like that into the world, just in case. What if it could somehow know and counter my plan? I turned my mind to another problem instead.

"The fruit of life," I said.

My teammates looked to me, waiting for me to explain myself.

"We know they function off similar principles to the Seeds," I continued. "The dimension tunneling to gather energy from elsewhere, and the power conversion that uses that energy to create some sort of effect in our world." I was simplifying it in the extreme, not even getting into the way the Seeds allowed the brain to offload the processing power to use and control certain Skills, but the basic idea was a good enough model. "The fruit could be very similar to, say, a thousand Seeds put into Resilience, except Seeds repair and replenish themselves, but the fruit doesn't. They siphon power from elsewhere and use that power to impose a static state taken from an initial reading. Superficially, it seems like the perfect counter to the Void. It might even help me retain my sanity, in addition to my physical well-being. The problem is, dimension tunneling is delicate and strenuous, and that's what's going to break down first. As soon as it does, the fruit will stop healing me. One fruit is recorded to have saved one particularly reckless warrior from life-threatening injuries almost four thousand times, but in that case lost potency after only seventy-five years."

"What are you getting at?" Jacky asked. "I don't understand."

"If we imagine the Void has similar destructive capabilities to a normal Chaos attack, how long do you think it would take me, or Behelaino, to impose life-threatening injuries on someone submerged within our power four thousand times?"

Torliam frowned. "Minutes, at most."

"Oh," Jacky said, her sentiment mirrored in the expressions of the others.

"So you need more than one fruit," Adam said.

I shook my head. "That might work, but I'm not willing to put you guys in danger by taking yours."

"We could ask the guardians for more."

I looked at Adam like one might look at a child who has just told you they want to be a dolphin when they grow up.

"We could threaten them for more, then," Adam countered, undeterred.

I didn't want to do that, though I had to accept the logic behind his argument. "We'd have to kill them, and I'm hoping they'll be more use to us alive. The woodland guardians ran me through a lot of different exercises that are supposed to help preserve me against the Void's effects, but I think I need to start training my Resilience, both mental and physical. I was hoping you guys could help with that."

"Do you think we'll have enough time for more training to actually make a difference?" Adam asked.

I shrugged. "It's not just about gaining levels in Resilience, I think. The Seeds within me have…instincts. I want to get used to what it's like to continuously protect the integrity of my body and mind against outside attack. I want to practice."

The *Swiftsure* arrived at the closest Shortcut in a few hours. Luckily, it was big enough to transport the entire ship with us still in it, so we wasted no time.

Ichi, who had never been on Earth before, was wide-eyed with amazement as he looked through one of the small windows at the suddenly panicking customs enforcement on the other side. "My Skill will be useful here, once it has time to catalogue the entire planet. Really, is this where *all* you humans came from? It is only as big as one, perhaps two, Estreyan world levels."

His smug superiority reminded me of Torliam, and I raised my eyebrow at my Estreyan teammate.

Torliam scowled back at me, understanding the comparison I was silently making.

Our arrival into the small customs facility had been unannounced, and it took some convincing and flashing of credentials to get us out without the usual inspection and days-long quarantine required for all alien matter arriving on Earth. They couldn't have stopped us anyway, but it would have been highly counter-productive to fight our way through.

From there, at high altitude and almost maximum speed, we arrived at the hidden island of the Remnants quickly.

They seemed to have been expecting us, or were at least not surprised by our arrival.

I was very surprised, however, to find both my mother and Reglium were there to greet us as we exited the ship.

Before I quite realized what was happening, Reglium had recognized Ichi, thrown forward a grasping hand, and clamped down on the other Estreyan with his body-takeover Skill.

Ichi stiffened and arched back like he'd been electrocuted, barely managing to remain standing upright.

"Peace!" Torliam called, raising a calming hand toward Reglium.

Reglium's glare wavered between Torliam and Ichi for a few seconds. "What is your meaning, brother? Do you not see who walks beside you? Or are you now taking up friendships with known criminals?" he sneered.

Torliam's face immediately contracted into a scowl. "I am no friend of his, but I am able to put aside my personal grudges for the fate of the world. He is free for now with the blessing of the Oracle. We are not here for you. Step aside, brother."

Reglium's glare grew only more severe at Torliam's dismissive words, but Ester said, "Do you think you know better than the Oracle, child?" and he was forced to comply.

Ichi shook himself lightly as control over his body and Skill returned to him. He gave Reglium a deadpan stare, like a hungry shark.

My mother kept a suspicious eye on Ichi as she passed by him to hug my brother.

I hesitated, unsure how to approach my mother, whether to wait for her to stop fawning over Zed or to simply move on. Meeting Ester's confident and ready gaze, I decided on the latter.

The rest of my teammates moved to follow me, but Ester held up a hand to stop them. "The inner sanctum is forbidden to outsiders. Wait here, please. We will not be long." She turned and led me away, surrounded by a seemingly unnecessary number of honor guards.

Eliahan, who walked with the honor guard, made several attempts at pompous small talk with me. I ignored him outright, addressing Ester instead. "You know why we're here?" I asked.

Ester's mouth pulled into a wistful smile as she stared into the middle distance. "Did you know that we were searching for the Champion when we were stranded here on Earth? This was before my own birth, of course. The Oracle Bestowed the youngest of that questing party with the sight and gave us a task, to be held above even fighting the Sickness or finding the Champion. Did you never wonder why we did not continue to search for our lost god or attempt to aid *you* in doing so? If not for this, we might have had the freedom to aid you, even if we could not make you aware of the full truth before it was time."

The Remnants' inner sanctum wasn't the ostentatious, semi-magical place I'd been imagining. Instead, it was a small, windowless stone room that *screamed* "unimportant." As we stepped through the door, I saw that they'd covered the walls in concealing, dampening, suppressing, and anti-scrying runes. They were strong enough to hinder Wraith, even though I was *already* inside the room. I had never noticed this little building before, and I was not sure if I had simply been unobservant during my prior stay on the island, or if the protections had kept me from placing any importance on the innocuous building.

"We were tasked to keep this secret. I advise you do the same, until the very moment you wish to make use of it," she said.

Sitting on the floor in the center of the room was a watermelon-sized, glowing power crystal, buzzing with so much confined energy I could feel it thrumming through the air.

"You've been working on this for the last few thousand *years!*" I said. I wondered for a moment how this could be more important than fighting Pestilence or searching for the God of Shaping and Molding.

She raised an eyebrow, probably guessing my thoughts. "A small knife to the brain is just as deadly as a large one. This may not seem impressive, but you must realize, Eve, this crystal holds enough energy to destroy the planet. Perhaps even twice or thrice over again."

"Enough to kill the Abhorrent?" I asked. "Is it possible to siphon the power back out of it? I mean, other than to power devices and the like? Could I use it to feed Chaos?"

She frowned sharply. "No, absolutely not. That is like saying the human body runs off warmth and electricity, so if you want to feel better you should electrocute yourself while standing in a fire. Do not attempt to channel this, Eve. Not even the gods attempt to use power not their own. It would be the height of foolishness."

"But—" I cut the rest of the incredulous statement off. Blue had used power crystals as payment before, because it could absorb the energy in them just like it did from light and warmth and emotion. "Ah," I finished simply. The quest hadn't told me to use the crystal. It was meant to be a gift twice over, and apparently, I knew the perfect recipient. What would Blue be able to do with that much energy? "Thank you," I said. "This will help."

Ester smiled wryly, staring at the crystal. "It had better. We have suffered enough for it. I will have my people pack the crystal for travel. You and your group are free to stay the night if you choose." She met my gaze. "We have fulfilled our duty and are free to act as we wish, even at the risk of our lives and bloodlines. Many of the Remnants will wish to aid you, if you have need of us."

"Is that all?" Eliahan said. "Will there be no Bestowment ceremony? We simply pack it up, and it is over, just like that?"

"It is just a power crystal. Do not be pompous," Ester said.

Eliahan flushed a little, but recovered quickly as Ester and I left, blustering at the other honor guards to pack the crystal quickly and securely.

I was walking through the compound to find my teammates when I came across my mother sitting in a small courtyard.

She stood, as if she had been waiting for me. Her face was a little pale, her expression subdued, and, to my surprise, she hesitated awkwardly before motioning for me to join her on the courtyard bench.

I did so silently, bracing myself for whatever she had to say.

"Eliahan favors you over Zed," she said.

I frowned. Was that somehow my fault?

"Looking at the two of them, it's obvious how inappropriate and damaging that attitude is from a parent." She took a deep breath, holding it for a moment before letting it out with the puff. "I've been hard on you. For a long time, not just since"—she waved her hand vaguely—"all this. I want you to know I'm sorry." She cleared her throat awkwardly, not looking at me. Before I could figure out how to respond, she spoke again. "I know you will risk your life again. Everyone around here has been talking about it, calling you a hero, a savior. Strange, hearing that about the daughter you still remember toddling around in diapers." She looked to me, finally.

I opened my mouth, then closed it again. "I suppose so," I said finally.

"Is there anything you need? Anything I can do for you?"

I shook my head. "I can't think of anything."

She gave me a bitter smile and looked away again. "I guess that's no surprise. But you'll do your best to be safe, right? You'll stay safe," she repeated firmly, as if saying it would make it so.

"I'll do my best. I prefer to be alive with all my limbs intact," I said, trying for a wry smile.

She let out an exasperated huff and stood. "You'd better. I expect you to bring your brother home safe and sound, too. And don't you think you should put more clothes on? Just because you have all those scales doesn't really make you *decent*." With a judgmental sniff, she walked off without looking back, but Wraith caught the glassy tears welling up in her eyes.

Chapter 15

Walls have ears.
  Doors have eyes.
  Trees have voices.
  Beasts tell lies.
  Beware the rain.
  Beware the snow.
  Beware the man
  You think you know.
  — Catherine Fisher

WE AGREED to stay the night, partially so Ichi would have time to catalogue the entire Earth with his Skill, and partially so the Remnants could examine the fruit of life.

The others had all been curious about what the Oracle's quest had been leading me to, but I shook my head, lips pressed together. "You'll know when it's time to use it. Before then, it's a secret. You never know who might be listening." I raised an eyebrow, my tone light, but they all understood the implication and stopped asking with not-so-subtle paranoia. Jacky and Birch even looked around as if suspecting an invisible person hiding in the room with us.

"However, it's worth noting that the Remnants are now... more free to help us than they were before. I'm not exactly sure what they might do, since it doesn't seem like they can help us locate the Avatar, but I don't want to waste any possible time or resources available to us, and I've been thinking." I rubbed my fingers against the tips of my claws, hesitating. "What happens after we defeat the Avatar? There are six more, and after that, the Abhorrent itself. We—we are going to have to deal with all of them."

They had known that, obviously, but something about saying it aloud was sobering.

Kris was the first to answer, her voice sounding very small and far away. "Do you think the stuff Testimony and Lore was saying, about there being one of us for each of the greater Trials, means there's an Avatar that…matches the Seal of Nine? One for the Veil-Piercer, Black Sun, Shadow, Summoner…? I really don't think I can handle one myself."

"I don't know," I answered truthfully. "It doesn't actually matter, though, except if that kind of link could give us clues to the Avatar's power. But, with so many previous versions of the Nine, there could be just as many different powers for the Avatars. I do know that none of us are going to be fighting alone, so it's not something you need to worry about."

"We need to better understand the warps," Zed said.

"Yes," I agreed. "I think understanding how the Abhorrent and his pieces work is the most critical piece of missing information right now."

"I've been talking to Pondslider," he said.

I tilted my head to the side slightly. "Do you think we could get the woodland guardians to help with the investigation, too? Maybe working together with the Remnants and the rest of our researchers on it?"

"I'll ask, too," Kris piped up. "I'll appeal to their sense of community and helpfulness, and Zed can appeal to their curiosity, make the warps seem like the next big scientific discovery. And if you ask the Remnants, Eve, I'm sure they'll be on it before you can even finish the sentence."

I smiled gratefully at her. "Good idea. I'll give them the contact information. The Remnants will be able to gather data and inter-face with the outside world for the woodland guardians—if the guardians agree. It doesn't require nearly as much from them as giving up the fruit did, so I'm optimistic."

We broke apart to set things in motion, and after my part was done, I found Sam sitting on the beach, looking out at the water and the faintly shimmering concealment barrier in the distance. I sat beside him, staying silent when I sensed him tense at my presence.

After a few minutes without me pressuring him, he relaxed. "I haven't come to an agreement with Black Sun," he said.

"Black Sun? Not yourself?"

He let out a humorless laugh. "Well, it's kind of hard not to think of it that way. Having Black Sun is kind of like having a split personality. I mean, I know we're still technically the same person, and I recognize that whether the Skill is active or not, but the two versions of me aren't the same, and neither of us wants to become the other."

"I'm not sure that's true," I said, frowning down at Sam, "about the two versions of you not being the same. Have you considered that maybe you can't agree with yourself, not because you're inherently a different personality under the effects of Black Sun, but because you're not being honest with yourself? The Sam with Black Sun turned on isn't perfect, but you make valid points when you're like that, you're less afraid. The Sam with all his feelings turned on understands consequences, both for himself and for others."

Sam rubbed roughly at his face. "You think all my problems go away if I just learn to *accept* myself?" he said incredulously.

"You can't just get rid of pieces of yourself," I said softly. "All parts of you need to accept the other parts. If Black Sun really does facilitate logical thinking, you should realize the negative consequences of your actions, from both your own response once the Skill wears off, and from your surroundings. And as normal Sam, you should be able to realize that there's a reason you find that Skill so addicting."

He glared out at the water.

"Keep trying. A little discomfort is worth the chance to grow. Besides, the worst that can happen is you don't get anywhere. Maybe…maybe try having a conversation with yourself? Switch

Black Sun on and off, get a feel for the details of what's changing at what level of activation. And also…" I hesitated.

"What?" His tone was still frustrated, but I could tell he wasn't directing the anger at me.

"Well, you're not alone. We've all done things we have nightmares about. I struggle with my choices, too."

He looked at me, finally, some of the agitation slipping from his face. "Right, I should have—I mean…yeah." He trailed off awkwardly, flushing all the way up to his sun-bleached hair. "Well, are you okay, about that…with Ichi, that is?"

"You get used to it," I murmured, looking out over the water. "It's like a callus, on the inside."

He didn't seem particularly appeased by that, but said nothing more than, "Right."

I wanted to stay there and watch the sun sink behind the horizon, but I couldn't help note each wasted second in the back of my mind, the pressure building under the weight of all that needed to be done until I stood and left him there to try and assuage the feeling.

I practiced withstanding Blue's drain in the Other Place while Adam shot me with increasingly powerful bolts of electricity. It…*sucked*. When I started feeling frustrated, tired tears building behind my eyes, I ended the training and went quietly to bed.

A sudden and visceral terror woke me in the night, and it took me a few ragged breaths to realize I was not in danger, and had not been the one having a nightmare.

I jumped out of bed, ran to the cabin next to my own, and burst into the room to find Torliam thrashing among torn blankets, drenched in cold sweat, the tendons in his neck standing out with tension. I reached out and grabbed him by the shoulders, yanking him up into a sitting position. I had seen flashes of the underground holding cell from NIX in my sleep, and I knew pressing him forcefully to the bed would only agitate him further.

I squeezed his shoulders, forcing myself to be calm even as he woke in confusion and fear, struggling against me. "Torliam, you are free," I said in Estreyan. "That is past, you escaped, you survived. I am here." I pressed him forward, and he allowed me to maneuver him till his head was between his knees.

He didn't need my instruction to know how to calm himself, taking deep, slow breaths and forcefully relaxing his muscles, one by one.

We didn't talk. There wasn't anything to be said, really. I doubted either of us would get any more sleep that night.

When Torliam's sweat had evaporated, I went back outside, but was surprised to find Zed lying on the roof of his own cabin, staring up at the stars. I hadn't noticed him when I woke up. How long had he been there?

I jumped atop the roof with a single leap.

Zed winced as I landed beside him, but didn't actually seem startled.

"Can't sleep?" I asked.

"Growing pains," he said shortly.

"Really?" I said, smirking. "Well, maybe you won't be such a short little human forever."

He was not amused, but didn't bicker with me like I'd been expecting. He must have not been feeling very well.

"Do you need Sam?" I asked.

"No. There's nothing he can do. I just want to relax a bit before we have to be on the move again, alright?"

"Alright," I said. "Well, let me know if you need anything. I'll just leave you be, then."

The sky lightened with pastel hints of sunrise, and I decided to see if any of the Remnants had breakfast ready. Instead, I found Gregor and Birch crouched by the corner of one of the cottages. A quick perusal with Wraith revealed that it belonged to Ichi. The boy was whispering to the tailos, who was communicating silently back with little touches to transmit telepathic thought.

I approached from behind, silently, then cleared my throat while standing over them.

Both jumped like they'd been struck by lightning, and while Gregor slipped immediately into his Shadow state and thus made no sound, Birch let out a yowl that drew more than a few glances.

"Planning something?" I asked.

Birch laid his ears flat and slunk down a little, looking around in embarrassment at his surprise, while Gregor returned to corporeality, pressing his hand to his chest and gasping. The boy glared defiantly up at me. "You're lucky I didn't panic and stab you," he said.

"Well, I need to work on my Resilience, anyway. I doubt you would have killed me. But no dodging the question, kiddo. I can't help but notice this is Ichi's cabin."

"We were trying to figure out whether we should poop in his bedroll, or just set the whole cabin on fire while he's asleep," Gregor said.

My eyes widened involuntarily.

He scoffed. "It's not like Ichi would *die*. Not like Uncle Blaine did," he finished bitterly.

I was speechless, trying to figure out how to respond to that, when Kris ran around the corner, her arms so full of various chemical containers that she couldn't even see over them. "I was thinking we should do something he can't just teleport away from. Something that'll *last*, you know?" she said. "Maybe we can make his teeth itch so bad he tries to pull them out."

My eyes widened again at the uncharacteristically vicious words coming from the tiny girl.

Gregor cleared his throat loudly, and Kris lowered the stack of chemicals to see me standing there. She paled, then tried for an innocent smile.

I snorted, torn between frustrated disappointment and chagrined amusement. "It's too late. I already heard you. Why don't you three postpone your evil plans and we go get ice-cream? They have some, and it's been way too long since we've had proper Earth ice-cream."

The three of them shared a wordless look, but Birch's happy chortle and bobbing nod decided it. He loved ice-cream almost more than he loved meat.

While we walked, I said, "I understand wanting revenge on Ichi. Do you understand why he wanted revenge on us?"

Both kids were silent at first, anger and sadness warring for dominance across their faces.

"We didn't know," Kris said. "If she was on our side, she should have *said* something. Otherwise *of course* we would think she was an enemy!" Her lower lip trembled, and she jumped atop Birch's back so she didn't have to walk so fast to keep up with us. She opened her mouth to say more, then closed it and swallowed hard. Her fists clenched around the fur at the base of Birch's neck. I half expected tears, but she blinked away the glassiness in her eyes.

Gregor shook his head, frowning. "I…I don't know. My feelings are confused," he admitted. "I don't know what to think or feel. It's sad that she died. But we weren't being evil to kill her, and it feels like he was being evil when he killed Blaine. But then I think how it felt when Blaine died, and I know *why* he did it. That doesn't *fix* anything though, everything's still wrong and sad and I really *hate* him." His voice fell to a whisper on those last words. He flickered into Shadow for a few seconds, then back, seeming calmer. "But I know we still have to stop the Abhorrent, and that's not really got anything to do with how I feel about him. So it doesn't really matter, does it?"

I reached down and held his hand, feeling equally relieved and guilty that neither of them seemed to have attached the blame for what they were feeling to me. At the same time, I felt a kind of melancholy. Kris and Gregor were asked to do so many things that they shouldn't have to, but it was easy to disregard the danger and the quests; they were of the Seal of Nine, just like the rest of us. But this…the mundane act of coming to terms with their uncle's death, and our alliance with his killer…it was the normalcy of it that made it stand out, the unfairness of a child being forced to grow up so quickly, to accept something even adults would struggle with. It was this more than anything that made me realize their childhoods had been taken from them.

WE LEFT the Remnants less than a day after we'd arrived on Earth. Tartarus was a long way away, and the Voids were even farther from the level's entrance. Ichi couldn't teleport with the ship, but if we took a Shortcut back to Estreyer and then left it behind, he could take us almost directly to the Voids.

The Remnants had given me the power crystal within a big, rune-embossed box that managed to contain any hint of the crystal's power, as well as completely block Wraith's ability to see inside.

They assured me it would protect the crystal from both damage and discovery.

I had trouble getting it to fit within my own backpack, and had to offload some of my other basic supplies, like food and water, to one of Kris's marionettes.

Gregor had handed out necklace-type containers for the fruit of life, one for each of us. "The chains will break before your neck does, but something could still apply enough pressure to suffocate you with them," he warned. "Still, you won't lose them, and we'll have immediate access to the fruit in case of an emergency."

"I designed the runes!" Kris piped up. "As long as we keep the fruit enclosed, we can wear them into the Other Place without Blue eating them, too. Some of the Remnant engineers helped," she added belatedly.

The Remnants gathered around to see us off, some of the warriors taking the opportunity to remind me, again, that they were available for whatever mission I could think to give. More than a few, those not as useful studying the warps, had wanted to come with us to Tartarus, but I'd refused them. I would call on them to fight the Avatar, but I didn't want to risk their lives before that. Plus, Ichi's Skill did have limits. The more people he teleported, the less distance he could cover, and all the marionettes counted as people, too.

Once we'd taken a Shortcut back to Estreyer and found a place to leave the *Swiftsure*, Ichi took us to Tartarus. The teleportation was instantaneous.

Wraith lurched, and I crouched down to ward off a vertigo-like sensation. I searched around us quickly for danger, and finding none, looked up at the real source of my discomposure. The sky was all wrong. Not because it lacked a sun or stars, though it did, but because it seemed to lack any end at all. It was the same reaction I'd had when, as a child, I'd realized the only thing keeping my feet to the Earth was gravity, and that "up" and "down" were really only figments of my imagination. I'd suddenly been terrified of falling off the surface of the Earth, even though I had no real reason to believe gravity would cease to exist.

My teammates, even the marionettes, reacted similarly. Only

Ichi managed to maintain his composure, and even he crouched a little, looking up.

"Thanks for the warning," Gregor said irritably, his lip curling up into a sneer.

"Words would have done little to prepare you," Ichi said. "Our destination is that direction," he pointed, "I could have deposited us directly in front of the Voids, but the area near the Voids is dangerous even for me, and it would not do to surprise the Warden, if we wish to live. I thought it best to approach cautiously."

Most of our supplies had been left behind on the ship, but Ichi had at least warned us that it would be dark, so we were all wearing headlamps. Some of us could produce light through our Skills, but that required concentration, and that we not be separated. We turned on our headlamps, checked our weapons, and started off in the direction Ichi had pointed.

Tartarus was apparently an absurdly gigantic cave with no ceiling. Drops of water fell from the empty sky occasionally, and had created stalagmites and little trickling streams that fed into the occasional shallow pool. There were no plants except for the sporadic patches of glowing fungus or mushrooms, but there were creatures.

Dead creatures.

Except they moved, so maybe not "dead."

There were little blackbirds with no flesh, whose feathers had fallen away from everywhere except the wings and tail, so I could see right through between the thin bones of their torso, shed snake skins that moved as if they were alive, and little puffs of wind that seemed sentient and scattered as we approached.

None attacked, so we let them be.

Eventually, we came to the bottom of a set of stairs. The stone steps climbed up into the darkness with nothing to support them. I looked up, following the stairs as they wove back and forth, turning and circling and even, at one point, making a loop like some sort of Escher-inspired roller-coaster. Wraith could sense farther than my eyes could see, but even it couldn't reach the stairs' destination.

"Is this it?" I asked Ichi.

"The Voids are above us. This is the path," he said.

"And the Warden?"

"It wanders. If we are lucky, we will not meet it. It is said to be undefeatable."

"Is it a god?" I asked. "Or a monster?"

"Both," Ichi said in a soft voice. "Or perhaps neither. Not much is known of it. Most who enter Tartarus do not return. I have never seen it."

Kris climbed atop one of her marionettes, settling into a harness built into its shoulders. "Maybe we can talk to it, like the woodland guardians. If it's a god, it will be sentient."

"If it moves to attack," I said, "our best bet is just to have Ichi teleport us away immediately."

Torllam frowned. "But we will need to get past it to reach the Voids. Also, I suspect this expedition will take some time, first to safely inspect the effects of the Voids, and then for Eve to attempt to understand them. If the Warden is hostile, simply running away will not serve our purpose."

"We'll fight if we have to." I hoped we wouldn't, as it would waste time and effort. But I wouldn't allow myself to fear this Warden. After all, if we couldn't even defeat a god, how could we hope to destroy an Avatar with a conduit of power right back to the Abhorrent?

I began to walk up the stairs, and the others followed.

We climbed for a very long time, till Gregor's legs started to ache and he needed to be carried by a marionette like Kris. Zed kept up with unflinching determination, as though he had dozens of Seeds in Strength and Stamina, though I knew, like any mostly-human being, he must be exhausted. He even played with the kids a bit, carrying them on his shoulders.

I was very aware that the entirety of Tartarus was cut off from the rest of Estreyer. We would be receiving no contact from anyone outside, with or without communication relay beacons. Anything could be happening beyond this endless darkness. The farther we went, the more that feeling that I might simply start falling upward scraped at my nerves. It was only when Jacky, who was more sensitive to gravity because her Skill allowed her to subvert it, announced that we were getting lighter did I realize it wasn't all just my imagination.

"There's something above us," she said. "I can feel it pulling on us."

Gregor frowned into the darkness above our heads, which the fun-house stairs disappeared into. "A mass large enough to have its own gravitational pull? Maybe a floating island?"

I shuddered as the stairs took us in a loop that we somehow didn't fall off of even as my head faced toward the direction I was sure at some point had been "down." "I think it's going to be a little more bizarre than that," I said.

We'd been climbing for another few hours—even I was starting to feel the mental fatigue—when the steps began to tremble ever so faintly. It was extra disconcerting because we were all feeling the effects of the gravity reduction by now. I sank Wraith into the steps and determined that the disturbance was coming from wherever we were climbing to, but it was still too far away for me to see or sense. "Let's move faster," I urged, paranoia lifting my scales like the hackles on a dog.

The trembling only grew more noticeable the higher we climbed, taking on the cadence of a rhythmic pounding like footsteps.

Then we saw the god walk out of the darkness.

He was upside down, his feet disappearing into the distance, confirming my second theory about our destination. But that wasn't what made my scales lift and my lips pull back in an instinctive snarl.

He was made of bones held together and filled in with billowing black ash. The upper half of his skull looked like a deer's, but the lower half was just an ovaloid hole of darkness that disappeared into the ash of his torso. At least a dozen arms poked out of his amorphous abdomen, each skeletal hand holding the handle of a cage. They would have looked like bird cages, except for their size and the remains of captured Estreyans disintegrating from age within.

I drew in an almost silent gasp of fear as something instinctive inside me cried "Danger!" As if to combat it, rage welled up and lent some chill to the blood pounding through my veins.

"Do you think we can talk to it?" Kris whispered. "It doesn't..."

The instinct to tell my teammates to start running as fast as thcy could warred with the instinct to crouch down and hide, hoping that the god would pass by unnoticed.

I bit my lip hard enough to break the skin, letting the taste of blood and the flush of pain in my cheeks speed my thoughts. "Look away," I warned, doing the same myself. I was wary of what might happen if we met the gaze of those empty eye-sockets directly. I searched with Wraith instead, looking for a way out. We were stuck on the staircase with nowhere to go but forward or back. Ink wings likely wouldn't last long enough to get us back down to the ground or up to the hidden land above.

I could attack the god, but without anywhere for my teammates to run to or attack from, it seemed a needlessly reckless move. And really, I was trying to stop being needlessly reckless, because I always seemed to regret it afterward.

"Ichi—" I started.

Before I could complete my command for him to teleport us away, the god turned its deer-like head toward us, those soulless, empty pits for eyes sweeping over the team.

It didn't need us to meet its gaze, apparently. It wasn't interested in talking, either.

In an instant, the world went dark, and silent, and *empty*. I tried to clamp dowh on my throat muscles to avoid letting out a scream, but found I couldn't even feel my own body, as if my mind had been ripped from it. Then, I really did want to scream, but I couldn't, because I had no mouth.

Interlude 4

After the call to his silent friends cut off, Reed called Demi again, and then tried Lucas.

Neither picked up.

He'd just grabbed the handle of his bedroom door, ready to go after them, when it turned on its own. Already on edge from everything he'd experienced that day, Reed let out a sharp scream of alarm and jumped back.

His dad poked his head into the room, raising one eyebrow, bemused. "It's time for dinner."

"Would it be possible for me to skip it?" Reed asked, unconsciously shuffling a little farther back when his dad smiled.

"No," the man said succinctly. "This is family time." The smile was wider now, just like the expression he gave the camera while reporting the weather. It reminded Reed of an iconic superhero from an antique comic book.

Reed knew clearly that things would go very wrong if he acted "abnormal" and tried to go against his dad. So, very aware of the silver knife in his pocket and ready to flinch away at the slightest sign of a mirror, he followed his dad down to the dining room, where his mom had just finished setting the table.

Reed's eyes flicked to the silver display cabinet in the corner, but he was too afraid to try to make them look at their reflections in a silver spoon or something.

In the end, he sat down to eat without doing anything, feeling like a coward. He consoled himself with the list of emergency numbers he'd copied to the link on his desk. As soon as dinner was over, he would keep calling and demanding help until he got a professional to actually listen and *do something*. He would save his parents, and his friends, too. It was even possible that one of the local enforcers would notice their calls in the record, or even had already responded. A team could already be on the way to help.

He tried to cheer himself with that bit of optimism, but watching his parents smile unnaturally and make forced small talk while he remembered the way his call with Demi and Lucas had gone silent made dread seep into his very bones.

He choked down as much food as he could despite his lack of appetite, and when he'd finished, asked to be excused.

"Don't forget your homework!" his mom called after him as he placed his dish in the sink and ran back up the stairs.

When he reached the hallway, a sound from his dad's office made him pause. The link on the desk was on, and it seemed to be playing the news. Thinking back to what Demi had said about the pedestrians entranced by whatever was playing on the billboard screen, Reed decided not to go in. Instead, he stood by the door and listened to his dad's familiar voice giving the weather report.

Did his dad leave that channel playing on purpose? Maybe it was some kind of clue. Usually the man said that watching himself on the screen made him feel awkward and phony, as if he were watching some actor pretend to be him.

"The forecast is cloudy with a chance of Cthulhu attacks," his dad's recorded voice announced, completely deadpan.

Wasn't that the joke his dad had made that morning before leaving? It wasn't the kind of thing you'd say unless you were making a joke. Had he done it on purpose, a plea for help? Could the parasite controlling him be stupid enough to think that was the *actual* forecast?

Frowning, Reed listened for a while longer. He noticed nothing else strange, so he continued on to his bedroom. When he'd been under the control of his own parasite, he'd consciously noticed nothing strange about his actions or those of the people around him, but Demi and Lucas had both showed signs of hostility when questioned, and Demi hadn't seemed to find anything strange about suggesting that he put on makeup with her, though he'd never so much as played with his mom's lipstick.

He sighed as he closed the door behind himself. He didn't have enough information, and gathering more was inherently dangerous, especially now that he was alone in lucidity.

He tried calling Demi and Lucas a couple more times, and when that failed, moved on to the emergency numbers. None of them were local, and the automated voice warned him that if he was currently in danger, he should hang up and call his local enforcers, and then thanked him for his patience as he waited for the next available human operator.

He ended up having to pee, which was an ordeal consisting of him blindfolding himself and feeling his way into the bathroom next to his room while holding out the silver butter knife like a weapon, then fumbling around blindly for a couple minutes.

When he got back to his room, he was still on hold, so he decided to see if there was anyone on the local EDF boards who had also noticed what was happening. It had started at least a few days ago, but might have been gaining influence even before that.

To his surprise, he did find a thread on the local boards which seemed to be relevant.

You are viewing thread: "New Horror-Themed Player, or Am I Going Crazy?"

ORIGINAL POSTER "HANGIN-WITH-MY-GNOMIES" SAYS:

So maybe I'm going crazy? I've got this little stream that runs through my backyard, and last night I went out there to catch my cat. I got pretty close to the water because I thought I saw him in the bushes on the other side, and with the moon reflecting off the water, I saw myself. Except there was some next-level horror film shit in the reflection, too.

It looked like a super thin, bald man with super

stretched out arms and legs, and he was perching on my shoulders like a monkey in a tree.

This wasn't like those stories you hear where you catch a glimpse of some ghost out of the corner of your eye for a second, but when you actually look there's nothing there. I stared at it for a good fifteen seconds, alright? I could feel it on my shoulders.

Then my cat came running up like it was being chased by a firecracker, and when I looked back, my reflection on the water looked just the same.

So, what do you think? Do I live near a new Player with some creepy-as-hell Skill, or am I going crazy?

I've gone out to the stream to look a few more times today, but I haven't noticed anything strange, except I can't stop imagining I feel something pressing down on my shoulders.

POSTER "55FINGERS" SAYS:

Definitely going crazy.

POSTER "STARVASCULAR" SAYS:

Perhaps you're especially sensitive to the supernatural? Has anyone died in your house, or maybe drowned in that stream?

POSTER "NOT JAMES BOND" SAYS:

Attention-thirsty much?

Well, I'll bite. If it is a Player, that's a pretty weird Skill. Still, it didn't harm you, right? Maybe they're friendly.

POSTER "ENFORCER DAWSON" SAYS:

Not James Bond, "They're friendly?" What about a creepy stretched-out bald guy secretly sitting on your shoulders says "friendly" to you? OP, if you really suspect Player involvement, call your local enforcers.

POSTER "HOLYSTONE" SAYS:

Players are all minions of the Devil. Hangin-With-My-Gnomies, if I were you I'd sit down and pray for protection. The enforcers definitely won't be able to give it to you if you're infested with demons. I hear there's a petition to publicly register all Players and those with the corrupted gene. Maybe if we did, we'd be able to avoid situations like yours.

POSTER "THOT PATROL" SAYS:

Oh. God. Well, I thought I was crazy. I saw something too. I bought this old silver teapot from the market, and when I polished it up, I saw myself without any skin. Well I was shocked and frightened, so I tossed it out my window and it's been sitting outside next to my house for the last few hours. Until I saw this thread, I was pretty sure it was just some sort of prank teapot that I was stupid enough to fall for and buy, but I was too weirded out to go pick it up. But now...I'm worried.

POSTER "HANGIN-WITH-MY-GNOMIES" SAYS:

Okay, guys, it gets worse. I'm the original poster of this thread. Except, I have absolutely no memory of creating it, and I'm actually having a hard time remembering what the topic is even as I write this. If not for the automatic notifi-cations I get whenever someone posts or follows here, I would have never known that my memory was wiped. I *swear* I'm not making this up. Something's going on.

POSTER "NOT JAMES BOND" SAYS:

OP, are you messing with us? It seems likely, but in the very small likelihood you are being serious, I feel obligated to advise you to call the enforcers. Unauthorized use of a Skill, especially a hostile Skill, on a civilian will land them in jail.

Reed was filled with adrenaline, which seemed to help to counteract some of the fatigue that had built up from all the stress. Finally, the call he'd been making was picked up by a person. He smiled as they introduced themselves in a tired voice. They would be able to help. It wasn't until Reed heard a small creak in the floorboards behind him that he realized he'd been so engrossed he forgot to be cautious.

"What are you doing?" his mom said.

He jumped and had to hold back a scream, turning to face her.

She was standing right next to him, looming over him. She was still smiling widely, though a muscle by her eye was jumping like her cheeks had cramped from the strain of holding the same exaggerated expression for hours. A meat cleaver shone ominously in her hand. "Didn't I tell you to do your homework?" she asked, tilting her head a little too far to the side to be natural.

Chapter 16

I have loved the stars too fondly to be fearful of the night.
— Sarah Williams

NORMAL PEOPLE DON'T THINK about how much they rely on their five senses. Humans can lose one or two and still function, but without all of them, we might as well be just a brain in a jar. Without the cadence of our breath or the thump of our heartbeat, even our grasp on the passage of time quickly loses its coherence.

My teammates' fear filtered through our blood bonds, only exacerbating my own. If not for Wraith, I might have succumbed to a panic attack. Eventually, some time before I wasted away and died, hysteria would have devolved into insanity.

Wraith had no sense of substance or warmth or vibration as it normally did, but I could still sense the glow of Seed power. It shone like the sun from the god's core, overpowering everything else. But without anything to ground me, all I could do was concentrate harder. I reigned in the Chaos that had begun to roil out of me and strained Wraith for clarity. As my mind adjusted, I became able to distinguish the god's core from its body. The cage I was imprisoned inside was technically part of the god's body, too. My teammates were held within their own cages, dim blobs of power that I could sense only faintly. I didn't sense any of the marionettes, either because they didn't have Seeds of their own, or because they'd been left behind.

Even as I clamped down on my panic, I felt some of my teammates doing the same. Kris was the fastest to regain herself, though Birch followed right behind her. Torliam seemed to calm in response to my own composure.

The rest of them were not handling the god's attack well. Adam was jerking spasmodically, arcs of lightning crawling over his body and branching out through the bars of his cage.

Gregor was flickering between his Shadow state and normal.

Jacky had grown so much that she was pressed against the bars of her cage, forced into a fetal position.

I sent a Window message to everyone who could receive one, which excluded only Torliam, Birch, and Ichi. I hoped that the VR chips still worked past whatever the god had done.

—Don't panic, guys. We're safe, he's just got us in his cages. Can any of you still sense anything? Wraith is still partially working for me.—
-Eve-

They seemed to find the appearance of the VR chip Window a comfort, but I could feel it wasn't enough. I remembered that more than involuntary spillover of emotion could come from the blood bonds. Torliam had, perhaps more than once, purposefully sent me anger through our bond, even before I had shared my blood with him in return. Now, I did my best to do the same, projecting forced calm and cold clarity.

It seemed to help more than the VR Window, and the backlash of panic from the others ebbed away.

—Veil-Piercer still works. I can see the cracks in the world, but that's it.—
-Zed-

—Summon is still working, too. But we're moving away

FROM THE STAIRCASE TOO FAST. I'VE GOT A COUPLE FLIGHT-
CAPABLE MARIONETTES, AND THEY'RE FOLLOWING US, BUT I'M
ABOUT TO LOSE MY CONNECTION TO THE REST.—
-KRIS-

I KNEW how devastating that would be for Kris. She kept the same spirits in the same bodies, usually. They had become her friends, and over time developed personalities. I could only hope she would be able to reclaim the same spirits after they were forcefully ripped from the marionettes.

—I'VE GOT NOTHING.—
-ADAM-

—EVERYTHING IS GONE EXCEPT THE VR CHIP.—
-JACKY-

WORKING QUICKLY, I created an updating, three-dimensional mini-map Window and sent it to everyone. Hopefully, it would help to give them a bit more grounding in reality, even though it was only the vague, glowing reproduction that Wraith had managed. Then, I pushed the Skill out to its limits, searching for anything that could increase our options. The Warden was the biggest god I'd ever encountered, the ground his feet walked on kilometers away. Wraith could barely reach it. There wasn't much cover down there, but the existence of somewhere to land, at least, would have had me sighing in relief if I could feel my lungs.

I spun up a plan, weaving ideas into something coherent almost as quickly as the Oracle wove her webs. I tested my idea by reaching out with a solidified tendril of Chaos and tugging on the bars of the cage next to my own. It swung gently, and though the bony claw holding the handle adjusted its grip slightly, the god did not retaliate or seem to notice my interference. I waited a few seconds to be sure, then adjusted Chaos's characteristics, disinte-grating a small part of one bar.

That got his attention. The hand holding that cage lifted as the glow of the god's power swirled and turned like a poked animal. The Warden examined the cage with his empty eye sockets, and then, with a swirl of black ash that felt like a grumble, lowered the cage again.

I was satisfied. Chaos would work against his body and the bars of the cages.

—Zed, get ready to use Veil-Piercer. I'm going to need you to open the biggest rip you can, then close it again immediately as soon as we're all in the Other Place. Everyone else, get ready to activate your wings as soon as I free you from your cages. The god shouldn't be able to affect us in the Other Place.—
-Eve-

I received a smattering of affirmative replies but Zed's return Window said:

—The Other Place still isn't very big. If we enter in mid-air, we might end up falling all the way through it and into whatever would be beyond the Veil without Blue. We could die.—
-Zed-

—We're going to have to make sure we stabilize our positions immediately and descend "up" to the ground slowly. It should be possible, with all of us working together.—
-Eve-

THE HANDS EXTENDING from the amorphous ash cloud of the god's torso didn't swing the cages back and forth very much as he walked, which meant there wasn't much more to the timing of it than waiting for Zed to pass close to one of the invisible cracks riddling the world.

He sent the Window as he activated his Skill, though I knew

from the flare of eerie power what he was doing even before reading the message.

—Now!—
-Zed-

The world tore open from his fingertips, a huge, jagged rent in the air spilling grey light that none of us could see into the darkness. It might've been my imagination, but I thought I felt the faintest hint of a chill. Mentally, I smiled, already snapping out with Chaos at the speed of thought.

Condensed tendrils grabbed the bars of all my teammates' cages while a huge black sheet of Chaos undulated out toward the rip in the world. Only slightly more than a second after Zed began to use his skill, part of the giant sheet of Chaos disintegrated into the surrounding air, binding it together, and then I forced it to contract like a giant jellyfish. This propelled it into the Other Place, and all ten of us were yanked after it, cages and all.

I hadn't been sure whether the god would lose his grip. To my dismay he did not, and ten of his fleshless arms were yanked along with us. The sensation of cold grew a little stronger, and though my eyes still didn't work, Wraith gained a little more utility, quickly filling most of the Other Place. The rip Zed had opened in the world was much bigger than I had anticipated, enough to fit half a dozen airships flying through side-by-side.

—Now!—
-Eve-

As soon as I sent the reply to Zed, he closed the rip behind us with a thought. Like a guillotine, it sliced directly through the giant bones of the god's forearms as if they were nothing more than soft butter.

My senses came searing back to life like someone had flipped a switch. It was almost as disconcerting as losing them in the first place. I barely managed to remember what I was supposed to be doing. Chaos ate through the bars of the cages and the giant pseudo-jellyfish expanded and contracted once more, slowing our fall. It was enough time for most of my teammates to activate their ink wings, and to grab Ichi out of the air.

"Blue, follow us to the ground!" I screamed.

The cosmic whale did not respond, but complied, creating air beneath us as the air above disappeared, a little bubble of Other Place following us down. We flew in tight spirals as we descended. Ichi almost tried to teleport us away once he'd recovered from the double shock of the god's attack and the effects of the Other Place, but I stopped him when I felt him gathering his power. I didn't know how his Skill might interact with Zed's, but I had a feeling it might be messy.

We hit the ground haphazardly, followed by a handful of marionettes who were either able to fly, or small enough they could hitch a ride on one of the others. Under Kris's control, they had slipped through along with us. She shuddered, tears slipping down her face. She must have lost contact with her other creations. We took a moment to catch our breath, though Ichi's teeth were already chattering.

Blue swam around us. "It is too bad you did not manage to capture more bits of that god. It was quite delicious."

I raised an eyebrow, looking around at the blizzard-like flurry of grey ash condensing within and adding on to the edges of the Other Place. Apparently it had been quite a large meal. Hopefully, it was enough to put Blue in a good mood. The rest of my plan relied heavily on the protection of the Other Place.

"We have to destroy the god," I said. "There's no way he's not going to notice us loitering around the Voids, and after all that I doubt there's any way he doesn't consider us his mortal enemies. We're safe in here for now, but we can't stay in the Other Place long-term, either."

Adam scowled, still twitching a little as random sparks jumped over his skin and crackled off his hair. "I agree. But how do you propose we do that? I have no idea how his power works, and even less than that of how we might counter it. He didn't require us to meet his gaze, he just had to *see us*. How are we supposed to fight under those conditions?"

I grinned, showing the too-sharp teeth at the edges of my

mouth. "Well, do you remember that attack Behelaino used against me? The one that wiped out half the mountainside…?"

WE DID some exploring of the upside-down floating island, peeking out of small rips in the Other Place to find our way around.

It wasn't hard to find the Voids, seeing as they were enclosed in blazing rings of fire that hung in the air atop gigantic, flat-topped pyramids that reached up—or was it down?—into the empty darkness. Carved stairs ran straight from bottom to top.

We'd been in the Other Place for over fifteen minutes, and Ichi was growing catatonic, blue-lipped and incoherent, so we stepped out into the real world, dragging him with us.

I took a moment to inspect the fruit hanging from our necks and the crystal in my pack. I had felt Blue's curious greed for them in the Other Place, but they seemed unharmed—undrained—the shielding around them doing its job.

I looked up at the fire-ringed Voids atop the pyramids and shivered, not because of cold but because of the otherworldly sensation of power tugging at my blood. It made me want to both flee and draw closer, a compulsion that didn't feel natural or my own. The Void itself looked like rippling tar hanging in the air, simultaneously innocuous and horrifying. I found myself worrying that the binding fires keeping the Voids constrained would somehow fail or run out of energy. It seemed inevitable. What could possibly contain that terrible power calling to my blood?

Adam grabbed me by the arm, and only then did I realize I'd been staring up in a daze.

I turned away from the pyramids, scales rippling with unease.

Ichi had regained some color, but the ground was already shuddering in a familiar cadence. "The Warden's coming," I said.

Adam nodded, scowling. "Do you think he can tell we're here?"

"Maybe. Or maybe he's just using common sense. We escaped, we injured him, and there's pretty much only one attraction on this entire level, right? Where else would we go, in the unlikely event his little trick didn't scare us off?" I said.

Kris, red-eyed and a little puffy due to tears that even the Other Place hadn't been able to suppress, looked longingly up the staircase, then clenched her jaw and turned to me. "Can you get him? Attack before he gets a chance to stop you?"

I hesitated, but shook my head. "Not yet. I need time to practice, and it would be best to attack from ambush, rather than out here in the open. He might have more abilities that he hasn't displayed yet, and now he knows his cages won't hold us."

Jacky, still larger than normal though she'd calmed down enough to shrink till she was only as big as me, hopped lightly on her feet, looking around and cracking her knuckles nervously. "What, then? Not many places to run or hide around here, yeah?"

"Back up the stairs," I said. "Kris's marionettes are still up there —or down there, or whatever—and if we move fast enough, there might still be some time to save them."

The girl's eyes widened, and then she gave me a tremulous smile.

"We'll have to stay in the Other Place as much as possible," I said, lifting a hand and setting a thin mist of Chaos aflame. "Let's try to keep him"—I nodded to Ichi—"warm and awake."

Ichi had managed to rise to his feet, but didn't look enthused about returning to the cold, grey otherworldliness of the Other Place.

Gregor sneered at the man. "Maybe Blue doesn't like him, either."

Ichi didn't retort, which only turned Gregor's sneer into a scowl.

Sam squeezed Gregor's shoulder. "Let's go," he said, but over the boy's head, he shot the Estreyan a similar look of dislike.

The climb back up to where we'd been attacked by the Warden was tense and unpleasant, and even the normally talkative Jacky and Zed were mostly silent. We exited the Other Place for short breaks, since I didn't have the mental control to keep a fire going while also trying to figure out how to emulate Behelaino's beam attack move. Controlling even my imitation version was very difficult, made more so because Blue kept siphoning off tiny bits of power and sending the whole thing cascading out into a destructive explosion. It required total containment until the final moment, and even though Blue *said* it was unintentional, it was impossible to build the kind of power I needed with the creature's interference.

When we found the marionettes, collapsed like abandoned toys across the staircase, Kris's tears returned. We stepped back into the real world, where she began frantically reaching around, grasping at the air. Reaching for their dispersed spirits, I guessed.

A handful of the constructs stirred, but the majority remained lifeless.

Her tears ran more heavily, and little Pino, the marionette with the bandanna and the beeping voice box, gave her a few awkward pats on the shoulder, then beeped in alarm when she hugged him tightly. She recovered faster than I'd expected, though, and ordered the remaining marionettes to carry the fallen. She even clamped down on the faint emotions I'd been feeling through our bond.

We rested there for a while, eating quickly in an attempt to recover some of the strength the Other Place sucked away so insidiously. It seemed the Warden really did have some way to track us, because every time we spent more than a few minutes in the real world, the vibration of his footsteps grew more noticeable as he approached our location. Without the marionettes to carry our supplies, we all had to load more onto our backs and into our arms.

When the god reached the edge of Wraith's range, before he became visible to the naked eye, I turned to Ichi, who was sitting a few steps down from the rest of us. "Now."

Ichi glanced over the whole group, and an instant later we reappeared at the base of the largest pyramid. "Might I stay out here with you? I do not think I will be necessary for the remainder of the plan."

I shook my head. "No. I want you there, just in case something seems like it's about to go wrong. As long as there's a small opening to the normal world, you should be able to get everyone to safety. Take them back to the place on this level where we first arrived if there are any surprises. Do *not* try to teleport if the Other Place is completely closed off, though."

Zed scowled at that. "What about you, then?"

"Ichi can come back to check on me a couple minutes later. I'll either have won or I'll be in a cage and need you to pop back and open up the Other Place for me again." The third option, that I would be dead rather than imprisoned, remained unspoken.

"I still think you should wait in the Other Place," he said. "We could just straight up surprise him."

"There's too much drain," I said, "and I need all the focus and power I can dredge up for this. You guys just keep him off me for a few minutes, it'll be fine."

"Be at ease," Torliam said. "Ichi will not wait *minutes* to return if we are forced to escape. He will do so instantly, appearing directly behind this shield." As he spoke, he activated one of the ink tattoos he'd grudgingly consented to receive, digging the black barrier into the stony ground. "This should protect him from the Warden's gaze. You will stand beside it, Eve, so that Ichi might see you and save you immediately."

"Alright, alright. That makes sense, assuming the ink barrier does prevent the Warden from imprisoning Ichi. Now, hurry up and get ready. It's not going to take the Warden that long to get back here."

As they did, I turned my concentration to my own part in the plan. I had found it impossible to build up power internally and then shoot off a beam of power directly like Behelaino. Instead, I needed to draw it out, condensing Chaos between both palms. I swirled the power forward and back, till it created a quickly rotating disk, then added more power as I increased the speed and condensed the size of the disk further. I thought of it kind of like a tiny slingshot.

Chaos pushed harder and harder against my control as it condensed, any minor deviation in the rotation enough to send the whole thing spiraling into a wild, wide burst of Chaos instead of the pure beam I was attempting to create.

Shuddering footsteps announced the god's arrival, but I ignored that as my teammates slipped into the Other Place and rushed off to meet him, leaving me in almost complete darkness. I had turned off my headlamp, hoping that without the light, the god might not notice me as easily. Perhaps he worked like Ichi and needed to be able to see to use his abilities.

I added more power to the whirling destruction between my

palms, trying to keep my arms from shaking. A couple minutes later a rip opened in the far distance, behind the approaching god.

Torliam's blue Skill snapped out at the god's heel, and my teammates were hidden again an instant later.

The Warden turned and looked for them, but only for a few moments. When he found nothing, he turned back toward me.

I clenched my teeth, breathing hard and ignoring the sweat dripping into my eyes. I still had some time. I couldn't see him yet, so hopefully he couldn't see me, either. We were still farther apart than we had been when he'd first attacked.

A moment later, another rip appeared off to the side. A rocket lit the dark like a flare, shooting out of the grey light and impacting against the cages where it exploded in a bright flash of fire and force. Again, they were hidden almost as quickly as they appeared.

The next time grey light spilled into the darkness, the Warden spun toward it immediately. A swarm of ink-bats spilled out, so thickly packed they made an almost solid cloud. They darted up to the god's head, moving faster than any real bat ever could, and harried its eye-sockets.

The god didn't bother batting them away. Its mouth seemed to grow impossibly deeper, though it didn't move, and the constructs were sucked into the gaping, howling hole with no chance to resist. None exited again.

Even as far away as I was, I almost stumbled at the sudden pull of wind the sucking force had caused. Chaos nearly escaped my control, and my hands burned uncomfortably as I crushed it back into shape. The skin on my palms began disintegrating as if I was holding my hands against a grinding wheel. Panting, I took a few sidling steps to the side, hiding myself behind the ink shield. Just in case.

My teammates popped out again, this time much closer. An incorporeal, fist-sized rock shot out and hit the god on his ankle-joint. The rock passed through the outer layer before regaining corporeality in the perfect spot to partially fuse the two bones together.

The god's steps hitched, but again, when he swung around and looked, they were gone. His massive head turned back toward me, and despite the distance and barrier between us, I felt like his black eye sockets and the gaping ovoid hole where the mouth and neck should have been were all watching me. The billowing black ash undulated as if something swimming beneath the surface had become agitated.

He started running.

I suppressed a gasp and strained against the whirling power within my hands, attempting to feed it even faster.

Pebbles began to jump from the crashing vibrations of the Warden's footsteps.

The skin on my palms was gone, and I felt the muscles deteriorating as well. As my fingers lost the ability to stay stiff, I bent even more of my will toward controlling the Chaos. It was part of me. It *was* me. I demanded *obedience*.

Chaos struggled for one final moment, as I poured out the last few drops of energy I could gather, the blood in my veins searing as it passed through and beyond me. Then, it obeyed, blackening past midnight and emptiness, past that last bit of luster that Behelaino's Chaos possessed, till it looked like nothing more than a hole in the world. My fingers had disappeared, and the whirling disk of Chaos now extended from lumps of flesh attached to the ends of my wrists. It didn't hurt any more.

I looked up.

The Warden's head was just visible above the edge of the ink shield.

I took a single step to the side, lifted my arms toward his chest, and with an exultant exhalation, released my power. It lanced toward him, a beam of anti-light piercing right through his chest and out the other side.

The beam frayed a little, expanding as the disk lost its compressing force and spilled outward, refracting off the god's body as it spilled out of his back.

There were no bright lights or overwhelming sounds from my version.

It was silent, and it was dark.

It continued for less than fifteen seconds.

When it was over, I stumbled. The ink shield had disintegrated from catching the edge of some of the spinoff, and I didn't have hands to grab anything for support anyway, so I fell to a knee, barely keeping from toppling over entirely.

The Warden, however, was in far worse shape.

His Seed core was deep within the black ash of his chest, and I'd aimed directly for it. It wasn't there anymore. Neither was most of his torso.

Without it, the ash fell away from the bones, which broke apart from each other, bouncing and scattering as they hit the ground with another earthquake-like rumble.

I closed my eyes against the sudden wind, opening them only once everything had settled again. All that remained of the Warden was a pile of harmless ash and bones.

Chapter 17

Everything tires with time, and starts to seek some opposition, to save it from itself.

    — Clive Barker

YOUR INTELLIGENCE HAS INCREASED!
YOUR FOCUS HAS INCREASED!
YOUR STAMINA HAS INCREASED!
YOUR CHARISMA HAS INCREASED!

I PUSHED up to my feet a little awkwardly, ignoring the VR messages. Struggle and desperation always seemed to push my Seeds to grow faster than anything else. Before learning more about how they worked, I might have been surprised that Intelligence and Charisma were part of what I'd just done. Now I knew that, beyond a certain level, Intelligence also represented the processing my Seeds completed to allow me to pull off complex Skill manipulation, and Charisma had a lot to do with sheer force of will, and also probably some connection to my status as a godling.

I pulled a few faint wisps of what power remained in me to my hands and set them alight with black flames, which began to rebuild the flesh and bones. The others would worry if they saw me injured.

A laugh, breathless and relieved, spilled out of me. I had never defeated a god so easily! I looked at the flames on my hands, so dark they almost seemed to absorb the light, and wondered if this was an indication that I was creating my own version of Khaos, becoming a new god. For a second, I wondered what my title might be if I did become a goddess. What concept was the Oracle trying to create with me?

I shook off the thought and walked toward the mountain of ash and bones.

In the distance, the Other Place opened and my teammates walked out.

We met in the middle, standing around the god's corpse.

Well, not a corpse in the same sense that a human would leave one. I could sense the faintest hints of Seed organisms spread throughout the mound of remains, about the same amount that would have been contained in one of the marble-sized Seeds NIX had given out. Given time, they would coalesce into a Seed core and multiply. It wouldn't be enough to control such a large body, but a small version of the Warden could rise from the ashes, literally.

I considered destroying even those remnants, which still wouldn't actually kill the Warden for good, but would seriously delay him from reforming here. I decided against it. We would probably be here for a few days at least, possibly more than that if I needed time to get control of the Void and myself before leaving as Behelaino had made me vow. This place had a Warden for a reason. After we left, I'd prefer to have him guarding the Voids again. It wasn't *safe* to leave them untended. I could feel it.

I hoped there wasn't another manifestation of the Warden patrolling out in the darkness somewhere. It would be very unusual for two manifestations of a god to live in close proximity to each other, but I couldn't imagine he would be happy to see part of himself lying in a broken heap at my feet.

Jacky grinned and whooped, leaping wildly into the air. She laughed till she started snorting, slapping me on the back. "Yeah!"

I actually managed not to be knocked off balance by her slaps, and they didn't even really hurt, to my pleasant surprise. I'd gotten used to wincing in advance whenever I saw one of her hands swinging my way.

Her laughter was infectious, and my teammates joined in the cheering. Even Ichi gave me a look of surprised respect, nudging the edge of the small hill with a quirked half-smile.

I took a moment to pull up my Attribute Window, checking my levels.

PLAYER NAME: EVE REDDING
TITLE: BEARER OF TESTIMONY
SKILLS: COMMAND, SPIRIT OF THE HUNTRESS,
TUMBLING FEATHER, WRAITH, CHAOS, VOICE

STRENGTH: 40
LIFE: 108
AGILITY: 51
GRACE: 42
INTELLIGENCE: 45
FOCUS: 44
BEAUTY: 23
CHARISMA: 58
MANUAL DEXTERITY: 11
MENTAL ACUITY: 45
RESILIENCE: 97
STAMINA: 47
PERCEPTION: 61

I looked back to the god's remains. Were the Attribute levels strictly accurate anymore? What did they even mean, really? Would the Warden have been only an 80 Strength, or a 150 Life? Chaos, or whatever it was becoming, seemed so much more significant than the still-mortal body I used to hold it, and really negated the significance of the more mundane Seeds. I could heal myself with a thought, burn away and completely reform a small island, and kill a god in a single attack.

It was a little reassuring, the idea that my potential was not bound by those obviously insufficient numbers, but only by the limits of my resolve.

As we made our way back to the base of the largest pyramid, Birch swept me off my feet with a burst of wind and sat me astride his back. He was still slightly too small to carry me naturally, as my feet dragged at the ground and there wasn't really room for his wings to move with me in the way, but he made up for that with concentrated bursts of wind that caught under his wings and helped each step turn into a short glide. He let out a loud roar that almost matched the flesh-rippling force I remembered from the adult tailos. Except *his* roar carried a fine mist of Chaos which immediately burst into firefly-like flurries of exuberant light.

I dug my fingers into the thick fur between his shoulder blades and found myself laughing too.

We stopped and set up camp at the base of the pyramid, so elated by our victory that we were able to ignore the feeling of unease radiating off the fire-bound Voids so far above.

Zed sat beside me, speaking through a mouth stuffed full of fruit leather. "When the Warden cut us off from everything, I could see this faint haze everywhere, not just the cracks in the Veil. I'm pretty sure it was the same Seed waste energy you can see, though obviously you're way better at it than me."

"Wow. I'm a little surprised, but that's definitely a good thing. Has your Skill progressed in any other ways?" I said.

He hesitated. "Well, a little. There's more than just the Other Place out there, different cracks."

I nodded. He'd told me about that as soon as he began to see the others.

"I can touch them, but after what happened with Pestilence I've avoided reckless exploration. But that's not why I brought it up. You've had Wraith for a long time, since before we even met Behelaino, and at first it wasn't even labeled as a Skill, right? So, where did it come from? Is Wraith a…naturally developed Skill, Eve? You just created it?"

I blinked a few times, chewing and swallowing before I answered. "I think so," I said, thinking back to the first hints of any special sensory ability, when I had been meditating under China's tutelage in the base we'd made of Blaine's basement back on Earth.

"Well, is that normal? Do Estreyans come up with Skills on

their own frequently? Whenever they talk about it, Skills always come from a Trial of some sort."

"I don't know," I admitted. "Maybe it's rare? Or maybe…well, maybe the Skill came from Seeds I had when I was born? Line of Matrix, and all that?" It was an interesting question, but I knew it wasn't *important*, not like the Voids reaching for my blood up above.

After eating till we almost burst, Ichi popped me out to the nearest communications beacon so I could call Queen Mardinest. "So convenient," I muttered under my breath.

To my dual relief and worry, Queen Mardinest *still* had no updates on the Avatar to report, so we popped right back into the disoriented-gravity of the floating, upside-down island in Tartarus.

We approached the Void at the top of the biggest pyramid. That hindbrain sensation of existential, otherworldly danger only grew stronger the higher we climbed, and Jacky ended up sending the kids back down with Sam when Gregor had a panic attack.

The burning ring of fire enclosing the Void gave out no warmth. According to vague records that were old enough to be more like myths, the containing fire had been created by a handful of the oldest gods working together. It wasn't something I could hope to replicate. I would have to contain the Void purely with my own willpower.

I hadn't asked the Oracle if her vision of the future had changed. Was I ready? Was this the right choice?

Swallowing hard, Adam set up the equipment we'd brought for this very purpose. We didn't have much hope that it would be able to decipher the true scientific nature of the Void, but there was good reason why this Aspect of Chaos hadn't been studied extensively before, so it didn't hurt to try. Really, though, we were hoping to discover more immediately pertinent information, like how likely it was to kill me.

I sat down, crossed my legs, and began to meditate, carefully exploring the call of the Void.

It took a couple hours for Adam to finish compiling the various readings and measurements. He frowned as he looked down at the data scrolling across his pad. "I don't understand what this means," he said, grinding his knuckles into his eye sockets in tired frustration.

I opened my eyes. "Well, collate everything and send it to anyone who might be able to help decipher it," I said. "In the meantime, we'll continue with the next round of testing."

Adam left the equipment where it was while Ichi teleported him away to do as I'd said.

I bit my lip idly, not hard enough to hurt, then turned to Zed. "Do you see anything?"

Zed squinted, his eyes wandering around in the empty air.

"What is it?" I asked impatiently.

"Pretty sure I can't see anything you can't. I can *feel* it, though. It's dangerous."

"We all feel it," Torliam agreed. "It is…unnatural."

Birch nudged his head into my shoulder, sending me memories of watching a science fiction film about the horrifying effects of black holes. "*Too dangerous. We run, attack from the flank. Find another way?*"

I met his human-like eyes. "I would, but we don't have another way," I murmured, then stood. "Let's talk to Blue. Not so close, though. Just in case."

We walked partway down the pyramid before Zed opened up a rip to the Other Place, and then Blue slowly moved his bubble of imitation reality back up to the top. The Other Place shuddered as soon as its edge reached the space where the Void was in the normal world and immediately stopped advancing. Blue swam around in agitation before slowing, one gigantic eye looking down at me. "This is one of your Aspects, morsel? Its infamy is well-deserved. I cannot eat this Void, nor is it meant for me to understand. Rather, it would devour me and all that I have gathered. I do not think you should enter."

I clenched and unclenched my fists. "Thanks, but I have to."

We exited the Other Place to find Adam and Ichi returned and on the verge of panic at our disappearance. Adam ran his fingers through his hair, which practically stood on end with static. "I thought the Void ate you all."

Picking up a pebble, I walked closer to the Void and tossed it in. The tar-like surface did not ripple or show any other sign of disturbance.

Ichi moved closer, his eyes warily trained on me and ready to activate his power at any moment.

Zed offered up a stick, a cast-off from Kris's work. I grabbed it with a tendril of Chaos. As soon as my power exited past my skin, the Void rippled, as if in recognition. I frowned and used the tendril of Chaos to poke the stick at the Void.

There was a faint tugging sensation, and when I tried to pull the stick back, gooey tendrils stretched away from the surface of the Void, as if it were reluctant to let go. They were powerful, and when I finally ripped the stick away, the part that had sunk into the Void was gone, not splintered or broken but just…gone.

I glowered down at the stick, my lips pressed together into a thin line. That wasn't exactly a surprise, I supposed.

I had been very careful not to pry too closely with Wraith, worried it might drive me insane like Behelaino said. I looked to Ichi, and when he nodded, I took a deep breath and poked with the stick again. This time I followed it with Wraith. I kept the sensory Skill confined to the area immediately surrounding the stick, or at least I tried. Wraith had no trouble sinking into the surface of the Void, but as soon as it did, it got lost. Control slipped away like smoke in the wind, my mind reeling with confused pain as Wraith sensed things that were not meant for a human brain.

I started to draw breath for a scream, and then the pain was gone, replaced by disorientation and weakness.

Ichi was leaning over me with an expression of suppressed concern, and we were outside of Tartarus, near the level opening. I climbed back to my feet, suddenly ravenous. Whatever the Void had done, it was almost as draining on my body's reserves as the attack I had used to destroy the Warden. I understood now why Blue had said it would devour him. I touched the fruit of life hanging from my neck. Would it really be enough to keep me alive?

"I'm okay," I said breathlessly. "Let's go back."

Ichi hesitated, looking me over, but complied when I gave him an irritated scowl.

"What was that?" Adam demanded when we reappeared. "Are you hurt?"

Torliam gave me a searching look, but could probably feel that I was no longer in pain through our blood bond.

I explained what I had felt, trying to keep the fear from my voice. That fear squirmed inside me like a slug, but I needed the others to be calm and reassured. It would be easier to master my own fear if I didn't also have to overcome theirs.

My teammates' faces had grown grim, but they were ready to continue.

When I felt settled, I ran down to our campsite and took a small backup power crystal from our supplies. Gregor had a power meter in the jumble of gear next to his bedroll. With a grin, I grabbed that, too. I tested the crystal quickly to make sure it was fully charged, then ran back up. "I have an idea," I said.

Staying well back from the surface of the Void, I used the tendril of solidified Chaos to tap the crystal's tip against the surface, yanking it back immediately.

I then inserted the crystal, which was now missing its tip, into Gregor's power meter. As I had guessed, it was almost completely drained, despite the fact that only one small portion had been in contact with the Void, and for less than a second.

But it wasn't *completely* drained.

ADAM IMMEDIATELY UNDERSTOOD what I'd done, grabbing for the power meter and starting to calculate how fast the Void absorbed power. It took a few more hours and a ton of tests to figure out the variables, but by the time we were finished, we had a semi-accurate calculation of the rate of energy dispersal within it.

It was not good news.

Not that we had expected it to be, I suppose, but it was still discouraging. We went back down to the camp and told Sam and the kiddos what we'd discovered.

"If we estimate the power the Seeds can produce by the measure of how much power my people are able to infuse into these same crystals, it is clear Eve will be at a deficit," Torliam said, sharing a grim look with Adam.

Adam's voice was gravelly with emotion. "Per my best estimate, the Void would consume Eve's power within a few milliseconds."

When put like that, it was starkly clear that I couldn't withstand the Void on my own, and even if the fruit of life could channel energy that quickly, which I doubted, the fruit's dimension-tunneling ability would burn out within only a second or two.

Gregor stared at me wide-eyed, looking pale and betrayed.

"Perhaps she can simply extend her senses into the Void for milliseconds at a time, building up her knowledge of it in stages?" Ichi suggested.

"She has to submerge herself in it," Zed said, staring at nothing. "Long enough to understand it. However long that is."

Ichi's eyes widened. He looked around at us. "Well, haven't you had experience with this type of thing before? What do you usually do when up against impossible odds?"

Jacky shot him an irritated glare. "We can't just pull miracles out of our asses. *Mierda*!" She tossed her head and snorted derisively.

I cleared my throat. "Actually…"

Everyone's heads swiveled to look at me with similar expressions of expectant surprise.

"Zed, if you would?" I waved a hand at the air.

He walked a few feet away and opened a rip.

I stepped through, creating a flaring white flame in my hand to put Blue in a good mood for negotiation.

As the others followed us into the Other Place, I motioned for Zed to close the rip connecting us to reality. It was a precaution born of paranoia. I wanted the Abhorrent's Avatar to have as little chance as possible of overhearing my plans and finding a way to sabotage them.

"I need your help with the Voids," I said.

"I refuse," came the echoing response.

"I'll pay you. Well." I brightened the fire even further, till my shadow stretched back dark and defined behind me. "Better than a thousand days of fire, I'd bet."

The alien creature swam closer to the edge, the draining force of the Other Place increasing its pull in a sudden gluttonous surge of cold and grey fatigue. "Speak."

I pointed to the power meter in Adam's hand, even as Blue drained the remaining dregs of energy from the unshielded crystal. "The Void has some sort of draining effect, in addition to whatever it's doing to destroy anything that enters it. However, as you can see, the effect isn't completely instantaneous. If we could feed energy into this crystal faster than the Void sucked it out, it might still be fully charged."

"This is an interesting theory, but I do not see how it is relevant to me. I am already helping you to train your resistance, though I doubt its effectiveness against the Void. What is it you are getting at, foolish creature?" Blue said.

I pulled out the rune-inscribed cube from my backpack, letting the fire hang in the air above my head. "Do you think enough energy to destroy the planet Earth would be able to keep me alive? Maybe with enough left over to expand your domain to its former size?" I placed the cube on the ground in front of me, the gentle sound of metal settling against stone seeming unreasonably loud.

The world pulsed with a greedy heartbeat, darkening as the edges of the Other Place closed in. "What is it you have brought me?" Blue said. The runes inscribed on the cube glowed as the creature tested their shielding effect. They wouldn't last forever, but I only needed them to hold out for the remainder of our conversation.

"A gift," I said simply, feeling the rightness of the statement. "But not one freely given. I'll need your help in return. Enclosed within this box is the largest power crystal I've ever seen. It's been being charged for approximately the last two thousand years. It should have more power than even the Void can drain right away. And as it is, it is useless to me."

"That's what the Remnants gave you?" Gregor whispered, shivering.

"A fitting gift," Blue said, suppressing some of the blatant avarice in its tone and gentling the hungry pull dimming even the light of my fire. "As you know, I am willing to bargain, for the right price. But I will not, cannot, drain the power of the Void, and I do not see how else you might expect me to be of aid. I have no more knowledge to give you, and I am much weakened after the…unfortunate occurrence during our fight with Pestilence." Blue's gaze turned to Zed for a moment, but it was no longer filled with ire toward the boy.

"I'm hoping you can help me in a different way," I said. "Are you capable of giving back energy as well as taking it? I cannot directly use the power of this crystal. The fruit cannot, either. But I know you can. If you are able to convert the crystal's power into the same type of energy our Seed organisms use, I believe the fruit of life could be powered well beyond its standard charge limit. It could heal me as many times as the energy provided allowed, with no need to reach elsewhere to gather power."

Blue circled the edge of the Other Place in seeming agitation. "Give back energy?" it repeated, as if the idea were alien and a little horrifying.

"In exchange for *more*," Zed interjected. "That's the kind of energy you wouldn't get from a tear in the heart of a hundred volcanoes, or ten thousand days of Eve creating a miniature sun in here for you. You could lose three quarters of it and still come out ahead, with the Other Place bigger than it was the first time I opened the Veil."

Blue slowed, his gigantic eye trained on the cube sitting on the ground before me. "And what would stop me from simply *taking* this gift now? I have no incentive to risk myself."

My voice came out slightly scratchy and deep. "You would regret it, creature of gluttony and curiosity." The crystal at my throat vibrated slightly, adding an undercurrent of promise to the words.

Blue let out a rumbling *humph*, but resumed circling us. "I may be able to convert the energy for you, but I am unable to guide its use, and I am imprisoned beyond the Veil. I have no way to help you once you slip into the Void, you uppity morsel."

"That is a problem," I admitted.

"Do you have some device that would allow you to store Seed energy, perhaps?" it asked.

"No." I wondered if the Remnants, or maybe the guardians, would be able to create something like that if I asked. But if so… why hadn't they already done so? That kind of thing would revolutionize the Estreyan world and be highly coveted. Even the guardians, less materialistic than most cultures, would find it invaluable. I resolved to ask anyway, just in case.

Though frustrated, my teammates weren't quite as hopeless when we left the Other Place as they had been before we entered. Zed, in fact, looked merely thoughtful.

When no one else had any more experiments to try, we returned to camp.

"It will take some time to receive answers back from those to whom we sent the data," Torliam said. He handed me one of our emergency meal kits and jerked his head toward my bedroll. "Take the time to rest. Whatever lies ahead, we will all need our strength, but you most of all."

I complied, knowing he was right. I leaned back, feeling the edges of the runic box that held the power crystal within my backpack. What would it take for me to actually use energy Blue converted? I had no natural power-siphoning abilities.

I resolved to question the woodland guardians via the communication beacon we'd left behind, but found myself falling asleep, and conceded that it would be okay to rest a little first.

Torliam was right. I needed to be completely and utterly rested before confronting the Void.

I was awoken by Kris's high-pitched scream. "No! I'm fucking done training!"

I snapped upright, Wraith cataloguing everything in the near distance in an instant.

Jacky was sweaty and disheveled, and must have just come from training. She stood glaring down at Kris, who scowled right back up at her, red-faced.

Those marionettes that were still animated shrunk back from their creator's anger, looking back and forth between her and Jacky.

Gregor stood awkwardly above his bedroll, datapad forgotten in his hand.

Birch blinked sleepily at my side.

Zed and Torliam stood together at the camp stove, a conversation obviously disrupted, while Adam and Ichi were both gone somewhere.

Sam was at his own bedroll, but his eyes were black and he practically radiated apathy, barely bothering to look toward Kris and Jacky before returning his attention to the datapad illuminating his face.

"You've gotta train," Jacky said, dismissing the young girl's vehement denial. She didn't seem to notice the angry tears gathering in Kris's eyes or the way the tiny girl's fists trembled with repressed emotion. "We can do it my way, or you can keep being lazy and I can *make* you do it my way, yeah? It's for your own—"

Kris's hand raised, one finger pointed at Jacky. "No." Two tears spilled down her reddened cheeks.

Jacky flipped backward like a possessed rag doll. She hit the ground at the edge of the camp and convulsed, tendons straining in her neck and veins bulging out from her skin. She spasmed strangely, limbs bending and flailing at inhuman angles, fingers curling and flexing independently. Her head slammed against the ground, the whites of her eyes bursting with blood as capillaries broke from the strain. She gasped as if suffocating.

Chapter 18

There is something at work in my soul, which I do not understand.
— Mary Shelley

I SPRANG TO MY FEET, reaching out toward Kris.

The girl flicked a glance toward me, and something inside me wrenched to the side.

I followed the burst of pain, instinctively turning into it to avoid having my spirit, which she'd just tugged on, ripped out of my body. I found myself pressed flat to the ground, any movement ready to send another burst of agony through me. This must be what was happening to Jacky. Kris was tugging at her spirit, and Jacky was unable to resist.

Torliam had met a similar fate, Gregor's mouth had dropped open and he was simply staring at Jacky in shocked dismay, and Sam hadn't moved, but he was at least looking toward Kris in interest now.

"It's not worth it," he said to her. "You always regret doing this kind of thing afterward. Even if you thought they deserved it beforehand."

Kris ignored him, lifting the hand that wasn't pointing at Jacky to scrub away the tears spilling down her face. "I'm not some robot!" she screamed at Jacky. "I need a break sometimes! If you want to train so bad, go train on your own, you stupid…scag!"

Zed stood dumbly, his hands twitching toward the guns at his waist, otherwise incapable of intervening.

I doubted Jacky could even comprehend Kris's words, convulsing as she was. She was bleeding from the nose, now, and starting to grow bigger, but her Struggle Skill didn't seem like it was mitigating the effects of Kris's attack at all, simply responding to Jacky's helplessness and fear. Was that what I looked like when under the influence of one of the Oracle's visions?

I stopped trying to fight against Kris's hold on my spirit. I needed to stop acting so much like a human. What god would let someone else control their spirit? It was mine, just as my blood and flesh and thoughts were mine, and only *I* could control them. I could feel her hold lessening, but before I regained my feet, Zed had come to a decision.

Instead of shooting, he ran to Jacky, reaching out to lift her. He'd probably intended to carry her out of Kris's range, perhaps shielding her in the Other Place, but he'd underestimated Jacky's strength.

One of her legs flashed up and lurched to the side, slamming him in the gut and lifting him off his feet.

He flew backward, bowed from the impact, and landed half a dozen meters away, somehow keeping from collapsing in a heap.

I stood and turned to Kris, ignoring the wrenching sensation of her Summon Skill trying to move me otherwise. "Stop," I said, Voice reverberating so hard through the air even the pebbles on the ground seemed to shrink down in fear.

Everyone froze, including Jacky.

Wraith sensed the glow of Kris's power fading away from Jacky and the others.

I let the silence settle heavily over everything, the only sounds Jacky's rough breaths and the faint crackle of the flame in the camp stove. After a few long, uncomfortable moments, I said, "Sam, heal Jacky and Zed," then moved to Kris's side. I knelt beside her so that I could look directly into her face rather than towering over her.

She glared back at me stubbornly for about two seconds, and then her face crumpled into tears as she began to shake.

Slowly, I reached out and gathered her in my arms, careful to ensure my scales didn't cut her as I hugged her to my chest, tucking her small head under my chin.

Sam checked Jacky first, turning Black Sun all the way off before touching her so he didn't end up making things worse.

My brother pressed gingerly against his abdomen and grimaced, but said, "I'm actually fine. I don't need healing."

I rubbed my huge, claw-tipped hand soothingly over Kris's tiny back as it heaved with the force of her sobs. "Get checked out anyway," I ordered. "You could have internal bleeding. You can't just shrug off hits like that like the rest of us. You don't have Seeds, Zed."

"I have nanites."

"It's not the same."

"It's just a checkup," Sam said, rising from Jacky's side and reaching out a hand to help her to her feet.

She accepted his hand silently, staring over at Kris and me.

Gregor, forgotten at the edge of camp, put down his datapad finally. He opened his mouth as if to say something to Jacky, but closed it again with a silent grimace, instead moving to stand with me and Kris. He put his much smaller hand on her back and said in a low voice, "We'll have a funeral for them, Kris. And gravestones. Eve can make them look all pretty. But maybe we can do it up above, somewhere where there's light. Not down here in the darkness. What do you think?"

Jacky let out a choked sound, meeting my eyes over the kids' heads. Her expression twisted with wretched self-recrimination, and she looked away, her arms wrapped consolingly around herself.

I was trying to think of a solution when, across the camp, Sam threw his hands in the air. "Fine, then! If you have internal bleeding and almost die in your sleep, I'm going to… I'll make you help with my volunteer clinic hours. On Earth!" He huffed and stomped away. "Like sister, like brother," he muttered under his breath, so low that I wouldn't have understood him if not for Wraith.

"I'm fine! Don't you think I know my own body? She didn't actually kick me that hard, it just looked dramatic. Save your healing for the people who really need it," Zed said, turning toward the pyramid stairs as if he, too, was going to stomp off in a huff.

The hair on the back of my neck lifted as I had a premonition. "Wait," I said. Voice didn't augment the command, but my tone was no less forceful for it.

Zed stopped, turning toward me slowly.

I could see the confirmation of my suspicions in his expression, though he tried to hide it. I'd known him his entire life, and with superhuman Perception, I knew every twitch and micro expression, could feel the beat of his heart through the pulse in his throat.

I hesitated, Kris still in my arms.

Gregor reached for her, and I let her go.

Her sobs had turned into whimpers as she'd exhausted herself. "Go to sleep," I whispered to her, giving her head one last gentle pet.

Gregor stumbled a bit, but managed to carry her to her bedroll, jerking his head imperiously for the marionettes to follow him. "Hold her hand," he ordered Pino as he tucked her into the fabric.

I wanted to say something to reassure Jacky, who had curled in on herself even more and was radiating shame, but I didn't know what, and whatever was going on with Zed felt more pressing.

He seemed to resist the urge to draw back from me as I approached, affecting an awkward smile. Any remaining hope of continuing his deception fell away as I reached out to touch his arm. He knew me, too.

With a touch, I sent Wraith past the barrier of his skin, searching through his body.

I stared at him, and he stared back. "Did NIX—" I stopped before even finishing the question. I knew NIX hadn't done this to him. He'd told us all when his VR chip gained command of the nanites and through them, the ability to augment his body. "You did this to yourself?"

He yanked his arm out of my grasp with more strength than he should have been capable of. "I needed to get stronger. Better. There's too much at stake."

I swallowed past the rising lump in my throat. "Zed, I saw... You augmented your bones, your muscle structure, your blood. You have an additional *organ* made of inorganic material!" My voice tightened as I spoke, till I was barely keeping myself from yelling.

"It's a backup for the heart and lungs. You can survive without most of your other organs for at least a little while," he said defiantly, lifting his chin.

"What about your nerves? What about your *brain*? What have you *done* to yourself?" I asked, losing the battle to keep myself from yelling.

He rocked on his heels, but didn't step back. "Light instead of electricity," he said. "It's faster. It's *better*. It's how the woodland guardians transfer their impulses, so I knew it would work. I'm not being reckless with it, I left the original nervous system in place with my initial experiments, till I was sure it was integrated properly."

"*Your brain,*" I repeated. "How can you tell me you're being safe when patches of your brain are—" I took a few deep breaths and forced my lips back down over my teeth, suppressing the snarl that had taken over my face without my realizing it. "How could anyone *safely* experiment on their own brain?"

"Holy shit," Gregor muttered behind me.

Zed pressed his lips together, a pinched motion that reminded me of our mother. "I simulated everything ahead of time. I programmed the procedure, safety precautions, and failsafes into the nanites, and I'm giving myself plenty of time to adjust to each update. Even if I were to pass out while they were working, which I haven't yet, I'd still be fine. They know what to do, with or without my oversight. I admit, something like this could never be *totally* safe, but the risks are worth it. I don't want look back after the Abhorrent has killed everyone and regret that I wasn't just a little braver, that I didn't do what was needed to *change* things. I'm making choices now, in the present, so that I can change the future. It's a chance to change the odds."

I let out a scoffing laugh, but he continued before I could say anything.

"You would have done the same thing. You *have* done the same thing. I understand why you're upset right now. Do you think I don't get it!? I know what it's like to stand there and watch my sister *dying*. But guess what? I'm *not* dying! And I'm doing what it takes so that we *all* don't die! I mean, seriously, Eve. Don't be a hypocrite. I saw you were missing half your fingers earlier."

"I can heal!" I yelled.

"So can I!" he shouted back. We glared at each other for a moment, panting. "And you couldn't always heal," he added, a little softer. "I imagined how much I might regret it if I let fear hold me back from getting stronger, and I decided that if I could so clearly imagine my regrets, perhaps I could just avoid them altogether in the first place. Being bolder might have left me personally worse off, if I made a mistake, which I haven't, but I didn't think those regrets would be anywhere near as severe as what I would feel if I knew I had been a coward."

"I'm not experimenting on my *brain*," I insisted.

"No, because your Seeds are doing it *for* you!" he screamed, losing any semblance of patience.

That made me pause, and I realized continuing to argue would bring no benefit. We both needed time to calm down. I ground my teeth together before spinning on my heels and stalking off, angry whips of Chaos flicking out of my skin as if they wanted to attack the air.

TORLIAM CLEARED his throat gruffly as I passed, scratching awkwardly at his beard.

I stomped off into the darkness, occasionally bursting out in angry mutters. I threw around some destructive waves of Chaos and created a few fireballs, but found mutilating the terrain wasn't really settling my internal turmoil.

I wasn't totally impractical. I understood Zed's need to grow stronger. But what he'd done was so far beyond the bounds of recklessness it left me speechless.

Using my Command Skill, which was based in my VR chip rather than any actual Seeds, I pulled up Zed's Attribute Window.

PLAYER NAME: ZED REDDING

TITLE: ONE OF NINE

SKILLS: VEIL-PIERCER

STRENGTH: 33

LIFE: 48

AGILITY: 22
GRACE: 18
INTELLIGENCE: 37
FOCUS: 10
BEAUTY: 11
CHARISMA: 9
MANUAL DEXTERITY: 25
MENTAL ACUITY: 22
RESILIENCE: 27
STAMINA: 38
PERCEPTION: 35

Zed had gone beyond the bounds of most humans. He was even stronger than a lot of NIX's Players.

I crouched down, raking my fingers through my hair and tugging at my scalp. How many things could possibly go wrong at once?

Wraith caught Adam walking up behind me, and I stood, turning to face him. An ominous foreboding filled my chest. Had I just tempted the gods of irony? "What's wrong? Did something happen?" I called to him.

He shook his head, waiting till he was closer to speak. "I thought I'd catch you away from the others. We haven't really had an opportunity to…" He scratched at his nose, looking away. "Ichi just took me out to gather the replies from the data we've recorded on the Void."

I relaxed marginally. "Oh, good." I realized he didn't know what had happened at the camp while he'd been gone. Either that, or what he had discovered was too important to wait for me to clear my head. I waited impatiently for him to tell me what the Thinkers and physicists had concluded.

"It has some vague similarities to what Blue does. By that, I mean that you're likely going to find it very difficult to maintain mental and physical solidity." He shook his head, fingers twiddling nervously. "The readings from that thing are off the charts. Literally. I'm worried, Eve. What if this is how things start to go wrong?"

"I understand, but I have some ideas. That's partially what the fruit should help to mitigate, and—" I cut off as he grabbed my hand, pressing something into it.

The necklace containing his fruit of life sat heavy in my palm.

"That one's mine. I want you to take it. It might help."

My eyes widened. I shook my head. "Adam, I can't—"

"I like you, Eve."

I froze with my mouth halfway open. His words were heavy with meaning, with *emotion*, and I felt the echo of it through our partial blood bond. He did not mean it trivially.

I was frozen, trying to process the sudden revelation.

He glanced at my face, and then away, fidgeting more quickly than ever. "You don't need to say anything. You don't even need to worry about it. I mean, I've known for a long time and I don't want anything to change between us right now, it's just…I wanted you to know in case—in case I lost the chance to tell you later." He cleared his throat. "Keep the fruit. You need it more than I do. I'm thinking it'll double your chances." He swallowed with some difficulty. "You have to come out of this okay."

He spun on his heel and walked away.

I remained frozen, staring down at the round locket in my hand. I was grateful, suddenly, that our blood-covenant wasn't mutual, because then he would know about the surging waves of awkwardness and embarrassment crashing over me.

Realizing I still had his fruit, I looked up, but it was too late to call him back. I would have to return it later. I breathed deeply, smelling old dust and mineral-heavy water, then tucked the fruit in a pouch at my waist. I gave myself a few more minutes to stare into the darkness, then scrubbed roughly at my face and let out a ragged sigh. I'd just awoken, so why did I feel so tired?

When I returned to the camp, I found Torliam waiting for me at the edge of the campfire's light. "What happened? Are you well?" he asked.

Torliam's questions echoed those I'd asked when Adam approached me, and I had to suppress another wave of profound awkwardness. I would actually have preferred it if Adam had yelled or complained or even attacked me. I would have known how to deal with that. Clearing my throat, I said, "Adam—he gave me his fruit." I didn't want to discuss it in any more detail than that, especially with Torliam.

My prevarication amounted to nothing though, because my blood-covenant with *Torliam* was complete. My mental barriers kept us out of each other's minds, but strong emotions could still leak through. Or perhaps he could just read it on my face.

"The human confessed his affection for you," he said.

I didn't respond, which was enough of an answer in itself.

Torliam's face turned white, then red with anger. "Where is he?" he growled. "I will—"

I groaned, cutting Torliam off before he could say exactly what he wanted to do to Adam. "Please don't make this any worse."

"Do not worry. I will not permanently injure him. I simply have some things to *discuss* with him," Torliam said, already striding off.

I rubbed at the muscles on the back of my neck, trying to release some of the headache-inducing tension gathering there.

I found Birch rolling around in my bedroll at camp. He perked up when he saw me, unapologetically shaking loose fur and feathers onto the fabric. He let out a happy sound and bounded to my side. Adam, Ichi, and Torliam were all gone, but everyone else was now asleep, except for Zed, who was standing at the top of the pyramid.

Crouching down, I buried my face in the soft ruff of fur at Birch's neck. "You don't have some terrible secret or violent drama you're about to spring on me, right?"

He let out a soft rumble, nudging me with his nose. There was a brief flash of scent, sound, and emotion. "*Comfort.*"

"Thanks," I said.

I settled down to meditate, working on the mindset exercises the woodland guardians had thought might help me maintain my sense of self, specifically, organizing and examining my emotions.

A few minutes later, I opened my eyes, feeling slightly deflated. I was, of course, doing almost the same thing Zed was. I was putting myself at serious risk for the chance of a power upgrade. The only difference between us, really, was that I was doing it openly, while he had kept it a secret.

Birch followed me as I climbed back up the pyramid. With

every breath I tried to push out some of my outrage, like a chimney releasing smoke.

The only thing I could really be angry at Zed for was the secrecy, which prevented the rest of us from helping him or keeping him safe.

When I met my brother's gaze across the plateau-topped pyramid, I said only, "You need to have Sam check you out." My brother gave me a suspicious look, clearly expecting more. "And I want an update on any future augmentations before you do them—and Sam needs to watch over the process—and maybe you should ask Gregor to check your simulations for unintended repercussions. Also…"

Zed rolled his eyes, one corner of his mouth pulling up in a small smile. "Alright. It can't hurt, I guess. Maybe they'll have some good ideas." Beside him, an opening to the Other Place hung in the air, and I caught a glimpse of Blue on the other side. Perhaps they had been talking.

"How did you figure out how to, or what to do, anyway?" I asked awkwardly, my claws combing through Birch's fur as a distraction. "I mean, scientists spend their whole lives researching post-human augmentation, right?"

Zed turned to stare at the tar-like, rippling Void. "NIX had a whole ton of research on it, which wasn't too hard to get my hands on with our new clearance levels. Then I repurposed some of my nanites to build a simulation chip in my brain. It's only the size of a grain of rice," he said quickly, "so don't worry! But really, the basic physical upgrades were super simple to figure out. You are around all the time. All I had to do was scan you a few times without you realizing it. Most of the stuff, except the backup organ and the improved nerve impulse transmitters, is copied directly from what you have. I'm surprised you didn't realize it."

"Oh." What else was I supposed to say? I was still a little angry, because I doubted a decade would have been enough time to research what he'd done thoroughly enough to be truly safe, but now I also felt foolish.

"That's the kind of thing it's really best to do all at once. The body is a very interconnected system. Of course, my nanites can't work with flesh material the same way Seeds can, so I had to get other materials to do the job. It'll require maintenance, and I had to do some tweaking so my body didn't think I'd been horribly injured and go into shock or have an immune response. As for my brain and nervous system, I did a lot of research to figure out how the woodland guardians were doing it. At least *my* thoughts are still all contained within my skull. You should realize, Eve, your brain isn't exactly running off flesh and blood hardware anymore, either. At least some of your processing power's being offloaded to wherever the Seeds are pulling energy from."

"I know," I said. "Do you still…feel the same? What about emotions and stuff like that? They're largely chemical, right?"

"There are analogues for that. I researched the guardians, remember? They don't have any chemicals, but I doubt you'd say they can't feel emotion. And…there's another benefit I didn't mention. My facility with the Veil-Piercer Skill may have deepened a bit more than I hinted." Zed cleared his throat. He looked around and stepped through into the Other Place, motioning for me to follow.

I complied, though not before casting a glance "skyward" as if praying for patience. Briefly, I wondered if the gods ever prayed to some higher being, but snapped back to the moment as Zed closed the rift, cutting us off from Tartarus.

"You need something to be able to access the Seed energy Blue converts, even beyond the Veil. I…might be able to do something about that, actually."

"How?"

"Pestilence had a kind of connection to the Abhorrent in his chest, a tether that was feeding him energy as long as he was outside the Other Place. I've been thinking… Why can't I just create something like that connecting you to Blue? It might also act as a safety line, something to let me drag you back out of the Void if you can't get out by yourself."

I stared, wide-eyed and entirely unsure how to respond. Was my brother's suggestion even possible?

He rubbed the back of his head sheepishly, shrugging when my staring became awkward. His voice still held a bit of pride when he said, "What? These upgrades I did weren't all for nothing, you know. Veil-Piercer was never *just* about the Other Place."

Interlude 5

Reed's mom reached forward and very deliberately said, "I'm sorry, my son seems to have been making a prank call instead of doing his homework," then pressed the button to hang up.

Reed shrank back from her, his eyes on the meat cleaver.

Her smile didn't waver. "You're grounded." A hand darted out for his arm, quickly snapping off the smaller link attached to his forearm. Then she scooped up his desktop link as well.

Normally, when he was grounded, she just took away his access to all non-academic Net pages. It was easy to do, since he was a minor. Taking away the entire link was something else. It contained all his credits, his identification, and even the homework she supposedly wanted him to do.

He didn't mention any of this, afraid of her reaction.

She stepped back, both links in one hand and the knife in the other. "You'll get these back when you've proved you know how to behave properly, mister." She glanced around the room as if searching for other contraband, and for half an instant, her gaze made contact with the mirror on the wall. Her body trembled, more like a convulsion than a shudder, and she almost fell.

Instinctively, he reached out to catch her. She was still his mom, after all, just trapped inside the parasite.

She jerked away and regained her balance, though the trembles remained for a few seconds and she looked pale and winded. The smile was gone from her face. "Now what do you say, Reed?"

He stared at her for a few moments in consternation, until her eyebrows rose challengingly.

"I'm sorry?" he guessed.

She nodded sharply, regained her smile, and left. He heard the telltale sound of his bedroom door locking after she had closed it. He hadn't even known the old lock had a matching key, and the fact that it locked from the outside was even worse. He felt like the crazy relative confined in the attic of some Victorian pulp novel, and cursed whoever had designed the old house.

When he was alone again, he stood to look in the silver mirror, blank-faced with shock. He'd just ruined everything. Without his links, trapped in an upstairs bedroom, how was he supposed to get help? He reached out and tried to pry the silver mirror off his wall, but as before, it wouldn't budge.

He started to pace, then sat down on his bed and let himself succumb to the urge to simply cry. He wasn't ashamed. If ever there was a time that warranted some crying, this was that moment.

When he was done, he felt empty, and that was actually better. "I won't give up," he whispered, a stubborn energy making him stand and move to the window. He looked down, gauging the possibility of injuring himself if he fell to the ground below. Maybe, if he dangled from the edge, or rappelled down with a rope made of his bedsheets, like he'd seen in the films…

But he would need the mirror. He didn't want to end up like Demi and Lucas.

He pulled the antique butter knife from his pocket. "Sorry, Dad," he murmured before stabbing it into the wall next to the mirror.

It took him over two hours to finish making preparations, being as quiet as possible and constantly ready to hide all evidence and pretend he was working on homework.

His mom didn't even come to let him out to use the bathroom, so he needn't have worried.

When night fell, he hid all his preparations under the bed and lay down. He couldn't leave until his parents were deeply asleep.

The house was old, poorly soundproofed, and creaky, and they might hear him otherwise.

As he waited, he thought over his plan, as far as it went. He also reviewed his preparations, carefully considering each item hidden away beneath him. Reed knew it would be dangerous out there, and he needed to be careful to avoid seeing something he shouldn't or tipping off any parasites to his purpose.

Tired, stressed, and at the edge of hope, Reed fell asleep.

The sound of a key scraping in the lock disturbed him and he jerked to wakefulness, disoriented, terrified, and furious at himself for, yet again, screwing everything up.

It was the middle of the night, and he could see the moon through his window, shining red through the smog and faintly illuminating his room. Reed gripped the slightly mangled butter knife under his pillow and made sure his blanket was completely covering his now-bare mattress.

The door creaked open to reveal his dad, which he hadn't expected. The man's gaze met his eyes in the dark without difficulty. He entered the room and silently closed the door behind himself. Instead of sitting beside Reed on the bed like he had when Reed was younger, the man moved to sit in the desk chair, hidden in the shadows where the beam of moonlight couldn't quite reach.

"Son, I know you're grounded because you were rebellious and didn't listen to your mother," he said.

Reed was silent, and the pause stretched out awkwardly. His hand was sweaty around the handle of the butter knife.

"Perhaps you're acting out because you're not getting enough physical activity. You need an outlet. Perhaps you should take up a…team sport. Like *track*." His dad's speech was more hesitant than it usually was, as if he was thinking hard about what he was trying to convey. "Yes, I think that's perfect. It's one of the most *normal* things a boy like you could do."

"Alright," Reed said tentatively, not mentioning that it was halfway through the school year and tryouts had ended long ago. He realized that the invisible parasites were probably using group activities like sports to secretly spread to new hosts.

His dad shifted in the dark, letting out what sounded like a restrained sigh of relief. "Good. I'm glad you agree. But you know, if you're going to make it onto the track team, you'll have to take up *running*. In fact, you should probably start…*running* as soon as possible, to prepare for tryouts. Most runners get their workout in first thing in the morning, which is totally normal, you know."

Reed couldn't help but notice that his dad kept emphasizing the word "running." The parasites were clearly reliant on keeping up a perception of normalcy, but this seemed like something else to Reed.

"I've unlocked your door so you don't have to wake your mother and me up when you go for a *run*." He heavily emphasized the word.

Reed nodded stiffly. "I understand." His dad was trying to help him escape, but, probably because the parasite was listening, wasn't able to be direct about it. How was the man even mentally lucid enough to fight like this? "Thank you," Reed added. "I won't let you down. I promise." He swallowed past the lump in his throat, hoping his dad understood what he meant.

"Good. I love you, son."

Reed had to swallow again a couple times before he could force the words out. "I love you, too, Dad." It felt like goodbye.

His dad stood, pulling something from the pocket of his robe and setting it on the edge of Reed's bed. "Here's your identification link. Your mother forgot that you would need it to turn in your homework at school. I told her we'd better give it back, if we don't want your teacher giving us an angry call."

Reed knew school didn't start again until the day after next, so really, this was his dad trying to help him again.

"It's still got a parental lock on it, but at least you'll be able to ID yourself if…well, if…" His voice had started to slow down, and he shook his head sharply, as if trying to get water out of his ear. "You'll have access to your credits, if you get too tired out there when you're running and need to call a taxi pod to drive you back home. Or, if you get lost, all official government services are still accessible, so you can use the GPS. You might need to *get help*." He was breathing a little harder, as if the effort of speaking was straining him physically. "That's all, son. Goodnight." He left without even giving Reed a chance to respond.

Run, and *get help*.

Reed repeated the emphasized words to himself in the dark, a mantra to settle his trembling hands. He waited an hour longer, sitting in his chair beside the window to make sure he didn't fall asleep again.

The moon was high in the sky by the time he stood to leave. His dad had left the bedroom door unlocked for him, but he was worried that the creaking of the floorboards and sound of the door opening would alert the parasites. It was safer to leave through the window. He'd already torn up and tied together his bed sheets into a makeshift rope.

Every sound as he opened the window, tossed down his backpack, and crawled out onto the ledge of the roof seemed abnormally loud.

He tugged on the makeshift rope, which he'd attached to the unused radiator pipe in his room, hoping it wouldn't suddenly rip and drop him as soon as he put his weight on it.

He ended up having to drop the last few feet anyway, as the bed sheets weren't long enough, but other than a faint twinge in his ankles, he was fine.

With one last look toward the house, Reed picked up his backpack and slunk away. He slid the butter knife partway up his sleeve so he could palm the blade in his hand and inconspicuously keep looking at it to ward off mind control.

It took him less than half an hour to get out of the residential district. He remembered what had happened to Demi and Lucas, so before he reached the more highly trafficked roads that would have billboard screens lining the sides of the buildings, he took out the silver mirror from his backpack. He'd had to carve out the entire piece of wall to get the mirror free. He'd covered up the hole with a poster and tossed the revealing chunks of plaster and wood out the window.

The streets were never empty, not even this late at night, but they weren't crowded, and Reed was able to keep to the shadows, using the mirror to check his surroundings and navigate forward. The plan, as far as it went, was to head straight for the nearest enforcer station and speak to them in person. If he could find even one enforcer who wasn't infected, or could help someone remove their parasite, then they could go rescue his parents before it was too late. It was, admittedly, a rather feeble plan, but it was as far as Reed had managed to get.

Words from one of the screens caught Reed's ear as he passed by it. Something about a press conference called jointly by Eve Redding and one of the Estreyan queens earlier that evening?

He turned his back so he could see the screen in the mirror, hoping no one dangerous noticed him.

He'd thought his situation couldn't get any worse, but that naive belief was torn away as he listened to the recap of the press conference.

There was another alien like Pestilence, the one who had used his powers to spread that horrible plague, and it was somewhere on either Estreyer or Earth, they didn't know where. They didn't even know what its powers were, except that they'd probably be different from Pestilence's, and that it was very dangerous. They were calling it an Avatar. The name didn't make sense to Reed, but maybe the subtitled translation of her speech had lost something in English.

The news anchor explained that there had been rioting already, and enforcers were struggling to deal with the panic, while many of the roads in bigger cities were experiencing blockages and wrecks as people tried to evacuate due to fear of the same spread of infection that had happened last time.

The Estreyan queen had tried to avoid broadcasting it plainly, but it was obvious they didn't know much of anything about this new aggressor. They had a plan, they said, but how good could their plan be when they didn't even know where the enemy was? He would have felt a lot better about it if Eve Redding was part of the press conference, but apparently she was off somewhere on a secret mission to stop the Avatar. Obviously, it would try to kill her and everyone else on the Seal of Nine, just like Pestilence had.

Reed looked around. Some pedestrians seemed anxious and hurried, but there weren't nearly as many pods on the roads as he would have expected if panic had led to an exodus. Maybe it was just because it was so late at night, or maybe the parasites felt fleeing in panic wasn't "normal."

This was probably why he'd been on hold so long the night

before when trying to call the national emergency services. The lines would have been swamped by calls from everyone who had heard the news.

He let out a shuddering breath, moving to lean against a wall in an alley from which the news channel was still visible. Would the enforcers or military even have the focus to spare for the parasites, with this much larger threat looming over everyone? What if they just…quarantined the whole place and decided to put it on the back burner, or something, rather than trying to fix the problem? Reed shook his head, trying to tell himself he was being ridiculous.

In the corner of the news channel screen, a film clip popped up as the anchor moved on to speculation about whether the strange warps that had appeared simultaneously with Pestilence's death had anything to do with this new danger. The clip was of their local warp, taken from the channel that broadcast a live recording of the phenomenon twenty-four hours a day.

Reed almost choked on his own spit again as he gasped.

A creature sat on a throne in front of the rippling warp that hung just above the concrete. Both the creature and the throne it sat on were made of something orange-ish and see-through, like amber. The creature's—no, the *alien's* face looked like a tortured, screaming human, its expression carved and unchanging. Grotesquely twisted, frozen faces seemed to be trying to escape its entire body, like souls condemned to hell.

A couple scientists passed by the edge of the screen. Both were twisted and inhuman, subsumed by terrifying parasites.

The news anchor didn't seem to see anything strange about that, but Reed noticed that a few people who glanced at the screen as they walked by suddenly stopped moving and turned to stare at the creature. Their eyes glazed over as parasites crawled *out of their shadows* and attached to them.

Reed clamped a hand over his mouth very carefully and turned so that even the mirror wouldn't show him the alien. He forced himself to breathe deeply and slowly through his nose, keeping his mouth covered to bottle up the terrified scream building inside him.

He had been wrong. Even his worst fear had still been naïve. It wasn't a Player, or an infestation of Estreyan monsters. The thing taking control of the minds and bodies of everyone around him was the new version of Pestilence. And it was specifically designed to keep anyone from ever *realizing* they needed to fight against it until it was too late. How was *he* supposed to stop it?

Chapter 19

Out of the night that covers me,
    Black as the pit from pole to pole,
    I thank whatever gods may be
    For my unconquerable soul.
    —William Ernest Henley

IT TOOK ZED ALMOST two days of constant experimentation to figure out how to connect me to the place Blue inhabited. The rest of us watched with mixed apprehension and impatience as his attempts to weave a tether out of things only he could see repeatedly unraveled into strange phenomena and dangerous effects that the rest of us *could* see. Sam had to heal Zed a few times, actually picking up a few novel types of damage along the way. One marionette got turned literally inside-out passing too close to Zed as he lost control again. After that, we gave the increasingly frazzled, exhausted boy a wider birth.

Outside of the Other Place, none of us mentioned what Zed was working on, or why. If the Avatar was somehow watching, it might figure it out on its own, but we certainly wouldn't make it easier.

Being constantly on edge as we waited for the latest disastrous backlash was only a moderate source of tension, however, compared to the strained interactions among the rest of us.

As we gathered for dinner, Jacky edged around the camp stove toward Kris. Her Struggle Skill started to make her grow before she tamped it back down again, and she kept popping all the joints on her body in rotation, sounding like some kind of nervous woodpecker. She cleared her throat. "Um, I'm sorry, Kris. I was being stupid. I've just been really worried that you or Gregor were gonna get hurt and I wasn't gonna be able to protect you. That's why I've been training you guys so hard. I shoulda realized, though, after what happened, maybe you wouldn't be in the mood to…" She cleared her throat again. "I'm not good with feelings and stuff, you know, but sometimes you just gotta hit something when it gets to be too much, yeah? I'm not gonna make you train with me any more if you don't want to. I know I screwed up. I—"

Kris, who had been staring up at Jacky from her seat beside the camp stove, suddenly hopped down and ran away.

Jacky stared after her, her mouth hanging open on aborted words, one hand raised as if to reach out for Kris.

"I'll go talk to her," Gregor said quickly, jogging after his sister into the darkness.

Jacky's hand fell back to her side, and she seemed to deflate like a popped balloon. "She hates me," she said, her voice thick with emotion.

"She doesn't hate you—" I started to say, but Jacky shook her head and ignored me, escaping from the camp in the opposite direction.

In the distance, Wraith watched as she threw herself into the middle of a violent kata, attacking invisible enemies and the stalagmites that grew up from the ground with blistering, explosive strikes.

Kris, puffy-eyed and red-faced, eventually returned with Gregor, who grimaced and shook his head at me when she wasn't looking.

Jacky kept training until Kris had fallen asleep, and then crawled into her own bedroll, shrugging my hand off her shoulder when I scooted over to talk to her. "Not right now," she whispered, cocooning herself up inside the blanket.

Catching me alone, Gregor told me, "Kris feels horrible about what she did to Jacky. Jacky apologizing just somehow made her feel worse? Which I don't understand, but Kris won't explain it to me. I think maybe she's just sad about her marionettes dying?" He shrugged helplessly, continuing in a wise tone like an old sage, "Sometimes you throw tantrums when it really hurts, even if you don't really *want* to, because you have to do *something* and there's just nothing else."

I remembered his own violent response to Blaine's death, and nodded silently, guilt wrenching at my internal organs. Actions always had unintended consequences.

Perhaps looking for somewhere, anywhere, to focus his frustration, Gregor sneered at Ichi as the Estreyan grabbed a meal kit from beside the camp stove. "I should have Sam poison his food," he muttered.

Sam's own hostility toward Ichi hadn't lessened even without Black Sun, though he showed it in non-torturous ways instead. As far as I knew he had yet to settle on conditions both versions of himself could agree to, and I'd even found him arguing with himself in the mirror. Maybe my idea had been futile.

Ichi spent a lot of time by himself, by choice, but also because the ostracism wasn't subtle. He was always within reach in case of an emergency, but he slept farther away from the camp than anyone else, stayed silent and watched the rest of us interact rather than joining in himself, and was always wearing a wry, sad smile that seemed to annoy almost everyone else.

I knew why he'd done what he had, but I couldn't forgive him, didn't want to sympathize with him, and had no plans to try and ease his discomfort or lift his mood. I didn't really care if that made me cruel or hypocritical.

Jacky and Kris continued to avoid each other, and though I wanted to force them to talk it out, I knew I couldn't. Sometimes people just needed time.

I'd been subtly avoiding Adam since his confession, which was difficult when we were all camping out in such close quarters, but I was able to avoid being alone with him again.

Torliam was not-so-subtly angry at Adam, the few words he deigned to speak to Adam clipped and derisive. "He acted selfishly,"

Torliam told me. "You need all your concentration to make it through the upcoming ordeal, *not* to be distracted by the burden of others' regard."

Adam was unrepentant, but spent as little time in Torliam's presence as possible, mostly doing experiments with the Void to try and figure out how it worked and what exactly was keeping it confined. I'd given back his fruit despite his protestations. "I don't need it, I have my own, and Blue can feed me way more power than a second fruit could. Keep it. Do you think I'll be better off if you were to die when we face the Avatar?" I let irritation slip into my tone, and he was unable to continue arguing. He'd tried to start a conversation a few times since then, and I tried to keep it from being awkward, but neither of us was successful in talking about anything but the pressing business at hand.

When Zed finally succeeded in creating the tether that would let Blue feed me energy, he decided to take a much-needed rest. While Zed slept, the Other Place closed, and the tether unraveled again, forcing him to recreate it from scratch when he finally woke. Gregor had been excited about the possibility of Zed creating a tether for each of us, but not only did it take a couple hours to weave up and require active maintenance and the kind of concentration that would leave Zed unable to defend himself in a fight, he could only create one at a time. Plus, Blue seemed to shudder at the very thought of *giving up* power, and had to be reminded constantly that it would gain so much more than it lost keeping me alive.

Now, the whole team was standing at the top of the tallest pyramid's stairs, doing our best to ignore the looming Void hanging above the center of the colossal structure. I'd trained for this, both mentally and physically, but I couldn't deny my fear, only try to keep it from being obvious to the rest of the team.

"How long is it going to take?" Gregor asked, standing beside Kris on the opposite side of the group from Jacky. "Do we have enough power?"

"I don't know," I admitted. "It should be enough, as long as I don't need more than an hour. Hopefully, I'll have learned what I need to much more quickly than that."

"Are you going to be able to get out again once you go in?"

"The connection Zed created will help with that, if I can't do it myself. He'll pull me back in twenty minutes if I haven't come back on my own already. Don't worry, I promise I'll be fine."

Gregor stared at me for a few seconds too long, his expression inscrutable. "You can't promise that," he said finally.

Once, he would have accepted my assurance unreservedly. Again, I registered that he was growing up, realizing the adults in his life were people, too, and fallible.

He turned and motioned to one of Kris's new egg-like rescue marionettes, and it quickly handed him a small balloon full of a fizzing blue liquid. "I think you should take this with you. Put it in your mouth. If It's bad In there, you can move all your Seeds to your brain and use Chaos to send this through the roof of your mouth into your brain tissue. It'll keep you alive even without a heart and lungs and stuff. As long as you can keep your brain intact and Zed can pull that back through, it'll be okay even if the entire rest of your body dies. You've only got about five minutes of oxygen after injecting it, though. I tried to make it longer, but…"

I stared at the fizzing liquid, slowly reaching out to accept the balloon.

"I know it might be difficult to get it into your brain. I would have given you a syringe you could insert at the base of your skull, but I'm worried anything outside your body is going to get disintegrated right away, and then you wouldn't be able to use it."

"Thanks," I said simply. I sat cross-legged on the ground and entered a meditative state. My mental mansion was no longer grey and gloomy and filled with terrifying ordeals. Bright spring light shone down from the sky constantly despite the lack of a sun, and a soft breeze kept the temperature from feeling too warm. I'd added more windows to the castle rooms, and mirrors, too, in defiance of my discomfort with them, and the combination sent energizing light cascading throughout.

I walked through each of the rooms, settling my thoughts and emotions, till I came to a room that featured only a full-length mirror. I stared at myself intently, and after a while raised a six-fingered hand and clenched it, feeling the rightness of the movement. My scales shifted as I took a deep breath and nodded to myself. What was left was only calm, alert readiness. The hint of cold rage wasn't something I could get rid of, but it buoyed me up rather than pushing me off balance. I opened my eyes and stood.

I turned to the rip in the world hanging beside Zed, took off my backpack, and removed the crystal from within. Meeting Blue's one big eye, I placed the crystal on the ground just inside the opening.

QUEST COMPLETED!

I pulled the fruit of life out of the pouch and held it up. "Here goes. Wish me luck, guys." Before I could let any sense of apprehension or discomfort at the nearness of the Void slip back into me, I popped the metallic, ozone-scented fruit into my mouth. I'd barely attempted to bite down on it when, as if responding to my intentions, it dissolved, slipping down my throat even before I could swallow.

I gasped, opening my eyes wide as my back arched and I almost rose off the ground with the euphoric force of it. The elixir of well-being and electricity crackled through every inch of my body, leaving me tingling and more *awake* than I'd ever been in my life.

I let out a heartfelt *whoop* of pure adrenalized eagerness, then shot my teammates a reassuring grin. "Whew, that's a rush." A quick scratch to my palm proved that the healing was in effect as it closed before even getting the chance to bleed.

Grim-faced, Zed turned to the large jagged portal to the Other Place and pulled some invisible things through the air, looping them over me. I felt no different until the last loop, as he gathered a handful of invisible threads and pressed them *into* my sternum.

"I felt that," I said. "It's…cold and crackly." It was like a combination of the Other Place and the lightning-burst of the fruit.

"That should mean it's working," he said. "If you—if you need to fight, or something besides just regenerating, you should have as much access to this power conduit as the fruit does. Don't hold back for fear of running out of Stamina."

"Thank you," I said, resting my hand lightly on his shoulder for a moment before turning to the others, running my eyes across them too quickly. I didn't want it to seem like I thought I would never see them again. "See you soon." We didn't need to waste any more time talking. We'd covered all the contingency plans for what to do when I came back out again already.

I turned, popped the fizzy blue balloon into my mouth, being careful not to puncture it on my sharp teeth, and walked toward the Void. Was this the point where the future could change? I shook that thought away. Maybe the future had already changed. I was prepared for this moment in a way I doubted would have been possible if I weren't actively trying to subvert the Oracle's vision. There was little we could have done to be more ready.

I stepped over the edge of the ring of fire and into the black-tar surface without slowing down.

I HAD EXPECTED pain within the Void. There was none. In fact, there was nothing at all. My mind reeled at the absolute emptiness, which was an alien sensation to a creature born with five senses who had then gained a sixth. I felt the chilled buzzing in my chest as the invisible tether connecting me to Blue channeled energy into me.

It was urgent that I understood the Void, and I tried to do so, but in doing so it felt as if the Void was seeping into me—eating me. Where it touched my flesh, I became it, losing form and matter and energy, any hint of what I had once been. Where it touched my thoughts, I lost them.

It wasn't an attack. There was no malice, no destructive force, no direction at all. The Void was the absence of all things, and the only thing with substance or thought there was me.

The rush of energy dissipated as fast as it could course into me.

As I experienced the Void, I became it. Time lost its meaning. Then, it was not the Void I had trouble understanding, but the Eve.

I forgot what I was doing, why I was there, who I was.

Even the tingling, cold well of strength that dwelt at my core began to detach from where I had once been.

I lost myself.

There was a tugging, dragging something with it. Suddenly, like a child birthed from the womb, everything was sound and light and smells and sensation, overwhelming to the point of pain.

The girl, dark-haired and flailing even as her extremities regrew and her scales reformed, screamed.

She was afraid.

Dark power spilled out of her, as if to devour the world.

Chapter 20

In the fell clutch of circumstance
    I have not winced nor cried aloud.
    Under the bludgeonings of chance
    My head is bloody, but unbowed.
    —William Ernest Henley

THE BOY with the black eyes and the touch which brought both healing and pain turned his gaze on the screaming girl, and she calmed, her destructive power receding.

Her own gaze was empty and unseeing, her body limp on the ground in front of the fire-ringed portal to emptiness.

The small boy-child, the Shadow, turned to the one with black eyes. "Something's wrong! She's hurt, fix her!" he demanded. He stuck a finger in her mouth, digging out a burst balloon covered in blue fluid that evaporated quickly on contact with the air.

Black eyes turned blue, but the girl did not move when he touched her. "There's nothing I can do," he said. "Whatever's wrong with her, it isn't physical. The fruit did its job there."

The boy whose fingers dug into the fabric of reality shuddered and sagged, pale-faced and bleeding from the nose, and the healer turned to aid him instead. As the boy's fingers loosened around the invisible power conduit, the scaled girl twitched and began to dissolve into inky blackness. With a horrified gasp, the boy regained his grasp on the power conduit, urging the creature beyond the Veil to continue feeding her regeneration.

The large one with the gold hair turned a glare on the tattooed one, whose skin crackled with nervous electricity. "Do you still think you were justified?" the large one asked, his words a growl.

The tattooed one did not respond except to sneer, but his fingers twitched nervously and the electricity crackled with a stinging bite. "Something's wrong with her mind?" he asked the healer. "Is it going to get better?"

"I hope so," the other boy responded distractedly, using his blood-borne power to reinforce the Veil-Piercer.

The beautiful girl bounced restlessly, cracking her knuckles and forcefully keeping herself from growing larger. "There's gotta be something we can do."

"Get me something to offload this damage onto. Maintaining this connection between Blue and Eve is hurting Zed, bad."

The girl nodded sharply, turning to the single outsider among them. "You take me. Somewhere with monsters I can knock out and bring back here, yeah?"

MY EYES WERE LEAKING, burning with a combination of dryness and tears from forgetting to blink, forgetting even that such a thing was possible. Shapes and colors moved blurrily in front of me, meaningless. The shapes made sounds, equally incomprehensible.

A cold, wet tickle on my hand preceded a burst of smell and sensation in my mind.

I jerked, the spasm moving me away from the cold tickle, but it followed, continuing to push thoughts that were not my own into me. My mind was far too jumbled to comprehend the outside thoughts at first, and it hurt to try, but after a while they cohered into simple feelings and impressions, warmth and wellbeing.

It felt good. I tried to hold on to that, but there wasn't enough of me to do so.

PILES of dead monsters lay against the stones at the base of the pyramid, each killed more gruesomely than the last to feed the power of the one who was keeping the Veil-Piercer awake and undamaged.

The Veil-Piercer was in turn maintaining the power conduit that kept the girl alive.

Fatigue stood out in the drooping shoulders and grey faces of the people around her.

The outsider, sitting away from the others at the edge of camp, watched as the girl once again started to dissolve into tar-like blackness.

The tailos scrambled back and away from where it had been pressing its face into her insensate hand.

The one with black eyes forced calm on her, and the creature beyond the Veil grudgingly fed her the energy to regenerate her mortal form.

"I doubt how long this will continue working," the outsider drawled, a muscle in his jaw jumping. "If her loss of control spills beyond our ability to contain, I would be willing to take her to the farthest edges of this world, where we might hope the destruction does not spread far enough to devour more innocent lives."

The others turned to glare at him with varying levels of vitriol.

The black eyes of their healer sparked with poorly suppressed anger. "She cannot leave Tartarus like this. She made a vow, and the rest of us did, too."

"I did not make this vow," the outsider said. "But if not that, then perhaps I could take the rest of you and leave her here."

"She's not gonna lose control," the other girl said, her voice full of fearful, angry prayer. "She's gonna get better and we're gonna fix everything. Keep your mouth shut or I'll shut it for you."

"There is optimism, and there is realism," he replied, unperturbed.

"You don't know Eve," the other Estreyan said, something unreadable undercutting the clear fatigue in his tone.

"Your confidence seems misplaced," the outsider muttered, but not loudly enough to draw more than a couple more glares.

"I want cake," the tiny girl said suddenly. She shot a look toward the outsider, her eyebrows rising in an approximation of imperiousness. "Why don't you make yourself useful and go get us some cake?"

THE FOREIGN THOUGHTS WERE BACK, but this time they were more complex than simple comfort and warmth. Fleeting moments of other emotions, other thoughts, interwoven smells and sights and sensations tied to meaning. These felt good, too, in their own way, and I tried to grasp them, but my mind had the coordination of a newborn baby.

Still, they sparked something within me, as if rousing a sleeping beast. It crept upward with a cold burn, like over-strong mint. Where it passed, I drew together like smoke into steel.

THE TINY GIRL sidled awkwardly over to the edge of camp, tugging on the other's sleeve. "Jacky, I—I'm sorry."

The other lifted her head from where it had been cradled in her hands. "What?"

"I'm sorry. I shouldn't have—I wasn't—" The little one's voice wavered, and she stopped to swallow before clenching her fists and blurting the rest out. "I shouldn't have hurt you! It wasn't your fault! I'm really sorry so please forgive me!"

The other girl gaped, then blinked away the tears gathering in her eyes. "No, it wasn't your fault, Kris. It was me. Me and my stupid training 'cause I don't know what else to do and I'm just scared all the time of what's coming for us and I want you to be—" She clamped a hand over her own mouth to stop the gush of words. "*Mierda*," she whispered, letting the hand fall away to scoop up the small one into an engulfing hug. "I'm sorry, too," she returned, finally.

The little boy snorted and murmured something derisive about "girls" from across the camp, but he was smiling.

The piles of gruesomely mutilated monsters at the base of the pyramid had grown higher.

The scaled girl, now lying on a bedroll next to the camp stove, shifted a little and made some small sounds, though her eyes were still unfocused.

The others gathered around with hope, grasping her cold hands and calling her name. She didn't respond.

THE TATTOOED ONE and the outsider snapped into existence among the others like a silent crack of lightning. "I found it," he gasped. "I just talked to Mardliest. We found the—" He cut off as the small boy jerked a hand across his throat in a slicing motion.

"Don't talk about it," the boy said. "We don't know if it can hear us."

The black-eyed boy looked to the Veil-Piercer and the grey tear in the world behind him. "We can't go into the Other Place and close it off. We already saw what happens to Eve if Zed lets go of that conduit."

The fair-haired Estreyan rubbed at his unkempt beard, pulling at the dark bags under his eyes. "Let us be vague, if we can, then, and hope that we are unobserved. We must have the information. Besides, no secret can stay such for long if more than one person knows of it. Even if we are not the ones to alert the enemy, others can do it just as easily. The true worry is that we bring its attention to Eve."

"*Mierda*," the other girl choked out, looking over the still-sleeping girl. "Do you think it knows what happened to Eve? Is that why it appeared?"

The tattooed one shook his head. "It didn't reveal itself. It's still in hiding, as far as we can tell, but my algorithms flagged an anomaly, and when we looked into it, evidence started piling up. It's very dangerous. Mind control, memory loss, that kind of thing. There might be a counter, but I don't want to mention it out loud. I'm about to go get something that might help us. Ichi will take me there, but I just wanted to make sure you guys were on guard to make sure nothing happens to Eve in the meantime."

"She needs to wake up," the tiny girl whispered, pale-faced.

No one responded to that, but grim looks were shared all around.

THE BEAST inside me continued to wake and unfurl, and where it touched I fused into cold steel, razor-edged.

Something new pushed into my mind, but it wasn't the scent-heavy thoughts from before. No, this had a familiar tinge to it, an emotion I recognized, a *taste* that brought to mind sky-blue glow and a deep voice. It was defiance. Anger. Strength in the face of despair.

It came and went, several times, along with the other thoughts that pushed through my skin with the touch of fur and a cold wet nose.

I began to recognize the people around me, understand the words they spoke, and have thoughts coherent enough to get to the end of them before they turned to smoke. Time had little meaning, as if I were in the grips of a high fever, but eventually, like a drowning person breaking through to air, I woke.

"How long have I been out?" I rasped, focusing with effort up at Torliam's astonished face.

Chapter 21

Beyond this place of wrath and tears
  Looms but the Horror of the shade,
  And yet the menace of the years
  Finds and shall find me unafraid.
  —William Ernest Henley

TORLIAM GAPED WIDE-EYED down at me, his expression absurdly, comically shocked.

I blinked eyelids that felt like sandpaper, trying to get my tear ducts to produce some moisture.

Slowly, his look of wide-eyed surprise transformed into an ecstatic grin, like the rising sun casting away the shadow of a long night. It was, perhaps, the happiest look anyone had ever given me.

I tried again to ask him how long I'd been asleep, but my throat was dry, and the first attempt at speech had irritated it. Instead, I ended up coughing in his face. The convulsions only made me aware that my whole body ached as if every muscle in it had been pulled apart and then sewn back together. Which, I supposed, wasn't too far from the truth.

"She is awake!" he roared, scrambling to get water for me.

The rest of my teammates appeared quickly. Jacky literally slid the last couple meters to reach my side, like my waking was some sort of extreme sporting event.

While the others were slightly less dramatic, they were no less enthusiastic, and I had difficulty processing the head-spinning onslaught of happiness and questions about my wellbeing.

Torliam cradled me upward toward the water like a child, bringing it to my mouth.

I gave him a glare and reached for the canteen myself, but somehow managed to *miss*, instead slapping him limply on the arm.

"Do not try to move just yet," Torliam said. "Sam?"

Sam's fingers were already pressed to the skin of my neck, as if he were taking my pulse. "She's fine—I think. Physically, at least. A little dehydrated, and she'll need food. We should probably try to keep her calm, too."

I frowned. Keep me calm? The way he'd said it hinted at fear, not simple concern for my wellbeing. "How long?" I repeated once I'd wetted my throat.

"Three days," Adam said after a bit of hesitation.

Three *days*? I wiggled my fingers and toes experimentally, then sat up. The movement sent the world spinning. Something dark and empty swam in the back of my mind. I attacked it instinctively with a rush of cold rage that raised the little hairs all over my body and brought a tingling flush to my cheeks. My fingers clenched with the futile desire to slice something, and when I exhaled, a faint mist of Chaos traveled on my breath.

The others scrambled back, and Sam's eyes instantly turned full-black.

"I'm fine," I said, attempting to project a tone of calm assurance. That set off another round of coughing, and I had to drink some more. Slowly and deliberately, I reached for the edges of the emptiness, the Void within me. Not reaching out for it, but feeling around its shape. It was power defined by its absence. If I touched it, acknowledged it in any direct way, it would consume my thoughts and grow within me, leaving less of me and more of it.

"Did you do it? Did you get it?" Zed said. His face was pale and grey except for red-rimmed and bloodshot eyes.

"Yes," I said.

My teammates indulged in another round of celebratory

whooping while I experimentally clenched and unclenched the rest of my muscles and looked around.

It was then that I noticed Zed still had the Other Place open, his raw fingers clenched around an invisible rope. Obviously I wasn't fully coherent yet, because I should have seen it right away. I decided to postpone standing up till I was sure I had the faculties to handle myself. Hopefully, it wouldn't take long. There was a lot to do. "Did anything happen while I was out?" I asked. "Any news on the Avatar?"

Wraith caught the look Adam and Sam shared behind my back.

"What?" I snapped, then winced as I caught my tongue on the too-sharp teeth to the sides of my mouth. I opened and closed my jaw, rolling it around and stretching out the muscles.

"I think you should take a little time to rest first," Adam said.

Well, that was unacceptable. I rolled my shoulders, and, with a deep breath, lurched to my feet. A brief burst of nausea and dizziness hit me once I was upright, but I managed to stay vertical.

Gregor eased up beside me as if ready to support me if I lost my balance, caterpillar brows drawn down darkly. "Are you okay?"

"You found something? You did, didn't you? Tell me!" I commanded.

"You must look in the mirror first," Torliam said, motioning to a full-sized, ornate mirror standing at the edge of camp.

I hadn't noticed it, either, and though I was about to insist that I was more than healthy enough to just *hear the truth*, the bizarreness of the request suddenly hit me, and I held my tongue. I turned and walked toward the strange mirror, Gregor sticking to my side like glue.

Ichi adjusted the angle upward so that I could see my face.

I stared into it, wondering what I was supposed to be looking for. I twisted around to catch a glimpse of my back. "I look... normal? What am I supposed to be seeing?"

"We found the Avatar," Jacky blurted.

Adam turned to glare at her. "What part of 'we need to be cautious,' did you not understand? Was it the *word* cautious?"

"She didn't remember anything! She's safe!" Jacky said. She turned to me. "If the Av—if *it*," she corrected with a glance toward Adam, "had erased your memory, you would have suddenly remembered when you looked in the silver mirror. Basically, if you see *it*, it makes you forget. It can also do some other things, but that only seems to be happening to the people living in the city around it."

Heady, dizzy triumph filled me, and I grinned victoriously. "That's great. That's *fantastic!* Well, what are we waiting for? I'm ready, let's go rip that scab on reality apart until it dissolves into primordial ooze."

"I do not think you are ready," Torliam said. I was about to snap back with a rebuttal, but he continued, "You made a vow, remember?"

That gave me pause. I couldn't break my vow. I had to be *sure*.

I looked down at myself, doing both a physical and mental inventory.

The results were undeniable. My frustration surged like an animal lunging against its leash, and I swallowed it back down. *Control.* Control must come first, and must come *absolutely*. I could not walk out of Tartarus with the emptiness ringing in the back of my mind otherwise. "Well, alright. At least tell me what you found, though. Is it safe if we discuss *it* in the Other Place?"

Zed gave me a pained smile, his fingers trembling. "As long as you're sure you're not going to dissolve into a puddle of Void as soon as I drop the connection between you and Blue. I won't be able to re-weave it in time to save you."

I looked from face to face, taking in their pale cheeks, dark eyes, unkempt hair—all the signs of their worry, their fatigue. To my surprise, that knowledge settled me, gave me a sense of belonging that I hadn't even realized I'd been missing. They were roots that would help to anchor me. They knew me. I belonged here.

I wanted to assure my brother that I would be fine, but hesitated to do so. "Give me a moment," I said instead, turning back to the mirror. I stared at myself a while longer, then sat down, crossing my legs and closing my eyes.

Meditation was harder than it had been in a long time, not because I couldn't calm down, but because my thoughts were slippery, like half-formed jello sliding through my grasp. Eventually, I succeeded, going back through the constructs in my mind, walking through the halls and rooms, setting things to right.

When I opened my eyes, I couldn't say that I felt *normal* again —I didn't—but I felt sharp and strong. "It's safe to let go," I told Zed.

He hesitated, but seemed to find some relief in the opportunity to rest.

Gregor still hovered at my side, and I gave him a simple smile, pressing a reassuring hand to his shoulder. "I'm okay now," I said.

He seemed unconvinced. "You almost choked on the balloon. I had to fish it out of your mouth. I didn't think of that, I'm sorry."

"No, it was a good idea. If I'd kept the balloon anywhere else, it would have disappeared instantly. It just turned out that a lack of *oxygen* wasn't really the problem."

Once we were safely enclosed within the Other Place, which was large enough, again, that I could not see its edges with the naked eye, I turned to the others. "Tell me everything."

Torliam and Adam opened their mouths at the same time, both cut off with a mutual glare, and then Adam spoke. "My algorithms found an anomaly. The Avatar is fairly clever, but I don't think she fully understands human nature. See, she—"

"*She?*" I interrupted.

"*It* looks kind of feminine. I saw a recording of her. I'll get to that, just let me explain." When I was silent, he continued. "So after the press conference Queen Mardinest held, pretty much every emergency hotline across both worlds was deluged with an absolute avalanche of panicked reports that people had noticed signs of the Avatar. You know how it goes, most of it was absolute bunk, just raccoons in their trashcans and people wearing hoods that obscured their faces while walking down the street." He waved his hand as if shooing away an invisible fly. "*Except* for one city, which had an abnormally *subdued* reaction. There were a few calls here and there, but a more normal amount, and very few of them about the Avatar."

"Which in itself is suspicious," I breathed.

"*Exactly,*" Adam said, a crackling wave of static jumping between his fingers as he gesticulated. "So my algorithm flagged an anomaly, and we looked into it. Turns out there were more than a few suspicious things happening, and we weren't the only ones who'd noticed. Some peoples' neighbors were acting strangely, and a few had seen things that were unexplainable, and I'm not talking about the weird weather patterns over the city. There were multiple calls to the local enforcers about monsters, parasites, mind control and memory wipes, all with a common theme. Mirrors, and the local warp channel. A couple of the reports were forwarded to the proper destinations, at first, though with everything that's going on, the specialists hadn't even started to investigate. Later reports were never filed, incidents never communicated through the proper channels. Still, any call made to the enforcers is automatically recorded, so we were able to comb their archives for more clues."

"Get to the point," Jacky urged, bouncing on her feet. She had no doubt heard all this already while I'd been asleep.

"My sentiments exactly," Ichi muttered from the edge of the group, drawing a few glares.

Kris pressed into Birch's side, and the tailos wrapped a wing around her, fluffing fur and feathers out to ward off the cold.

Zed's head dipped down and then jerked back up, his eyelids drooping. His gaze wandered in Adam's general direction, failing to focus.

"The Avatar's power propagates through observation," Adam said, grinding his teeth a bit. "Gregor and I saw her through the remote monitoring systems when we first went to examine the data from the warps. She had seated herself on a throne directly in front of one of the warps on Earth. Despite looking right at her through the screen, at the time I remember being absolutely certain the Avatar was not there, and that everything I was looking at was completely normal. Upon looking away, I immediately forgot seeing her at all, and was left only with the surety that everything about the warps was normal."

Gregor shuddered, rubbing at his forehead.

"Others, those who live in the city near the warp, reported seeing, under certain types of reflections, monstrous, parasitic—well, we're not sure if they're invisible, or simply illusions. They push the mind control and memory loss a bit farther, as well as controlling their hosts to keep them from any alarm about the Avatar or its actions. Each parasite seems to take a different form.

One woman reported that hers, a raven that had pecked at her skin until it opened up a hole big enough to nest inside, became visible in the reflection from an antique silver platter. She was able to remove the parasite, at which point she beat it into a pulp with the platter, reportedly killing it. When she tried to tell her husband about what had happened with the intention of getting him to look in the platter as well, he attacked and attempted to kill her."

"Okay, well, that sounds objectively awful," I said, imagining an entire city full of people covered in invisible creatures gnawing, biting, and pecking at them. "What else?"

"A young girl reported seeing a monster rise out of her mother's shadow while she was watching television. We're not sure if that's accurate, because other reports seem confident the effects propagate by looking through any normal mirror. A couple of teenagers made a report saying the parasites, when removed but not killed, disappear back into non-silver mirrors. Upon looking in any normal mirror, the parasite will reappear from the person's shadow and attempt to take control again. In addition to reflections from relatively pure silver, reflections in running water have some chance of revealing the deception, and one woman reported seeing visions of the truth in a quartz basin. The parasites seem to be spreading to those in closest proximity to the Avatar first, with no reports outside Leighton."

"Proximity?" I said. "It's definitely not based on length of exposure? Or the Avatar's… *focus*?"

"It is possible," Torliam said. "But if that were the case, I would expect some of the senior researchers on other warps to be affected, and none have been. We ourselves would have been ideal targets."

"What about other types of reflections? Glass in windows, shiny things?" I asked.

"There have been no reports of this, even among those already aware of the effect and prepared for the danger. We're not sure if this is because the Avatar can't do it, or because maintaining frequent eye contact with a true-silver reflection wards off the effect. Some reports to the enforcers have indicated that the parasites seem to be confused when around those using true-silver, and will not notice them unless their attention is forcibly drawn."

"But it's also possible the Avatar can use any non-silver reflection at all, in addition to any image of…herself?"

"It is," Adam said.

"How long have you known?"

"About thirty-six hours, on Estreyer."

"What's being done? They must have a response in motion?"

Adam shifted on his feet. "We've turned off all visual monitoring of the warps, taken down all the channels that were playing them, and are in the process of force-crashing any film clip containing warp imagery we can find on the Net. We've quarantined those we know have been exposed through their work, whether or not they've shown signs of being affected. There's a quarantine team on route to Leighton now, and hopefully we're not too late to keep anyone with a parasite from escaping. A few people left the city after the press conference, but just like the call volume, the whole place has been abnormally calm."

Torliam cleared his throat. "We have been moving as fast as we can. There has been some…*resistance* from Earth's leaders. They distrust Queen Mardinest."

"For good reason," Sam interjected, scowling. "She wants to raze yet another Earth city to the ground."

"She has not authorized that," Torliam said quickly. "But yes, she believes that to be the best course of action. The Avatar's power is not fully understood, and that has raised some worry that she will be able to use those who have been influenced to further propagate her power, or manifest within the body of any affected person to escape our attempts to kill her. My mother thinks some sacrifice is necessary, for the greater good."

"For the greater good," I mouthed silently. I hated that term. I remembered the last time the Estreyans had destroyed an entire city, during the invasion. The memory caused a residual pang of guilt and horrified grief.

No. I could not allow that to happen again. "I seem to remember that everyone who was affected by Pestilence was cleansed as soon as we killed him. Not only that, we have both your Skill," I said to Torliam, "and his." I jerked my head to Ichi. "If the Avatar tries to escape, we will simply find and follow her instantly.

We're going to *save* the city and the people in it, not *condemn* them."

"How?" Jacky asked, grinning expectantly.

I hesitated. "Er, I'm going to need some help with that part."

The others continued to stare at me expectantly, though with varying levels of enthusiasm.

"We need to change our strategy. Stuff keeps blowing up in our faces and sending us careening from one emergency to the next. We've been stuck being reactive. That's not all our fault, but now that we can see what we're dealing with a little better, I think it's time to just…fix things. Get down to the root of the problem and rip it out. The Abhorrent is making life unpleasant for me. I want to kill every last one of its minions, and then go after It directly. If it runs and hides, I want to flush it out of its den. And then I want to exterminate it like the infestation it is."

<hr>

Interlude 6

<hr>

Now that he understood what was really going on, Reed severely regretted not throwing caution to the wind and ripping the parasites off both his parents while Demi and Lucas were still there to help him, even if he'd had to smash his parents over the head with a chair or something. He'd felt helpless, and thought waiting for real help might even be safer for them, but now he doubted the enforcers would be able to do anything to help after all, which meant he'd only condemned his parents to—to what? Were they slaves? Soldiers? Food for this "Avatar"? Reed kept his trembling hand clamped over his mouth, forcing himself to breathe through his nose despite the wild, trapped scream that kept trying to rise up through his chest.

He had *promised* to get help. Reed forced himself to lower his hand and push away from the wall. He couldn't let his dad down. His dad was counting on him.

Keeping his eyes firmly down and away from the billboard screens, he moved out of the alley. His link still had access to non-entertainment services, so he called a taxi pod, setting his destination as the nearest enforcer station. Maybe Demi had been right, and they had all been subverted already, but if not, or if he could find a chance to save one, getting an enforcer on his side was the fastest way to fix this. They'd be able to call in help, let the military know where the Avatar was.

As the taxi pod pulled up beside him, he hopped in and confirmed his destination with the automated system, ignoring the smell of urine and plastine only *mostly* masked by bright, chemical lemon.

He returned his attention to his link. His mom might have cut off his access to most of the Net, but there were ways around that, which most kids his age were well-acquainted with. Simply routing his link's identification matrix through a foreign, third-party system would bypass the restrictions, though without a verified identity he wouldn't be able to make purchases or calls, or post online. But he would be able to access and view any Net page that didn't require confirmed identification—like the Earth Defense Boards.

First, he checked the thread "New Horror-Themed Player, or Am I Going Crazy?" for more relevant posts. There were a couple, but none that gave him any new information about how to deal with the invisible parasites. He would have posted his own experience in case it helped others, but he couldn't. He thought back to the film of the warp, and the creature enthroned in front of it. That had to be where all the parasites were coming from. Maybe it was responsible for the clouds, too.

He took a moment to access the satellite weather service, zooming in on Leighton and the surrounding areas. As he'd suspected, the extra-thick, unchanging cloud cover only covered this city. Maybe people outside it were still safe, their minds free of the Avatar's influence.

He returned to the thread "Seal of Nine Movements & Government Mobilization."

He skipped over the original post and the first couple pages of response, looking for something new, something relevant.

POSTER "SNOWBELLS & WHISTLES" SAYS:

What if the eclipse had something to do with it? I heard there was *also* an eclipse on their world, at what was practically the same time, and if you think about it, doesn't that seem a little strange? Because I also heard that relative time moves faster for them, whatever that means. What if...like, it's some sort of doomsday calendar

Ragnarok type thing? Or, we've all been exposed to deadly radiation and they're trying to figure out how to tell us we're all going to die. Or there's an asteroid hurtling toward Earth and the Estreyans don't want us evacuating to their world.

POSTER "BITE-SIZED DRAGON" SAYS:

Did you actually read what you wrote before posting, Snowbells? That's the most ridiculous thing I've ever heard. An eclipse signaling Ragnarok? Deadly radiation? An asteroid that's going to wipe out humanity? It's like you took the worst parts of several bad science fiction films and smashed them all together.

POSTER "CHINCHILLI" SAYS:

The radiation and asteroid are obviously just random ideas, I agree. But I've been thinking about it, and I don't think the eclipse theory is that ridiculous. They have *gods*. Like you'd expect, those gods have unimaginable powers, and I know for a fact Eve Redding has spoken about one she calls the "Oracle." Getting an omen of something big from an eclipse is *not* the most far out there idea. The timing is very suspicious, mainly.

But it doesn't actually matter *how* or *what* sent everyone scrambling. It could be the eclipse, or it could be some tea leaves in a weird shape, or it could be the discovery of an ancient doomsday calendar. The important thing is *why*?

I'm not the type that thinks our governments, any of them, are some paragon of goodness and honesty. Power leads to corruption, and as far as I can tell, the Estreyans are pretty much just humans with superpowers, which means they have the same problems as us. So I don't expect them to tell us the truth about what's going on.

What worries me is they're not being subtle enough about it.

They don't care if we notice, because whatever they're

doing is too important to delay, too massive to keep it under the radar.

POSTER "BANDUD, OF THE LINE OF NANAEL" SAYS:

Greetings, Earthlings. I, Bandud, am an Estreyan visiting your small planet. I am learning your culture by participating in your customs, such as these communal forums of free thought and speech.

I keep abreast of the news of my homeland, and your fearful natterings led me to curiosity.

None of the Seal of Nine have been seen in many days, and no one knows where they might be, or at least those who do are not talking about it.

This is not necessarily cause for alarm, but generally, as they are of quite great interest to my people, our reporters pay very close attention to their comings and goings. Even so much as a stroll down the street to stop at a food stand will be considered newsworthy. Rather than trivialities like that, the most recent headlines have been scandalous or entertaining speculation as to their whereabouts.

POSTER "DEVON MILLER" SAYS:

Bandud, if you're actually an Estreyan, you should probably talk to one of the mods about getting verified. There have been a slew of accounts popping up and pretending to be Estreyans, all of which did varyingly bad jobs of disguising that they were actually weenies in their mother's basement getting off on feeling important.

Which means without the tag, pretty much no one around here is going to take you seriously.

Including me.

POSTER "BANDUD, OF THE LINE OF NANAEL (VERIFIED ESTREYAN)" SAYS:

I thank you for your advice, Earthling "DEVON MILLER."

POSTER "MAXXX" SAYS:

Wait, you guys have tabloids, too? What kind of "scandalous and entertaining" speculation has there been?

POSTER "BANDUD, OF THE LINE OF NANAEL (VERIFIED ESTREYAN)" SAYS:

"MAXXX," it is to my surprise as well, the similarities between our two peoples, despite your appalling weakness and fragility.

Some of the more garish news outlets will run pure speculation, such as that Jacqueline of the line of Santiago has run off with a foreign prince. The others hunted them down and are now subjecting him to a pseudo-Trial to determine his worthiness for such a prize.

One news segment hypothesized Eve Redding may have become addicted to crushed basilisk-scale dust, and went into seclusion to try and detoxify and regain control of herself. It is known to make people moody, and Queen Mardinest would not have wanted Eve destroying the castle and surrounding neighborhoods in fits of pique.

Another article claimed a source had told them Torliam of the line of Aethezriel and Adam of the line of Coyle were fighting for Eve Redding's favor. Adam has been very jealous of the blood bond between Torliam and Eve, which of course is common knowledge. Obviously most of the populous supports Torliam's suit, but Eve herself was once mostly human, so Adam still felt he had a chance. The queen grew fed up and locked them all in the dungeons to work out their issues.

Not that I read these articles or watch the news segments *myself*, of course. It is just impossible not to notice.

Reed rolled his eyes and was about to continue scrolling when the taxi pod drew to a halt. He fumbled a bit in his haste to turn off the foreign service he'd re-routed his identity matrix through, then paid by swiping his link over the scanner in front of him.

As he exited the vehicle, he almost looked around in curiosity, but stopped himself before he caught more than a glimpse of the nearby buildings. Instead, he pulled out the silver mirror and used it to scan his surroundings. He was in front of the enforcer station closest to his house. Most of the buildings around him were dark and closed up, but the station was still brightly lit, doors ready to slide open as soon as he indicated any intention of walking through them.

Reed put the mirror away and palmed the scratched and dented antique butter knife.

He walked through the front doors, pausing just before reaching the lobby and turning around with his hand held up close to his face to do a quick sweep of the room. He didn't want to make it too obvious what he was doing, but was somewhat reassured by how Demi and Lucas had both found it difficult to notice him while he was actively looking in the silver mirror.

The lobby was big, with a lot of desks, but more of them were empty than he'd expected, even for the night shift. His class had gone on a field trip to this station when he was younger, and there had been dozens and dozens of active enforcers on duty at the station. Still, there were a handful of enforcers at their desks now, and a couple more he glimpsed in the background, in offices or through windowed doorways leading into the bowels of the station. He supposed the rest must be out patrolling or responding to emergency calls.

Of the few who remained, none of them were free of the Avatar's parasites.

In fact, they were horribly, almost completely subsumed.

If he were able to get one of them free, would they even be useful? Maybe, if they had a top of the line medbot available—and they probably did, but even then—*maybe*.

Still, they didn't need to be able to fight, as long as they were coherent enough to call in reinforcements from elsewhere.

"Can I help you?" one of the enforcers called, looking him over somewhat skeptically, too tired-looking to really pull off *suspicious*.

Reed, keeping his head down, turned around and shuffled a little closer to the man. That only gave him a better view of the weapons at the man's waist, and—his eyes widened—was that a *gun* just laying there on the desk? He looked away from it quickly. "Umm, I'm here to report something sensitive. I—I need to talk to an enforcer, alone."

"Alone?" the man repeated, narrowing his eyes. "How old are you, boy?"

"Fif—" Reed swallowed. "Fifteen."

"Why are you out here at this time of night?" Something about the man's tone seemed more hostile than concerned.

Was that the parasite, reacting to something *abnormal*? Could it —could it *tell* that Reed wasn't infected? "My dad sent me," he said. "He told me it was your...*normal job* to take reports like this. I need to talk to you, or one of the others, alone, because I, um—"

"You can trust all of us here," the man assured him, eyes still narrowed. "Are you here to report a citizen guilty of misconduct? If you give us a name, we can bring them in to get treatment from our anti-deviance device."

"Anti...deviance device?" Reed repeated slowly.

The man gestured toward the far wall, to an area that wasn't visible from the entrance.

Reed almost, *almost* turned to look, but caught himself halfway through the instinctive pivot. He could see a hint of something shiny from the corner of his eye, and carefully kept himself from looking at it directly.

"You seem a little out of sorts, young man. The anti-deviance device can help with almost anything, you know. Special technology. Why don't you take a peek yourself? Works through eye-contact, you know." The man smiled, probably what was supposed to be an encouraging, sympathetic expression, but all Reed could think of was the hellfire and brimstone creature he'd seen in the butter knife's reflection.

Reed turned and ran, slamming back through the front doors faster than they could open on their own. He veered left and sprinted down the sidewalk, his backpack bouncing against his back, the butter knife clutched in his fist like a weapon. Mindless terror carried him through the first few blocks, and then he realized how reckless he was being. He turned into the darkest alley he could find, slipping the butter knife back up his sleeve so that just the tip was peeking out.

He kept his head down, hood pulled up, and his eyes on the reflection and his feet. Despite the pounding of his heart and the clawing pressure in his lungs urging him to *flee,* Reed kept his pace to a fast walk.

He meandered mindlessly for the next quarter hour, taking a winding path in an attempt to avoid cameras and throw off pursuit. Would they know who he was, just from him walking into the station while wearing his link? Would they come after him, try to drag him back and force him to look in their "anti-deviance device?"

He shuddered. Obviously, his idea to get help from the local enforcers was a bust. He'd probably just made everything a thousand times worse. But how was he supposed to get help?

He paused in an alley, pulling up the list of emergency numbers on his link again. He redialed the one his mom had made him hang up on earlier, then kept walking while he waited for someone to pick up, his mind racing. He'd been stupid to think the local enforcers could help against something like this. What he really needed was the big guns, shock and awe, the type of power that was actually *meant* to fight apocalyptic, world-ending threats. He needed the Seal of Nine. Eve Redding and her team would know what to do. They would be equipped for something like this. Samuel Hawes had a healing Skill that could work literal miracles, and they'd be able to command the other Estreyans to help, too.

But there was no way they'd take his call directly. In fact, whoever was on the other end of this emergency line might require some sort of proof. How backed up with reports and supposed sightings of the Avatar were they, to have this kind of wait time on emergency calls? How was he supposed to get them to take him *seriously* over the phone?

He stopped on the side of the road, hailing another taxi pod. It took him to the nearest skyrail lift, and he anxiously rode the elevator up, shifting from foot to foot, sick and jittery and feeling like he had to pee, though he knew that was only nerves.

When he got to the concourse, he stopped to examine the other people milling about with the knife's reflection. Some of them, the nervous and tired ones, often those with a little extra luggage or traveling as an entire family, were clear of the parasites. He contemplated going up to one of them and revealing what was going on, asking for help, but what could they do that he couldn't? What if they drew negative attention from the parasites? Instead, he bought a one-way ticket out of the city, and stood well away from the others while he waited.

When the skyrail car arrived, he blended into the pile of passengers and found a seat in the back corner. He was *still* waiting for the emergency line operator to pick up his call. He switched on the ID routing application again and returned to the EDF boards, leaving the call ringing in the background. He skimmed through page after page, only stopping to read the posts that seemed relevant.

You are viewing thread: "Seal of Nine Movements &
Government Mobilization"

POSTER "THE MEG" SAYS:

My husband is an enforcer. They've been stocking up on supplies for the emergency shelters, doing inspections and inventory, and making sure the sirens work and the air filtering is ready to go. No one wants to open up a shelter containing half the city's population and find everyone inside suffocated again. Inspections like that are a normal part of the job. But it's not normal for the timeline to be so *urgent*, or for all the inspections to happen at once. My husband thinks they're getting the shelters ready to use, and soon.

POSTER "HOLY PAJAMAS" SAYS:

I heard a lot of the Empowered on Estreyer are being called in for very hush-hush "quests." Can anyone confirm?

POSTER "LEVENEVES" SAYS:

I'm always surprised by the number of conspiracy theorists hiding in the woodwork of the Net. Why is everything with you people some sort of doomsday sign? Our treaties with the Estreyans are holding strong, and that Pestilence alien trying to turn everyone into rabid zombies was *killed.*

POSTER "CHINCHILLI" SAYS:

It's not a conspiracy theory that the national guard has been pulling people in for "drills." Way too many people, all at once. Interpret that how you will, but these things are actually happening. Basic math will tell you it's not standard procedure, especially not when it spans so many different regions and fields.

Reed realized many of the posts in this thread had been made before the press conference announcing the Avatar's existence was released. As soon as that came out, it was all anyone, anywhere, was talking about, and the thread had blown up with a couple hundred more pages of posts since then.

ORIGINAL POSTER "ANTIGONE" SAYS:

For any who doubted something was going on, they just released a press conference from Queen Mardinest of Estreyer. There's a second alien just like Pestilence, and it's here, presumed hostile. Watch the press conference <u>here</u>.

I wish I had been wrong.

My hands are shaking as I write this. I wish I could wake up, and it would be back to yesterday, or back to a couple years ago, before we knew anything about extraterrestrial life at all. But I know I'm already awake. This is the real world. This is real life. And we, normal humans? We're the background characters. The redshirts. The death toll given only in numbers, not faces or names.

POSTER "ZODIAC DRAGON" SAYS:

Not "just like" Pestilence. She didn't say that. It's just the same species. Did you notice the wording when she asked people to report sightings of suspicious phenomena or unexplained happenings? They don't know what the hell it can do, or where it is.

As for the rest of your comment, I empathize. The shelters aren't going to do jack shit against something *like* Pestilence. Someone up the thread made a comment about evacuating to Estreyer. Do you think they would allow that? I for one would feel a lot safer if all my neighbors were superheroes who might at least be strong enough to hold that thing off for a second or two while I run away, instead of being forced to huddle in an underground stadium with a hundred thousand other terrified, helpless humans.

POSTER "SNOWBELLS & WHISTLES" SAYS:

Wait, so this other type of alien species also has different Skills, basically? I mean, they didn't say it outright, but why else would they not just tell us to look for people coming down with the plague and then trying to eat each other?

I don't mean to sound crazy, but isn't that sort of… suspicious? I know we all saw footage of the one they called Pestilence, and it was made out of bugs, but I've *also* seen footage of it disguised as a little girl that just suddenly… bursts into cockroaches and shit. Are we totally, *totally sure* Pestilence wasn't a crazy Estreyan they just didn't want to admit was one of them? Or even one of their gods? Like, they've got "good" gods, and even those ones basically kill anyone who asks for a Skill to test if they're "worthy." What makes us all so sure they don't have evil gods, too?

POSTER "THE MEG" SAYS:

I've been praying. I don't know if I actually believe it'll help, or if there's just nothing else I can think to do that will be any better.

They acted like Pestilence was working alone, that after defeating him, it was all over and everything was fine. But if there are two, that means there's more, right? Maybe a whole society of them, somewhere out there in the solar system, and they have a grudge against humanity. How are we supposed to win a war against creatures like that?

POSTER "NOT-A-CONSPIRACY-THEORIST" SAYS:

People, stop panicking. There isn't actually any danger. They're doing all this so they can get us to agree to passing more restrictive, invasive laws, "for our protection." Looks like it's working. If you want to know the real truth about what's going on behind the scenes, there's a whole list of videos telling the truth, here.

POSTER "BREAKFAST SOUP" SAYS:

So, getting back to the original point of this thread (you can talk about the press conference and the Avatar specifically in the thread devoted to that), it seems clear Eve Redding and the Seal of Nine disappeared to deal with this. Are they on a quest, do you think? But I don't understand why they can't just kill it the same way they did the last one. Maybe they're on a quest to *find* it?

POSTER "FIGARO" SAYS:

Could it be a child of the last one? Do we even know how that thing reproduced?

POSTER "HOLY PAJAMAS" SAYS:

I think this situation is a great argument for why the human military should all be Empowered, or Players, or whatever you want to call them. Without Skills, our soldiers stand basically no chance against something like this. We don't have enough Players to comprise an entire army, not unless we combine forces with other countries. Relying on the Estreyans for extra manpower makes us look weak, and how long before they decide they'd like to take advantage of that?

When the skylift car slowed to a halt, Reed looked up from the screen, feeling sicker than when he started reading. The crowd filling the concourse was thicker than he would have expected, and as he shuffled into the press of bodies, he caught a brief glimpse of an armored enforcer standing near the wall. A cold weight settled in his stomach.

He tried to convince himself they were just there to make sure people didn't panic and cause injuries trying to escape the implied danger within the city. But when he, as subtly as possible, pushed his way toward the far wall near the emergency exit and used the butter knife to examine the whole of the concourse behind him, he saw that the crowd was passing through two enforcer-guarded checkpoints. Each checkpoint hosted a large standing mirror, and those among the crowd who seemed confused or anxious to get through the choke point immediately grew calm once they looked into one.

He noticed that the part of the concourse where boarding passengers would normally stand was empty. Instead, all the passengers seemed to be circling around to the other side of the station, queuing up for the return trip to their original locations. No one was leaving the city.

He looked around in paranoia, but no one seemed to have noticed him.

Out on the concourse, a man with dark glasses and a long white cane was dragged, literally, into a small office next to the ticket station. The door closed and the blinds were pulled shut so Reed couldn't see, and from where he stood at the back of the crowd, he couldn't hear if there were any screams from within.

Some of the others were alarmed at this, but the enforcers were not perturbed, and neither were any of the passengers with invisible parasites. Together, they kept anyone from resisting or escaping.

Reed didn't hesitate a second longer, slamming into the emergency exit doors and hurtling down the stairwell. He hoped he hadn't drawn any attention to himself, but that thought only made him run faster. Still, he managed to exit onto the sidewalk with a semblance of calm, keeping his head down and scouting out his surroundings with the knife.

For a moment, he felt lost. What was he supposed to do now? He did a quick search for the closest enforcer station outside of Leighton, then roughly calculated the distance against the exorbitant price of yet another taxi pod. He had enough credits. He could make it there, and back again if he had to. There wouldn't be enough left over to even hope to bribe a self-respecting enforcer, though, even if he could find one that didn't have tentacles growing out of their ears, or gnashing, teeth-filled mouths all over their body.

He raised his head, holding back a grimace at the particularly disgusting parasite he saw from the corner of his eye. A couple taps on his link hailed a taxi pod. It was only a few seconds later that a chill crawled up his spine.

Very slowly, keeping his eyes forward, he turned his head toward the man he'd just noticed.

Bulbous, mucousy flesh surrounded whoever had once been beneath, only the polished black shoes and dress-pant hems making it obvious that a human was under there at all. The flesh dripped, forming a slowly growing, sizzling puddle on the concrete.

Reed shuddered.

He was not looking in either of his two silver mirrors.

That parasite was openly existing in the *real world*. Was he the only one who'd noticed? Or, perhaps, the only one around who wasn't infected.

He must not have successfully kept the look of horror off his face, or maybe he'd gasped or something, because the man turned toward him.

Reed did not bolt immediately. He turned his face away, keeping the parasite barely visible out of his peripheral vision, and started walking away.

The huge blob of acidic snot and tumorous flesh followed, taking steps a little too large to be casual.

Then Reed bolted. He ran like his life depended on it.

The parasite was quicker than it should have been for its size, and Reed, sprinting down the sidewalk, had the stray thought that the person inside would likely be injured from pushing beyond their limits.

The street below the skyrail station was fairly empty, but the resounding screams of shock and expressions of horror told him he was not the only one who could see the hideous monster chasing him.

Many people barely reacted at all, and he knew they must have parasites of their own.

Reed jerked to the right, running through a small alley. He looked for something to push into the path of the panting, slobbering creature behind him, but there weren't any convenient rubbish bins or crates lining the sides of the alley like there always were in action films.

He pushed himself as fast as he could go, but the footsteps behind him kept drawing closer. "Help!" he screamed. He burst out of the end of the alley, his backpack tugging against his shoulders as the monster almost grabbed it.

Reed jerked to the side, ripping free, but he'd been thrown off balance and was going too fast. His legs got tangled, and he tripped over his own feet. He almost fell, managed to catch himself with an animalistic scramble on all fours, and then felt the burning grasp on his ankle as the monster caught him.

He lashed out with a desperate kick, his shoe sinking into squishy flesh, then ripped his leg away. He managed to make it another couple steps, noticing with vague horror that there were more of the parasites on this street, the nightmare creatures stretching and twisting into sight around their hosts even as he watched.

The monster behind him hadn't been deterred at all by Reed's kick to the face, and he knew with certainty he couldn't escape.

He threw himself into the street, sprinting across with the last of his strength, heedless of the taxi pods hurtling past.

The parasite followed.

Reed was almost to the other side when the edge of a taxi pod clipped his heel and sent him sprawling. His head hit the concrete curb with a crunch he felt all the way through his body, and he bounced from the momentum, but behind him he heard the wet, bursting, shattering as the parasite and its host collided with the taxi pod directly.

There was no moment of wooziness that slowly faded to oblivion. No, Reed felt a burst of sick, *broken* pain, and then he felt nothing.

Chapter 22

It matters not how strait the gate,
  How charged with punishments the scroll,
  I am the master of my fate,
  I am the captain of my soul.
  —William Ernest Henley

OBVIOUSLY, the Oracle's threat to kill me if I ever summoned her again through predetermination was a bluff. I was the last hope for existence, after all. The Oracle could simply not show up if she really didn't want to meet me.

I needed the help of the gods, and Behelaino wouldn't be useful for what I had in mind. The Oracle was the only other god I could feasibly access.

Before I had even realized I'd made up my mind to try and get a message to her again, a Window popped up in front of my face.

It was a simple string of letters and numbers.

They were Estreyan coordinates, much more complicated than the simple latitude and longitude coordinates of Earth, for obvious reasons.

My teammates were busy preparing to attack the Avatar, and there was no time to waste, so Ichi and I went alone.

We arrived in a familiar place. Heavy fog filled the surroundings, cutting off visibility any farther than a dozen meters out and pooling on the ground up to knee height. Loose strands of hair floated upward, as if we were underwater. The thick air caught in my lungs and I broke into a series of choking coughs. Even after I found my breath, my lungs seemed to rattle with every inhalation.

The ground, mostly concealed beneath the fog, was jagged and sharp, crystalline. This was the place where we had met the Goddess of Testimony and Lore, who had given us Skills and labeled us the Seal of Nine, who had marked us—*branded* us—with the crystal symbols.

We walked forward. The fog in the air thinned as we went, settling toward the ground, and the sun came out, shining off the fog and hints of crystal with almost blinding brightness.

We found the Oracle standing at the edge of a crystal valley as the sun rose.

Ichi stayed well back as I approached her.

I stopped at her side, looking down on the valley. I was captivated by the sheer *scope* of it, endless beauty stretching out before me for days, almost like the feeling I got when looking up at the stars. I felt small next to it. Heavy fog spilled over the carved-out side of the valley's ridge, running down the walls like water, eddying around chunks of bright, colorful crystal. The clear morning sunlight glowed off the tiny particles of fog in the air, giving everything a softness that contrasted poignantly with the sharp glitter of crystal and the rainbow beams of refracted light.

Even if I lived a thousand years, could I ever see all the wonders of Estreyer? Would I even see my next birthday?

Without turning to the Oracle, I said, "I know how to do what needs to be done. I need your help making sure *I* live through it."

She turned her head slightly toward me, even the music of her body totally silent for once.

"You said your true strength was looking back, not forward," I said.

"Yes," she answered, her voice a low whistle of wind through reeds.

We kept our voices low as we discussed a solution to my upcoming problem, though sound didn't carry well through whatever gases made up the air on this level, and I felt no sense of the unease I associated with being watched in secret.

"Will it work?" I asked.

"It can work."

That was the most I could hope for, I supposed. I hesitated for a moment, but decided to be bold. "Will any of you fight with me? Any of the gods? We could use the help."

There was no hesitation in her response. "We will not."

"Why?" I couldn't keep the frustration out of my voice. All of them, powerful enough to create Estreyer, to breathe life into the Estreyans, and what were they *doing* with that? Manipulating mortals into doing their jobs for them. Perhaps they couldn't defeat the Abhorrent directly, but it sure seemed like they weren't trying very hard to help us either.

"Why?" she echoed, her trilling, reed-flute voice sounding somehow pitying. "Just as Pestilence was able to corrupt the God of Knowledge, making of him a weapon for the Abhorrent, so too could Tempest spread its madness to the gods. We need only look on it to be lost to it."

"Tempest?"

"You know its power, and you know its location, so too may you know its name. Yes, this Avatar is Tempest, and it is insidious. Still, the mortals are not abandoned. The gods do not go to war for fear of becoming a weapon of the enemy, but that does not mean we field no weapons of our own." She spoke slowly, enunciating every word as if to impress their significance on me.

That didn't ease my frustration, and my scales shifted aggressively while I consciously kept from making a fist. You couldn't do that with claws without hurting yourself. There wasn't much more to say, and the Oracle left, walking into the mist we had come from before disappearing with her cocoon of white threads.

I expected Ichi to teleport us back to the capital right away, but instead he turned to walk along the lip of the valley, his expression contemplative.

I followed, keeping a wary eye on him.

"In a handful of days, our alliance will be over," he said.

"Yes." I remembered the feel of Blaine's blood and brain matter splattering the side of my face.

Ichi's eyes met my own. The corner of his lips lifted into a mocking smile, and he laughed softly. "I see the bloodlust in your eyes. Will you attack me, then, as soon as you no longer need me?"

"Only in self-defense," I said, my tone a dark contrast to his false amusement.

"Oh, perhaps not directly, not physically, but through the court of public opinion, with accusative words and misleading questions?" He paused, my silence enough confirmation for us both. "And if I, in turn, wish to accuse you of the murder of my lover, to have you stand trial for the justice *you* deserve, who would stand by my side against the savior, the Spark of hope? None of them can see what you really are." His tone had grown bitter by the end.

He was probably right, I conceded silently. Aloud, I said, "Perhaps we will both be dead in a handful of days, and then we'll be even."

He let out a short, humorless laugh. "One can hope." Mid-step, he teleported us both back to the castle, and just as quickly left me alone.

OVER THE NEXT FEW DAYS, we were terribly busy preparing for our attack on Tempest. Information regarding the Avatar kept trickling in, and I'd had a chance to watch several of the videos that Adam had archived, reflected off a silver mirror to prevent Tempest from attacking me or infecting me with one of her invisible parasites. We weren't even sure if she could do so all the way on Estreyer, but we weren't taking any chances. She had a vaguely feminine shape, and looked like hundreds of tortured, frozen faces encased in amber. We hadn't yet seen her move from her floating throne.

Despite the looming battle, knowing what we were up against had bolstered morale on both Earth and Estreyer. Hunting for an enemy we knew was there but couldn't find had been like jumping at shadows, but knowing the thing's name helped people to reconcile the idea of our enemy in terms they could cope with.

Our preparation to go after the Abhorrent had borne fruit. Pondslider had called me the day before, yelling into the microphone as was her habit, as she seemed to forget that we could talk across such vast distances without raising our voices. Or maybe she was just excited. "We have done it! The biggest breakthrough in three generations, and of course I was invaluable to the process. We will need the whale, and a large source of power, and Zed. The warps exist beyond the Veil as well, and with the boy, we can reach them."

My scales flexed and my eyelids fluttered with excitement, but I tried to keep my tone controlled as I asked. "You figured out the warps?"

Her vulpine grin was answer enough.

Now, with a moment to breathe before we took a Shortcut back to Earth, I decided to check up on my teammates to see if there was anything I could help them with, even if that was just a conversation, a chance to express what they were feeling and gain comfort from me.

Adam first. After all, he was the one I had the pressing, unresolved issue with.

I could have reached through the entire castle with Wraith, but I tried to give people some small measure of privacy, so instead I pulled up his location with my VR chip. He was at the edge of his room in the castle, maybe on the balcony. Except he was with Jacky, which made me hesitate, but almost as soon as the thought of postponing our conversation for a little longer entered my mind, the little dot representing Jacky made a beeline out of the room.

While I walked, I thought about his confession. I already knew my answer, but wondered if it was the right one. I remembered the first time we'd met, in the darkness of the ratmen Trial. I thought about the way he always sneered pessimistically at my plans, yet somehow ended up ready to fight at my back when the time came, often with just the little bit extra we needed to make everything work. He'd comforted me when I woke from a nightmare, shared with me moments of wonder in the face of despair, and didn't want to *use* me like the majority of the world seemed to want to.

I loved Adam, and I knew he loved me, beyond anything romantic. We were true friends.

I stopped in front of his door, knocking politely, not loudly or quickly enough that he would worry there was an emergency. He seemed surprised to see me on the other side, and I gave him a small smile.

But when I tried to imagine being with him, I couldn't. I could feel the depths of coldness within me, the screaming ache of regret, the sharp, bright joy of pointed teeth and the claws tipping my fingers, and could not imagine his happiness surviving, were I to turn all of that on him.

I followed him to the balcony. His tattooing equipment was still scattered around. He must have been giving Jacky more tattoos.

I wondered if he truly understood what he had asked from me. Independent of whether it would be *good* for us, did he actually *want* that?

He waved for me to sit down and wordlessly cleaned and prepped his supplies while I watched. He knelt in front of me, pressed his fingers to the partially scaled skin of my ankle, and began to give me a small tattoo. After a while, he looked up and raised an eyebrow at me, more kindness to the expression than challenge.

Then again, maybe he did know me, I thought. Maybe he understood exactly what he wanted. He'd been at my side longer than anyone except Zed, after all. "I don't think I can give you what you want," I said softly. "I've never thought of you like that, romantically," I said, my cheeks tingling with the force of my embarrassment. "And even if I had…there's no *room* left for anything like that in my life."

He nodded slowly. "It's just that? There's no one…else?"

He was talking about Torliam, I knew. Even I wasn't oblivious enough to miss that, and suddenly their bickering made a little more sense. "I don't—" I hesitated.

He was nodding a little, even before I finished.

"I don't know," I admitted. "But certainly not *now*."

"Okay, I get it. I mean, I kinda already knew. I just didn't want to regret not even trying, you know?" It wasn't really a question. "We're still friends," he assured me, "and don't go letting it get awkward. I've got your back, you've got mine, and I'm still going to tell you when you're doing something stupid." He returned his attention to my ankle, muttering, "Which will likely be quite often."

I snorted, but settled back in my chair and let him work.

Once he'd finished, I ordered him to get some sleep, then went to find Torliam in the auxiliary war room, where he'd been working almost constantly.

He looked up from the datapads strewn on the table in front of him when I entered. "How did it go?"

I knew he didn't mean with Adam, but the Oracle. "I talked to her. There's a way that might work, and she agreed to help. She'll come to me when it's ready. Do you need to use my face for anything?"

He perked up at the offer, immediately shoving a few of the datapads into my arms. "Yes!"

Being the savior of mortal-kind—a war hero—did wonders for getting people to do things they didn't want to, sacrifice more than they felt reasonable, and mobilize quicker than they otherwise would have admitted was possible. Torliam was famous, too, but many humans distrusted him, and on Estreyer, he lived at the heart of a web of political tension, mostly because of his mother. The humans saw me as one of them, and if I'd wanted to declare myself Supreme Leader of Estreyer, there might have been some protestors, but they would have been in the minority.

I tried to tell Torliam to sleep, but he shrugged me off. "I have too much left to do, and with the way things are progressing on Earth, we do not have time to wait."

"We'll be leaving in a few hours. There are other people to help coordinate things. And those people *aren't* going to be fighting by my side."

"Those people are already helping, and there is still more work to be done. They also do not have the authority to declare treason if someone refuses to send the requested aid."

I rolled my eyes. "You haven't been declaring treason, anyway. And if that's the issue, just temporarily give your helpers that authority. We can review any accusations for accuracy when this is all over."

He didn't respond, which meant he was at least considering it, but by the way he was still scowling down at a datapad when I left the room, I doubted he would actually step away to rest.

With a sigh, I left him and went to Kris's workshop, nodding to the scrambling Estreyans that had filled the palace over the last couple days, and who were actually *too busy* to make a big deal of my presence.

The workshop, too, was overflowing with activity, though most of the ruckus came from the marionettes working in assembly lines to create more of themselves, which Kris put the finishing touches on and then brought to life with a spirit pulled from the ether.

She was in the bowels of one of her rescue pod marionettes, aviator goggles pulled down, laser-created sparks splashing against the leather protective gear she wore.

I deliberately decided not to disturb her in the middle of whatever that was, and turned to the far wall of the workshop, where Gregor had taken over with a small chemistry lab.

He was ordering some of the marionettes around, but wasn't in danger of cutting off a limb if I distracted him, so I navigated through the organized chaos to his side.

There were several identical stations, each equipped with the standard hotplates and glassware I associated with chemistry and mad science from the films, but also a few exotic machines that spun and flashed and rumbled, and what I thought must be a very expensive three-dimensional printer.

Gregor conducted in imperious tones and blistering insults, and the marionettes created the fizzing blue liquid, which went into the injectors created by the printer. The end result was boxes upon boxes of blue-filled vials, and more boxes of thick electronic half-collars. The collars would automatically clamp down around the back of a human neck, scan, and then accurately inject the compound into the base of the skull, from where the compound would disperse throughout the brain. Gregor hadn't found a way to keep it from being partially washed away by the natural flow of blood, but people who were getting proper blood flow to the brain probably didn't need it anyway, and it would give those in truly critical condition a chance to be stabilized or forcefully healed if standard medicine had no answer to their injuries.

"Status update?" I said.

He huffed irritably. "We're running well behind the necessary numbers. Apparently it takes quite a while to get factories up and running, etc. That's all the excuses I'm hearing, anyway," he said, waving his hand dismissively in the air. "I'm doing my best to make up for it, but there just isn't enough time, and my setup here is much too small. If not for Kris"—he shook his head—"it would be impossible."

"Hopefully we have enough healers coming in to make up for it." I considered for a moment how hopeless the situation would have been if we were on Earth with the Avatar. At least here we had five times as long to prepare as she had to wreck everything. It still wasn't nearly enough time. "And what about *you*?"

"There's not really much I can do last minute to get any stronger, except for taking the fruit of life." He touched the metal container hanging from his neck. "I'm ready, though. I'll do my part, and when you do yours…we're going to win," he said, his voice firm. He patted my hand. "Don't worry, Eve. Also, maybe you should get some sleep before we leave?" he added, then turned away to berate a marionette that had chipped one of his glass beakers.

I let out a soft snort of amusement, then turned to his sister, who was finally crawling out of the rescue pod marionette.

She waved her hands in the air, and it gathered five of its limbs under itself and rose. It swayed a little, as if disoriented, but she just motioned vaguely to the other marionettes that had been helping with its creation and turned away, leaving them to handle getting it acquainted with its new body and purpose. She pulled up her goggles when she saw me.

"Eve! Is it time to go already? I haven't hit the quota yet!"

"No. I'm just checking in with everyone. There's something I want to talk to you about."

She scowled suspiciously. "I'm going with you. You can't make me and Gregor stay behind. Plus, you need my marionettes, and I have to be there to keep them going."

I'd opened my mouth to keep talking, but closed it again, waiting a couple seconds while she glared at me, hands on her hips. Finally, I said, "That's not what I wanted to talk about. It's the fruit."

"Oh." She deflated a little, hands falling down to her sides. "What about them?"

"You know they might cause…*complications*, if we ever manage to find a way to get you back to full size. I'm just… I want you to be safe, but I also want you to be sure this is what you want. It's difficult, being trapped in a body that doesn't feel like your own."

She took a moment to consider my words before responding. "I'm getting used to looking like this," she said. I couldn't tell if it was fatigue or bitterness in her voice. "But…I've been working with a lot of spirits lately, and I think I have an idea how to fix my body. I'm not sure if the fruit will interfere or not, but if it does, all we need to do is drain it of power, right? Cut off a limb and let it regrow a few times, maybe. I'm sure it would hurt, but Sam could probably help with that…" She caught the look of horror on my face and rolled her eyes. "Well, maybe not that. But don't worry, I know about the possible downsides."

Only partially mollified, I said, "Well, alright. What's this method of fixing your body you came up with?"

She turned around at some beeps from Pino, who gestured to the shell of another rescue pod waiting for her. "It's kind of a long explanation. Let's talk about it later, alright?" Before I could respond, she'd already hurried away.

I sighed, rubbing my forehead. A quick check of the time told me we had about six hours till the full-scale attack on Tempest was scheduled. I needed Sam. He could force everyone to get some sleep—the kids especially. I didn't care how valuable the oxygenating compound or rescue-oriented marionettes were, being completely strung-out from days of frantic preparation and worry was not the correct way to enter a life and death battle, especially for children who were human enough to still need almost a full night's rest.

I found Sam in a room off one of the castle kitchens. Horribly mutilated animal and plant remains filled half the space, and his healing abilities were fully charged.

He actually looked refreshed, and I supposed that was a side effect of such a ridiculously high Resilience level combined with said overflowing healing ability.

He was eating from a large platter of food, and when I entered, he patted the seat beside him and pushed the platter between us so we could share.

I plopped down with a sigh, immediately shoving enough food into my mouth to fill one cheek with just enough space left over to talk impolitely around it. "How are you?"

"Good," he said with a small smile.

"Yeah?"

"Yeah." He nodded firmly, his smile growing a little bigger. "I'm terrified, of course. But other than that, I'm actually doing…*good*. I took your advice with Black Sun, and I think I found an answer. It actually helped a lot, having to go back and forth so often while you were out of it. Black Sun—kinda like Harbinger, it's like the Skill was literally made to tempt me to be the worst version of myself." He chuckled sardonically. "But it can also let me do good I couldn't ever have hoped for otherwise. It's the kind of struggle that will never just…go away. And it's going to be hardest when the negative emotions are naturally more prevalent. I was never a fighter—I mean, never a *warrior*—and I've been thinking about what comes after this, what kind of life I want for myself, and I think it might be different what I would have expected. I've changed, and to be honest, even if I screw up sometimes, I like this version of me better. I can make things happen, not just go along for the ride while life happens to me."

"I think I know what you mean," I said. I would never, could never, choose to go back to being a powerless human. In a way, it would be kind of like death. I wasn't sure if that was a healthy attitude or not.

"Dealing with negative emotions isn't going to go away just because I live a mundane life," he continued. "Black Sun gives me the ability to deal with more, if I don't abuse it. And I'm thinking, after this is over, I don't want to settle down and pretend I'm okay being who I was before all this, even if it was easier. It's not like I was *happy* then, just comfortable. You know my parents are rich?"

I shrugged noncommittally. I hadn't *not* known, but Sam didn't really talk about his home life, or his past.

"Well, money only solves money problems, and not even always then. My parents want me to take over the company. Probably more than a little of that has to do with the fact that I'm famous now, and it'd be good for stock prices. I doubt I'd really be in charge, more of a figurehead they think is inept and insecure enough to be puppeteered by them and whoever else." He shuddered visibly. "Instead, maybe I'll go places where people *need* me, and actually do something useful. There should be plenty of opportunity for that, given the amount of shitty places in the world."

"I can see that. You, doing that, being that."

He'd returned to the food, which both of us had stopped eating without noticing. "I like looking in the mirror and respecting myself. And I've got some regrets, so... maybe it'll help me to balance the scales."

I shoved a little savory pie into my mouth. "Therapy might help with that, too." I said it in a joking tone, but we both knew I was serious, and maybe the conversation would have continued, and I would have been able to ask Sam about the things that had scarred him so before we met, but Zed hurried into the room, success and excitement shining on his face.

"I've been talking to Blue," Zed said. "It wants to make another bargain with you."

Chapter 23

One need not be a chamber to be haunted. One need not be a house. The brain has corridors surpassing material place.
   — Emily Dickinson

"MY DOMAIN IS MUCH BIGGER NOW," Blue stated, the edge of darkness pressing close to my left, while a grey replica of the palace, the grounds beyond, and a good portion of the city stretched out to my right.

"I can see that," I replied. I couldn't even begin to estimate how much energy I had consumed to build and rebuild my body as it turned to nothing within the Void, but more, much more, had been left for the cosmic whale when we were done. "What is this bargain you wish to make?"

"You wish to evacuate the citizens of this city plagued by the Avatar. Now that my hoard is more bountiful, again stretching beyond the edge of sight, I could be useful to you."

I wished the creature would speak plainly. I wasn't sure if its mind simply worked differently than ours, or if it enjoyed playing these little games, but Blue was never one to jump straight to the point. "How so? And why are you offering?" It was not in Blue's nature to give without taking. It was a creature of gluttony and greed, and the Other Place was very aptly named its "hoard."

"I have extensive control over this replica. It need not exclusively match the physical features of your mortal realm. I am able to create rapid movement with only moderate inertial forces. In essence, *transportation*. If the boy can open multiple cracks through the Veil for me, I could hypothetically transfer living or nonliving objects from one crack to another much quicker than would otherwise be feasible. The increase in speed between an injured person and your healers would more than make up for what small amount of energy I drain from them while transporting them, and would likely save many mortal lives." Blue waited, floating in the darkness beyond the edge of the Other Place, one gigantic eye focused intently on me.

I could feel the draw of cold, that constant hunger as Blue couldn't stop itself from tugging at my warmth even as it tried to bargain with me. "That would be useful," I agreed. It would depend in large part on Zed's ability to keep multiple rips in the Veil open at a significant distance, but if he could do even three or four, it would make evacuation of the citizens so much easier. "And in return?" I asked.

"One large boon, to be granted by you once the Abhorrent is defeated. A vow that cannot be reneged on."

My eyes narrowed. "That's vague." I doubted Blue didn't actually know what it wanted, so the fact it was disguising its request in the form of a boon was suspicious. "I prefer to make more specific bargains."

"I shall not request anything unjust. Only, perhaps, difficult. If you are to fall to the Abhorrent, I will receive nothing." The gargantuan creature swam past and around the grey replica of the palace, its huge, indistinct body moving with surprising quickness. Its eye returned to peer down at me. "I do not think you can afford to refuse my aid. Without me, joining together all the warps to open the door to the *breaks* will be much more difficult. Perhaps even impossible for you mortals."

The creature was right. "I will accept no boon that endangers me or mine," I said.

"Then it will be up to you to fulfill my request safely," Blue replied.

I ground my teeth together, but nodded. I was desperate for

any help I could get, after all. We made the vow, the creature's aid in exchange for a boon, and I returned to the real world, a bit of chill remaining in my spine, unsure that I'd made the correct choice. I consoled myself with the assurance that whatever Blue wanted, it couldn't be nearly as bad as what the Abhorrent would do, and whatever boon Blue could ask of me would not preclude me from mitigating action after said boon had been fulfilled.

I got Sam to "help" the others get a few hours of sleep, and then we went to the airfield where the *Swiftsure* was waiting for us.

I grinned at the sight of the motley group waiting to board another of the transport ships we'd commandeered. The woodland guardians had sent a contingent of warriors into the outer Estreyan world for the first time in what was probably millennia, and I still wasn't quite sure how we'd gotten them to agree.

Pondslider, taller than many of the others of her kind, noticed us first, and waved excitedly, running over to Torliam and expounding effusively over all the airships, gesturing wildly as she spoke. She carried a wooden death-static launcher over her shoulders and a heavily loaded belt full of esoteric tools around her waist.

Not all of the others were so enthusiastic to be away from their village, especially not on a mission that would certainly prove deadly for some of them. They were drawing looks from the other groups boarding their own ships, both Estreyan and human, and one of the woodland guardians was glaring fiercely at anyone who caught his eye.

As soon as we'd found the Avatar, quite a few humans—soldiers, politicians, and strategists—had been invited to Estreyer to take advantage of the time differential between the two worlds. On Earth, only about half a day had passed since I had been suitably in control to leave Tartarus, while on Estreyer we'd had nearly three days to prepare. It didn't feel like nearly enough.

The *Swiftsure* wasn't the last ship to leave, and this Shortcut wasn't the only one sending a constant stream of fully loaded ships through, but almost everyone deemed absolutely necessary was already waiting for us. We arrived at Leighton within half an hour, which seemed like an eternity, but also not nearly enough time, according to the dread in my belly.

I took a last look around at my teammates as we entered the

queue for one of the openings in the outer quarantine bubble. I could feel their fear, a sickness adding to the chemical turmoil in my own veins. This fight would not be like Pestilence, who was cut off from the Abhorrent and being drained by the Other Place. Tempest might be young, but she grew stronger with every passing moment, and the Abhorrent could feed as much of its power into her as she could take.

"This is it," I said, pushing my sharp-edged purpose back through our blood bond to them. "No fear." Within me, the cold abyss consumed my own fear—of losing them, of failing, of not being ready—leaving behind only the anger with which I would annihilate my enemy.

Leighton was a large city. The double layer of quarantine bubbles surrounding it seeming almost impossibly massive. The inner quarantine bubble isolated the Avatar and the city itself, including the swollen purple and grey storm clouds hanging low over the downtown skyscrapers. Between it and the outer bubble, to the north of the city, were the sprawling refugee camps and medical centers, as well as the staging areas for the military and volunteers. People scurried around like frantic ants and ships floated in the air in loosely organized groups and queues. There were thousands of us.

There had been reconnaissance and rescue teams going into the city since shortly after the quarantine had been established, skirting the edges, where there was less of Tempest's corruption. Things had gotten worse, much worse, since Adam and the others had found her.

We'd thought, at first, that her powers were mental. Illusions, "metaphors," maybe. Then the first of the reconnaissance teams had reported the horror-film monsters in the real world, crawling out of that invisible dimension they'd been hiding in, like a fractal growing from two-dimensional to three, a sliver one moment and bulbous flesh the next. They had attacked the rescue teams and any nearby citizens, or at least those not under Tempest's control.

Some of the teams had reported even stranger things—disorientation and surreal moments that we suspected were another aspect of the Avatar's powers. She was only growing stronger. We couldn't wait any longer.

The cargo doors of the *Swiftsure* opened, spilling out marionettes carrying supplies for the emergency camp, in addition to their own weapons and medical gear. When they were finished delivering the supplies, many of them would join one of the other rescue or reconnaissance teams. As long as Kris wasn't cut off from them somehow, like being separated by the Other Place without any rips to the real world for her Skill to access them through, her marionettes could move kilometers away from her. If she strained, it was enough to cover about a quarter of the city around her.

Torliam accepted an incoming call on the *Swiftsure's* comm system from one of the lead coordinators of this makeshift emergency camp, who looked both tired and wired enough that I suspected they were taking some artificial stimulants to keep going. That stuff was dangerous, whether it was a chemical or Skill-based stimulant, but both the human and Estreyan military would approve things like that in times of dire need. "Fifteen minutes from deployment," the coordinator said, either not recognizing who he was speaking to or not caring. "You're in the G group. Line up and your coordinator will approve your entrance once we open up some holes. Have you been fully briefed?"

"Yes," Torliam said.

"Says here you're on the front lines, not search and rescue. Do you have the cognitohazard equipment?"

"We do," Torliam said.

"Gear up, then. And good luck." The coordinator cut the call abruptly.

We did a quick check of our gear, both the old and the new. Our armor was adorned with a handful of what had once been silver coins, polished down to a gleaming sheen meant to draw the eye with bright flashes and provide a constant clarifying effect from the silver reflections, so long as we stayed together. The visors we wore had been created with Blaine's help to protect us from the golden light of the God of Knowledge. Now, they would filter out the Avatar herself, with reflective striping on the inner sides to act as a quick slap of self-possession with the barest glance.

Those of us who used weapons carried them openly, and I carried the power of a god within me, its dark tendrils curling just beneath my skin.

We flew to the edge of the inner quarantine barrier, where the teams who would actually be going into the city were already gathered, most in ships, a few on foot or riding Estreyan mounts. Barrier specialists were preparing to open holes for us to enter.

I ran my fingertips idly over the circlet on my brow. "Open the side door," I murmured to Torliam.

When he did, I let Chaos spill out of my skin in a faint mist, taking control of the air around me. I stepped out of the ship deliberately, walking up onto an almost invisible platform of my power, till I was high enough to be visible to all of the gathered soldiers and ships. I'd promised Queen Mardinest I would give an inspiring speech, but as I looked down on these people, all of whom were risking their lives, many of whom would be dead before sunrise tomorrow, the vaguely memorized cliches I'd prepared no longer seemed appropriate.

I spoke at a normal volume, but Voice strengthened and carried my words to everyone below. "Today is, perhaps, the most important day of our lives." The people below stilled, turning to look up at me. "The survival of two worlds depends on what we do here today. We are here not only to protect the innocents within this city, but to protect every individual you have ever met, and all the rest that you haven't. And for this goal, you are risking your lives. By your bravery and selflessness, our worlds may yet be saved. But I will not lie to you. Many of us here today will die, lives sacrificed for the protection of all that is good in this world against the eldritch forces of darkness.

"We will be diving into hell. Do not be surprised by the monsters and demons you will see. The Avatar is strong, and her power is an abomination, turning bodies and minds against their owners, a devouring of the self. Save those who can still be saved, but do not throw your lives away in vain. Do not remove your protective goggles. Do not gaze in mirrors. Do not trust anyone who is not wearing their own goggles, be they civilian or soldier. Stay with your teams, protect your fellow comrades, and remember your equipment. Remember your objectives, and listen to the instruction of those guiding you."

I was supposed to be encouraging, courage-inducing, I remembered. I pushed even more power into my voice, trying to instill a little of my own resolve into the core of all those who heard me. "There could be no greater cause for which to lay down our lives, and though some of us may not see the sun rise tomorrow, I promise you, we will not lose this fight. Defeat is unthinkable. The abomination cannot be allowed to exist. Any sacrifice is worth it, for if we lose this fight, we lose *everything*. So we will not lose. Each of us has our part to play, and we must all vow that we will not fail each other. I vow this. I will not fail you."

I took a final deep breath and said, a little softer but with no less conviction, "You are all heroes."

I gave a single nod to the men and women controlling the barriers, then climbed down from the air and returned to the ship. A few minutes later, we were given the cue to fly through the opening in the barrier in front of us, and the *Swiftsure* darted through.

We knew exactly where we were headed. The warp, where Tempest, the latest manifestation of the Abhorrent's will, sat on her throne and gathered her power.

As we breached the edge of the city, a flash of lightning broke the clouds, and with the echoing clap of thunder, rain crashed down like the fist of an angry god.

Interlude 7

Reed woke to a grating feeling in his head and the surety that his brain was trying to pound its way out of his skull.

A hand on his neck pulled his head forward, and then something really *did* shift. He gasped and tried to jerk away as pieces of his skull settled and fused, but he could barely move.

The pain subsided, and he turned his head to the side as his stomach rebelled.

The person kneeling over him helped turn him so he didn't choke on the mouthful of bile that surged up. It took him a few seconds to regain his composure.

He shoved himself away from the ground and into a sitting position, leaning against the nearest building. Reed reached up to feel where his head had cracked against the curb. It was sticky with fluid and crusted with dried blood, but it didn't hurt, and no part of his head squished or shifted unnaturally when he applied pressure.

"You will be fine," a woman's voice said.

He used the wall he'd been propped up against to crawl to his feet and turned to look at his rescuer. She was geared up strangely, a visor over her face and sleek body armor covering the rest of her, with a few shiny disks that he realized after a few seconds of staring were *silver*. "Did you just..." He cleared his throat and looked around quickly.

The body of the parasite-controlled man who'd been chasing him lay in the street a few meters away, twisted and broken. Dead. Reed had been pulled out of the street, where a pool of blood—his blood—had gathered at the base of the curb, and into an alley. The sky was so dark with swollen, bruised clouds that he couldn't tell if it was day or night, and the world seemed to have aged a decade while he'd been asleep.

"I healed you," the woman said. "Though your dreams for the next few months are probably going to consist of a lot of pain and nightmares, maybe some sleep-walking or night terrors. It's the trade-off."

Sirens for fire alarms and crashed pods screamed in the distance. A block away, a group of people wearing similar gear to this woman were stripping the parasite off a struggling man and forcing him into a nearby hovering heli-pod, which already held a handful of other unconscious people.

Reed looked back to the woman. "I—I'm—what's going on?" He brought up his arm to try and check the time on his link, but its screen was shattered and refused to respond.

"Reconnaissance and rescue raids," the woman said simply. "Come along." She reached for his arm, jerking her head toward the waiting heli-pod.

"It's the Avatar," Reed blurted as she tugged at him, frantically reaching down to pick up the silver butter knife from the sidewalk.

"We know," she said.

"Oh, of course." He raised the butter knife and looked around in it, trying to settle himself. She was wearing silver, she'd just healed him, and her teammates were saving someone from a parasite.

"Don't worry, we've got it under control. We've got teams coming in from around the world, and the Seal of Nine is gathering up a huge group of volunteers from Estreyer. They'll be here soon. They're going to wipe that thing off the face of the planet. In the meantime, we're here to save as many people as we can."

"How long was I out?" Reed rubbed at the crusted fluids that had dried on his face, forcing some of it to flake away.

"It's just about noon. Can't say how long you were lying there, but by the state of your head I'd say at least a few hours. You're lucky you didn't bleed out. Anyway, make sure to get that sleep. You need to have the dreams, alright?"

He nodded distractedly, climbing into the heli-pod and seating himself in an empty space along the side. He found himself speaking again as a way to distract himself from the unconscious people within, some with blood running from their noses. "Are you going to heal them, too?"

His rescuer and her teammates grabbed onto the bars sticking out of the heli-pods exterior surface as it rose up a little and moved down the street. "Nah. Don't have enough power for that. We'll get them back to the rear camp where the medics can deal with them. I've got to save my energy for the critical cases."

The heli-pod's pilot leaned around to call to the others, "I'm getting some static. Nav systems don't like this place, and our coordinator's not responding to my pings."

"It's getting worse. You think the alien bitch is trying to cut us off?" one of the others hanging off the side yelled.

"She doesn't like us nibbling away at her," another said with a dark grin.

When the heli-pod stopped for them to save a few more people with perfectly visible parasites, Reed waited inside it silently. By the time it started moving again, now almost completely full of unconscious people who'd been rescued from the parasites, he felt a little more settled.

"My parents are pretty deep into Leighton. On the east side. Do you know what the situation is like around there?"

It was one of the other soldiers who answered him this time. "We haven't sent any teams that deep yet. 'Specially not to the east side. Too close to the warp and that...*thing*. Stuff starts getting weird the closer you get." The man shuddered, his visor disguising his eyes but not the sudden pallor of his skin.

Reed's fingers tightened around the butter knife, cold and clammy. "I see. What about the people affected by a parasite?" He motioned to the unconscious forms in front of him. "Are they okay? Is it...dangerous, when you free them?"

"It can be, for some of the worst. Of course, here on the outskirts it's not as bad, but the exhaustion is severe. Extracting them from the cronenberg suits doesn't really hurt them, it just lets their bodies respond to the stress they've been under. Far as we can tell, none of them are sleeping while they're in there."

Another of the rescue team members shuddered. "Awake, the whole time... You think they're aware of what's going on?"

Reed shook his head. "I don't think so. At least, I wasn't. My friends and I did a little testing, once we realized silver could protect us. For the early stages at least, you're kind of hypnotized, you don't notice the strange things around you or in how you're acting."

"That's some small relief," the woman said. "Impressive, that you managed to get free of the Avatar on your own. Almost got out of the city, too, if not for that nasty head wound."

"How long until the rescue teams get to the people farther in?" Reed asked.

A couple of them shared a look. "We're restricted to the outskirts for now, until Eve Redding gets here with the rest of the reinforcements. Then it'll be a full-scale raid while her and the Seal of Nine fight the Avatar."

Reed blanched. "Is that...safe? Will you be able to evacuate everyone?"

They shared another loaded look. "Don't worry, kid, just leave it to us. We'll get you settled in at the refugee camp and they'll take care of you till you're back with your family."

Reed's heart was pounding, and he felt sick. "Where is the camp?"

"To the north, just a few miles beyond the edge of the city. The Estreyans have a quarantine force field up, so everyone at the camps is protected from the stuff inside."

Reed adjusted his grip around the butter knife, then lifted it up to take another look around. When the heli-pod descended so the others could jump off to grab a woman slapping bloody handprints across the concrete side of a building, he slipped out behind them and ran down the street, dodging around the corner before any of them could notice.

He paused, taking a moment to retrieve the bigger mirror from his pack and look around with it. Things looked much the same in its reflection as they did in real life: creepy, ominous, and tainted. He shuddered, sure that the changes to the real world that had once only been visible in reflection could not be a good thing. But, reassured that nothing was hiding, invisible to his eyes, he took a moment to figure out his next move. Without his link, he couldn't contact anyone, and would also have trouble navigating this unfamiliar part of the city. He didn't want to risk going back to the skyrail, either, if it was even still running with all the chaos.

But he had to save his family and friends. It was on him, since no one else would do it, and he'd failed to bring help. His eyes swept over the street, some of the lanes blocked by wrecked or abandoned pods. His gaze caught on a multi-passenger pod, an older, rectangular model made to seat at least nine. The door was sitting open, the taillights indicating it was still running.

The thought to steal it would normally never have even occurred to him, but now, he jogged over to it and jumped into the front seat with barely a perfunctory glance to make sure it was empty. He quickly punched in an emergency override to the input screen, allowing him to take manual control of the steering. He heard the quick snapshot of a picture being taken, and then the pod began to let out soft, timed beeps.

The pod would send his face and location to the enforcers. Misuse of an emergency override could be prosecuted by up to ten years in a labor camp, but he figured everyone had slightly more important things to worry about at the moment. The override was meant for emergency situations such as this, though he suspected the manufactures had predicted something more like failure of the auto-navigation systems rather than the total breakdown of civilization.

With some effort, he tore off all three mirrors, then retook his seat and maneuvered the bulky passenger pod down the cluttered, sometimes entirely blocked streets as quickly as he could, only bumping into or scraping past things a few times.

At first, he was almost sick with adrenaline, but there wasn't much he could do for the parasitized citizens he passed, and he didn't have the medical training to help the injured.

He flinched a little every time he saw one of the Avatar's parasites, hoping they wouldn't notice him. A couple chased the pod, but none could keep up with it, and most ignored it in favor of continuing whatever incomprehensible activity they'd fixated on, like muttering to themselves, scratching at the walls with shards of broken glass, or throwing themselves relentlessly against a closed and locked door. Likely trying to get at some poor, uninfected person barricaded within, he thought. He kept his eyes away from windows and billboard screens, and kept his butter knife clenched in one hand on the steering wheel, angled to reflect his own face and keep him sane.

His body couldn't keep up the deluge of chemicals into his bloodstream, and so, after a long while and a few detours, he arrived tense and half-exhausted outside Demi's apartment building. Pieces of the walls were crumbling, cobwebs hung from the flickering lights, and rust-colored stains slipped down from the corners of the walls. As he made his way up the emergency stairs, he caught glimpses of the hallways through the plastine doors, the small windows looking onto each level like a screenshot taken from a horror film.

Through one, he saw a small parasite, covering the form of a little girl with black-buckled shoes being literally dragged down the hall by someone much bigger. She wasn't struggling. Reed could not see her face past the worm-like, pulsing flesh that surrounded her, and he wondered if she was dead. "Passed out," he muttered to himself, the words a prayer. "She's just passed out from exhaustion. Sleeping."

Another door showed a thin man, stretched too tall and hunched over to avoid bumping into the ceiling, writing something on the walls in what looked like blood. The hall lights flickered, and in between one blink and the next Reed thought he saw the hallway itself twisting open like a warped tunnel, dark shapes flitting through the shadows as something looked back at him. He threw himself away from that door and pushed himself faster up the stairs. He paused on the landing between that level and the next to take out the silver mirror and look around with it for a few seconds, gritting his teeth against the choked whimper vibrating in the back of his throat. He had to keep going. He was their only hope.

One door was propped open by a body. He knew it was a body because of the blood splattered everywhere and the bits of cloth still covering parts of it. One foot still wore a shoe, but the rest... He looked away before he could take it all in, swallowing and holding his breath as he ran past, even though it made him light-headed with the need for air.

After that, he tried not to look around so much, until he reached Demi's floor. To his relief, the hallway on her level was free of parasites, though there was a smell coming from under one of her neighbor's doors that reminded him of singed hair and pork. *Human*, he thought before he could stop himself.

He rang Demi's doorbell and covered the camera with his finger.

Her mother answered, cheerful as always, and so he greeted her with equal cheerfulness, his finger still over the small camera.

It would have been abnormal for her to refuse her daughter's best friend entrance, and so she let him in.

He gripped the very tip of the butter knife, the rest up his sleeve, and forced his face to remain neutral and composed when a parasite opened the door. It looked like a spider made out of hair, fangs, and too many dark, beady little eyes. The parts of their living room he could see were covered in slowly dripping web and smelled sickly sweet, like he imagined blood mixed with honey might smell. He slipped off his shoes and padded down the hall to Demi's room, just like every other time he'd been there, resisting the urge to look back at her mother with the knife's reflection.

He paused at Demi's door, wondering if he should knock or take her by surprise, since they would shortly be in a physical struggle. Then, he remembered the huge vanity mirror in her room, and had to let out a weak laugh at his own stupidity. What if her mother had placed a mirror in the entranceway, capturing his eyesight before he had a chance to react? He needed to be more careful. "I'm not cut out for this," he muttered to himself, knocking politely on his best friend's door.

Her mother was still down the hall, staring at him.

Demi opened the door with a sultry smile that he could barely see under the mass of slimy hair covering her face. A wave of rotten stench hit him, floating out from her bedroom. Her parasite was fully visible, which would at least make it easier to fight.

He pulled his backpack around, one hand resting on the silver mirror within, the other palming the butter knife. He kept his head turned away from the vanity, and as soon as Demi closed the door behind him, he tossed the silver mirror at her face and tackled her.

They fell to the wet carpet with a mucky splash, and he pressed the mirror to her face despite her efforts to push it away, just to make sure she couldn't avoid seeing herself in it. With his free hand, he stabbed the butter knife into the drenched, bag-like gown and used it to pry the living cloth away from Demi's skin, tearing it in the process.

She whimpered in horror, and he took that as a sign that her mind was clear and let the mirror fall away from her face so he could use both hands to tear her free.

He stabbed the parasite a few more times, and, to his surprise, it seemed to respond to the damage with pain. It bucked against him, then tried to crawl up his arms with strangling force, and then, finally, to escape across the room toward Demi's vanity. He didn't let it, stabbing and slicing and *ripping* until it fell still.

He was panting when Demi laid a trembling hand on his shoulder. He jerked, then took in the blood running from her nose and the sickly pallor of her skin with guilt. "Oh, god, Demi, are you okay?"

She nodded. "Better, now. Could you go get our medbot, though?"

He scrambled to comply, nodding hurriedly.

"Keep your eyes *down*, Reed," she added weakly as he darted away.

He returned with the clunky, old-model medbot and the poorly-stocked medic's case he'd found beside it, kneeling on the soggy floor by Demi's side while its diagnostic limbs prodded her.

"What happened?" he asked softly.

She shook her head, rubbing at the black makeup smudged under her eyes with a shaky hand. "I saw something. I wasn't even looking at the screens, I just saw a reflection of them."

"The Avatar?" he whispered.

She let out a shuddering laugh. "Yeah. Shit. It was way worse than before. I came home and... *I'm* the one who did that to my parents, Reed. I made them look at the local warp channel. Then it just got worse." She motioned to her room. "*Don't look*," she repeated quickly. "I was doing something to spread the mirror world. It might still be able to hurt you."

To Reed's relief, the medbot only prescribed sleeping pills and electrolyte-heavy hydration. "You're okay," he said. "Your parents are going to be okay. I've got a multi-passenger pod outside. We'll get them into it, and then we'll go to Lucas's house, and then mine. The rest of the world knows about the Avatar. They've got refugee camps just outside the city with medics and healers, and they're saving people. We just need to get everyone and make it there."

"Okay. Is it—Are the camps safe from the Avatar?"

"The Seal of Nine is on their way, so just a little while longer and all this will be over."

She nodded jerkily, one hand fumbling around till she found the dropped silver mirror. Speaking quietly, they planned their next move, and then left the bedroom to surprise and overpower her parents. It was much easier, with both of them, but things didn't go exactly as they'd hoped.

Her father passed out entirely when they removed his parasite, and Demi panicked until Reed explained what the rescue team had told him. "He needs rest, and maybe an IV for dehydration," he said.

Her mother was better, but only slightly, and neither was capable of walking down to the waiting pod on their own.

Reed forced Demi to eat and drink quickly, doing the same himself, though he could barely taste the energy bars, and the juice coated his tongue with a lingering film.

He stuffed both their pockets with what medical supplies he'd been able to raid from Demi's bathroom, and then they dragged her parents back down the stairwell, each supporting an arm and letting the adults' lower halves drag and bounce behind them.

He thought back to the article he'd read about countering mind-control Skills, but when he looked around, he let out a low laugh that felt like broken glass in his chest. He doubted the author of that article had meant it for, or even considered, a situation like this.

Reed drove to Lucas's house while Demi kept an eye out for danger with the silver mirror, several times urging him to close his eyes while verbally guiding him past dangerous obstacles, such as a stack of televisions on the side of the road, all showing an image of the warp and the enthroned Avatar sitting before it. He hoped it was overkill, but neither of them were willing to take unnecessary risks.

Reed took this time to explain everything that had happened to him since Demi and Lucas lost lucidity. He hadn't had even a moment to consider what he'd accomplished so far, but Demi's grunts of disbelief and gasps of fear and appreciation as he told the story made him realize just how lucky he'd been to make it this far.

To their combined dismay, they didn't find Lucas or his family at their house. Mostly because the house itself was gone, burned down to the foundations and still smoldering.

Demi covered her mouth with a trembling hand. "You don't think…"

"No," Reed said, trying to convince himself as much as her, "they would have escaped. Try calling him."

Lucas didn't answer.

Demi tried again, but the call failed entirely as her link lost service. She smacked it angrily. "He's still got his parasite." Demi's voice was thick, and she swallowed convulsively, then bounced a little in the passenger seat. "Your house next. Let's not waste any more time."

Some part of Reed wanted to protest, to get out and look through the ashes, but the thought of *finding* something there quickly killed that urge. As they drove away, lightning flashed and the rain clouds finally broke.

He pushed the pod faster, maneuvering a little more recklessly, trying not to imagine what they would find at his own house. He should have found it easier to navigate as he grew more familiar with the streets nearest his home, but it was the opposite. The streets twisted in ways only a deranged city-planner would have thought up, the intersections becoming maze-like and confusing. If not for Demi's help and her mind, kept clearer by the silver mirror, he doubted he would have ever made it.

The rain was punishingly heavy. By the time they arrived, the sewer tunnels along the sides of the streets were filling, which meant the roads would soon be flooded. Lightning flashed, leaving crimson echoes in his eyes and growling, angry thunder shuddering through his bones.

The house was still standing, but as Reed stepped into the rain, blinking up at it, it seemed to lean over him hungrily. The wrought-iron fence gating his front yard was rusted. It creaked as he pushed it open, the sound half old metal and half anguished scream. He jumped away from it immediately, hurrying past the postage-stamp lawn and decorative hedge, both withered and dead.

"Let's hurry," he said, metallic rain running into his mouth.

They stepped warily into the house. His parents hadn't turned on the lights, and with the storm outside, it was grey and gloomy within. Mold and mushrooms sprouted in patches on the ceiling, fluttering gently as if breathing in his scent.

They found his parents at the base of the stairs, across from the kitchen.

His dad lay on the ground, half propped up on the bottom steps. His face was pale, his eyes closed, but he still looked like a human to Reed's eye.

His mom stood over the man, the long, pleated skirt of her dress smeared with crimson. Her parasite was fully visible. Her stubby, simplified puppet hands smeared thick, almost-black blood over the wall, her movements frantic and jerky.

Reed and Demi both stared silently for a few seconds before the woman noticed their presence.

She stilled, then turned slowly toward them.

The gaze of her black, button eyes held an almost physical weight as it landed on them, and the porcelain, tombstone teeth displayed by her never-ending, peachy-cheeked smile were clotted with stringy chunks of blood.

"Welcome home!" she exclaimed. "I've been decorating. What do you think?" She stepped away from the wall, gesturing to the words scrawled across it.

But Reed's eyes were drawn to what her skirt had been hiding.

A large kitchen knife sat buried in his dad's abdomen. Thick blood pooled underneath and around him. The edges of the puddle were smeared, partially wiped away. Reed's eyes flicked back to his mom's puppet hands, then to her mouth, then to the wall.

His mind read some of the words before he could truly register what his eyes were seeing.

What kind of angel screams in the shadow of your footsteps?
What kind of evil—

Demi yanked on his shoulder, trying to drag his gaze away from the words—and almost succeeding.

One eye remained trained on the bloody, jagged words against Reed's will, turning in its socket even as his head jerked away, till the blackness of the inside of his eye-socket cut off its view of his mother's infectious work.

Chapter 24

Darkness becomes me.
— Sha Du

THE *SWIFTSURE* HAD BEEN CREATED from a creature that swam the depths of an Estreyan ocean. A little rain—even a lot of rain—didn't impede our ship in the least.

We paused for a few minutes, hovering in the air at the edge of the city while the other ships flew in. The combat-oriented teams' ships hovered behind us, waiting to follow our lead.

Ichi took Zed, teleporting to a handful of predetermined rendezvous points—intersections and other places where we predicted heavy concentrations of civilians—where Zed would open a series of doors to the Other Place, scattered across as large a section of the city as he could handle. The other rescue teams would get people to Blue, and it would get them to the refugee camps.

After a few minutes, Zed popped back into the ship with Ichi, drenched and breathing hard. He sat down immediately and closed his eyes, fingers twitching as if trying to grab something. After a few seconds, he nodded. "Okay, they'll hold." Keeping so many distant cracks open was a strain on his Skill, and I reminded myself that we couldn't expect him to be able to pop himself or any of us into and out of the Other Place while keeping the other tears open for the evacuations.

Still, Ichi could be similarly useful. We'd considered putting him on rescue duty, as he could transport large groups of people even more quickly than Blue, but in the end our own group's interests won out. After all, if we didn't defeat the Avatar, everything else would be in vain.

Torliam nodded, and we headed south-east, straight toward the warp that occupied what had once been a small square with a fountain, where now Tempest had made her throne. A handful of combat-ready ships followed behind us, bearing the most powerful warriors and those with the most singular and useful Skills.

The bedlam below grew more obvious as we moved from the outskirts into the city proper, the maze of streets filled with wrecked or abandoned pods and the lurching, strange-gaited creatures that had once been people.

We had no desire to waste time, but Torliam flew relatively slowly, carefully. Reconnaissance had shown Tempest's power was more than just the mind control and parasitic monsters, and we were wary of traps and unexpected attacks.

We were right to be wary, but when the danger came, it was from a completely unexpected direction. As we had flown through the storm, I had several times been warned of an impending lightning strike by the gathering of electricity in the surrounding air and the tingle of little hairs rising up all over my body, allowing us to outmaneuver the attacks.

There was none of that, this time. Something in the air contracted a millisecond before, and then we were struck.

I didn't understand what had happened at first. I was blind, and deaf, and my body told me I was falling, careening toward my sure death. Ghosts ran their fingers over my skin and pressed their screaming lips to my ears. My intestines writhed within the sheath of my stomach.

Then the impact, like a bug on a windshield.

My mind was tossed adrift while the ghosts turned to swollen-bellied flatworms and tried to burrow into my orifices.

I needed no coherence to recognize this attack, and responded with deep-seated instinct, tearing them apart and burning away what remained. When my vision returned, still spotted from the flash of light, the mirror on the inside of my visor settled my mind, and I drew Chaos back under my skin.

The *Swiftsure* had crashed. The walls rippled around us, the flesh of the ship writhing and bunching, tearing at the inorganic mechanisms that had been carved into and melded with it.

Adam was standing, his hair smoking and crackling with electricity, and, with a wild look on his face, he tore Kris out of her seat harness, yelling something I still couldn't hear past the ringing. A smoking crater in the floor beside him showed where he had redirected the majority of the lightning strike.

Kris was limp, but Gregor was a shadow, running around to the others and cutting them free with a flicker of his daggers.

I stood, almost falling again when the ship heaved beneath us, and lunged toward the cockpit. Outside, I felt for the other combat ships, and found them similarly downed.

Torliam pushed himself shakily up from the control panel. The shadows twisted around him, made eerie by another, more distant flash of lightning, and for a moment I thought I saw something solid unfold within them. But then he shook his head and coughed, and the shadows returned to normal.

"Are we still flight-worthy?" I screamed at him, leaning over so he could see the movement of my mouth.

The ship bucked under us again, this time with a convulsion that set metal to screeching and shattered the cockpit window. The grey walls bulged, and I saw the outline of crooked fingers press against it, as if something monstrous was trying to break through its flesh.

That was enough answer for me. I grabbed Torliam by the shoulder and yanked him out of the pilot's seat. "It's the Avatar. We have to get out, right now."

I sent the same message to the others in a VR Window, and slammed a drill of Chaos into the side door, forcing it open.

Birch screamed in alarm as crimson mist poured out of Kris's mouth, but Sam was already there, his hand on her forehead, and whatever he did snapped her eyes wide open, her back arching as if she'd been hit with a defibrillator. Birch clawed at the mist, and it shredded and dispersed.

I waved the others out, and they jumped and ran, but I had to physically drag Torliam from the ship. He couldn't seem to turn away from the mangled remains of the *Swiftsure*.

"Get the marionettes!" I screamed to Kris past the crashing rain and echoes of thunder. "Cut your way out if you have to!"

The ship convulsed again, stingray-wings and tail fluttering, and then shuddered into the air.

I wasn't sure if there had been multiple lightning strikes, or if ours had jumped from the *Swiftsure* to the other ships, but the simultaneous crashes had taken out a large part of the city block around us. Two of the other ships had collided with each other on the way down, and were in even worse shape.

I sliced into the *Swiftsure's* belly with whip-cords of condensed Chaos, and the marionettes took advantage of the opening, prying apart the ship's wriggling flesh and pulling themselves and what supplies they could through the wounds. "It was the lightning," I said. "She doesn't just use mirrors. *Shit.*"

The shapes of hands and faces pressed out from the surface of the *Swiftsure's* skin as it turned toward us, clawing and biting at the grey flesh as if they could rip their way out.

The other ships were similarly coming back to life, each with their own unique, grotesque mutations. One began to fray apart as if made of countless razor-thin ribbons. Another grew knobby bone spikes as its wings and tail cracked and stretched to create three asymmetrical, broken-looking legs. Yet another seemed to literally turn inside-out, crushing those within until their blood and viscera seeped out through the seams.

I used a few tendrils of Chaos to cut through the ships, creating openings in their bellies to let any survivors slip out. "And she doesn't just infect *people*," I murmured. The ships turned towards us, their malice clear and oppressive. I raised a clawed hand toward the *Swiftsure*, but Torliam reached out and gripped my forearm.

"Is there no way for us to cleanse her? We have silver—"

"Does the *Swiftsure* have eyes?" I asked, more harshly than intended.

He said nothing.

I turned back to the ship, and with a slow wave of my hand, turned it to dust. The rain washed what little remained of it away.

"The Avatar is afraid," I yelled, loud enough for my own teammates and the rest of the warriors following us to hear. "She wants to keep us from getting close."

"Then let's get *closer*, yeah?" Jacky yelled back with a wild grin.

I looked over the men and women gathered around us for injuries or signs of Tempest's power. A couple of the other teams' members were struggling with parasites, but others were already helping them.

Sam nodded to me, black-eyed.

Kris climbed atop Birch's back and Gregor into one of the marionette's arms, grim-faced and squinting through the rain.

"I won't let her strike us again," Adam said, pulling an extendable metal rod from his backpack.

Torliam cast one last, heartbroken look to where the *Swiftsure* had been, then pushed the wet hair away from his face and steeled himself.

I waved a hand for the others to follow, then loped deeper into the city, my teammates, the marionettes, and the other combat teams following.

THE AVATAR TRIED to keep us from finding her.

We knew where the warp was and had studied maps of the city, so it should have been easy to navigate, even on foot and surrounded by all that pandemonium, but she seemed able to deform the fabric of reality around us, or at least our perception of it, twisting the organized city streets into a surreal web of tangled asphalt. She also threw her monstrous servants at us, swarms of innocents ready to give their lives just to slow us down.

The other combat teams orbited my own, handling most of the attacking parasites as well as the follow-up to ensure their victims were extracted alive. Players, Estreyans, warriors from the Remnants, and even a few of the woodland guardians did their best to keep me and the other members of the Seal of Nine safe and supported.

Vigor coursed through my veins and strengthened my muscles with giddy power, courtesy of a support Skill boosting my abilities, and together we ripped through the city like the whirling blades of a meat processor. I tore a globulous mass of little flesh-balls with toothless mouths and round, shiny eyes off a man, letting him drop to the ground behind me, propped up enough that he wouldn't drown. The parasite itself got no such consideration, and was burnt to nothingness by the hungry black flame of Chaos.

In their insidiousness, Tempest and Pestilence were similar.

Both used innocents as their puppets, spreading like a disease through both the mind and body.

The buildings leaned in above us, like the fingers of a stiff hand attempting to curl into a fist. Street lamps twisted to follow as we passed, their flickering lights like the eye of a cyclops. The water rushing past our feet pulled at us, the current changing direction swiftly and erratically as it attempted to disrupt our footing.

The woodland guardians, being smaller than even humans, began to have trouble with the strength of the current, so Kris assigned them marionettes to ride atop, the same multi-legged, cockroach-like model that we'd used to sneak around their village. The woodland guardians didn't have Skills, but they had runic devices for both attack and defense, and those death-static tubes, which even the parasites couldn't defend against.

Another parasite sped toward us, driving a half-wrecked pod, and might have crashed into us if not for one of Kris's larger marionettes sideswiping it hard enough to send the pod spinning out of control and smashing into a building.

The street signs became unreadable, letters morphing and transposing their places. My sense of direction spun like a compass following Tempest's magnet, and without the sun or other clues to ground me, I had no way to reestablish it. Our visors were fitted with communication and locating equipment that linked back to our coordinator at the camp, but any attempt to contact them resulted only in static. We had expected that, at least.

Despite the dizzying effects of Tempest's power as it merged with reality, Wraith spread out over a large enough area to partially stabilize my sense of relative space, and the mirror in my visor kept my mind firmly separated from the surreality. Really, though, it was Torliam's Skill, cutting through Tempest's deceptions like the hot rays of the sun through morning fog, that allowed us to push ever closer to the Avatar hidden in the midst of the city.

"Please, help me, help me," a woman moaned nearby, having slipped past the other teams. Black and crimson ribbons were sown into her skin, stitching her up like a corset. Blood seeped slowly from each hole and was quickly washed away by the rain. Otherwise, she looked quite normal, and I couldn't tell what part of her exactly was a parasite, or if, perhaps, she was just a cruelly wounded woman sincerely asking for help.

Sam pressed a hand to her forehead, and her eyes rolled back. He caught her as she collapsed, digging his fingers into her skin and ripping it away. An entire outer layer of skin, hair, and ribbons tore away, revealing a completely different woman underneath, unconscious. "Cruel," he murmured, breaking the window of one of the pods lining the street and settling her in the front seat.

I caught a glimpse of movement from the corner of my eye, but when I turned to look, I saw nothing. I considered for a moment that it had only been the rain running over my visor, but decided in a situation like this, no level of paranoia was too high. I turned my head forward again, focusing on my peripheral vision.

In the window of the buildings to either side, people pounded on the glass, their mouths open as if screaming, their colors slightly washed out.

I checked with Wraith, but found no hint of any invisible presence. After walking a while longer, watching as their eyes followed me, I realized they were only there in the *reflection* of the street. I shuddered. Was this another aspect of Tempest's power? Were those real people, trapped in a mirror world? If so, what would happen when we killed her? Would they be set free, or trapped on the other side forever?

I pointed out what I'd noticed to my teammates.

"I would rather die," Adam said, shuddering viscerally and shaking his head, as if to dislodge the image from his eyes.

"They'll be freed once we stop her," Sam said. "Just like Pestilence."

"*If* they are truly trapped," Torliam said. "Perhaps it is only a ploy to discomfit and distract us from our goal. Do not lose focus."

The closer we drew to Tempest, the more drastically she warped the world around us, till each intersection was like a kaleidoscope, and the streets twisted like snakes.

But the heart of her power was stationary, and we were determined.

We passed a few rescue teams along the way, but not nearly enough to make up for the density of parasites the Avatar was congregating to herself. There should have been more, and I could only assume they had been stalled or diverted like she had attempted to do to us. Wraith could sense the mind-controlled citizens migrating inward all around us, some moving to cut us off, others seemingly moving for Tempest just like us. I would have called for reinforcements to try and save them, if only our comms had been working. As it was, these people could very easily end up collateral damage, crushed between Tempest's power and our own. Our combat teams couldn't stop for long enough to handle rescues in these numbers.

"We're getting close," I said.

Torliam nodded, grim faced. "Yes."

Finally, we trudged around a corner, the water in the streets a river pushing against us. The buildings leaned in over and in front of us, but I could see a city square, its small fountain, and the rippling distortion that hung in the air. Where Tempest sat upon her dark throne, I saw only a black blur, as the visors filtered my vision of her as best they could.

We weren't sure if Wraith counted as eyesight for however Tempest spread her influence, so to be safe I kept the sensory Skill away from her, skirting the edges of the square.

"You see the connection to the Abhorrent?" I asked Zed.

"In her chest, where her heart would be if she had one. It's bright," he said.

I settled that knowledge firmly in the back of my mind.

This time, I felt the gathering power of the lightning strike. I crouched down, keeping my head just above the water, and covered my eyes, counting on Adam to disburse the electricity without our team being zapped like fish in a pond.

Whatever the lightning did, Wraith was not immune to the attempted subversion of my senses, but this time I knew to go for the silver right away, contracting everything down to my focus on that true reflection. By the time my sight cleared, I was already standing, Wraith again spread out through our surroundings. Because of that, though Tempest likely meant for the parasites that stepped out from every alley and doorway and pod lining the streets around us to seem as though they'd appeared from nowhere, I clearly sensed their reveal.

"Not so impressive," I murmured.

While most of those around me were still prone or blind, Chaos lashed all the way down the street, arced over the heads of those standing between us, and dug into the obscured body of the Avatar.

Beside me, Adam was crackling with electricity, having fallen to his knees. The diverted bolt of lightning had left a smoking crater in the wall of the building beside us.

Zed leaned against one of the marionettes, his eyes unfocused and his fingers grasping at empty air, trying to keep his control of all the openings to the Other Place, which would close without his continued focus.

I considered telling him, and maybe Kris as well, to stay back and away from the fight. But Zed still had his guns, so could still be useful beyond his Skill, and Kris's control over her marionettes was strongest when she was close. More than that, I was afraid of what might happen to them if I let them out of my sight in this place, with this enemy. "Close in," I said instead.

As if on cue, the parasites between us and Tempest threw themselves at us. Some bellowed in rage, some screamed for help, and some were silent in bodies that could no longer make human sounds, but all were grotesque, molded carefully to prey on the deep-seated fears of a mortal mind.

The warriors around us rose to the challenge, the effects of their Skills flashing and singing as they charged into battle.

Tempest's puppets fell like wheat before the scythe, the parasites ripped from them and tossed into the unquenched black flames that I let trail behind us, or shot by yellow death static from one of the guardians' oversized energy tubes.

The water was too high, the current too strong now, to leave anything helpless in it. Zed opened up another small rip to the Other Place, his fingers pale and trembling as he did so, and the marionettes helped him feed people into it. Blue whisked them away in batches.

The endless wave of parasites may have slowed us, but they did not stop us. We moved inexorably forward, and I thought, perhaps, that would be how this went. Us, moving inexorably forward. Her, ineffectually attempting to stop us, until, eventually, we rolled over her like a wave.

That was not how it went.

Halfway up the street, the parasites thinned out. That seemed wrong, confusing. I tried to figure out what was causing the dissonance, and, as if passing through an obscuring veil, I saw the flesh-rune.

It was three-dimensional, and made of bodies. Parasitised citizens had been strung up in the air and bound together into an amalgamation of limbs and flesh that stretched to create a skewed, polygonal shape.

Red tinted my vision. I blinked, then saw my eyes in the strip of polished silver inside my visor. Blood dripped from my tear ducts, seeping from the burst capillaries of my sclera. "Don't look!" I called to the others, turning my head away.

I had to grab a handful of the surrounding warriors with condensed cords of Chaos, as well as a couple of my own teammates, and yank their heads away when they didn't seem to hear me. "Keep your eyes on your silver," I yelled. "Let everything else be peripheral."

Jacky turned her back on the corrupting flesh-symbol. "Those poor people. Can we—Are they still alive?"

"Yes," I said. I turned to Kris. "Have your marionettes take them down and back to the Other Place."

She nodded, the spirits of the marionettes already moving.

"Let's go," I said, turning back to face the square, only a few hundred meters away now. "Every second we wait is a second she grows stronger."

Tempest had stood from her throne, and though I couldn't see her clearly, she seemed to be looking at me. I thought I could feel her gaze moving across my body, trying to bore through the protection of my visor and into my eyes.

I took another step forward and received another shock as I

passed a second previously invisible barrier. There were other parasites scattered among us, lurking on the sidewalks, between the abandoned pods, and crouched on the roofs. Their cores glowed with Seeds. She had taken Players and Estreyans under her control.

I hadn't noticed them with my sight *or* with Wraith, and I realized suddenly that this is what she'd done with the lightning strike, simply disguising its real effect with the appearance of the more mundane parasites.

I thought of the other lightning strikes I'd seen and heard all around the city. Perhaps this—subverting those who'd come to fight against her and her efforts—had been her purpose all along. Most, no matter how powerful, would not have the ability to protect themselves against something like that.

I cursed aloud, sending the location of all the new enemies to my teammates in a mini-map Window. I wasn't sure if everyone else had noticed them, and I didn't want my teammates to be taken off guard. To my relief, the precaution was unnecessary, and the whole street immediately exploded as shocked combatants attacked and protected against parasites with similarly extraordinary powers.

The water dragging past my shins bit with sudden, impossible cold, freezing outward from me in a crystalline pattern as one of the parasites did some sort of dance of supplication toward the heavens.

I shattered the ice and jerked my legs out to stand atop the little iceberg amidst the swirling river that had once been a street.

A rippling purple orb floated toward me, the air shrieking around it like tearing metal. I backhanded it away without even touching it, and when it hit a nearby building, the orb popped, leaving a huge spherical part of the structure simply gone, sheared through with a razor's edge.

Gregor sliced a flying, membranous creature out of the air with his Absurdly Sharp Blades.

A marionette yanked one of the woodland guardians out of the way of a crushing blow, while one of her new rescue models injected oxygenating serum into a Player whose body had been ripped in half just under the armpits and then ferried him back to the rip Zed had created to the Other Place.

Jacky punched a literal crater into a parasite with a grossly distended, torn belly, sending viscera and pale little spider eggs exploding everywhere.

Torliam was calmer, his light blue power spreading out all around us, ready to lash out where it was needed, and, from the vibrations Wraith could feel in the air, also shielding us from two different types of sonic attack.

Ichi's eyes were wide, his face pale, but that didn't stop him from popping around the battlefield just in time to disappear people out of harm's way half a second before they would have met their death.

Birch was using Chaos to impressive effect, thick tails lashing out of his body as he jumped around with Kris, dealing devastation everywhere he moved.

"Cover me!" I yelled.

Both Zed and Adam moved to my sides, my brother sniping anything that looked my way with small rockets while Adam surrounded us with hungry ink creatures, eels in the water and razor-edged raptors darting through the air.

No matter what she could throw at us, what she was doing to reality, my goal hadn't changed. Kill her, and all the smaller problems would be solved, or at least solvable with time and effort.

I held my hands up, palms facing each other a few inches apart, and poured power into the space between. It spun and built, struggling against my will and my hands as I compressed it.

The last time I'd done this, it had been a fight. Chaos had bent to my will, but not without extracting its price in flesh and pain. My power was still wild and hungry, but I was too used to getting my way. I was the master of my self, not simply some vessel for a godhood. This dark, destructive power *belonged to me*, and no part of me would disobey my will.

The condensed ball of Chaos built faster this time, and I spared some concentration to step a little higher into the air so I could aim at the square without hitting anything unintentional along the way.

She drew in a few dozen minions as a shield all around her, all of which looked more or less like normal people, perhaps hoping I would hesitate.

I released the beam of black destruction, and it cut through everything between us without distinction, reaching the Avatar faster than even my Perception could follow, only fraying a little as it refracted off her body. For a moment, reality itself seemed to glitch around me, sound and light disappearing, the twisted hellscape around us blinking out of existence. For a fraction of a second, I saw without the Avatar's influence.

The clouds lightened. The rain was a drizzle instead of a flood. The buildings around us, while mostly destroyed, did not pulse with fleshy life or seem to reach for us with malevolent hunger. The parasites became people, still in the midst of aggressive movement but suddenly clear-eyed. For a moment, I hoped.

But it was only for a moment.

My beam of anti-light dissipated.

Tempest stood in front of her throne, her form twisting surreally even through the obscuring visors as she pulled power and mass from her own shadow to replace what I had destroyed.

I felt her gaze boring into me again then. A sound rose up from the water, the stones, the very air around us, at first low and grating but morphing into a shrieking wail as reality began to break apart under its force.

I coughed out the air in my lungs and tried to keep my organs from shattering within the casing of my flesh and bones, as I felt the tingling foreboding of the eldritch monster preparing to smite us.

I turned to Adam, but his lightning rod was thrust into the old brick of the half-collapsed store beside us.

I let myself fall out of the air, wrapping Chaos around myself and my teammates as best I could, reinforcing it into a repelling barrier.

It mattered not at all.

Lightning shattered through us, through the earth, the sky, and the space between atoms.

Something twisted and moved, leaving me deeply nauseous in a way that had nothing to do with my stomach. Wraith was just as disoriented as my physical senses, and it took me several panicked seconds to scrabble to my hands and knees, and then upright. I spluttered disgusting water out of my mouth and looked around.

I was somewhere else, near the corner of a street I didn't recognize, kneeling under the bare, knobby branches of an old tree. I was alone, or mostly so, except for the scattered parasites turning toward me with sudden and malicious interest. With a thought, I tried to find my teammates with my VR chip. Their little icons were there, scattered through the city, but flickering around confusedly as the Avatar interfered with the localized signal between our chips.

The tree above me bent down, scraggly branches grasping for me even as I regained my footing and slapped it with an irritated wave of Chaos. "Fuck," I spat, trying to gain my bearings. Mind control, warping reality, and now twisting space… What else could this Avatar do?

A stifled scream slipped past Reed's clenched teeth. He slapped a hand to his face, covering his left eye, as if that would somehow help. It had been *caught* by the words written in blood on the wall and refused to follow when he turned his head, so that while his right eye was facing forward like normal, the left eye was turned as if to see the inside of his own skull. The muscles inside his eye socket screamed out in pain, and he struggled to turn his eye forward again.

When it felt like it was facing the right way, he opened his eyes, blinking and trying to focus. He saw double for a few moments as his left eye shuddered and struggled to sync with the right, but eventually managed blurry success.

Demi had moved to stand protectively in front of him, and he realized then that he'd fallen to his knees.

He stood and moved to her side, nodding without looking at her. "I'm okay."

His mom was looking at them still, her head tilted too far to the side in exaggerated confusion.

Behind her, his dad's chest rose and fell shallowly.

Still alive, Reed thought with profound relief that almost knocked him back to his knees. "Yank forward, hold her down with a knee to the back," he murmured.

He caught Demi's curt nod out of the corner of his eye.

"*Now*," she snapped, springing forward even as she spoke.

Reed followed half a second behind, some small part of himself embarrassed that even now, with his own parents in the balance, he never quite managed to properly take the initiative when he should.

His mom struggled violently, almost managing to throw them off and giving Demi what would surely become a black eye. She screamed, gnashing oversized porcelain teeth. "*What—what kind of demon—*"

Reed smashed her face into the floor and pressed his fingers into her larynx till she choked to keep her from completing whatever she'd been trying to say. Those strange questions were a weapon, just as dangerous as a mirror, and he didn't want to find out if hearing one would be as bad as reading it.

As soon as they got the parasite off her, Reed's mom collapsed to the floor with worrying stillness. He tossed the butter knife to Demi, and while she stabbed at the parasite trying to crawl away, he checked his mom's pulse and breath.

He found both, but they were weak. "Get our medbot," he snapped to his friend, rolling his mom onto her side, her head supported by her right hand, her left arm out straight in line with her body; they'd learned this "recovery position" on a school field trip to the hospital. It had seemed silly at the time, cartoonish even. Demi had joked that it would be useful the next time she caught Lucas looking at her boobs, because she would knock him out. They had both laughed at Lucas's flushed face and embarrassed, guilty glare. It didn't seem funny now.

While Demi hurried off, her head down and the knife raised, he scrambled over to his dad.

Reed's hands fluttered over the knife buried in the side of his dad's stomach. He wanted to pull it out, but he thought maybe he shouldn't, in case it was stemming the bleeding. Unless it got jostled, it probably couldn't make the wound any *worse* if he left it in. He pressed his fingers to his dad's neck, the reassurance of the quick heartbeat there countered by the cold, corpse-like feel of the skin.

There was a sound he couldn't quite make out in the distance, or maybe an unexpected silence, and for a second, the world flickered back to normal. His dad was still bleeding on the floor, but actual healthy light came through the windows, his house returned to the unassuming historical wood floors and wallpaper he remembered, and the dead parasite that had been feeding on his mom disappeared from the corner of the living room where Demi had tossed it.

It was only a second, and at first he thought it must be the Avatar getting past his defenses, but then Demi yelled, "Did you see that?"

He knew it was probably only wishful thinking, but he thought, maybe, the Avatar hadn't done that on purpose. Maybe they were fighting it, like the woman who'd rescued him earlier had promised, and it would all be over soon.

The medbot, a much more expensive model than the one Demi's family had, led them through basic first aid with the blood clotter and pain-relieving spray, confirmed that Reed definitely shouldn't move the knife, and told them his mom was in a coma, not simply sleeping. It recommended urgent admission to the nearest hospital or clinic for both parents, tried to send out a request for an ambulance, and then threw an error code, going into a loop of failed attempts to request emergency transportation.

They raided every piece of real silver in the house, filling their pockets with the smaller pieces and duct taping the larger, flatter ones to their bodies in a mockery of armor. It might help protect against parasites, if any that attacked them would automatically see their own reflection.

Demi was uncharacteristically quiet as they handled all this, until she finally said, "What your mom was writing on the wall... I think I did something like that, too, in my room." She pressed a hand to her forehead, her expression pained.

Reed watched her carefully in case he needed to make her look at some silver, but she shook her head and looked at the dinner platter he wore as a breastplate without prompting.

The tension around her eyes eased. "It...helps her. The alien. *Tempest.*"

That *thing* wasn't a she. It wasn't a person, or even an animal, that would live and feel and play and die. It was like a virus, or a natural disaster. But it *wasn't* a *she.* The alien had no right to such a label, and it grated on Reed that Demi would use it for the Avatar.

He wanted to snap at her, to tell her so, but instead he said, "What do you mean?"

"She's trying to spread. I did it for the same reason I made my parents look at her. She wants people to *see*." Demi shuddered and lifted her thumb to her mouth, nibbling at the nail, a nervous habit she'd long since kicked.

By mutual, silent agreement that they were already terrified enough, Reed and Demi didn't continue the conversation.

They carried both his parents out to the multi-passenger pod, laying them along the benches rather than strapping them in upright. His dad groaned—they couldn't help but jostle him a bit —but didn't wake. Reed talked to him, told him it would be okay, that he was safe and mom was safe, and they were going to a place where people could help.

All four were totally drenched by the effort, and as Reed returned to the driver's seat, he rubbed his fingers over the fabric of his damp shirt, frowning at the feeling and peering out through the windshield where the wipers swept back and forth in a futile effort to keep his field of view clear. The water was tinted red, and despite the bruised, angry veil of the clouds above, he knew the color wasn't some trick of the light. Even as he watched, the red grew deeper, the raindrops moving a little slower.

"It's raining blood," he said to Demi, the surreal statement spoken with the same tone he would have normally used to tell her to grab a coat, since it was cold outside.

"Hurry," was all she said in response.

Reed had to navigate with heavy use of the silver mirror to confirm the names on the street signs, and had a few tense arguments with Demi about where they actually were. The mirror helped, but its power to protect them seemed to be weakening, perhaps because the horrific contamination wasn't just on the other side of a reflection anymore. His mind was clear, it was reality that was being suffocated by hell.

Eventually, they worked out a system where they would agree on a series of navigational steps ahead of time, based on a significant landmark that was still recognizable and their memories of living in this city for years, and then follow the navigational steps despite confusion or dissonance that suggested otherwise.

This led Reed to turn into what appeared to be an alley, but was actually a four-lane street, then he drove through a small dip that had been disguised as a foreboding chasm of darkness. None of that would have been an issue if not for the parasites, which filled the streets in even greater numbers than before.

He had to slow down to avoid killing them as he forced the pod through the streets, and a few even attacked the vehicle. The pod was old and sturdy, and though it was disturbing, he thought they would make it. Then one parasite plastered itself to the window and shrieked, "*What kind of evil grows in the flesh of your eyes?!*"

Reed swerved, scraping the side of the pod along a lamp-post to roughly dislodge the parasite while Demi shoved the mirror into his face. His ears hurt, and the sound of nails on chalkboard overwhelmed everything for a few seconds. He touched his ears. His fingers came away bloody, but the grounding effects of the silver mirror steadied his mind, and despite the blood, he'd retained his hearing.

It wasn't till one of the parasites used a Skill that Reed realized how well and truly screwed they were. The parasite, a big, troll-like thing, raised one muscled arm. Neon-blue swirls of light built around the appendage, the color almost searing against the grey gloom and crimson rain staining the world. The parasite slammed the arm into the ground, and the asphalt between them cracked and broke, as if something was tunneling through it.

Reed slammed on the accelerator pedal, but both he and the pod were too slow. The pod lurched as the fissures reached them.

The parasite lifted its other arm, those neon swirls building again.

Reed kept the pedal stomped all the way to the floor, and the pod groaned and shuddered as it scrambled for speed, bulldozing other pods out of the way as he clipped them and even smashing into a few parasites who didn't manage to get out of the way in time.

It wouldn't have been enough, except for the Estreyan ship that shot by overhead, firing a spray of projectiles that hit the Empowered parasite and sent it crashing to the ground.

"Shit, shit, shit!" Demi spat, slamming a fist into the dashboard.

Only then did Reed notice the urgent error codes the pod was flashing across its control panel, and the loud warning beeps. The attack had damaged their power line. The battery was draining quickly.

He turned to Demi, eyebrows raised manically high, his fingers white-knuckled around the manual steering wheel.

"There's no way we make it all the way out of the city in this," she groaned, shaking her head violently. "We're going to have to switch vehicles."

"How? They're everywhere! It's not safe to stop moving, let alone get out and try and transport *them*," he jerked a thumb toward the back seats, where both their parents rested, unconscious.

She bit the edge of her thumbnail, rocking back and forth for a few seconds. "What about a parking garage? If we can get into the control station, we can have a replacement vehicle brought right to us, and I doubt there'd be many parasites in there. They're all out *here*," she finished with a wave to the surrounding streets.

"That's a good idea," Reed agreed. "They even have wheelchairs, I bet."

"Don't look so surprised," Demi said distractedly, not even looking at his face. "I'm either right or I'm right."

It was a well-used line from when they would bicker as children, and it set Reed a little more at ease, a nugget of normalcy in a world turned inside out and upside down. "The only problem is, I have no idea where the nearest parking garage is. Do you?"

"*Shit.*" She returned to gnawing on her much-abused thumbnail, then yanked it away from her mouth and glared at it, as if the old habit's reappearance offended her.

They entered a large intersection, and on the cross-street appeared their salvation.

An Estreyan rescue team, complete with airship, stripping people of their parasites and hauling the unconscious bodies through a side door.

Reed turned the pod so quickly it tilted a little to the side, then grimaced as his dad moaned again when the pod settled back down. "It's okay, Dad! I found help." His voice broke on that last bit, and he swallowed, focusing on the Estreyans turning toward them.

A couple gripped their weapons or raised their hands in a way that might have been a gesture of surrender if they were human and couldn't shoot deadly superpowers out of their fingers. One who was maybe the leader waved at them to relax, probably noticing his and Demi's lack of parasites.

The pod skidded to a stop beside the ship, and Reed spilled out of it, the sudden *smell* of the bloody rain almost making him gag in surprise. Still, he managed to babble out their situation and a plea for help, and they were quickly accepted.

Some of the Estreyans were wearing visors, while others had small silver disks attached to a fitted headset, so they could look down and to the side to see their own reflection. Most of them also had what looked like polished silver coins set into their armbands. Reed was relieved to see they knew the necessity of silver.

Demi nudged Reed in the side and he followed her gaze to the strangest member of the alien team, a small creature that seemed to be made of turquoise pebbles and polished turtle shells. It carried a huge wooden tube, which seemed to be some kind of weapon. The Estreyans were tossing each removed parasite to the little turquoise creature, who would point his tube at them, and the parasites would collapse to the ground, dead.

Reed blinked a few times, then elbowed Demi back. "Don't *stare*."

"All will be well, young human," the apparent leader said, glowing slightly through old-style plate mail armor that made Reed self-conscious about the makeshift silver armor he and Demi had taped onto themselves. "We will aid you." His accent was really strong, but Reed could still understand him with enough concentration.

Reed cleared his throat awkwardly and bowed to the man. "I am Reed from the line of Phillips. Well met," he said, copying the standard Estreyan greeting he'd read about on the Net. He hoped he'd got it right.

A few of the Estreyans laughed, but the leader smiled heroically and returned the greeting. "Penacor of the line of Bane. Well met."

All around them, the rest of the team continued to fight against the parasites and throw unconscious humans into their ship, but Penacor barely spared a glance to the chaos, which Reed decided was actually reassuring, because if this Estreyan wasn't worried, that meant he could protect them.

"The Veil-Piercer has opened many doors to the beyond, and brokered an agreement with a powerful spirit on the other side. We must merely get to the closest door, and it will transport you to safety."

One of the others glowered and muttered something in Estreyan, which caused the leader to grimace. "We will find our way, through the power of justice and righteousness, Deodor. Do not doubt, my friend."

Reed guessed that Deodor had been skeptical they could properly navigate to this "door." "So the Seal of Nine are here? Are they fighting the Avatar?"

The leader nodded, idly reaching out one massive hand and tearing a snarling, blade-covered parasite off someone who'd tried to attack them. "Aye. They fight against Tempest even now, and are soon to be victorious, I have no doubt."

"Okay, that's great and all, but our parents need help, like right now. Especially his dad," Demi said, her arms crossed and one hip cocked out confidently, though her voice was strained. "Are your healers going to be able to deal with that knife wound?"

A giant Estreyan woman with some sort of telekinetic Skill smiled at her. "Do not fear. The Seal of Nine has provided us with an...air potion. It will keep his brain breathing, even if his wound is otherwise fatal. I will move them, and see to it." The pod's door slid open at a wave of her hand.

"An air potion?" Demi mouthed to Reed incredulously.

Reed shrugged. "Things may be lost in translation," he muttered. He was halfway to letting himself feel a real sense of relief, almost believing that they were safe, when another ship barreled out from between the multi-story buildings surrounding them.

It clipped a row of windows as it banked to a stop in mid-air, sending grimy glass down into the flowing blood on the sidewalk.

Parasites clung to its sides.

At first Reed thought they were attacking the ship to bring it down, but then the ship turned toward them, and Reed saw its *face*, cadaverous and sunken and entirely too *human*. None of the other Estreyan ships he'd seen looked like that.

The ship's expression twisted with malice, and that's when he realized it was a parasite, too. Which meant that—

One of the humanoid parasites clinging to its side opened its mouth—the mouth running vertically from its neck to its groin and filled with rows of shark-like teeth—and spat what looked like a little rock at them.

The telekinetic woman waved her arm through the air, slamming the little rock sideways into one of the buildings lining the street.

The point of impact pulsed and rippled, then grew a couple dozen thin legs and arms that wriggled and grasped at the air.

The parasites clinging to the other ship were Estreyans, too. "We need to get out of here!" Reed screamed to the rescue team.

Demi grabbed his arm and pulled him behind the pod, crouching down and peeking out around the front.

Both their parents were still inside, with the pod's side door open and facing the parasitized Estreyans, leaving them helpless and exposed to any attack that might slip past the rescue team. Reed yanked open the driver's door and checked the battery cartridge's remaining energy level.

It was almost dead. But he didn't need much.

Ignoring Demi's hissed questions, he jumped into the pod and executed a tight, three-point turn, leaving the open side door facing the rescue ship's belly.

He didn't need to explain any further to Demi, as she was already unbuckling his dad by the time he'd got out and moved around the pod. Together, they dragged his dad out and shuffled toward the ship, heedless of the fighting all around them.

One of the Estreyans noticed their efforts and used a Skill to harness their dad in a glittering crystal, which then lifted the man into the ship and deposited him in a glowing, sarcophagus-like tube. "For his wound," the man said, gesturing to his stomach.

"Thank you," Reed gasped, turning back to the pod for the remaining three unconscious passengers.

He slipped, catching himself with a splash of iron-and-rot-water that got into his panting mouth.

The parasites were screaming, closing in on the rescue team with reckless abandon. Someone had killed the infected ship, though he'd been too busy to notice how.

As they drew closer, their screams gained coherence past the sounds of battle and the crashing blood rain. "*What kind of demon feasts on the corpse of a thought?*" he heard.

Reed lifted his forearm, where he'd taped another butter knife, and tried to look in it, but it was covered with blood. Stumbling to his feet, he frantically wiped it away until he could see himself, and the silver blocked out some of the nails-on-chalkboard sound reverberating through his head.

He turned to Demi, to make sure she'd been able to do the same, and found her on the ground behind him.

A parasite writhed up from behind her. It seemed to form from the very blood she lay in, clotting into globules as it enveloped her.

But Reed's eyes were drawn to the way her teeth were clenched till the tendons stood out on her neck, and the *hole* in her side that she was trying to hold closed, pressing her hands to it as if she could replace the missing ribs and keep her organs from spilling out.

Her eyes were on his, and she moved her mouth as if to say something, but no sound came out, and he couldn't quite read her lips.

He was kneeling beside her before even realizing he'd moved. "Keep your eyes open!" he was screaming, slapping a hand against the silver dinner plate on his chest as he slipped his arms underneath her back and legs.

He heaved upward and managed to lift her, along with the parasite, and stumbled toward the rescue ship. He lunged up and into the side hatch, toward the glowing tubes in the back. He used his knee to nudge one open, then lowered her inside, pausing to rip the parasite off her. "It's going to be okay!" he shouted hoarsely.

He closed the transparent lid over her, and the brightness of the glow increased. He took a moment to meet her gaze, trying to keep his expression confident, so that maybe she could draw some comfort from it.

Then he turned away, throwing himself back out the hatch and to the pod where his mom and Demi's parents still waited. He paused to stab the globulous, bloody parasite a few times, till it stopped trying to wriggle away.

The rescue team was failing, most already either injured or struggling with parasites of their own.

Their attackers seemed to put particular emphasis on ripping away the silver they'd been wearing, tossing it beneath the blood-river rushing through the streets. They were still screaming their bizarre riddles.

The turquoise and turtle shell alien was killing them with its wooden tube, apparently unconcerned for the people being controlled underneath, but even as Reed watched, it was struck from the side with a bright red bolt that *exploded* it, sending fragments everywhere.

He turned back toward the passenger pod, slinging his mom's arm over his shoulder and dragging her out. The current almost pulled them down, but Reed managed to brace them against the side of the pod. Doubt filled his mind like smoke in a burning house. Even if he could get them into the Estreyan ship, who would fly it? If a parasite got it, too, it would surely kill or reinfect everyone inside it…

Still, Demi and his dad needed those healing capsules, or they might die before he could get them to a healer, so he needed the ship.

He was dragging his mom into the ship, painfully slowly, when he saw a creature made entirely of bone spring around the corner of a street a few blocks away.

It landed lightly in the intersection on flexible feet that reminded him of the springy prosthetics amputee athletes used. It was thin, and its limbs were abnormally long. Its arms, tipped by huge, dagger-like claws instead of fingers, hung down past its knees. It paused for a couple seconds, its expressionless face turned toward them, and then it sprang.

It landed in the midst of the battle with only a single jump, swinging a thin arm around so quickly its claws whistled through the air, bisecting the crimson raindrops.

Reed instinctually threw himself to the ground, as if somehow that would save him from this horrifying parasite, but, to his surprise, the blow did not land.

Not on him, at least.

The bone creature had attacked one of the parasites, clipping its hamstrings. Its claws were too sharp to tear away the parasite from the Estreyan below, so instead it leaned forward and bit down on the monstrous cocoon. With a jerk of its head, it tore away the Avatar's minion, and then it used its claws to shred it to bits before whirling on the next enemy like an avenging devil.

Reed climbed back to his feet, watching what he had thought was a parasite protect them from the others. None of the still-lucid Estreyans attacked it. Was it another strange alien, like the one made from pebbles and shell had been?

He settled his mom into the ship, then returned for Demi's parents, moving as quickly as he could. To his dismay, despite their new ally, the rescue team was still losing.

Even as he dragged Demi's mother into the ship, he watched Penacor collapse under the combined onslaught of two parasites, one of whom had been his ally only minutes before.

They weren't going to make it.

He stumbled on trembling legs back toward the pod. He just needed one of the Estreyans to survive—just one—anyone who could fly the ship once he had it loaded.

His weary eyes trailed over the corpses of Estreyans and parasites alike, and caught on a cylindrical shape. The tube weapon that killed without light or noise.

Without consciously considering what he could possibly do with the artifact, Reed waded through the muck and picked it up. He slipped the straps over his head, settling it to his body. Numbly, he pointed it at the nearest parasite, which was screaming into the telekinetic woman's bleeding ears. It had two handles on the side, which he'd seen the little alien pulling earlier.

Reed grabbed them and pulled, and the parasite slumped to the ground, landing on top of the Estreyan woman.

He turned and found the next enemy, yanking the handles again.

The bone creature landed beside him, narrowly saving him from having his head sliced off.

He was screaming, he realized, though he could barely hear the sound of his own voice over the rain and the screeching chalkboard and the death all around.

He yanked on the handles again and again. Sometimes it worked, sometimes it didn't, and he had to wait and pull again, either because he'd missed or because it needed time to recharge. Without knowing how it worked, he couldn't be sure.

Soon, it was just him and the bone alien still fighting to protect the ship, standing back to back in front of the open cargo hatch, and he knew they were all going to die.

He kept screaming, though he was pretty sure his voice was gone, because being silent as he died and let them all down would have been just *too much*.

The parasites were closing in, dodging his shots, sniping at them.

Something exploded behind them, the blood that sprayed up from the force doing nothing to disguise the sound of concrete buckling and breaking.

It wasn't until the encroaching parasites all froze, then fell away from their hosts in shards and dust and the occasional slurry of meat that he realized the sound had been something new arriving.

The Estreyans slumped to the ground, and without them in the way, he saw the figure standing tall within a crater of buckled concrete, the blood river not even reaching her knees.

Dark, prehensile tendrils grew from her body and wove through the air around her, and the rain slid off her scaled body as if repelled. Her eyes pierced through the gloom and the rain, so bright and icy they seemed to be lit from within.

Reed carefully turned the tube weapon away from Eve Redding, swallowed hard, and lifted a hand to give her a small wave.

Eve Redding strode toward Reed, the dark tendrils he recognized as her Skill drawing back into her body. The tingling heaviness in the air around her didn't dissipate, but he was pretty sure that was just the effect of her presence. She probably couldn't walk down the street without people stopping to stare at her, even if she hadn't been a seven-foot-tall warrior princess with claws and scales.

She paused, picking one of the visors the Estreyans had been wearing out of the blood. A too-fast-to-be-human flick of her hand sent the blood spraying off of it, and she slipped it onto her face, covering those unnerving eyes.

She gave him a perfunctory nod, then turned to the bone alien. "Can you find Kris?"

It nodded.

"I need you to take me to her."

It nodded again, pointing one long, sharp digit into the distance.

"Wait!" Reed blurted, worried that she would shoot off with the bone alien and leave him in the middle of a war zone with a ship he couldn't fly.

She turned back to him, one eyebrow raised.

He almost quailed under the impatient force of her stare. "Umm, there's no one left to fly the ship, and there are injured inside, not just unconscious. Can you…send help?"

Her eyes flickered over his shoulder into the ship, to the pod, and then to the alien weapon he held. "You're not a Player?" she asked, as if she already knew the answer.

He shook his head, resisting the urge to shrink back as a small frown puckered the skin between her eyebrows.

"At least it'll get me out of the rain," she muttered. "Get inside and go through to the cockpit."

Shuddering with a combination of cold and relief, Reed turned to the pod, still needing to move Demi's dad onto the ship, but Eve's Skill was active again, a couple tendrils already grabbing the man while others reached into the ship ahead of her.

She opened storage hatches on the walls without even looking, one of her tentacle-like appendages grabbing a couple vials of bright blue liquid attached to mechanical collars. She pressed them into his hands while opening a door he hadn't noticed earlier and walking through to the cockpit. "The emergency stabilization pods will let you know if their hearts stop. If they do, follow the instructions and inject those into the base of their skull. There are healers at the camp that will be able to fix anything else, as long as we keep the brain alive."

Reed trailed after her, holding the bright blue vials like the precious, fragile miracle they were.

"Sit there," she ordered, pointing to the chair nearest the pilot's seat, again without looking, as if she knew where everything was without even needing to see. She placed her hands on a control panel and said, "Recognize security level zeitolon override," then rattled off a long string of letters, numbers, and fake words.

The ship rose a few feet, and Reed hurried to take off the tube weapon and attach it safely to a mount on the wall before strapping himself in. He'd barely used the thing and was already paranoid about accidentally shooting someone with it.

She took the controls and steered the ship, grim-faced.

The bone alien crouched between the two of them, still tall enough to see over the dashboard and through the window. It pointed a finger, and they shot off in that direction.

"You're a civilian?" Eve asked.

"Yeah. I—I live near here."

"Clever use of silver. You figure that out all on your own?"

He looked down self-consciously. "Yeah. I have—*had* a silver mirror in my room. I saw some things and figured out what was happening. Well, actually I thought it was a Player," he said with an awkward, derisive laugh. "I tried to let someone know, get help, but it was too late. The enforcers were already turned, they were keeping people from leaving Leighton, and I tried to call the national emergency lines, but…" He shuddered at the thought of his mom, coming up behind him with a meat cleaver. She could have done the same thing to him she did to his dad. "Me and my friend managed to get our parents out, but not before my mom stabbed my dad. And then my friend got hit by a Skill. And my mom's in a coma—she was really deep under, writing those *questions* on the wall with my dad's blood…" He forced himself to stop talking, pressing a trembling hand against his mouth.

The bone creature pointed again, guiding Eve down to a small courtyard surrounded by apartment buildings.

In the middle of the courtyard, standing atop a bench, was a small form that he recognized as Kris Mendell, another member of the Seal of Nine. The courtyard was filled with dead, extracted parasites, and a group of people were working to fight off and free those that remained on a host. Two smaller marionettes guarded the miniature girl, whose hands were waving about as if she was directing the fight.

When the ship lowered to hover beside her, its side door opening, all the people turned at once and followed Kris into the ship, falling in line like trained soldiers.

Only the marionettes followed Kris as she moved into the cockpit.

"Using humans? Pretty impressive. Will they be alright?"

The girl nodded, sparing Reed a look that he couldn't quite decipher past the visor concealing her eyes. "A little sore, maybe, but nothing the healers can't deal with. I was careful to make sure I didn't damage the connection of the body to the spirit. So what did Tempest do to us?"

"Space-warping, I think. The city's under her control. She's absorbing it into her domain. Can you get your marionettes to search for the rest of the team? Lead them to the rooftops."

Kris jerked her head at the bone alien, and it moved away from the cockpit, going to stand beside the two marionettes near the wall. It was only then that Reed realized it, too, was a marionette, and he looked at the tiny girl with even more respect.

"You can't find them?"

"The chips work on a local area signal. I'm getting something, but it's not very accurate. I could use some help. I don't want to let her power up any longer than absolutely necessary."

"I'll try. Hopefully we can find Torliam." Kris jerked her thumb toward Reed. "Who's the kid?"

He wasn't sure how he felt about being called a kid by someone both younger than him and one quarter his size, but he supposed if you were on a list of "people who've saved the world at least once," you could call anyone whatever you wanted and they should probably just shut up about it.

"Civilian. Found him protecting the ship. Figured out silver all on his own. Might even have been one of the whistleblowers we used to figure out what was going on."

He cleared his throat. "Hi, I'm Reed."

She nodded. "Kris."

He resisted the urge to say, "I know." Because of course he did.

Everyone did. Little kids dressed up as Kris for Halloween. He looked between her and Eve, wondering if anyone would ever believe him if he tried to tell the story of meeting them.

"Reed," Eve said. "Tell me about the Avatar. We did as much reconnaissance as we could, but you've been living here. Don't leave anything out. What has she been doing?"

He was hesitant at first, wondering what he could tell her that would actually be useful, but eventually he just started listing every strange thing he'd noticed, leaving out only the more personal bits of his story. He was interrupted frequently as they picked up the other members of the Seal of Nine, each of whom had been fighting off parasites when they found them. Seeing them in action, even from afar, was completely different than watching the film clips spread throughout the Net.

Jacqueline Santiago hit hard enough for the sound of impact to reverberate through the air, so hard he could *watch* the shock-waves travel as they shook the crimson raindrops.

Reed almost peed his pants when he accidentally saw Sam Hawes' eyes. The man's visor was held in his hand, revealing black orbs that sent the parasites around him tumbling and sliding to the ground with only a look. When Sam walked into the cockpit and learned what had happened to Reed's dad and Demi, though, he turned back around and used his healing Skill to stabilize both of them.

Birch—the telepathic winged cat—had green eyes with human-shaped pupils, which shone with obvious intelligence. The creature preened under his awed gaze, nodded at him, and reached out to pat him on the head with one wing.

Adam Coyle had tattoos covering most of his body, and a scowl that never left his face, but when he asked everyone if they needed their ink shields renewed, the concern was obvious in his voice. With his hair wet and flattened instead of springing up wildly, he actually looked kind of sad.

Prince Torliam of the line of Aethezriel was *gigantic*. Eight feet tall, maybe, and broad, too. He nodded kindly, pressed on Eve's shoulder as she gave up the pilot's seat to him, and introduced himself to Reed with a light accent and a voice that seemed like it was meant to roar battle cries at the head of an army—probably while riding a unicorn or something.

He flew like a *madman*.

Reed almost screamed when the ship twisted into a barrel roll to avoid an attack from the street below. Eve Redding, he thought, had been flying like a grandma by comparison.

She didn't seem bothered at all, though, standing behind Torliam with her stance wide for balance and her arms crossed. Misty, thin waves of blackness wafted out of her bare, mutated feet, which must have somehow been sticking her to the floor.

Reed's eyes flicked back up to hers, though he couldn't see them through the visor, and she *smirked* at him. He felt himself flush from his neck to the tips of his ears.

If Eve hadn't urged him to continue, he might have fallen silent in the presence of people who were powerful enough to literally change the course of the world through the pressure they exerted. With them all together, he again got that sense of physical pressure, a tingling of potential in the air ready to snap into movement.

"I think I understand the common theme," Eve said as he finished.

Reed wasn't the only one who focused on her as if she was about to reveal the secrets of the universe.

"Her powers are likely fed through observation. There is a connection between thought and reality, and she has some way to feed on it, taking power from the observer while sending some piece of her own power back through the connection. First, the mirrors and the warp channels. She was still weak at that point, thus the need for *normalcy*. Then, her minions capturing and turning others, keeping word from leaving Leighton. She was trying to be cautious, still. She didn't start going full-out until it was clear we'd caught her, when we placed up the quarantine barriers. By that point, she was powerful enough to start subsuming the city itself. The questions? They're describing her. *She's* the demon that feasts on the corpse of a thought."

Reed shuddered as an echo of that grating shriek sounded in his ears.

The others did the same, and Eve nodded. "See? Thinking of her as she is, describing her to ourselves. It's dangerous."

"How do you fight something like that?" Jacky said, her fists clenching and unclenching repeatedly. "How are we supposed to kill her if we can't *think* about her?"

"I can do it," Eve said, her voice almost a whisper. "I know how."

They picked up the last member of their team, an Estreyan Reed didn't recognize.

"Take us to the edge of the square, right to her," Eve said.

The man seemed like he was going to protest, but she gave him a hard look. "There's nothing she can do to us if we barge right in that won't be just as bad if we try to tiptoe up again. This time, there's no need to bother with reinforcements, either."

Torliam tapped something into the ship's console that was supposed to send it back to the refugee camps on autopilot and gave Reed some rudimentary instructions about how to fly it in case of emergency.

All of them gathered together.

Kris took the tube weapon, which was taller than her, off the wall and strapped it on with a nod to him.

Then they disappeared.

"Teleportation," Reed mused, nodding to himself and carefully tightening his hands over the ship's controls.

Demi was going to be *so pissed* she'd missed all this.

Chapter 25

I am the voice of the voiceless; Through me the dumb shall speak.
Till the deaf world's ears be made to hear. The wrongs of the word-
less weak. And I am my brothers keeper, And I will fight his fights;
And speak the words for beast and bird. Till the world shall set
things right.
— Ella Wheeler Wilcox

ICHI'S TELEPORTATION could still be disorienting, despite
having felt the effects of his power dozens of times. My mind
insisted there should be some kind of wrenching, or *feeling*, associated with such absolute movement.

The little city square, built around an old stone fountain, was
almost unrecognizable. The fountain ran with blood, spilling over
the edges and rippling over the cobblestones. Flowers and vines
made of flesh bloomed through the blood in a riotous tumble,
pulsing excitedly.

The clouds above were a sick, deep purple—in spots almost
black. People screamed in the faint reflections of the windows of
the surrounding buildings, pounding futilely on the glass as if to
break out of the mirror world. I took it all in with a thought,
Wraith moving to fill the space with barely restrained hunger.

But of course, the center of this tableau was Tempest.

She stood from her throne and turned toward us, her movements slow and self-assured. Regal. Instead of the blurry blackness of before, she and her throne were visible. Unfocused, but visible. Behind her throne, the warp hung in the air like a mirage.

She smiled as our eyes met, and I could feel her almost childish *glee.* "You've come," she said. Her voice was achingly, overwhelmingly *normal.* It made my ears hurt.

My teammates winced and stumbled, pressing their hands to the sides of their heads.

I turned my head toward Ichi. "Leave."

He hesitated, then shook his head, clenching his jaw. "I can be of use, still."

"You'll die if you stay."

"Even so."

Tempest shifted, cocking one hip out and crossing her arms, the pose of an irritated teenager. "It's too late to leave now." She reached out a hand, dug her sharp fingers into the air as if sinking them into the skin of reality, and tore.

I felt it happen, the severing.

To Wraith, it was as if a cage had been dropped over us, confining my senses to our immediate surroundings. Behind me, the others flinched, gasped, and screamed in turns.

All around us was a chasm of darkness just like that of my vision, and floating, isolated in the middle of it, the little city square. We had been severed from the rest of the world in a true sense. Except, I could just make out the real world, sliced right through and separated from us by a few hundred meters of abyss. We were a little bubble tossed out into a dark, stormy sea, with no way to return to shore.

Zed shot me a look, and I saw a flicker that looked like a message Window trying to open, but I wasn't able to read it.

I shook my head, and his jaw tightened in frustration. I could only assume he'd been trying to warn me about whatever Tempest had just done.

I let out a slow, deep breath, steadying the faint trembling of my fingertips and forcing my pounding heart to slow a little. Beneath the rippling pool of blood, from the soles of my feet, I let Chaos seep out of me, a slow, inexorable wave. If you really wanted to win, you didn't wait around while the enemy grew stronger, after all. You prepared a bullet to the back of the head while they were still distracted.

She grinned.

I slipped my visor off, letting my head hang as I dropped the useless protection into the blood with a small splash. The rain had ceased, but the fountain produced enough blood to keep my feet submerged.

"Given up, then? I am no Pestilence, to be defeated so easily. You will be mine, just as this space is mine."

My teammates were silent, though I could feel the fear and confusion washing back to me through the blood-covenant we'd established so long ago, a bond that I now used to give them a little of my strength, letting it trickle out from that cold abyss within me.

I raised my head, looking right at Tempest. "I don't need you to focus on her at all," I said. But I wasn't talking to her. "In fact, feel free to ignore her," I continued, despite the burning sensation in my eyes.

Tempest was…normal. No, she was grotesque, all sharp angles and pain and tortured souls encased within a body made hard by time, but still transparent. Her expression wavered so quickly it was hard to pin down—terror, rage, confusion, one after the other, and all mixed together.

"I need you to focus on *me*. Remember who I am, please," I asked my teammates. In case I can't remember for myself, I added silently. They had been with me through everything, and knew me best.

"What—" Adam started to ask, scowling suspiciously at me. He never finished his question, because a stubby-fingered, deformed hand reached out of the blood fountain, gripped the edge, and crawled out. It was followed by others, too many to have been hiding submerged beneath the surface, as if they were being formed even as they appeared.

I sensed no human hosts within them.

A wave of Torliam's sky-blue power, incongruous against the backdrop of this hell-realm, dealt with the first handful easily, crippling arms and legs. But more bubbled up.

"Do you know who I am?" Tempest asked, her voice like nails

through my eardrums.

I ignored her, waving to the minions that were no doubt meant to distract. "I'll let you guys deal with those. They're made of fear and flesh, nothing else, so there's no need to hold back."

My teammates fanned out around me, and I fed them strength as Tempest's petulance turned to anger and she tried to rip at their minds.

While the rest moved, both Tempest and I were still. I could feel the tumult within her, whereas I was calm. Tempest was different from Pestilence in another important way. She was young —inexperienced. Despite her abilities seemingly being catered to stealth, an insidious spread that left no clues and, without revealing itself, left no way to combat it, she'd thrown away her greatest advantage.

She should have been less greedy.

The opponent that could have defeated me would have taken the time to learn to understand humans. They would have understood what it meant to act normally and simply done it, not attempted to sledgehammer the world into the shape of "normal." They would have been subtle, taking those who were two degrees away from the most influential individuals around the world first. They would have used their influence and understanding to create lesser threats that would force me to divert my attention from them. They would have hid, and waited, till I began to wonder if they existed at all, and grew complacent.

Her eagerness—her *greed*—would be her downfall.

I let the spill of Chaos flow faster, no longer attempting to disguise it. It burned where it touched, transforming and cleansing and *fusing* with what had once belonged to her.

This place was hers. I needed it to be mine. I didn't want to be in a mini-realm that suddenly ceased to exist when Tempest died, or be stuck here forever, or fall for whatever trap she had planned, whatever that little spark of sneaky smugness she'd broadcast when she broke this place off from reality meant.

She realized what I was doing, a little belatedly, when the solid silver beneath my feet began to repel the spill of blood. Her expressions continued to flicker unnaturally, but the anger was apparent in her gaze. "You dare?" she hissed.

The nightmare monsters bubbled up from the fountain even faster, so thick they created an almost solid mass. Despite the lack of Estreyan or Player hosts, they had power of their own, straight from their creator. To look at them, to touch them, to hear their screeches, was to be corrupted.

My teammates still wore their visors, the silver in which helped, and for the rest they drew on their own willpower and my shared fortitude, but despite their power as warriors, they were at a disadvantage when Tempest's influence permeated the very air they breathed.

Kris had only the three marionettes, but she used them to full advantage, the two smaller ones protecting her while the larger one sliced through everything it could reach. The woodland guardians' death static weapon hung around her neck, and she used it to full effect, sprays of neon yellow burning the life from any monster that stepped away from the others.

Ichi jumped from place to place with the erratic speed of popping corn kernels, death on the edge of his sword with every swing.

Birch bit and tore and roared, a miasma of Chaos following him as he pounced on parasite after parasite.

The flesh flowers and vines pulsed and twisted into the air, creating that same fractal flesh-rune we'd seen earlier.

"I dare," I agreed, letting the black flames flare hungrily and surge toward her. Fighting so directly against her influence, trying to subvert her domain, was intense and draining, requiring almost all my concentration. I pushed as fast as I could, knowing she had a connection to the Abhorrent feeding her, while I could only rely on myself. The flesh runes and the abominations they'd grown from burned away. Blood disintegrated where my power touched and could not return to the space I'd marked as mine in silver.

Silver, scientifically, had no reason to be so effective against her. I suspected it worked as it did for the same reason the gods and the Abhorrent existed as they did. We told fairytales about silver and its use against the hidden, the evil, the corrupted. Silver was pure and powerful in our stories, and so, to a creature who existed within the confines of the stories we told ourselves, it was effective.

Tempest pushed back against the advance of my power, her

own will a pulsing, sucking morass that ate away at my efforts like acid, that tried to ooze past my defenses and poison me.

With my rage to feed them, the flames burned high and hot and bright.

The silver spread outward inexorably, reaching the feet of my teammates, steadying them.

Torliam's power crushed down on a group of monsters like a hammer, then washed over the fountain to attack their source.

Sam slipped through the fray with seeming ease, his touch bringing destruction to his enemies and constantly stabilizing his teammates, not allowing the faintest hint of injury or fatigue to linger on them long. His eyes flickered with deepest black in tiny flashes, like an old, silent, black-and-white film.

In addition to the ink shields my teammates employed, protection springing from their skin wherever and whenever it was needed, Adam had created an army of ink creatures. Some swam through the air, others tunneled through the ground, and some darted around with speed too fast for the eye. They rained down destruction on everything indiscriminately, tearing at the ground, the buildings, and the flesh flowers on the far side of the square as if it was all as dangerous as the nightmare creatures.

The silver licked at Tempest's toes, and, as if that was too much for her, she sprang forward. Everywhere her twisted body touched upon the smooth cleanliness of my domain, pieces of her shattered like hard candy.

She swiped at my head with her angular, pointed fingers, and I caught her wrist, the force of our collision shuddering through my body and sending a shock-wave bursting out from between us.

The faces trapped under her surface all turned to focus on me, expressions contorting grotesquely with terror, fury, cruelty, and again, that *glee* that felt closer to true evil than anything I'd ever experienced.

I blinked, and the blood welling in my eyes spilled down my cheeks. I squeezed her wrist harder, and dug Chaos into her with the speed of a striking snake. It burrowed into and branched out within her, spilling flames beneath her skin.

Tempest screamed and yanked back, her arm shattering up to the elbow, large pieces of it falling away and bursting against the gigantic silver mirror beneath us. The damage didn't last long. The angles of her arm twisted through space, the broken pieces shivering into view as if they'd never been gone, merely out of sight.

As she reformed, I attacked again, slamming thorny whips of condensed Chaos into her limbs, wrapping them around her body and ripping away everything I could. Meanwhile, the edges of my domain continued to expand.

When the silver sheet reached the fountain, it faltered. I could feel the Abhorrent's power feeding it, a deluge that pushed back against my control with the crashing force of a waterfall.

Tempest attacked me again, moving faster this time. She twisted space, or herself through space, I couldn't tell. Her limbs and body moved in ways I couldn't follow, slipping between perspectives, and I felt as if I were a two-dimensional creature trying to combat something that moved in three dimensions.

My skin split, my scales shattered, and blood ran from my nose, my ears, and my eyes. Dodging was impossible, running pointless.

I couldn't match her in that way, but I refused to let that matter. She was insidious poison and the sharp edge of a dangerous thought, but I was the sky on a moonless night, an ocean without end, and I ripped as much damage into her flesh as she into mine.

She plunged a hand into my side, and my flesh wriggled and bulged.

I jerked away, shearing off a chunk of my own torso with Chaos, letting the flesh fall to the ground, still squirming. My scales rippled with visceral disgust, which only grew stronger as the flesh broke apart into hundreds of maggots that burrowed into the ground, leaving the silver filled with little irregular holes.

She grinned knowingly. "Afraid?"

My eyelids fluttered with malice as I delved down to the core of that cold rage and flung it outward. It surged over her throne, which crumbled into nothingness. The fountain collapsed on itself, leaving a silver floor so smooth it looked like spilled moonlight, and the nightmare corpses blew away like ash on the wind. Silver spread all the way to the edges of this tiny little realm, butting up against the chasm of darkness she'd inserted between us and the real world and settling there.

"Do you know who I am?" she asked, as she had earlier. Her

words were unhurried, but she couldn't hide the insecurity behind them. She was, perhaps, beginning to understand the folly of her hubris. She couldn't understand completely, yet, of course, but I would teach her.

"*I am the angel that screams in your shadow.*" The words came from everywhere and nowhere, tearing at the bindings of reality even as they tore at my mind.

I knew the brain didn't have pain receptors, but I swore I could feel jagged fingernails scratching at its meat.

"*I am the evil that grows in your eyes.*"

A living rot bloomed behind my eyeballs, black filaments digging into the flesh and burrowing through into the back of my eye sockets, reaching around as if trying to sprout out from under my eyelids.

"*I am the demon that feasts on the corpse of your thoughts.*"

Toothy worms ate their way through the folded cortex of my brain and burrowed into the white matter beneath.

Blood welled up around my feet as she began to overwhelm what progress I'd made.

Behind us, my teammates screamed as her words consumed them. They attacked her recklessly, without regard for their own wellbeing or the danger of friendly fire, thrashing like wounded beasts in a snare.

Jacky's fists crunched against Tempest's sides, her chest, her face, shattering the amber.

Tempest did not break.

Gregor's blades whipped through her legs half a dozen times in the space of two seconds.

She did not fall.

Adam released his tattoos, the knotted, fractal designs expanding between us, trying to force her away from me.

She stood steady, holding me to her.

A gentle blue rain fell down around us, scouring her as if to sterilize her creeping rot.

Her hundred amber-trapped faces hissed with derisive laughter.

Kris reached out and yanked, tears spilling down her face and mixing with the blood leaking from her nose.

Tempest's spirit, if she had one, did not respond.

Zed's silver bullets tore into Tempest's joints, the base of her neck, and her head, sending shards spraying off, but they reformed before the next bullet had even left the chamber. His face was twisted with desperate hopelessness, and his eyes flickered down to the center of her back. His expression hardened, and he took a step forward.

Ever-so-slightly, I shook my head.

He stopped, letting out a scream so raw it tore at his throat. He clawed futilely at the air, unable to sink his fingers into any invisible seams within this realm.

Ichi, the raw orbs of his eyeballs seeping blood, blinked toward her. His power flared for a moment. Then he gasped and collapsed to the ground, dead, the flesh of his burst eyeballs dripping out of their sockets. Sam leaned down over the Estreyan, but it was far too late.

Birch roared loud enough to rattle my brain and burst my eardrums, and Chaos spilled out of him, so thick and heavy it looked like a living mass in the air. It ate into Tempest, coiling around her like an anaconda and trying to swallow her head.

That did something, maybe—distracted her for a moment, at least—and blocked her gaze from meeting my own.

I was afraid.

But I was also angry. Still angry. Always, always *enraged*.

I reminded myself of my goal—to kill the Avatar with as little collateral damage as possible. I remembered my vow to Behelaino. I *promised* myself that I would exert control. I would follow the plan.

My throat felt raw, as if I had been screaming, and my voice was hoarse when I spoke. But that did not diminish the weight of my words. The crystal at the base of my throat vibrated with power, and I spoke truth into being. "I see you," I said.

Tempest seemed to realize the danger, releasing her hold on me, her eyes widening as if in slow motion as she tried to lunge away.

My clawed hand plunged into her chest and gripped firm around the place where her heart would have been, if she had one. "I see you, and you are *nothing*." I released the Void.

Chapter 26

Now I am become Time, the destroyer of worlds.
— Robert Oppenheimer

IT BLOOMED out from me effortlessly, confined only by the strength of my will and the cold depths of my anger.

Tempest screamed, the sound of which was enough to send my teammates to their knees.

It meant nothing to me.

The Void ate her away from the inside. I could feel the power pouring in from elsewhere to replace what she lost, even more quickly than the Void could siphon it away. I couldn't sense the power conduit that tethered her to the Abhorrent, but I didn't need to. Zed had told me where it was. I couldn't destroy it, or indeed affect it in any way, but, again, I didn't need to.

I only needed to erase the parts of her that the tether connected to. It was like a power plug, useless without an input socket. Destroying her from the outside in would never reach it. She would heal too quickly.

But from the point of contact, the Void bloomed, turning all that was her into itself, starting with the only truly essential part of her physical form.

She tried to escape, willing to tear her own body apart to do so, but I refused to release her, my grip absolute.

"Nothing," I repeated, the whispered word cutting like a scythe through her hubris.

Her gaze met my own, filling, finally, with understanding, and then with fear.

The Void bloomed.

The touch of the Abhorrent was severed.

Tempest finally ripped away, a gaping hole in her chest that didn't heal, her crumbling, shattering edges no longer twisting back into wholeness.

But the Void was bloomed, and did not wish to return to a seed confined in the back of my mind, ignored and untouched.

It rippled against my will, and I sank to my knees. I lost my breath, my touch, my sight, and the memory of ever having such. It touched on a spark of anger, but that was not consumed.

The cold surged up and swallowed the Void, reminding it that it, too, was part of me, and no part of me could act against my will.

As breath shuddered back into my lungs, I opened frigid eyes to see Tempest standing over my kneeling form.

She was heaving, as if she needed air, trembling at the edges, and yet a triumphant smirk was slashed across her face. She raised her arm to strike.

It never fell, as, instead, a splash of glowing yellow struck her back.

Her eyes didn't widen, her mouth did not gasp open with surprise. She had no time for any of that, as she was dead. One second passed. Two. And then she disintegrated, dissipating so completely she did not leave even a speck of ash behind.

The warp hung in the air as ever, rippling indifferently and confusing my senses. I looked away.

Kris lay behind where the Avatar had been, propped up weakly on one elbow, the tube weapon's handles clenched in tiny fingers stripped of flesh. There wasn't much left of her at all, her legs completely missing, and her torso held together by carved pieces that had once belonged to her two smaller marionettes. The glow of her Skill dimmed as she stopped controlling herself like a puppet, collapsed back, giving me a grin, and let out a single, rattling breath past the blood in her lungs.

The Void had not been sparing. I could see it in the broken, half-eaten forms of my collapsed teammates and the crumbling of the silver world around us. Sam moved first, his hand flopping over and restarting Birch's heart, which I could see begin to pump, as the missing half of his body left it exposed to the air.

The fruit had done their job, but were spent, it seemed.

Ichi's body was completely gone.

I wasn't *happy* about his death, but, especially with the anger steadying me, I couldn't feel particularly bad about it, either. There was a balance, that was all.

Sam spread his touch around, healing the worst of their injuries first, just enough to keep everyone alive.

I reached for the blood bond between us all, feeding what I could into it. I didn't have much left but the cold, and that wasn't meant for mortals.

The world crumbled a little more, my silver tarnishing.

"Zed," I said. "Can you reach through?" I pointed to the black chasm separating us from the rest of reality.

The augmented muscles and bone beneath his skin were show-ing, the replacement organ in his chest pulsing and oscillating as it handled the job of his wrecked heart and lungs. He limped toward me, but stopped over Kris's body. "Is she…"

"Yes." Her heart had stopped, her lungs did not pump with air, and the brightness of her mind had dimmed.

Sam gasped, running to Kris's side. "N-no, no, no," he murmured, the words spilling out of his mouth so quickly his tongue tripped over them.

Gregor, perhaps the least harmed out of everyone, let out a low, guttural scream.

I watched, blinking tiredly.

Zed gave me a strange look, anger and grief mixed, and then pushed past me to the edge of the chasm. His fingers sank into to the darkness, and like a pane of glass shattering, it broke. The town square, now little more than a flat pane of polished silver, settled back into reality without even a whisper.

The sky was clear, as if the sick clouds above had never been.

The air was clean, free of the smell of blood and rot. Crashed and abandoned pods filled the streets, and much of the infrastructure had been damaged or destroyed, but the walls did not pulse with flesh, the street lamps did not stare into your soul, and blood did not overflow the sewers and cascade through the streets. The people were themselves.

My teammates were crowded around Kris's body, tears streaming down their contorted faces, their bodies racked by heartbroken sobs.

Gregor yanked on my arm, sobbing incoherently for me to do something, to work a miracle.

I sighed, pressing a clawed hand to his head, then looking away when he flinched from the cold weight of my gaze. "Calm down," I said, my voice loud enough to carry over their combined sorrow. "She's not dead. She just needs a new body."

I slipped between their huddled forms and crouched in front of her, pushing the marionette pieces away from her chest.

A small, shimmering purple and gold orb was nestled in the meat there, thin streams of her Seeds filtering out of the surrounding flesh and coalescing into the main mass. "See? She hinted to me about this, but I didn't understand at the time. This time, let's make sure to get her a form that fits her better, alright?"

KRIS'S BODY-DEATH had left the team somewhat subdued, with no real room to celebrate our victory. Besides, we all knew it wasn't over yet. We quickly, though tiredly, jumped into action, contacting our coordinator to call for aid, most urgently healers, followed by a barrier team, a group to make Kris a new body, and all the runic engineers from the Remnants and woodland guardians that had been working on the warp project.

That's how, some hours later, I found myself sitting in a hastily-erected military tent on the edge of what had been Tempest's square. I was too paranoid that something would go wrong, that the Abhorrent had some trick up its sleeve, to leave the warp site. I would be there to catch and crush any anomalies.

My teammates had all been healed and then checked over again by Sam, and they were with me, some passed out from exhaustion, some sitting in front of the little camp stove with me, watching the flame more for comfort than for warmth. My own wounds had already healed without the need for help.

We'd previously explored several avenues of growing Kris's body to a normal size, and so now, when we needed it, it was easy to gather a group able to weave something suitable together. One of them was the Remnant woman who'd given her flesh the last time something like this happened. She had sniffed with pointed offense when it was suggested that Kris's current diminutive form was in any way lacking—other than being dead, of course.

They were in an adjacent tent, with a small awning connecting the two side doors, and would be finished with their task soon.

I had impressed upon them the need for the body to continue to grow and mature properly, in all ways indistinguishable from a normal mortal form.

They'd agreed with many nods and deep bows, assuring me they could handle the project, they were honored, they would not let me down, and whatever other platitudes they thought I wanted to hear.

Outside, at the edge of the silver square, a large rip to the Other Place hung in the air, radiating cold and grey light, allowing the runic engineers to scurry in and out. A similar group of engineers worked in the real world, setting up a complicated runic device based on a "merging of quantum field theory and metaphysics," according to Pondslider, who'd had to get some of the more technical jargon translated into English by one of the Remnants when she tried to explain the theory to me.

They believed they understood how the warps worked. "Many keys to a singular door," she'd said. Using identical runic devices on the *exact same* warp, one version of it in the Other Place, the other in the real world, would create a resonance that would spread throughout all the warps. A sympathetic response would allow them control over what was "essentially the same key," only separated by distance, and allow them to open the door to the *breaks*, where the Abhorrent lived.

The engineers had tried to explain the theory to me in several different ways, but I only grew more frustrated as none of the explanations seemed to totally fit with each other. "You will see,"

Pondslider had promised me when she arrived, patting me on the knee like one might a slightly stupid grandchild. "We will handle the hard work, you just use the tool and go fight."

Even with the cold still settled in my bones, that drew a small smile from me, which seemed to satisfy her.

The setup was slow, as the team in the Other Place had to take frequent breaks to mitigate the chill and exhaustion Blue caused, but Pondslider had poked her head into the tent not long ago and told me they would be ready soon.

The Remnants seemed to have a healthy fear of Blue, but the woodland guardians bickered with the gargantuan creature exuberantly, many declaring themselves fast friends with it and waving off its bluster and threats as it watched them set up the runes and materials with distrust. Just like when we were trying to find the entrance to the God of Shaping and Molding's realm, the place beyond the Veil was the key, and Blue's domain allowed us to actually interact with that space. The warps pierced through more dimensions than even the woodland guardians could verify, and had given the Abhorrent a chance to slip a piece of itself through during the eclipse. Blue had only agreed to allow any tampering with the version of the warp in the Other Place after being assured several times that a repeat of its last brush with the Abhorrent would not happen.

I stared into the little camp stove's fire, slowly rolling the plan around in my mind again, a kind of meditation to help me remember even if I lost my ability to reason.

Torliam sat near me, exhaustion pulling at his features more strongly than gravity ever did. He'd had no rest after the fight, being expected to speak to the politicians and military leaders who wouldn't accept debriefing by someone with a "less important" position, but who Queen Mardinest was too busy to talk to.

"Are you not tired?" he asked me.

I shook my head. "No. Fatigued, a little, but not sleepy. I'm not sure that I will sleep again."

He eyed me as if considering an appropriate response to that, but in the end only nodded.

Sam, too, no longer needed much sleep, and wanted to watch over Gregor and Jacky while they rested, periodically going into the adjacent tent to check on Kris's body and the Seed core still nestled within in. He would stare at it for minutes at a time, as if reassuring himself the shimmering orb was *her*, that she would wake up the same person, unharmed by the damage to her previous body.

Zed, by comparison, was both droopy-eyed and jittery, as he needed to sleep but refused to do so, and threatened to shoot Sam if he tried to force the issue.

Birch was curled up asleep at my side, and would wake and eye me distrustfully if I shifted, making sure I was not trying to leave without him, even for a few minutes.

Adam had passed out shortly after we exited the silver city square, but was awake now, huddled up in a blanket and furiously pushing ink into the skin of his now-bare arm. He did not like the plan.

"You are not responding to what has happened as I expected," Torliam said finally. "Do you need…" He hesitated again, finally settling on, "Are you well?"

"It is the godhood," I said, giving him a small smile of reassurance.

The others turned to me with interest.

"Does that mean you're a goddess now?" Zed asked.

"Maybe? I'm not sure where exactly the line between godling and goddess is. I had to use it to deal with the Void, and it's very cold and *focused*. It leaves no room for things outside of the goal, like extraneous emotion."

"Is that permanent?" Adam asked. "Once you're a goddess, you can't feel 'extraneous emotion' anymore?" It was obvious by his tone that this idea upset him.

"It's not permanent, I think, as long as I don't keep drawing on that well of power. And it's not like I can't feel *anything*. It's just hard to think about or focus on anything that doesn't contribute to accomplishing the goal, because the goal is the most important thing in the world. So," I let out a deep breath, "it's very important to set the right parameters for success before dipping too deep into the godhood. I need to be thorough and clear."

Sam nodded slowly, his face the only one that held real understanding. "You're making promises to yourself. Promises that, as a god, you have to keep, even if they would seem useless and silly when the time to follow through comes." It was, in a way, very similar to what he had done with Black Sun.

I kept silent the thought that it would also allow me to do things that I otherwise would have recoiled from in instinctive horror, like jumping off the edge of the world with nothing to catch me, or lobotomizing myself.

Pondslider stuck her head past the canvas door flap. "Everything is ready. We only wait for you now."

I stood, and had already taken a few steps toward the entrance when I remembered Kris was not yet transferred to her new body. Something inside me surged impatiently against the thought, but I forced myself to say, "We'll do it after Kris wakes up." I still had enough sense to realize I might regret it later, if I didn't wait to see her.

Pondslider bobbed her head up and down. "Good. Pay respects to the honored creator. We will, too. Then we will go ahead with your stupid plan and wake up a new death-bringer."

We didn't wait long. It had only taken this long because they had checked and double checked the runes drawn over the floor and dry-rehearsed the joint Skill-work till they were sure there was no chance of screwing up and earning my wrath.

Kris's new body seemed too large, at first. She blinked a few times, and one of the Estreyans who'd helped to create her body rushed over with some water for her to sip through a straw. "Is everyone else okay?" she asked, but before waiting for a response she made some experimental sounds, obviously surprised at the deepness of her voice, as opposed to the high-pitched piping created by the tiny lungs of her old body.

She sat up and looked down at herself, then around at all of us. Her open mouth quickly stretched in a dazzling smile, and she sprang to her feet, patting her body, stretching out her arms, and feeling the top of her own head as if that would tell her how tall she was. She turned to Gregor. "I'm bigger than you again!"

The boy paled, then swallowed. "Revenge is immature. Let bygones be bygones…?"

She laughed, putting her hands on her hips and leaning back dramatically, like an evil cartoon character.

Gregor moved to hide behind Jacky's leg, but he was smiling. "Glad you're okay," he mumbled.

She nodded, moving around again experimentally. "I guess I'm basically immortal, huh? Pretty cool. I should just keep a room full of clones ready to be activated in case of my untimely demise."

There was a moment of silence.

Jacky frowned, looking around. "Seriously? No one's gonna say anything to that? Why do *I* have to be the mature one here and veto the clone vat room?"

Adam raised an eyebrow. "Why do you need to veto it? I think it's a good idea."

"Are you *kidding*?"

They descended into comfortable bickering, pulling the rest of the team into their increasingly outlandish hypothetical arguments and counterarguments.

I smiled, watching Sam try to mediate, while Zed played both sides, saying whatever outlandish thing had the best chance of escalating the drama at that moment.

Soon, though, that urge to complete my goal forced me to remind them what was waiting.

As we walked back out into the square, now surrounded by a smaller spherical quarantine barrier, the woodland guardians greeted Kris happily, congratulating her on her miraculous revival. I saw her struggle to keep her smile in place as she interacted with them, the absence of her own cadre of marionettes very conspicuous. Of all those she had brought to Leighton, not a single one remained. Most had been cut off from her power and severed from their bodies when Tempest disconnected the square from conventional reality, and the rest fell when she did, her will no longer present to sustain them. By now, it was too late to hope to retrieve any of their lingering spirits.

Adam caught the direction of my gaze and murmured, "She'll be okay."

"I hope so."

He scowled. "I'm more worried about *you*. Have you considered we might only be bringing unnecessary trouble on ourselves, giving the Abhorrent a chance it wouldn't otherwise have? There isn't another eclipse like the last one scheduled for thousands of years, and its single shot at successfully getting another Avatar into the world just *failed* when we killed Tempest."

Torliam's sharp hearing caught this, and he moved to my other side, frowning. "Even if this is true, walking away now does not solve the problem. The Abhorrent can afford patience. Even if it can use no other method than the warps weakened on the day of a joint eclipse between our two worlds to attempt once again to escape the *breaks*, our world will not be truly safe, and I worry there will not be any worthy to face it alive at that time." He looked at me, probably silently amending the statement, because I might live for a very long time, indeed.

I ignored the twinge of unease that thought caused me. "The Abhorrent isn't so easily stymied," I said, remembering the sense of it I'd gotten from the third puzzle band's vision. It was the hand of darkness, the conductor watching from beyond the edge of the board. This was not checkmate yet. "We can't keep letting it take the initiative and just react to whatever it throws at us. If we want to *win*, we have to go on the offensive."

"Kick its ass, *chica*," Jacky said, hopping over to pound me on the shoulder.

The runic engineers brought both incomprehensible arrays to life, one in the Other Place, and one in the real world. The warp rippled as if being vibrated.

Some Estreyans with powerful destructive Skills, along with those whose Skills could be used for containment, stood around the barrier. They would likely be useless against any Avatar that I—or my teammates—couldn't kill, but both worlds' various leaders had insisted on their presence, very apprehensive about my plan to willingly open a connection to the *breaks*. A few cameras took in every angle of the warp, not broadcasting anywhere, but recording for future use in case such information became useful.

While the engineers evacuated with haste, Zed and I entered the quarantine barrier. It wasn't much, but it would do something to protect those outside, if something went wrong. "Are you ready?" I asked as we moved to stand in front of the warp. The two of us would have no such protection.

He nodded, rubbing his forehead in a way that reminded me of our mother. She wasn't here, and probably wouldn't even find out about this second part of the battle until after it was over. I felt guilty, but it was much too late to delay the plan now.

With one claw, I pricked a spot on the back of my wrist. A single drop of blood welled out. It wasn't hard to take control and hold that drop hovering in the air, since little particles of Chaos saturated my bloodstream. "Here," I said, floating it over to him.

He looked from it to me questioningly.

"A Bestowal," I said. "Kind of, anyway. If it works correctly, it'll last only long enough to help you complete a single, small goal. I was thinking you could use it to help you focus on the Avatars."

With a nervous—or perhaps simply disgusted—grimace, he opened his mouth and let the drop fall on his tongue. He shuddered and his eyes widened, cheeks flushing with color and his back straightening, as if there wasn't enough space inside him to contain this raw power.

I watched carefully, worried at the strength of his reaction, but he let out a huge puff of air and a half-laugh of surprise.

"Is that what it feels like to you? It's like…being filled with mint-flavored lightning. But cold." He grinned, bouncing on his toes.

"That was just a tiny taste. There's an abyss filled with that stuff inside me. I haven't touched the bottom yet." I turned toward the warp, coating my hand with a thick layer of Chaos, and then doing the same to his entire body. "Whenever you're ready."

Zed's hands hesitated in front of the vibrating warp, staring at it as if he could see the secrets of the universe. "I'll only keep the door open while we're searching. As soon as we're out, it closes. Don't want any nasty surprises."

"Don't worry," I said, understanding the risk he was taking. "I'll protect you with my life."

He raised his eyebrows, turning his head slowly toward me. "I'd rather you protect me with something else. Like your fists? Or Chaos?"

I laughed, and it felt good. "Duly noted."

Turning our thoughts to the target, we reached through the warp simultaneously. The sensation was indescribable in a completely different way than the nothingness of the Void, but I was careful not to let it distract me as Zed stabilized the warp and opened the door to the *breaks*. I focused on the two Avatars I had known, and the six others like them waiting somewhere beyond.

"Got it," Zed said, just as my fingers closed around something solid.

We pulled back, and dragged a twisted, squalling infant through onto Earth. It had orbs of fire for eyes and blonde hair that glowed like the sun. It turned its burning gaze upon us, the shock on its face quickly giving way to malice, its tiny body already growing larger as it pulled power from the Abhorrent.

Chapter 27

Something wicked this way comes.
— William Shakespeare

THE CHILD-LIKE CREATURE held between Zed and I exploded with light almost too bright to stand within Wraith's senses, though my physical eyes caught only a couple flashes. This light was much whiter and harsher than Seed glow, of which the Avatars didn't have any in the first place. I suspected some sort of radiation attack, but didn't wait around to confirm that.

I reached out and plunged my free hand into its chest, reminding myself again of the vow I'd made to control the Void, and how *absolutely unacceptable* it was to hurt Zed with this power, especially now that he no longer had the fruit to sustain him if I did.

Void bloomed inside my fist, ready to consume, to take all it touched and make it nothing, and I felt it begin to expand, but I was ready with the cold, unconquerable anger. I would not allow the Void free rein.

This Avatar died quicker than Tempest had, either because it was weaker, or because I'd learned from the last attempt.

The cold lingered, and it was only my promise that Zed could not be hurt that let me think to ask he be checked out by a healer, in case that light had been radiation and any of it had slipped past the Chaos I'd layered him in.

Sam learned a new type of damage when he touched us, which meant it probably had been radiation, and also that we shouldn't spend a ton of time hanging out in front of the warp after this, unless we could find someone with a Skill that could neutralize radioactive material.

That was only a minor detraction to the overwhelming, joyful exuberance expressed by everyone watching from outside the barrier. Despite the danger and our attempts to ward people off, Players and Estreyans and even a few humans surrounded the quarantined area, ready to risk their lives for a chance to experience the historic moment. People cheered through tears, screamed till they were hoarse, and kissed anyone close enough to grab with two hands. There was no more room to actually see what was happening, but the crowd continued to grow, pressing up against the cordon beyond the barrier.

Their presence made me uneasy. "Let's hurry," I said.

The second time was even easier than the first.

We searched, we found, and we pulled. My eyes widened as I found myself holding the sweetest little baby ever, though it didn't seem to be either a boy or a girl, and in fact didn't have genitalia at all, which was strange but didn't matter because there was *love* in its eyes and I knew I needed to protect it and keep it by my side always. This child *belonged* to me and was the key to all happiness. I hesitated. I did.

"Don't," Zed implored me, his voice cracking as tears welled in his eyes and spilled down his face.

"I *promised*," I whispered, digging a hand into its sweet, precious chest and letting a bloom of blackest Void disconnect it from the Abhorrent.

The child disintegrated, and my knees almost buckled with horror. *What had I done?* I drew breath to wail…and the Avatar's compulsion dissipated. I gasped instead, staggered by the force of my compelled emotional reaction, as well as its sudden disappearance.

Zed swayed on his feet, and I steadied him with a hand on his shoulder. "That was the worst one so far," he said, and I understood what he meant.

If not for the strength of my predetermination, I could never have killed that creature. And that was only a few seconds after it had entered this dimension. How strong might it have been after a week, after a *year*? That thought was horrible, but the realization of just how *far* the rage suffusing my being would allow me to go was worse. If I had to, to reach my goal, would I kill Zed? Gregor? Torliam?

I paced back and forth, forcing my scales to settle down and hugging my arms to my suddenly chilled body. No, I reassured myself. I wouldn't have done that to anyone I truly cared for. Because the whole *point* of my goal was to kill the Avatars and the Abhorrent behind them. I would never truly desire that for those I cared for. Even in the worst case scenario, where for some reason it seemed necessary, I would search for another way, and if I couldn't find one, I would mold one into being from sheer willpower.

Zed hesitated the next time we lifted our hands to reach into the *breaks*. "I think I felt something the last time. Not an Avatar."

My heart hammered within my chest as I anticipated what he was going to say, but I waited silently for him to finish.

"It was hungry," he whispered, his lips barely moving, as if it might somehow hear if he spoke too loudly. "I think it might have noticed what we're doing."

There was only one creature beyond the *breaks* that knew hunger. "Did it find us?" I asked.

"No. But it's searching. We need to be quick, in-and-out."

I nodded grimly. "Let's grab two, if we can."

Zed hesitated, but agreed. "Kill them *posthaste*, okay? If we get a bad combination, things could spiral out of control real fast."

We were quick, though I didn't know if that was due to experience, or if somehow the remaining Avatars were growing closer to us, which would logically mean the thing behind them was growing closer, too.

The infant I focused on first had an eyeless face and withered limbs, its huge head lolling atop an almost stick-thin neck. It still turned its face toward mine, and I could feel its gaze travel across my skin as clearly as if someone had tickled their fingers across my face. "I speak only truth," it said in perfect English, its voice the susurrus of an entire forest's leaves rustling together in unison.

I sank my claws into its chest, but it didn't even seem to notice. Its flesh parted around my hand and flowed back together like water. I imagined that might have made it hard to kill with conventional attacks, either Skill based or with weapons, but Void could destroy more than the physical.

"I have seen your death, and it is me," it said. There might have been more, but it was dead by then, and I'd grown only colder and harder as I drew on the strength of a godhood to control the Void.

I wasn't sure if the Avatar had been talking about itself, in which case obviously it did not speak only truth, or if it was a mouthpiece for the Abhorrent. I could imagine that an unkillable creature that spoke only the most terrible, destructive truths at the right time, in the right ears, might be enough to send the world spiraling to an auto-cannibalistic end.

But that was an idle thought kept to the back of my mind, for I was already focused on the other Avatar, held by my brother.

It was the first to seem completely normal, except for having one white eye, and one black. Both were wide with surprise and fear. "Please stop," it said. "I can be reasoned with. Answer my questions correctly and I don't have to attack you. I'm not like them, I wasn't always bound to the Abhorrent and—" Its words choked off as I wrapped clawed fingers around the source of its power and erased the connection.

I turned back to the warp immediately. Zed shifted uncomfortably, rubbing away goose bumps on the arm nearest me. I imagined he could feel the terrible, cold force of my purpose. "The last two," I said, unblinking.

This time, I, too, could feel the hunger of the Abhorrent, sense its searching thoughts as it grew closer. I'd worried, before we started this, that the Abhorrent would find some way to stop us before we could get all of the Avatars. I wasn't sure if this was better, or worse. Zed and I yanked our hands back simultaneously, the door to the *breaks* snapping closed faster than a bear trap.

We had the last two Avatars, and nothing more. In my hands I held a black chick the size of a toddler, still covered in fuzz instead of feathers. I noted vaguely that it was the first to not mimic humanity in at least some superficial way, but this fact had no bearing on my goal.

I followed the same procedure as the times before, digging into its chest with a clawed hand, but before I could release the Void, the avian creature…died. It disintegrated to ash between my fingers.

I stared down at the pale, powdery remains in my hands, nonplussed. That wasn't how it was supposed to work.

A black flame flared to life at the edge of the square, almost reaching the quarantine barrier. This flame was not like that of Chaos. It flickered with hints of dark green and purple, and I could feel the heat on my face even from so far away.

The people nearest the sudden conflagration stumbled back in surprise, at first. The Avatar emerged from the fire, whole and healthy, and larger than before, some of its down replaced with small feathers. It was a phoenix. Even as the flames died down around it, they sprang up elsewhere, most relevantly on Zed.

My brother screamed in surprise that quickly morphed into pain as he spontaneously combusted as if in retribution for my attack on the Avatar.

Chaos lunged for him in a great wave, my own flames thankfully powerful enough to smother the Avatar's. But it had hurt him, all the same.

With barely a thought except for anger, a thick, solid spear of Chaos burst from me, spearing into the black phoenix's chest and releasing a bloom of the Void Aspect from its point. The creature squawked in surprise, but this time, disappeared fully and for good, leaving no ash behind and reappearing in no sudden conflagration.

I found it much more difficult to snuff the Void out when it was so far from my body, and though I succeeded, the effort left me lightheaded with the aftereffects of sudden desperation followed by relief. I could not use the Void like that again. To do so would be reckless, an obvious betrayal of my vow to Behelaino.

Only then did I notice that others besides Zed had caught fire as well, as their tortured screams and the panic of the crowd around them filtered through the veil of my focus.

Most of the healers we'd had on hand were off helping with the rescue efforts or working at the refugee camps, but Sam was here, along with a couple others, and I did not have time to worry about anyone else.

I turned to search for the last Avatar, which had surely grown more powerful already.

I found it walking toward the barrier as if to escape, though for some reason those closest to it on the other side were not frantically backpedalling in terror.

I let a couple tendrils of solid Chaos wrap around my body and whip me toward it, so that I landed between the Avatar and the barrier. I punched my hand toward its chest, but stopped cold when I saw her face, the tips of my claws barely piercing her skin.

"China?" I whispered, looking down into big blue eyes. The cold urged me to keep pressing, to let the Void bloom in my hand, one last time. But that didn't make sense. A powerful wave of confusion dampened my thoughts, everything slowing as if I was filled with dark molasses.

She'd started to nod, even as my mind jumped to her sister, also dead because I couldn't protect her. She frowned, as if confused. "Don't you know who I am, silly?" she asked, smiling and tilting her head to the side. "You did kill me, after all. Got me all twisted around till my spine—you let Pestilence get me, there wasn't even a body left when he finished." Her tongue had seemed to trip halfway into her sentence, catching itself on a completely different statement.

I frowned, suspicion overpowering confusion, and, for a single instant, Blaine flickered in her place.

I plunged my hand into the creature's chest, and, with one last exertion of will, destroyed it.

I turned to Zed, who, thankfully, had had enough presence of mind to stumble over to the edge of the barrier. As soon as the last Avatar was dead, the barrier team created an opening for him, and he fell into Sam's arms, shuddering as his wounds were transferred and healed.

Many of the observers had run away by now, but those that remained were loud enough to make up for the smaller numbers. They called my name, and then in waves like a catching fire, it became a chant of "Godkiller," over and over till the sound must have spread halfway across the city.

I ignored them.

My goal wasn't yet met, and the satisfaction of completing a critical part of the plan warred with the urge to keep the momentum going, to pursue my purpose. I moved to Zed's side, examining him with both my eyes and Wraith. "Are you alright?" My concern stemmed both from personal concern for my brother as well as my need for him to be strong enough to help me with the next step of the plan.

"Your shield helped," Sam said with barely a wince as patches of his own melted, twisted skin healed from the assumed wounds. "As did smothering the fire right away. The people who burned longer..." He shook his head. "I don't know what kind of fire that was, but they're lucky to be alive, and likely still would have died of complications, without powerful healing Skills at hand. Zed is going to be okay, though I imagine the pain won't be forgotten anytime soon."

"Can you still connect to the *breaks* one last time?" I asked, looking down at my brother's pale, sweaty face. "I want to catch the Abhorrent before it gets away."

"EVE, don't you need to rest? After...all that?" Zed jerked his head toward the warp vaguely. "This is the Abhorrent we're talking about. You won't get a second chance." He pressed his lips together, obviously holding in harsher words. "I know you're being compelled to take action, but I think you should be reasonable about this."

I rocked back on my heels, looking away while I tried to pause and process his argument. Zed, at least, was obviously tired, and he was the only person in the world that could allow me back into this dimension if I entered the *breaks*. I bit down my frustration at his earlier refusal to take a nap, nodding stiffly, instead. "Okay. You sleep, first. I will make sure I am fully prepared, as well."

He let out what he probably thought was a subtle sigh of relief. "Roger. How about we wait till the morning? The Abhorrent will still be there."

I grudgingly agreed.

A few guards had to keep the crowd from rushing us as the team returned to our tent, and once inside, I was grateful for the noise-cancelling Estreyan technology built into its fabric walls.

Zed stuffed his ears with noise-cancelling earbuds and collapsed onto a cot, while the rest of us moved into the adjoining tent where Kris's new body had been created.

The others sat on chairs or the supply crates lining the walls, but I paced over the runes drawn on the ground, trying to soothe my agitation with the delay by telling myself that this was a necessary step, too.

Torliam tapped listlessly on a datapad, and at first the others made token efforts to occupy themselves, as well.

Kris and Gregor discussed the retrieval of the bodies of her marionettes. Adam worked on replacing the tattoos on his arms. Jacky fidgeted until Adam snapped at her with irritation, then sat by Birch and poked at him until he snapped at her fingers.

The attempt to avoid the topic on everyone's mind only lasted a few minutes.

"Was that all of them?" Kris asked. "No more Avatars?"

"Eight lesser Aspects revolving around a single base concept," I said. "The only one left is the Abhorrent."

"It's not right, you going by yourself," Jacky said.

"I am going into the *breaks* alone," I said firmly, forcing myself to stop pacing. "I will need to use the Void fully, I suspect. It's not safe for anyone else."

Adam glared at me. "You almost lost control of the Void out there. I don't know if the others saw, but yeah, I noticed. Those things," he jerked a thumb toward the warp, "were weak, compared to the Abhorrent. How are you supposed to control the Void if you have to pour any more power into it?"

"It's not about pouring power into the Void, truly. The Void's sole purpose is converting 'not nothing' to 'nothing.' Using it against the Avatars isn't any more difficult than using it against the Abhorrent will be, except with the Abhorrent I just have to be a little more *thorough*. Besides, you were skeptical about my plan to kill all the Avatars, too, but it went great."

"This is different," he insisted, the fresh ink on his forearms seeming to shift under the skin as he flexed his fingers like he wanted to strangle me. "You weren't doing that alone. We were all there, ready to have your back as soon as you needed it. Also, my concerns about pulling through the Avatars were *valid*. If anything had gone wrong, we could have been playing right into the Abhorrent's hand! At full power, any one of those *things* would have been just as bad as Pestilence."

"Exactly!" I snapped back. "If they had gotten a chance to come over on their own terms, they would have systematically destroyed the world. The radiation of a sun, without an atmosphere or magnetic field to protect the planet. Someone who made everyone who ever met them love them so much they'd do *anything* to protect them and keep them happy, regardless of the consequences. A creature that hands out prophecies designed to drive people to their own destruction. One that you can actually kill, but who is reborn in exchange for the painful deaths of thousands or millions every time you do. Another that—" I broke off, tossing my hands up. "The point is, we killed them before they got a chance to do any of that."

"We're only worried for you," Sam said, surprisingly placid even without the use of Black Sun. "You'd probably be on the other side of this argument, if any of us were the ones planning to do this."

I opened my mouth, then closed it, gritting my teeth together. I was agitated when I should be calm, to reassure them. "I know. I'm—"

"Are you coming back?" Gregor asked, his fists clenched and his jaw raised, as if to receive a blow.

"I am coming back," I said, conviction in my tone.

He stared at me shrewdly, then nodded when I didn't look away from his gaze. "At least you believe that."

"Can't you have Zed make a tether for you, like he did when you were going into the Voids?" Jacky asked, her knees bouncing restlessly.

"He would have to keep the warp open to the *breaks* to keep a tether active and attached to me. It's too risky. Something could come through. He'll open them again once I've had time to destroy the Abhorrent."

Torliam set aside his datapad. "What you said when we battled

Tempest… You asked us to remember who you were," he said, his gaze penetrating.

"The Void makes me forget," I said simply. "I thought it might help to have an outside reminder."

He nodded as if he'd expected that answer, rubbing a hand roughly over his bearded jaw. "Do you need someone to do that for you when you fight the Abhorrent?"

"I already said. I'm going in there alone."

"No, that is not what I was alluding to. You have a partial blood-covenant with all of us, and a complete one with me. Perhaps we would be able to act as a stabilizer, should you need it. I have done so in the past, though in no circumstance quite so dire. We might not enter the breaks with you, but we could remain ready on this side of the warp, grounding you as soon as you reenter the world."

"Oh," I said softly. "Yes, that's actually a good idea."

The others pounced on this way that they could help, and Torliam walked them through his idea. By the time Zed woke up, they'd all gotten a crash course on focusing their thoughts and utilizing the blood-covenant bond. Torliam had even requested someone with a support Skill for the mental Attributes be brought in to help them.

True to his word, Zed returned with me to the warp in the morning. As my other teammates gathered around the edge of the barrier, he reached up to the warp. "Ready?"

"Yes."

Really, his Skill was invaluable. In many ways, he was the true key to our ability to fight the Abhorrent and its minions. Without the Veil-Piercer, I could list a dozen ways we would not only have died, but simply failed to move forward due to lack of options. In a way, Zed was also the catalyst for me gaining that first Seed of Chaos. Before he'd been pulled into NIX's game, I'd been prepared to run—and keep running.

"I'll be waiting," Zed said, then reached out with one hand and opened the door to the *breaks*.

I plunged through as fast as I could so that he could close the door behind me. I did not want to chance the Abhorrent escaping back into the mortal dimension.

The *breaks* between worlds were nothing like the Voids; they were *full* of things, they were just infinitely far away and incomprehensible, both beautiful and terrible. The expanse twisted like a fractal and collapsed like a dying star and I felt like one of Adam's ink constructs—a two-dimensional being suddenly given three-dimensional form and unable to comprehend the new sides of the world I was seeing.

However, I had experienced the incomprehensible before, and my time within the Void helped to put the *breaks* into perspective.

It could be worse.

At least I could use Chaos to create my own air directly inside my lungs. Still, I couldn't imagine being trapped here for eternity. I could understand why the Abhorrent would want out.

As if that thought drew the being—and maybe it did, in a place like this—I felt its ravenous attention find and lock on to me.

A couple minutes passed, by the count of my heartbeat, and it arrived. As if molded by the Abhorrent's presence, the space around us settled into something slightly more palatable to my mortal mind. Darkness, interspersed with colorful dust and spots of light. It was a view of space from the perspective of an impossibly large existence, the galaxies nothing more than clumps of sparkles I could cup in the palm of my hand.

The Abhorrent itself…looked like me. Perhaps it had taken my form because it had no true semblance of its own. Or perhaps it was just a creepy power play.

A surprise like this might have horrified me once, but now I was no stranger to fighting something that wore my own skin. It meant nothing. I forced my irregular, pounding heartbeat into a steadier rhythm and let my power build in preparation for an attack, every ounce of my concentration focused on the being before me.

It raised its hands, mouth quirking to the side in what would have been a wry smile, on a human. The Abhorrent might have looked like me, but that was only on the surface. It was as if someone subtly the wrong shape was wearing my skin like a costume. Its movements were practiced, a little too exaggerated and lacking in the tiny contradictions and nuance that gave humans the sense of a soul shining through from within. "Peace, girl. Why the rush to violence? We have only just met, and you do not know me."

Alright, I had not been expecting that.

I stared at it silently, still ready to snap into action at the smallest trigger.

It waved a hand, and the stars around us twisted, forming two chairs and a table made of darkness cornered by points of light. Atop the table appeared a chess board, black and white, and too familiar. "Play a game with me, and let us sit and converse while we do so."

I recognized the chess board from the Oracle's vision, and felt an instinctive aversion to the horrible defeat I'd suffered on it. "And if I prefer to fight?"

It shrugged stiffly, awkwardly. "If you refuse, I will run, and keep running, till you grow weary of the chase. I can continue until you forget your own name, let alone why you are hunting me. I have a glut of patience, so much I would vomit it out if I could." It smiled, tilting its head to the side. "Do not look so surprised. I am not some rabid animal slavering for blood. I enjoy intellectual stimulation and interesting conversation, and I have not had the chance to play against anyone but myself in so long…"

I was sure it was a trap, but…its threat was pretty compelling. I sat down.

"I'll be black, you be white," it said, and the chess pieces appeared on the board. These ones were not marked with either the Abhorrent's symbols or those of the Seal of Nine. "White moves first."

I knew the rules to the game, but I was by no means an expert. Briefly, I wished Gregor were here, because he could probably beat me with only one second per move while keeping the entire game in his mind, predicted ten moves ahead. I moved a pawn forward. I hoped my supposedly superhuman Intelligence and Mental Acuity would serve me passably.

"Must we be enemies?" my doppelganger asked, moving its own piece. "I have no quarrel with you except for the feud against my very existence that the gods have so selfishly inflicted upon you with their manipulations."

"Is it a feud against your existence? I thought it was only your *presence*."

It rolled its jaw. "You must realize this place is a prison, for those such as us—those who have tasted *life*. You cannot tell me you, too, would not attempt to return if by some chance or malice you found yourself trapped here."

Well, it was right. But that changed nothing. "That's irrelevant. I am not you," I said, thinking over my next turn carefully, and then taking even longer to actually move the piece, mostly out of spite.

"Rather than condemn me for something that I had no control over, decided in an instant upon my awakening, is there no option for rehabilitation? I am open to change. I am willing. You—"

"Willing to change your very nature?" I scoffed. "That sounds like death."

It paused, frowning at me. "You have destroyed these Aspects of myself which the mortals find so disagreeable—though they were formed from the very psyche of those same mortals, and dwell in the hearts of all mankind." The lips pressed together in perfectly plastic repressed frustration. "Perhaps they could be replaced by other Aspects. Love, forgiveness, peace? I have heard these things are desirable, and I would cooperate fully."

Bullshit. "Aspects are only different faces of the same root concept." I pointed at the Abhorrent. "Again, would that not be *death* to you?"

Its frown sharpened into a glare. "And why should I die? Why should I be exiled? I did not bring fear into the world. I did not create death. I am an inherent part of life. Through me, all good things are given *meaning*. Without the darkness, what is the light?" The words were spoken vehemently, its anger the first real emotion it had exhibited, I was sure. Still, the auxiliary muscles in its face remained unnaturally still, as if the skin was plastic, or deadened.

"We make plenty of our own darkness. We don't need yours, too." I shrugged with feigned nonchalance, intensely aware of the supremely powerful eldritch being I was antagonizing over a game of chess that may or may not be some cryptic trap.

It did not respond, the frustration I sensed from it sliding back beneath the surface. The game progressed a few more turns in silence. The Abhorrent was winning. I found this more distressing than I should have.

"I know some of your story, godling," it said finally. "Chaos and Control, or like enough. That is your power, scavenged and hoarded in the face of adversity." It looked up at me, raising one eyebrow.

I remained silent, allowing the expectant pause to turn awkward.

"Destruction and Domination are alternative names for this. Do you think the gods will allow you to exist among them, without my threat to make you tolerable?"

That was the first thing the Abhorrent had said that really made me think. I hadn't considered that possibility before, and though I didn't feel particularly suspicious of a betrayal by the very gods that had helped me to where I was at that moment, there might have been some merit to the idea. The Oracle was a manipulator, and the Void I wielded to combat this ancient enemy was so feared that even the original goddess in control of that Aspect was not allowed to touch it. But I distrusted the Abhorrent more than I ever could the gods. I'd seen its Avatars in action, after all. "I don't care," I said finally. "If I need to, I'll fight them, too."

It sighed with frustration. "But would it not be better, if you needn't fight at all? I would be more than willing to accept a truce. I would not harm you and yours, and you need not aid me in any way, only simply allow me to be what I am. Do you think I desire complete destruction? No. I too, need the light to balance my darkness." It took my knight. The board was growing bare of my pieces, my options narrowing as the Abhorrent pushed me closer to checkmate. "Do you truly care what I do, if it does not affect you or those you value? I would promise their safety and your own. As you know, creatures like us are bound to our truly-given word."

That was a lie. I might be bound by my vows, but it was not.

It must have seen that knowledge in my face, because it shook its head with contrived exasperation. "For a creature of Chaos, do you have no *give*? Are you decided to fight me with no regard to reason or sentiment?"

I considered lying, but what would be the point? "I am adaptable. I am not mercurial. I resolved to kill the Abhorrent. As long as you are it, and it is you, this will not change."

Rage flitted past under its skin, and it threw its head back with a harsh laugh. "Kill me? I am an amortal being. Does your bravado spring only from the depths of your ignorance? Even the gods of your dimension could not kill me, even were they gathered together as one."

I lifted a pawn, rolling it between my fingers. "Then why are you afraid?" I asked. I reached all the way across the board and knocked over the black king with my pawn, an audaciously illegal play.

It stared at me for a full second, entirely expressionless. Then it surged across the table, teeth bared and claws going for my throat.

Chapter 28

Reality is shaped by the forces that destroy it.
— D. Harlan Wilson

I DID NOT FLINCH BACK from the Abhorrent's attack. Instead, I opened my mouth wide, and wider, till it gaped open impossibly wide, a black hole of a maw that would swallow the world. It was a fear I'd seen long ago, in the Fear Trial I had to go through before confronting the God of Knowledge. Now, I drew it out of my mind to use against another, in this place where thought so easily molded reality.

I cannot imagine the Abhorrent understood my intention.

It tore at my insides on the way down, but did not seem to be trying to *resist* being swallowed. Perhaps it imagined that its nature would corrupt me from within, as more than one of its Avatars had tried to do. Obviously, such a strategy was core to its being, one of the conceits that defined it.

But there was a Void inside my stomach.

The Abhorrent fell in, disappearing into the tar-like, ravenous blackness without even a ripple.

That wasn't nearly enough to kill it, whatever power source it existed on easily keeping pace with the Void. But I'd expected that.

The real purpose of the Void wasn't to kill the Abhorrent. It was to isolate every part of it from the outside.

During our chess game, it had said something very incisive. The Abhorrent came from us, and it dwelt in the hearts of all mankind. It was amortal. It had never been alive in the same way things from my own dimension were, and so it could not die like them. It embodied a concept, and I could not erase that concept from existence without ripping apart reality at the very seams. It would be the destruction I sought to avert, if not worse.

But I had thought of a way around that.

For a moment, at least, the Abhorrent existed only within me, and I existed outside the mortal dimension.

A concept had to have someone to conceive it, or it didn't exist.

And with the Void, it was easy to erase entire parts of myself.

I would have balked from this, without that cold, unflinching purpose to focus my will. My thoughts still shied away from the truth of what I was doing. But the Void was eager, and I had carefully outlined the parameters of exactly what parts of me should cease to exist.

The Void bloomed in my thoughts, and where I touched it, I became it.

I felt the Abhorrent's shock within me, then its panic, then its rage. It scrabbled for an edge to the Void, but had no anchor or purchase, and so remained futilely trapped. The panic returned, and only at the last, when I had almost forgotten there was anything inside me at all, only then did it feel despair.

I smothered the Void, as I had promised myself I would, meditating on the idea over and over until it required no conscious decision from me to do so. I am not sure how long I stayed like that, floating in the incomprehensible expanse where once had been two chairs and a chess set that I no longer remembered. The cold shifted, eventually. It had purpose, still.

I was not finished.

As if the knowledge was a breath of cleansing wind, my thoughts cleared and drew back together. I had to follow the plan. Even if I didn't understand what exactly I had done, or what purpose the following steps held.

I searched within myself for anything that was not me, particularly around the stomach and brain area. I found nothing, so I patted my stomach and thought very hard about returning to the warp.

That part was easy, but what to do from there stymied me. I reached out to touch the warp, and as if in response, a doorway opened. I fell through it, landing on a patch of smooth, tarnished silver. I stood, carefully, smiling up at the person I suddenly recognized as Zed.

My thoughts rattled a little and began to settle, connections reforming faster than I could control. I let out a tremulous breath and grinned brightly around at my teammates, who were spread out around the edge of the barrier, sitting cross-legged with their eyes closed and their hands resting on their knees.

"I think it worked!" I said.

They sprang to their feet, laughing and cheering.

Gregor wiped at suddenly wet eyes, and Adam actually shared a huge smile with Torliam. Sam pressed his hands to his face, crouching as if so relieved it made him dizzy.

Zed turned to the warp with a calculating expression. He reached out, barely touching his fingers to its surface, and then went through a few complicated, folding and knotting gestures. The warp shimmered, and then, without any fanfare, disappeared. "It's done." His voice was soft, but held all the finality of a true end.

"You did it!" Jacky yelled, bouncing up and down like an exuberant balloon.

"I'm not sure exactly what 'it' was, but I think that was part of the plan."

Everyone looked a little confused, and for a moment, I felt the gaping hole in my core self, a sense of loss that I couldn't quite grasp, because there was nothing for it to connect to. My silly grin only grew brighter.

I wasn't sure why I was smiling, because I certainly didn't feel much other than confusion and a deep, abiding cold, and the expression felt kind of strange to my cheek muscles, but I couldn't remember whatever emotion my face was more familiar with showing, so a silly grin would have to do.

Interlude 9

Reed slept for almost sixteen hours once he finally got through all the questioning and into a cramped tent with an open cot.

Demi and both his parents had received extra-special healing, and so woke up earlier than him, despite their injuries.

When he woke, his mom and dad, along with Demi and her parents, pestered him to explain what had happened while they were unconscious that led to him flying an Estreyan ship out of the city and to the safety of the refugee camps. He made them update him on what he'd missed while sleeping, first.

Lucas and his family were still missing, but Reed's parents said no bodies were found in the remains of his friend's house, so they were all holding out hope. The quarantine barriers were still up, but the city looked normal again, at least from a distance, and word was they would be allowed to move back home and start rebuilding in a week or two. Rumors were flying about what had happened in the city after their escape, including that the Seal of Nine had obliterated between one and a couple dozen Avatar-aliens. Some of whom may or may not have been babies. Or phoenixes.

Needless to say, Reed took these rumors with a grain of salt.

"Lucas will never again get to complain about us geeking out about Skill-users," he promised Demi as he began recounting what had happened from the beginning.

His father interjected when Reed talked about how he'd thrown

Reed and Demi out, only to later help him escape. "I can barely make sense of my memories of that time. The parasite was in control, but I had some idea about what was going on. There was a lot of struggle, because to some degree, it could recognize my thoughts, so getting around its control even a little required a lot of mental discipline." They didn't know why the parasite hadn't been able to fully control his father, who had eventually ripped it off himself—only to be stabbed by their mother.

When Reed got to the part where he met Eve Redding, their mouths dropped open in unison, and there was silence for about five seconds before his dad and Demi were yelling over each other, demanding that he continue with the details of the story. Of course, they interrupted him with constant questions while he tried to do so.

When he explained that he'd actually met the entire Seal of Nine team, Demi almost cried.

His dad wanted him to do a guest interview with his news station. "I plan to gouge them hard enough to top off my retirement fund," the man said, shooting Reed a wink when his mom gasped and slapped his arm.

"Howard! Have you forgotten Reed's *college* fund?"

They were all being so loud they drew the curiosity of more people, until Reed ended up trying to tell a whole group of people how Eve Redding stuck her feet to the floor with Chaos so she didn't fly off when Torliam of the line of Aethezriel sent the ship into a barrel roll. More than a few people thought he was making the whole thing up for attention.

Demi leaned forward, her expression deadly serious as she pressed her fingertips together. "Reed. Can Eve Redding either confirm or deny the rumors about Dr. Deer?"

Reed stared at her. "No, Demi. We didn't talk about that. Why would that come up?"

She gaped back at him, as if he was the one being crazy. "It would come up when you *ask* her? The biggest ongoing mystery of the decade, and you just…didn't think to mention it?"

"How would she even know about Dr. Deer? She's not a local. She lives on *Estreyer* most of the time!"

The two of them fell to bickering, each argument as much a

joke to see who could keep a straight face the longest as a distraction from their circumstances, which, considering the last couple days, weren't actually too bad. If Reed could just find a way to access the Net, everything would be perfect. He really wanted to see if anyone had posted more *reliable* updates on the Seal of Nine.

455

Chapter 29

Do not stand at my grave and weep. I am not there, I do not sleep.
— Mary Elizabeth Frye

MY TEAMMATES, my *friends*, were happy with my successful return at first, but that soon changed. They thought I was acting strange, and I admitted that might be true, but there wasn't much I could do about it.

Adam had glowered at me as I shoved the delicious confection known as "toasted marshmallow" into my mouth till my cheeks bulged. "Alright, Eve. We get it, you succeeded, we won, we saved the world, and you somehow entirely wiped your memory of the details, but..." He pointed an accusing finger at me. "You've been grinning like a loon for the past three hours. *No one* is that happy. And not to be rude, but, *especially* not you."

I swallowed, nodding, and shrugged. "You're right, I think. But I seem to have erased a big part of my personality along with those memories of whatever I actually did inside the warp, so... What can you do?" I tossed up my hands, winked at him, and used Chaos to spear another marshmallow and hang it over the delightful little camp stove's flame. "Also, I seem to be missing a large swath of my memories from the last few years, mostly to do with the bad guy we were fighting. I *think*."

"The bad guy," Adam repeated incredulously.

There was an awkward silence, which I ignored, and then Zed said, "What do you mean, you erased part of your personality?" His voice was slow and tightly controlled, like a leash holding back a snarling wolfhound.

I almost giggled at the image, impressed with the strange thoughts my brain sometimes connected to each other. "*Yep.*" I popped the "P" saucily. "I erased a big chunk of my personality. Thoughts, memories, you know. I'm sure I had a good reason for doing it, but I admit now I am feeling a little confused."

You could practically see the…*something* wash across them all. Their faces twisted up in various ways to express the opposite of a smile, their heartbeats and breathing sped up, and they shared speechless looks with each other.

I studied their faces carefully, then tried to mimic Torliam's expression, squeezing my eyebrows together and letting the corners of my mouth fall down. I wasn't sure if I'd got it quite right. It still didn't feel natural on my face.

Gregor's eyes welled with tears, and he leaned forward, holding his stomach like he was feeling nauseous from too much candy. Except he let out a loud gust of air, then looked up at me with the tears spilling fast and thick down his cheeks. "What did you *do* to yourself?" He started choking and hiccupping, and Jacky pulled him into her lap, rubbing soothing circles into his back.

"This was the plan?" Adam asked intently.

"Yes. Well, there's still one step left, but I can't do anything about it right now. Is something wrong with Gregor?" My eyebrows puckered, just a little, and I realized with excitement that I'd discovered one of my natural expressions!

"What is the last step?" Torliam asked.

"I take something from the Oracle and use it to…scan my brain from the past? I've labeled that step 'De-lobotomize.'"

"Oh, *thank god!*" Adam said, flopping backward. "Well, what's taking her so long? This is basically unbearable."

It didn't seem so bad to me, but I didn't say anything because everyone else immediately agreed with Adam.

Still, I could take a hint. I stopped smiling, letting my face settle with the same cold stillness I felt inside. That was more natural, anyway.

When the Oracle finally came, it caused quite the scene. There was nearly a mass panic when thousands of thin threads began pouring up through the silver floor of the city square, knitting themselves into the Oracle's nest. It wasn't every day that an Estreyan god suddenly appeared on Earth, I supposed. And, from a certain light, her cocoon was a little ominous looking. Still, when my team didn't immediately charge into battle, the gathered people lowered their guard, though perhaps they did not abandon their wariness.

Torliam marched me toward the spiderweb egg-sack as the Oracle stepped out of it. He was holding me by the elbow, like a father walking his daughter down the aisle at a wedding. I think he worried that I might not be capable of walking the thirty meters from the tent by myself. Stopping a respectful distance from the goddess, Torliam bowed, squeezed my arm reassuringly, and stepped back to the others, who had gathered just outside our command tent.

Without preamble, the Oracle held her hand out to me, presenting me with a small, blueberry-sized ball of Seed material, several different colors swirling through it. I felt only a vague curiosity. "This is a joint Bestowal, created by a handful of the gods for you, and you alone. It is a token of thanks, and a measure of our regard," she said in her musical voice.

The plan, which at some point I had *promised* myself I would follow, urged me to swallow the Bestowal and use it to regain what I had lost. But I wasn't so sure I wanted to follow the plan. I was not stupid. I had lived a hard life, where silly grins and childish playfulness were out of character. Within that shimmering ball lay a plethora, a smorgasbord of pain.

If I didn't *have* to go back to being so very mortal, *should* I?

I wavered, but I knew that I had once valued these bits of myself enough to ask for the Oracle's help. I'd carved this plan into my mind with a promise that shaped the world as I spoke it.

I felt a spark of hope through the blood-covenant bond with my teammates. It offset the cold—a natural, perfect counterpart. It felt…*good*. Maybe there would be some of that in there, too.

THE BESTOWAL WORKED QUICKLY. It turned out there was almost as much hope in that little shimmering ball as there was pain. There was no sudden onslaught of *emotions* or anything, I just felt like myself again. My full self.

I couldn't remember actually erasing the Abhorrent, since the Void seemed to have caused some damage to my short-term memories, but I remembered *planning* to do it, and I remembered the aftermath. It didn't matter if I remembered the Abhorrent now, or any of the concepts associated with it, because there was no longer any actual being that matched those memories and could use them to anchor itself to existence.

My teammates teased me about how I'd acted while "temporarily lobotomized," but luckily we were too busy dealing with the aftermath of the events in Leighton for them to get too much mileage out of the joke.

The cold anger receded from my bones with time, settling back into the abyss within me, ready to be called on at will. Even without it, though, I was now technically a goddess.

I had taken to spending time in the refugee camp, as my presence there seemed to bolster the confidence of the displaced, and I had the good luck to happen upon the young civilian, Reed, when walking through one day.

He'd looked like he was about to pass out due to the amount of blood rushing into his face when I waved and greeted him by name, and then somehow blushed even harder when his female friend shamelessly flirted with me. Local Net connections were down, but the boy had somehow managed to get access to a satellite internet receiver, and he happily relayed all the online gossip about me and the other members of the Seal of Nine.

Apparently, the gods themselves were some of the worst rumormongers. They were rejoicing all throughout Estreyer, raining down Bestowals and blessings over the land and talking to any old mortal they happened to see about Eve Redding, Goddess of the Unconquered, the Unbowed, and the Unbroken.

"It could be worse," I suppose, I'd told him with a sigh.

He grinned evilly. "Oh, you mean people praying to you? Because that's a thing."

"No!" I gasped with horror.

"*Yes.*"

"Do they not understand the concept of…alien Seed goo?" I said, flapping my arm vaguely in the air.

"No. My grandfather used to say, 'Everyone has the right to be stupid, but most people abuse that privilege.' And you have to admit, once you've seen someone heal with a touch, or burp fireballs or whatever, the idea that some powerful being could listen to the thoughts addressed to them and maybe respond isn't so crazy."

I was beginning to realize why so many of the gods lived in extreme seclusion and tried to kill anyone who came to ask them a favor, and decided never to mention in public that I had the ability to give Bestowals to worthy questers.

To my profound surprise, the person who stepped in and made all this a little bit more bearable was my mother. Apparently, after our little talk about favoritism, she had appointed herself the head of my PR and Marketing team. "It is still the same field of work," she told me. "But now for better pay and something I care about."

She made me look good to the public, but most importantly, she did so while keeping me from having to parade myself around to supposedly important people all the time. After all, it would be a very serious slight to suggest that Eve and Zed Redding's mother was not good enough to meet with you in her extremely busy offspring's place. Things got better between us, and maybe, someday I would admit that parts of me were definitely passed on from her—even some of the good parts. Just, maybe I wouldn't admit it aloud.

The members of my team—really just my *friends* now—settled into roles that fit them a little more comfortably than "saviors of the world," though they'd always be that, too.

Jacky trained warriors in combat forms specialized to their Skills, gave the kiddos rides on her shoulders, and took up building custom motorcycles that looked like something out of a science fiction film. It reminded me of the first time I'd heard her really laugh, when we were just setting up our base in Blaine's basement and Sam had been so shocked to learn she'd "borrowed" a motorcycle.

Sam traveled to remote parts of both worlds, offering his services to those who needed him most, but who had no way to come to him. Sometimes, he even did more than use his Skills to heal, using his authority as one of the Seal of Nine to mete out justice to those who deserved it.

Birch and I took a trip with some of the others to the desert level where I'd met his pack. We explored the remains of the copse his packed had lived in, and he attacked the nearby retchin in a fit of grief and rage when we found only bones and the occasional bit of cracked eggshell. Later, we traveled to a few other places rumored to host tailos, but we didn't find any others. That didn't stop me from promising that we'd keep looking, though. Estreyer was a big place, with many levels where those like him could be living in seclusion.

The woodland guardians set up a home for us in their village, and though we didn't live there full-time, the kids and I stayed there often, frequently accompanied by Torliam. The woodland guardians tutored the children in runic engineering and metaphysics, and allowed Torliam to research and publish papers about their history and culture.

Queen Mardinest still wanted Torliam to take the throne after her, and Reglium still bitterly despised his brother for it, but Torliam remained adamant that he wouldn't. "I have done my duty to this world. The rest of my life will be my own to do with what I will. There are no shortage of those who wish to wear the crown. Some of them may even be good leaders."

We took Gregor out of school and hired various expert tutors for him, as well as letting him enroll in whichever classes at the local academy interested him. He loved the freedom to learn at his own pace and around his particular interests, and even made some friends, though none of them were his own age.

Kris remained in school, and with a normal-sized body and an open aversion to anyone who treated her like a celebrity, she made friends, too, though she always seemed more at home with the woodland guardians than she did around her own species. We had buried and held a funeral for the marionettes she'd lost, and once she'd had time to get over her grief, the itch to use her Skill was too great to resist. Slowly, she built up a small group of meticulously-crafted marionettes, and over time, their spirits gained personality and individual purpose and became her companions, too.

When the kiddos had breaks from classes, Torliam often invited us, and whichever other members of the old team were free, to accompany him on his research trips around Estreyer. Sometimes he did legitimate research, but I suspected some of our trips were secretly more about sightseeing—him introducing us to the wondrous, beautiful places and people of his world.

Zed had some trouble settling to a more normal lifestyle, but eventually returned to school and got a couple different doctorate degrees in genetics and cybernetics. He'd always wanted to be a medic and join the Peace Corps, but without a healing Skill, I think he felt unsatisfied with his capability in that field. Instead, he worked to cure new and genetic diseases, rebuild ruined bodies, and redefine the limits of humanity. Sometimes, I thought he might end up doing more to mold the future than the rest of ever had, or would.

Out of all of us, Adam had the most trouble, feeling unmoored without some enemy to fight or goal to achieve. He did some traveling, maybe a little too much drinking, and eventually fell into a job somewhere between private investigator and government-sponsored hacker. He would give me a telling smirk sometimes, when certain scandals or sudden turns of misfortune to the rich and powerful came up on the news or in conversation. I had no doubt any government who hired him was in just as much danger from his prying fingers as his legitimate targets. An organization like NIX would never slip past him.

I finished paying Blue its thousand days of fire, and when it found a way for Zed to open up a small tear in the heart of a volcano, we did that, too. Blue did not mention the boon I owed it, though I felt like the smug creature liked the idea of having such an advantage over me. One day, I was sure it would cash in its favor, and I probably wasn't going to like what it asked for.

Sometimes, I would be doing something normal, like picking Gregor up from his tutoring session at the local academy, and there would be a moment when I shuddered with the feeling of an axe waiting to drop over my neck. This mundane existence, where my life or the lives of those I cared about being endangered was the rare exception rather than the rule, sometimes seemed surreal. I had nightmares about waking up in the past, in a world still subject to the ever-present fear of the Abhorrent.

On the other hand, I also had nightmares about waking up an old lady and realizing that I hadn't accomplished *anything* of actual value since the whole saving-the-world thing.

I still had things to do, after all. Promises to keep, and people to look after.

I didn't bother to check my Attribute levels anymore, because they didn't actually mean much. I was Eve Redding, and no quantity of numbers could define me.

Very occasionally, I gave out a Bestowal to someone I thought deserved it. My power was a double-edged sword, and wielding it required true commitment. It was best used only by those who knew exactly what they needed, but just needed a little help to achieve it. All Bestowals were temporary, meant to complete a singular goal and no more. No Skills. *Certainly* no godlings.

Someday, maybe someone would find a way to open a doorway to the *breaks* between worlds again. But that wasn't something anyone could stop, even if we left warnings against it. Curiosity was a part of human nature, as was their fear of the dark.

THIS CONCLUDES the *Seeds of Chaos* series. Thank you for reading.

Want to read more stories by me? Check out A Practical Guide to Sorcery.
"In a world where magic is a science, Siobhan is a genius.
But even geniuses need schooling."

It's a free to read web novel, a new chapter every week.

IF YOU HAVEN'T ALREADY, join my newsletter and become part of the Inner Circle.

I will send you new release updates, exclusive content like pre-release or deleted scenes, as well as news about giveaways or contests I'm doing (signed paperbacks, posters, etc) and other cool stuff I think you might enjoy. Sometimes I tell weird stories about my life.

https://www.azaleaellis.com/newsletter/

Blurb:

In a world where magic is a science, Siobhan Naught is a
genius.

But even geniuses need schooling.

Siobhan has just been banned from the country's only magical university. As the unwitting accomplice to the theft of a priceless magical artifact, she has suddenly become a wanted criminal. There are fates worse than death, and if caught, she will face them. Unwilling to give up on her dream of becoming the world's most powerful sorcerer, she resolves to do whatever it takes to change her fate.

Even if it means magically disguising herself as a man and indebting herself to a gang of criminals to pay for University tuition.

With the coppers after her, the pressure of trying to keep her spot in the devilishly competitive magic classes, and the gang calling in favors to repay her debts, Siobhan will need every drop of magic she can channel.

Chapter 1 - Escape via Unexpected Transmutation

Siobhan

Month 9, Day 28, Monday 1:00 a.m.

FOR ONCE, Siobhan felt grateful that the average person was such an imbecile. The coppers were no exception, even in a big city like Gilbratha. Shivering in the dark, she took another peek out of the alley behind the inn, tugging down the hood of her ratty, stolen cloak. She had to be sure the ambush they'd set couldn't snap shut around her. The coppers were positioned at both street corners, and she guessed they were waiting in the inn's common room, and probably outside her door as well.

The coppers had the right idea, staking out the room her father had rented for them.

Siobhan would have preferred not to return to the inn, but she had no choice. Her belongings, including her grimoire, were there. She couldn't afford to lose what little she had. Lucky for her, the coppers had apparently failed to consider the fact that she wasn't a blazing idiot. She wouldn't simply walk, oblivious, through the front door.

As far as Siobhan knew, the room was still undisturbed, probably because they'd noticed the rudimentary alarm ward she'd set on the doorframe. Tripping it would have alerted her to the manhunt's progress and kept her from walking into their trap.

Either that or they'd subverted the ward and were waiting for her in the unlit room, the more obvious guards only serving as decoys, encouraging her to discard her vigilance.

Siobhan grimaced, looking up at the dark, many-paned window on the second floor. She would just have to be careful. *'Climbing a building can't be so hard, can it? It's not as if I have a choice, after all.'* With a nervous breath and a very careful twisting of her thoughts away from the possibility of falling, she crossed the alley. Her hands reached for the wooden slats, and she began to climb, fitting fingers and the tips of her boots wherever she could.

The wood was faintly damp, and in more than a few places it had bred a slimy film. When she reached the second floor, her right hand slipped, but she managed not to cry out, despite breaking most of the nails on her left hand as she dug her fingers even harder into the crevasse. *'And it took so much effort to grow those stupid nails,'* she thought wryly. *'I guess I really never will fit into high society.'* She shuffled sideways till she reached the window of the room she'd left that morning, a time that now seemed a lifetime away, full of innocence and hope.

Bracing the toes of her boots between the wooden siding panels, she peeked in, moving her head slowly to avoid drawing notice. Her fingers trembled on the edge of the sill with the pressure she placed on them, and she was excruciatingly conscious of how close she was to falling backward. She saw no one within, no inky shadows that looked more suspicious than any other.

Siobhan had placed the alarm ward over the window as well, but that didn't matter, unless they were very much cleverer than she was giving them credit for. If they *were* that clever, she would simply have to run, again.

No, the bigger problem was her lack of formal training or experience with breaking and entering. The latch was locked from the inside. She was sure there were spells that could reach through a barrier and undo a simple latch-lock. However, she didn't know any of them.

That would have posed a problem, if not for the versatile nature of sorcery.

'*I can't let something this trivial stop me,*' she thought, glaring at the wood-bordered glass panes. '*I need my grimoire.*' She made sure her feet were stable, then released one hand's death grip on the windowsill. Her cold, clumsy fingers fumbled in one of the pockets of the ratty jacket she wore under the even more ratty cloak. She pulled out a soft wax crayon and carefully drew a small Circle on the glass, completely enclosing one of the hand-sized panes. That was where the magic would take effect.

There could be no gaps in the Circle. Mistakes could be deadly.

Though she shook with the effort, Siobhan slowly drew a larger Circle around the first, dragging the crayon over the wooden divisions between the panes with careful precision. That was where she would write the Word, the instructions that would help guide the magic to the right purpose.

She drew a third, small Circle on the windowsill itself, then connected it to the outer Circle on the glass with a line. That was a component Circle, where she would place the Sacrifice, which would be consumed as she cast the spell. She wrote the glyph for "*fire*" within it, though she would sacrifice no actual fire. It was close enough to the *idea* of heat to work. More fumbles into her many pockets turned up a vial of honey, of which she tipped a sluggish drop into the component Circle on the windowsill. Next, a small, rolled-up ball of similar stickiness—spiderweb. She reached for a wad of cotton, but found she had none.

Biting back a curse, she reached again for the wax crayon and wrote the glyph for "*silence*" in the space between the two overlapping Circles on the glass. She didn't know the glyph for "*stillness,*" but she did know "*slow,*" so that's what she wrote. She squeezed in what further detailed instructions would fit, but it wasn't much. Finally, Siobhan drew a pentagon within the inside Circle.

She made the mistake of looking at the ground below and had to swallow down her lurching stomach and steady her trembling legs. Magic required concentration. She couldn't allow her circumstances to dull her wits if she wanted to succeed. '*Grandfather didn't teach me to be the type of sorcerer who has* performance problems,' she thought, sneering at her faint reflection in the glass. '*He also didn't teach me to make up spells out of desperation…*' This thought popped into her head unbidden, and she pushed it away. Untested spells were always dangerous. It was always safer to copy a spell you already knew to work, which, ideally, had been proven over generations of regular use, than to try something entirely new. If the magic rebelled and she lost control, she might die.

But she was desperate. '*It's a simple enough spell. Surely at least some sorcerers have done something similar before. And even if the magic turns wild, it only means I must control it all the more tenaciously.*'

She glared at the spell array she'd drawn and let her Will spill out into the world, activating the spell. The magic took hold of the windowpane, and she winced. The array was proving its inefficiency by letting off a glow. She focused harder, and the light dimmed, though not enough to be truly stealthy. Siobhan could only hope that no one was watching, because the glowing spell array would be obvious against the darkness.

After hurriedly wrapping her free hand in a fistful of cloak, she gave a sharp jab toward the glass. On the bright side, there was no loud shattering of glass. On the not-so-bright side, that wasn't because her spell had successfully muffled the sound, but because the force of her blow had been too weak to break the window.

Siobhan drew back her fist and punched harder. This time, the windowpane broke. The sound of shattering glass was muffled, and the shards slowly floated down toward the grimy floor inside, like feathers.

'*Feathers, that would've been a good component. A couple might have eased the Will-drain,*' she thought, releasing the mental effort that kept the spell going. Where the component Circle had been, both the honey and the blob of spiderweb were gone. The whole spherical area within had frozen so solid she knew it would burn her skin and break away from the wall if touched. The air became visible as it passed over the spot, little particles of water turning to ice in an instant.

She'd used up all the heat. Such inefficient spellwork was

embarrassing, and a little frightening, because if the spell had run out of fuel she could be dead. Still, it was the best she could do in that moment, and it had worked.

Siobhan reached through the newly created opening, and with a simple flick of her finger, opened the latch. It creaked. She froze, waiting for a response. None came, except for a sudden chill from the pebble tucked into the lip of her boot as her ward alerted her of the intrusion. Gingerly, she pulled open the window, leaning back in a way that made her sick to her stomach to allow it to swing outward. She climbed into the room, careful not to set her booted foot down on the shards of glass below.

An effort of memory brought to her mind's eye the state of the room as she and her father had left it, and a look around confirmed that nothing seemed to have changed. She hurried to gather her things, and only remembered at the last moment that one floorboard creaked when stepped on, just in time to avoid it.

She grabbed her small pack, which contained her grimoire, a little box of spell components, and her spare Conduit, as well as her extra, more worn set of clothes—the ones she hadn't wanted to wear to the University—and hairbrush, which was free of any hair of course, as Grandfather had taught her.

She gathered up her father's things next. What was light enough to carry, anyway. Finally, she did a quick sweep of the inn's lumpy straw beds for stray hairs or other pieces of themselves they may have left behind, a well-practiced spell burning anything relevant to smokeless ash.

As she was finishing, the telltale footsteps of a copper sounded from the stairs below, the copper hobnails in the soles of their boots clicking against the wood.

Siobhan made sure her packs were tightened securely to her body and returned to the window. A piece of glass, invisible in the shadows, cracked under her boot. She froze.

Outside the door, someone's weight shifted, boots shuffling over the wooden floor.

She scrambled to crawl back through the window, made awkward by her load. To her relief, the door didn't burst open, as she would surely have been caught halfway through maneuvering back outside.

"Investigator," two men greeted, the nervousness of those who knew they had not been quite as vigilant in their task as might be desired apparent in their voices.

"Anything to report?" a third man's voice replied perfunctorily, the scratch of a sore throat roughening the sound.

"No, Investigator," came the jointly spoken reply.

The man let out a wet cough. "We've got the wardbreaker here. Occupants are listed as one Ennis Naught and his daughter, with no proof of a license for thaumaturgy, so we're good to ward-break." After a pause, he added in a low grumble, "*Six hours* later."

One of the guards let out a nervous laugh as Siobhan leaned back and closed the window. She reached through the opening she'd created and re-latched the lock, then stared at the broken windowpane in dawning horror.

"Planes-damned Crown bureaucracy," the guard said with an awkward laugh. "Always making our jobs harder, am I right?"

The investigator didn't reply, but there was more nervous shuffling, and then another set of footsteps and the dry sound of chalk scraping against the other side of the door.

Siobhan held back a stream of invective as she shuffled along the wall, trying not to let the packs drag her over backward. '*I hope you find your hide burned by a fire demon from one of the greater hells, Father,*' she thought. '*How dare you put me in this position, you criminally irresponsible, thieving, sorry excuse for a caretaker. If Grandfather were still here, I would never be reduced to climbing down the side of some flea-ridden inn to escape from the coppers. Grandfather would never have used me as a decoy to evade capture for his own feckless crimes!*'

Distracted by her own mental tirade, one foot placed slightly wrong was all it took for the packs on her back and the immutable force of gravity to undermine her hold on the wall. Siobhan fell backward.

She suppressed a scream, experiencing a moment of terror before landing on the mucky cobblestone of the alley below. The impact knocked the breath from her lungs with an audible "oomph!"

The packs, filled mostly with cloth, had cushioned her fall. She arched her back and pulled at the air, her hands scrabbling at nothing as her mouth gaped like a fish. '*Oh, I've killed myself,*' she wailed mentally. '*What an ignominious end, dashed upon the ground…*' The tiniest bit of breath filtered into her lungs, and that led the way for more. Once she was sure that her back hadn't snapped like an incense stick from the fall, she sat up and stumbled to her feet, only to freeze as a light shone from the window above.

They must have broken the ward on the door, since it hadn't alerted her to the intrusion.

A quick mental argument about whether it was more stealthy to press herself against the side of the building to be more difficult to spot, or to remain frozen to avoid drawing eyeballs to suspicious movement in the darkness, yielded no good answer. She was left no time to think of a better option, because one of the people above hurried directly to the window and looked out.

When they shone a beam of light out into the alley where she stood, all thoughts of stealth vanished and Siobhan bolted.

Shouts followed her, and as she skidded around the corner into the street, the copper at the end of the block saw her and gave chase.

Instead of cursing, Siobhan saved her breath for escaping.

"Halt!" the copper yelled.

She ignored him, darting around the nearest corner and sprinting blindly down the alley. This part of the city had only the rare crystal streetlamp illuminating the darkness, which worked both for and against her.

The copper's clacking footsteps echoed loudly behind her, and were soon joined by others as his associates gave chase.

She scrambled around another corner, her boots slipping in something rancid and slimy as she rushed deeper into the maze of poorly planned and haphazardly constructed buildings. Behind her, red light flashed as a magical projectile impacted against the wall she'd just passed. A stunning spell.

'*At least they aren't trying to kill me,*' she thought, somewhat hysterically.

Her heart in her throat, Siobhan pumped her arms and legs even faster. She had no idea where she was going. If she'd had time, she would have scouted the surrounding area before going back for her things, but she had barely managed to find the inn again after escaping from the University. She'd been right not to wait any longer, or the coppers would have entered the room before she did, and what few resources she had just recovered would have been lost. She was tiring quickly. She'd never been particularly athletic, and sprinting at top speed for any length of time while carrying a third of her weight in luggage was shockingly difficult.

She came to a "T" shaped junction. Another frantic turn around the corner sent her stumbling over detritus hidden by the dark. She went sprawling forward, scraping her palms against the stone and slamming her chest into the ground, which only made her much-abused lungs ache even more.

Siobhan scrambled back to her feet and found herself facing the sudden end of a short alley. There was nowhere for her to run. She spun around, hoping for the alley to extend in the other direction, but found that to be a dead-end as well. Her only way out, the alley she'd just come down, led straight back to the chasing coppers.

Her breath came fast and her head whipped around as she searched for something, anything that would allow her to escape. '*Do I have a spell that could help me here?*' She could think of nothing. From the sound of the shouts and clacking footsteps, she didn't have the time to draw out a Circle and the Word to guide a spell even if she knew one that might help.

When a window at the other tail of the alley screeched open and a man's head popped out, already looking at her, her heart jumped as if it meant to crawl up through her throat and escape her body.

Instead of calling out that he'd caught her or pointing a battle wand at her, the dark-haired man waved her over. "Hurry," he called in a low voice.

Siobhan hesitated less than a second, since a suspicious stranger on the poor side of the city, who was at least nominally willing to help her, was sadly the best option currently available. She dashed across the alley, cringing as she briefly exposed herself to the approaching coppers.

Another blast of red light shot out toward her from the tip of a battle wand, but the aim was off. The spell splashed ineffectually against the wall once again, leaving a subtle scorch mark and a puff of steam behind. That one had been more powerful than the last.

She grabbed the dark-haired man's outstretched hand. With their combined effort, she scrambled up and through the window, her packs scraping against the frame and snagging for a single, panicked instant before releasing. Siobhan tumbled to the floor, wild-eyed, and the man immediately closed the window and moved further into the building. While she struggled to regain her bearings, he was picking up a small oil lantern from the floor, the flame within illuminating the darkness with a dull orange flicker.

"Follow me," he said, the words fully enunciated and carrying the kind of confidence that told her he hadn't even considered that she might do otherwise.

She complied, noting the upright way he moved and the expensive fabric and cut of his suit. This man wasn't one of the poor locals, but unless he was leading her into an elaborate trap, he also wasn't a copper. She looked for signs of sorcery—the many pockets filled with component materials, or a jewel clear enough to be a Conduit. Despite the fashionable cut of his clothes, his pockets didn't seem to hold anything, and he wore no jewelry. That alone didn't mean he wasn't a thaumaturge of some sort, but he was unlikely to be a sorcerer, at least.

He led her out a side door into another narrow alley, then into a building on the other side. Once the door was shut behind them, he peeked out a small opening in a boarded-up window, and after a few seconds, sighed in relief. "We should be safe to wait them out here." He hung the lantern on a nail sticking out of a nearby support beam, then turned to face Siobhan. He was clean-shaven, wavy hair falling over his forehead in a way that made him look slightly boyish, but which was offset by an angular jaw. His lips curled up at the sides, giving him an ever-so-slightly amused expression as he stared back at her.

She backed up to a safe distance from him.

He let out a soft snort, as if offended. "I assure you, I mean you no harm."

"Forgive me if your words do not reassure me in the slightest," she said, still more than a little breathless.

He spread his hands, holding them up in an innocent pose. "I have helped you evade law enforcement at my own risk. What more can I do to reassure you?" Despite his words, something about the amusement in his low voice communicated clearly that he was not a danger to her only because he *chose* not to be.

Siobhan was very conscious of the leather book pressed against the skin of her back and the amulet hanging down from one of the cords around her neck, both disguised by her clothing. '*Maybe he does have a Conduit, and it's simply hidden.*'

She glared at him, chin raised high. "Perhaps you can explain how you found yourself so conveniently placed to come to my rescue." Siobhan was tall for a woman, but very aware that without magic she stood little chance of defeating most opponents. Unfortunately, her Will was almost exhausted, and confined within such a small space, without even a battle artifact, she wouldn't have enough time to cast any serious magic before it was too late. She slipped the packs' straps off her shoulders in case she needed to move nimbly. They would just be extra handholds for someone to grab her with.

He stared at her assessingly. "I am a philanthropist."

Siobhan's eyes narrowed. "You're a criminal," she said, her tone daring him to deny it.

He slipped his hands into his pockets and grinned. "Then we are alike, no?"

She looked him up and down, mentally calculating the cost of his outfit, which was probably worth as much as the Conduit in her pocket. His stance was arrogant and assured, like her own, but hers was the result of conscious training and self-discipline, while his was natural, a product of inborn arrogance and a lifetime of privilege. She didn't bother to hold back her scorn. "No, I think not."

Rather than offending him, this sent one side of his mouth curling up in amusement. "So you're evading law enforcement out of…innocence?"

She had no response to that. '*I've been unwittingly implicated in a life-ruining crime, but I'm innocent, I swear!*' didn't seem likely to convince him, assuming she saw a point to defending herself, which she didn't. '*Even if he believed me, it's too late to change things now.*'

The man didn't let the awkward silence stretch out. "Perhaps you can agree that, for the moment, our interests seem aligned?"

"I know *my* interests. What are *yours*?"

His expression turned a little more serious. "You have made quite a name for yourself in a very short time. The city is abuzz with it—" He cut off as the eponymous sound of copper-nailed boots striking against the cobblestones resounded through the alley beside them.

The coppers weren't running this time.

When she heard them pound on a nearby door and demand entrance, Siobhan thought she might be sick. "Is there another exit?" she hissed, reaching into her jacket to clasp her Conduit, though she knew once they found her, all hope was lost.

He shook his head with slow finality, the last of his nonchalance burned away.

In the alley, they heard the coppers break down the other door when no one answered.

Her other hand reached up to press against her chest, feeling the amulet against her skin. She looked around, but there were no windows except the boarded-up one by the single door.

The man peeked out through the gap in the boarded window again. "We have less than a minute. Is there anything you can do? A spell? Something to hide us, or perhaps a big blast to knock them out of the way and leave them unable to give chase?"

"No, no," she said, patting the pockets of her jacket, hoping to prove herself wrong. '*Why did Grandfather never teach me any battle spells?*' she wailed to herself. '*Is there any magic besides sorcery I can employ?*' Her mind ran through its repertoire of knowledge—everything Grandfather had taught her, the things she had picked up from other thaumaturges while traveling with her father, and the things she had experimented with.

She had some minor healing salves in her pack, and the medallion hanging from her neck would protect her from certain dangers, but none of the magic she knew was particularly offensive, and of the spells that might be useful, she couldn't cast any of them quickly.

Magic was the answer to almost every problem, but only if you were very, very good at it. Her ignorance and lack of skill damned her.

The coppers were at the door. One slammed their fist against it. "By order of the Crowns, open up!"

The man ruffled his hair till it stood on end, took off his jacket and unbuttoned the collar of his shirt, then moved to stand between her and the door, his knees dipping slightly as if to prepare for sudden movement.

'Does he plan to fight the coppers? What can he hope to do, unarmed against a battle wand?'

The wood shuddered under another pounding fist.

Siobhan's free hand clutched at the artifact. *'I think I'm going to pass out.'* When the copper's first concussive spell on the door cracked its wood, her eyes closed in a reflexive flinch. Her mind settled instinctively into the perspective that allowed her to channel her Will, and she reached out for what little power she had access to without a Circle. Her body flushed with a warm tingle. *'Oh no, I really am going to pass out…'*

The second attack broke through the doorjamb, sending the door itself slamming against the wall and splinters of wood flying through the room.

Her attempted rescuer flinched, raising his hands before the threat of the copper's extended battle wand. His pose showed that he meant no harm, but his knees were still slightly bent, perhaps hoping to take them by surprise.

A uniformed man and woman stood in the shattered doorway, both breathing hard.

Siobhan resolved that she would attack if he did. She might not be particularly useful in a fistfight, but at least she could help even the odds, and maybe keep one of them from calling for reinforcements while the man fought the other one.

The copper's female partner stepped around him, shining a lamp over both of them. The woman looked around suspiciously, her eyes flicking around the dark corners of the room and then settling down to glare at the two of them.

Squinting against the bright light, Siobhan unclenched her fists, leaving her Conduit in her pocket, and raised her hands into the air. Her eyes flicked down to the battle wand holstered at the female copper's hip. *'That artifact likely contains more of those stunning spells. Meant to incapacitate, not kill.'* Perhaps if she lunged for the woman fast enough, she could steal it and use it against her and her partner. '*The wand can't be that difficult to operate, surely?*'

She plotted out her vector of attack in a blistering fury of concentration. '*I can do this. I can.*' Two steps forward, duck down to avoid the spell from the male copper, spin to reach the woman's side and simultaneously use her as a partial body shield. Snatch the wand—

"Have you seen anyone come this way? Tall, dark-haired woman. Might have been wearing a hooded cloak. A thaumaturge," the woman said.

Siobhan blinked. '*Is this a joke?*' Her hood had fallen down around her shoulders, revealing her face and hair. The woman was looking right at her. Perhaps their description of her appearance was somehow incorrect, maybe of someone older than her, or with some sensationally evil feature, like glowing red eyes. Siobhan carefully didn't look at the packs on the ground, which were more evidence of her identity.

Her rescuer turned to look at her, and the momentary widening of his eyes when they landed on her, combined with the pinch of pain caused by too-tight boots that had fit fine only seconds before, gave Siobhan the last clue she needed.

"Heard footsteps goin' into the buildin' 'cross the street," she said, hoping her flinch at the sound of her own voice hadn't been noticeable. The sound was scratchy and deep, unmistakably male. She cleared her throat, doing her best to imitate the Gilbrathan poor people's accent. "There was this bright light, a green one. We figured it best to stay out the way." She wasn't an actor, but with singularity of purpose, a simple change in mannerisms wasn't so difficult. She hoped she didn't seem suspicious, as she hadn't prepared for this. Still, better to speak less, to give them less chance to notice something amiss.

"You didn't open the door when we called for entry," the male copper said, the words an accusation.

"We were…occupied. You broke it down before we had the chance," her rescuer said, adjusting the waistband of his pants with obvious awkwardness.

'*He's insinuating I'm a prostitute,*' Siobhan realized, not having to act to adopt an embarrassed expression.

The male copper grimaced with faint distaste, but the female's eyes narrowed as they roved over Siobhan's body.

Siobhan's clothing was covered in pockets, but that style wasn't reserved only for magic-wielders. Plus, the state of her clothes and the obvious lack of wealth and hygiene didn't evoke thoughts of a powerful thaumaturge. She had taken off the few trinkets she normally wore, and her Conduit was safely tucked away. She was wearing trousers rather than a skirt, and if they rode a little high on her ankles and loose around the hips, that only suggested she couldn't afford tailoring.

The woman pointed her wand at Siobhan, and Siobhan tensed again, thinking her deception had been discovered.

However, instead of ordering her to lie down on the ground with her hands behind her head or shooting her with a stunning spell, the woman fiddled with the artifact's controls for a couple of seconds, then cast an almost invisible wave that washed over Siobhan and prickled against her skin.

The spell irritated her nostrils and eyes, forcing her to blink back tears. *'Some kind of revealing or nullification spell?'*

The copper lowered her wand. "Across the alley, you say?" She nodded to her partner, who hesitantly lowered his own wand, though he kept his glare trained on Siobhan's rescuer. Despite their obvious mistrust, an out-of-place gentleman committing no obvious crime with a ragamuffin homeless person apparently didn't compare to the urgency of finding Siobhan. After a final admonition to report any sightings of the "rogue and dangerous thaumaturge," and to be sure to avoid her for their own safety, the coppers left.

Siobhan waited to be sure the coppers were gone before examining herself. Instead of her skin's normal ochre, she had grown even paler than her rescuer, and when she tilted her head down to look at her body, light blonde hair fell into her face. The fine strands were cut short, to just below her chin, rather than the normal dark mane that grew past the small of her back. Her boots pinched uncomfortably around larger feet, and she was fairly certain she had grown taller as well.

The man settled the door back in its frame and then looked her transformed body up and down. "You cast an illusion of a man over yourself? It's not what I expected, but, I admit, it is quite impressive."

Siobhan shook her head, wide-eyed. "It's not an illusion," she said. '*And I didn't cast it*,' she continued silently.

YOU CAN BUY A Practical Guide to Sorcery: A Conjuring of Ravens now.

Also by Azalea Ellis

Seeds of Chaos Series (Complete)

Book I: Gods of Blood and Bone

Book II: Gods of Rust and Ruin

Book III: Gods of Myth and Midnight

Gods of Smoke and Stars: A Seeds of Chaos Adventure—Available free to newsletter subscribers

Book IV: Gods of Ash and Amber

A Practical Guide to Sorcery Series

Book I: A Conjuring of Ravens

Book II: A Binding of Blood

Book III: A Sacrifice of Light

Book IV: A Foreboding of Woe — Coming Soon

Codename: Moonsable (Patreon Exclusive Sidestory)

The Honeymoon Suite (Patreon Exclusive Novelette)

The Catastrophe Collector: A Practical Guide to Sorcery Series

Book I: Larva — Coming Soon

More books may have been published since you purchased this copy.

Here's a Quick Link to All my Books.

About the Author

I'm the type of person that often has a wacky, shocking, or silly–but totally *true*–story to tell about my life.

(Like the time my brother and I were chased through a secluded strip of woods in the middle of the city, for over a mile, by a naked man with an erection.)

(Or the time a trucker threw an open bottle of pee out his passenger side window without looking right as I was walking by. You can guess what I got splashed with.)

I've got an active imagination that tends toward the outrageous and the macabre, which led to me being voted "most likely to borrow someone else's car to transport a dead body."

I write books about things that interest and excite me. I'm always in the middle of teaching myself something new, and if I'm not overwhelmingly busy I tend to get antsy. I believe that the impossible is only so if we believe it to be so. Therefore, nothing is impossible.

If you'd like to get updates from me, both about my books and about what I'm up to from time to time, the newsletter is the place to be, as I tend to be very scarce on other social media.

https://www.azaleaellis.com/newsletter/

For more information:
www.azaleaellis.com
author@azaleaellis.com

www.ingramcontent.com/pod-product-compliance
Lightning Source LLC
Chambersburg PA
CBHW032110110726
47902CB00003B/536